D0092570

Please turn the page for more reviews. . . .

"GRAFTON KEEPS PULLING OUT SURPRISES— AND PULLING US IN."
—Entertainment Weekly

"Sue Grafton fans are in for a real treat with *O Is for Outlaw*. . . . New readers will benefit from the details previously unwritten, while longtime fans will be intrigued by the new look at Kinsey's life."
—St. Louis Post-Dispatch

"Highly recommended . . . Kinsey is sassier than ever, the supporting characters are amusingly eccentric, and the mysteries, both past and present, are intriguing."

—Library Journal

By Sue Grafton

Kinsey Millhone mysteries:
"A" IS FOR ALIBI**
"B" IS FOR BURGLAR**
"C" IS FOR CORPSE**
"D" IS FOR DEADBEAT**
"E" IS FOR EVIDENCE**
"F" IS FOR FUGITIVE**
"G" IS FOR GUMSHOE*
"H" IS FOR HOMICIDE*
"I" IS FOR INNOCENT*
"J" IS FOR JUDGMENT*
"K" IS FOR KILLER*
"L" IS FOR LAWLESS*
"M" IS FOR MALICE*
"N" IS FOR NOOSE*
"O" IS FOR OUTLAW*

*Published by The Ballantine Publishing Group
**Published by Bantam Books

"O"
IS
FOR
OUTLAW

Sue Grafton

BALLANTINE BOOKS • NEW YORK

A Ballantine Book
Published by The Ballantine Publishing Group
Copyright © 1999 by Sue Grafton

All rights reserved under International and Pan-American Copyright Conventions. Published in the United States by Ballantine Books, a division of Random House, Inc., New York, and distributed in Canada by Random House of Canada Limited, Toronto.

Ballantine and colophon are registered trademarks of Random House, Inc.

www.randomhouse.com/BB/

Library of Congress Catalog Card Number: 00-108982

ISBN 0-449-00378-7

This edition published by arrangement with Henry Holt and Company, LLC

Manufactured in the United States of America

First Ballantine Books International Edition: May 2000
First Ballantine Books Domestic Edition: January 2001

10 9 8 7 6 5 4 3 2 1

FOR MY GRANDDAUGHTER, KINSEY,
with a heart full of love

The author wishes to acknowledge the invaluable assistance of the following people: Steven Humphrey; Detective Peggy Moseley, Los Angeles Police Department; Captain Ed Aasted and Sergeant Brian Abbott, Santa Barbara Police Department; Pat Zuberer, Library Clerk, Barbara Alexander and Betsey Daniels, Librarians, Ronetta Coates, student, Louisville Male High School; Beverly Herrlinger, Curriculum Coordinator, Jefferson County High School Admissions Office; Ray Connors; Kathy Humphrey, Communications Director, California State Senate; Marshall Morgan, M.D., Medical Director, Emergency Room, UCLA Medical Center; H. Ric Harnsberger, M.D., Professor of ENT/Neuroradiology and Director, Neuroradiology Section, University of Utah Medical Center; Barry and Bernice Ewing, Eagle Sportschairs; Lee Stone; Harriet Miller, Mayor, City of Santa Barbara; Danny Nash, Jefferson County Clerk's Office, Louisville, Kentucky; Erik Raney, Deputy, Santa Barbara County Sheriff's Department; Kevin Rudan, Resident Agent, Secret Service; Don and Marilyn Gevirtz; Julianna Flynn; Ralph Hickey; Lucy Thomas and Nadine Greenup, Librarians, Reeves Medical Center, Cottage Hospital; Denise Huff, R.N., Cottage Hospital Emergency; Gail Abarbanel, Director, Rape Treatment Center, Santa Monica/UCLA Medical Center; Jay Schmidt; Jamie Clark; and Mary Lawrence Young.

To the reader,

Just a brief note to clarify the time frame for these "alphabet" novels. For those of you confused about what appear to be errors in my calculation of ages and dates, please be aware that *"A" Is for Alibi* takes place in May of 1982, *"B" Is for Burglar* in June of 1982, *"C" Is for Corpse* in August of 1982, and so forth. Since the books are sequential, Ms. Millhone is caught up in a time warp and is currently living and working in the year 1986, without access to cell phones, the Internet, or other high-tech equipment used by modern-day private investigators. She relies instead on persistence, imagination, and ingenuity: the stock-in-trade of the traditional gumshoe throughout hard-boiled history. As her biographer, I generally avoid mention of topical issues and date-related events. You'll find few, if any, references to current movies, fads, fashions, or politics. This book is an exception in that events connect back to the Vietnam War, which ended in 1975, eleven years before the incidents described herein. Given narrative requirements, I populate historical actions with fictional characters and project wholly invented persons into academic institutions and political arenas, in which their "real-life" counterparts will doubtless dispute their presence. In my view, the delight of fiction is its enhancement of the facts and its embellishment of reality. Aside from that—as my father used to say—"I know it's true because I made it up myself."

Respectfully submitted,
Sue Grafton

1

THE LATIN TERM *pro bono*, as most attorneys will attest, roughly translated means *for boneheads* and applies to work done without charge. Not that I practice law, but I am usually smart enough to avoid having to donate my services. In this case, my client was in a coma, which made billing a trick. Of course, you might look at the situation from another point of view. Once in a while a piece of old business surfaces, some item on life's agenda you thought you'd dealt with years ago. Suddenly, it's there again at the top of the page, competing for your attention despite the fact that you're completely unprepared for it.

First there was a phone call from a stranger; then a letter showed up fourteen years after it was sent. That's how I learned I'd made a serious error in judgment and ended up risking my life in my attempt to correct for it.

I'd just finished a big job, and I was not only exhausted but my bank account was fat and I wasn't in the mood to take on additional work. I'd pictured a bit of time off, maybe a trip someplace cheap, where I could lounge in the sun and read the latest Elmore Leonard novel while sipping on a rum drink with a paper umbrella stuck in a piece of fruit. This is about the range and complexity of my fantasies these days.

The call came at 8 A.M. Monday, May 19, while I was off at the gym. I'd started lifting weights again: Monday, Wednesday, and Friday mornings after my 6 A.M. run. I'm not sure where the motivation came from after a two-year layoff, but it was probably related to thoughts of mortality, primarily my own. In the spring, I'd sustained damage to my right hand when a fellow dislocated two fingers trying to persuade me to his point of view. I'd been hurt once before when a bullet nicked my right arm, and my impulse in both instances had been to hit the weight machines. Lest you imagine I'm a masochist or accident-prone, I should state that I make a living as a private investigator. Truth be told, the average P.I. seldom carries a gun, isn't often pursued, and rarely sustains an injury more substantial than a paper cut. My own professional life tends to be as dull as anyone else's. I simply report the exceptions in the interest of spiritual enlightenment. Processing events helps me keep my head on straight.

Those of you acquainted with my personal data can skip this paragraph. For the uninitiated, I'm female, thirty-six years old, twice divorced, and living in Santa Teresa, California, which is ninety-five miles north of Los Angeles. Currently, I occupy one small office in the larger suite of offices of Kingman and Ives, attorneys at law. Lonnie Kingman is my attorney when the occasion arises, so my association with his firm seemed to make sense when I was looking for space. I'd been rendered a migrant after I was unceremoniously shit-canned from the last job I had: investigating arson and wrongful death claims for California Fidelity Insurance. I've been with Lonnie now for over two years, but I'm not above harboring a petty desire for revenge on CFI.

During the months I'd been lifting weights, my muscle tone had improved and my strength had increased. That particular morning, I'd worked my way through the customary body parts: two sets, fifteen reps each, of leg extensions, leg curls, ab crunches, lower back, lat rows, the chest press and pec deck, along with the shoulder press, and various exercises for the biceps and triceps. Thus pumped up and euphoric, I let myself into my apartment with the usual glance at my answering machine. The message light was blinking. I dropped my gym bag on the floor, tossed my keys on the desk, and pressed the PLAY button, reaching for a pen and a pad of paper in case I needed to take notes. Before I leave the office each day, I have Lonnie's service shunt calls over to my apartment. That way, in a pinch, I can lie abed all day, dealing with the public without putting on my clothes.

The voice was male, somewhat gravelly, and the message sounded like this: "Miss Millhone, this is Teddy Rich. I'm calling from Olvidado about something might innerest you. This is eight A.M. Monday. Hope it's not too early. Gimme a call when you can. Thanks." He recited a telephone number in the 805 area code, and I dutifully jotted it down. It was only 8:23 so I hadn't missed him by much. Olvidado is a town of 157,000, thirty miles south of Santa Teresa on Highway 101. Always one to be interested in something that might "innerest" me, I dialed the number he'd left. The ringing went on so long I thought his machine would kick in, but the line was finally picked up by Mr. Rich, whose distinctive voice I recognized.

"Hi, Mr. Rich. This is Kinsey Millhone up in Santa Teresa. I'm returning your call."

"Hey, Miss Millhone. Nice to hear from you. How are you today?"

"Fine. How are you?"

"I'm fine. Thanks for asking, and thanks for being so prompt. I appreciate that."

"Sure, no problem. What can I do for you?"

"Well, I'm hoping this is something I can do for you," he said. "I'm a storage space scavenger. Are you familiar with the term?"

"I'm afraid not." I pulled the chair out and sat down, realizing Ted Rich was going to take his sweet time about this. I'd already pegged him as a salesman or a huckster, someone thoroughly enamored of whatever minor charms he possessed. I didn't want what he was selling, but I decided I might as well hear him out. This business of storage space scavenging was a new one on me, and I gave him points for novelty.

He said, "I won't bore you with details. Basically, I bid on the contents of self-storage lockers when the monthly payment's in arrears."

"I didn't know they did that on delinquent accounts. Sounds reasonable, I suppose." I took the towel from my gym bag and ruffed it across my head. My hair was still damp from the workout and I was getting chillier by the minute, longing to hit the shower before my muscles stiffened up.

"Oh, sure. Storage unit's been abandoned by its owner for more'n sixty days, the contents go up for auction. How else can the company recoup its losses? Guys like me show up and blind-bid on the contents, paying anywheres from two hundred to fifteen hundred bucks, hoping for a hit."

"As in what?" I reached down, untied my Sauconys, and slipped them off my feet. My gym socks smelled atrocious, and I'd only worn them a week.

"Well, most times you get junk, but once in a while you get lucky and come across something good. Tools, furniture—stuff you can convert to hard cash. I'm sure you're pro'bly curious what this has to do with you."

"It crossed my mind," I said mildly, anticipating his pitch. For mere pennies a day, you too can acquire abandoned bric-a-brac with which to clutter up your premises.

"Yeah, right. Anyways, this past Saturday, I bid on a couple storage bins. Neither of 'em netted much, but in the process I picked up a bunch of cardboard boxes. I was sorting through the contents and came across your name on some personal documents. I'm wondering what it's worth to you to get 'em back."

"What kind of documents?"

"Lemme see here. Hold on. Frankly, I didn't expect to hear so soon or I'd have had 'em on the desk in front of me." I could hear him rattling papers in the background. "Okay now. We got a pink-bead baby bracelet and there's quite a collection of school-type memorabilia: drawings, class pictures, report cards from Woodrow Wilson Elementary. This ringin' any bells with you?"

"*My* name's on these papers?"

"Kinsey Millhone, right? Millhone with two *l*'s. Here's a history report entitled 'San Juan Capistrano Mission,' with a model of the mission made of egg cartons. Mrs. Rosen's class, fourth grade. She gave you a D plus. 'Report is not bad, but project is poorly presented,' she says. I had a teacher like her once. What a bitch," he said idly. "Oh, and here's something else. Diploma says you graduated Santa Teresa High School on June tenth, 1967? How'm I doin' so far?"

"Not bad."

"Well, there you go," he said.

"Not that it matters, but how'd you track me down?"

"Piece of cake. All I did was call Directory Assistance. The name Millhone's unusual, so I figure it's like the old saying goes: apples don't fall far from the tree and so forth. I proceeded on the assumption you were some-wheres close. You could've got married and changed your name, of course. I took a flier on that score. Anyways, the point is, how d'you feel about gettin' these things back?"

"I don't understand how the stuff ended up in Olvidado. I've never rented storage space down there."

I could hear him begin to hedge. "I never said Olvidado. Did I say that? I go to these auctions all over the state. Lookit, I don't mean to sound crass, but if you're willing to pony up a few bucks, we can maybe make arrangements for you to get this box back."

I hesitated, annoyed by the clumsiness of his maneuvering. I remembered my struggle in Mrs. Rosen's class, how crushed I'd been with the grade after I'd worked so hard. The fact was, I had so little in the way of personal keepsakes that any addition would be treasured. I didn't want to pay much, but neither was I willing to relinquish the items sight unseen.

I said, "The papers can't be worth much since I wasn't aware they were missing." Already, I didn't like him and I hadn't even met him yet.

"Hey, I'm not here to argue. I don't intend to hose you or nothin' like that. You want to talk value, we talk value. Up to you," he said.

"Why don't I think about it and call you back?"

"Well, that's just it. If we could find time to get to-gether, you could take a look at these items and then come to a decision. How else you going to know if it's worth anything to you? It'd mean a drive down here, but I'm assuming you got wheels."

"I could do that, I suppose."

"Excellent," he said. "So what's your schedule like today?"

"*Today?*"

"No time like the present is my attitude."

"What's the big hurry?"

"No hurry in particular except I got appointments set up for the rest of the week. I make money turnin' stuff over, and my garage is already packed. You have time today or not?"

"I could probably manage it."

"Good, then let's meet as soon as possible and see if we can work somethin' out. There's a coffee shop down the street from me. I'm on my way over now and I'll be there for about an hour. Let's say nine-thirty. You don't show? I gotta make a run to the dump anyways so it's no skin off my nose."

"What'd you have in mind?"

"Moneywise? Let's say thirty bucks. How's that sound?"

"Exorbitant," I said. I asked him for directions. What a hairball.

I showered and flung on the usual blue jeans and T-shirt, then gassed up my VW and headed south on 101. The drive to Olvidado took twenty-five minutes. Following Ted Rich's instructions, I took the Olvidado Avenue exit and turned right at the bottom of the off-ramp. Half a block from the freeway, there was a large shopping mall. The surrounding land, originally given over to agricultural use, was gradually being converted to a crop of new and used cars. Lines of snapping plastic flags defined tent shapes above the asphalt lot where rows of vehicles glinted in the mild May sun. I could see a shark-shaped mini-blimp tethered and hovering thirty feet in the air. The significance escaped me, but what do I know about these things?

Across from the mall, the business establishments seemed to be equally divided among fast food joints, liquor stores, and instant-copy shops that offered passport photos. There was even a facility devoted to walk-in legal services; litigate while you wait. BANKRUPTCY $99. DIVORCE $99. DIVORCE W/KIDS $99 + FILING FEE. *Se habla español.* The coffee shop he'd specified appeared to be the only mom-and-pop operation in the area.

I parked my car in the lot and pushed into the place, scanning the few patrons for someone who fit his description. He'd indicated he was six foot two and moviestar handsome, but then he'd snorted with laughter, which led me to believe otherwise. He'd said he'd watch the door for my arrival. I spotted a guy who raised a hand in greeting and beckoned me to his booth. His face was a big ruddy square, his sunburn extending into the V of his open-collared denim work shirt. He wore his dark hair combed straight back, and I could see the indentation at his temples where he'd removed the baseball cap now sitting on the table next to him. He had a wide nose, drooping upper lids, and bags under his eyes. I could see the scattering of whiskers he'd missed during his morning shave. His shoulders were beefy and his forearms looked thick where he had his sleeves rolled up. He'd removed a dark brown windbreaker, which now lay neatly folded over the back of the booth.

"Mr. Rich? Kinsey Millhone. How are you?" We shook hands across the table, and I could tell he was sizing me up with the same attention to detail I'd just lavished on him.

"Make it Teddy. Not bad. I appreciate your coming." He glanced at his watch as I slid in across from him. "Unfortunately I only got maybe fifteen, twenty minutes before I have to take off. I apologize for the squeeze, but right after we spoke, I hadda call from some guy down in Thousand Oaks needs an estimate on his roof."

"You're a roofer?"

"By trade." He reached in his pants pocket. "Lemme pass you my card in case you need somethin' done." He took out a slim Naugahyde case and removed a stack of business cards. "My speciality is new roofs and repairs."

"What else is there?"

"Hey, I can do anything you need. Hot mops, tear-offs, torch-downs, all types of shake, composition, slate, clay tile, you name it. Corrective and preventative is my area of expertise. I could give you a deal . . . let's say ten percent off if you call this month. What kind of house you in?"

"Rented."

"So maybe you got a landlord needs some roof work done. Go ahead and keep that. Take as many as you want." He offered me a handful of cards, fanned out face down like he was about to do a magic trick.

I took one and examined it. The card bore his name, telephone number, and a post office box. His company was called Overhead Roofing, the letters forming a wide inverted V like the ridgeline of a roof. His company motto was *We do all types of roofing*.

"Catchy," I remarked.

He'd been watching for my reaction, his expression serious. "I just had those made. Came up with the name myself. Used to be Ted's Roofs. You know, simple, basic, something of a personal touch. I could have said 'Rich Roofs,' but that might have gave the wrong impression. I was in business ten years, but then the drought came along and the market dried up—"

"So to speak," I put in.

He smiled, showing a small gap between his two front lower teeth. "Hey, that's good. I like your sense of humor. You'll appreciate this one. Couple years without rain and people start to take a roof for granite. Get it? Granite . . . like the rock?"

I said, "That's funny."

"Anyways, I've had a hell of a time. I hadda shut down altogether and file bankruptcy. My wife up and left me, the dog died, and then my truck got sideswiped. I was screwed big time. Now we got some bad weather coming in, I figured I'd start fresh. Overhead Roofing is a kind of play on words."

"Really," I said. "What about the storage space business? Where did that come from?"

"I figured I hadda do something when the roofing trade fell in. 'As it were,' " he added, with a wink at me. "I decided to try salvage. I had some cash tucked away the wife and the creditors didn't know about, so I used that to get started. Takes five or six thousand if you want to do it right. I got hosed once or twice, but otherwise I been doing pretty good, even if I do say so myself." He caught the waitress's attention and held his coffee cup in the air with a glance back at me. "Can I buy you a cup of coffee?"

"That sounds good. How long have you been at it?"

"About a year," he said. "We're called 'pickers' or storage room gamblers, sometimes resellers, treasure hunters. How it works is I check the papers for auction listings. I also subscribe to a couple newsletters. You never know what you'll find. Couple of weeks ago, I paid two-fifty and found a painting worth more than fifteen hundred bucks. I was jazzed."

"I can imagine."

"Of course, there's rules to the practice, like anything else in life. You can't touch the rooms' contents, can't go inside before the bidding starts, and there's no refunds. You pay six hundred dollars and all you come up with is a stack of old magazines, then it's too bad for you. Such is life and all that."

"Can you make a living at it?"

He shifted in his seat. "Not so's you'd notice. This is strictly a hobby in between roofing engagements. Nice thing about it is it doesn't look good on paper so the wife can't hit me up for alimony. She was the one who walked out, so up hers is what I say."

The waitress appeared at the table with a coffeepot in hand, refilling his cup and pouring one for me. Teddy and the waitress exchanged pleasantries. I took the moment to add milk to my coffee and then tore the corner off a pack of sugar, which I don't ordinarily take. Anything to fill time till they finished their conversation. Frankly, I thought he had the hots for her.

Once she departed, Teddy turned his attention to me. I could see the box on the seat beside him. He noticed my glance. "I can see you're curious. Wanna peek?"

I said, "Sure."

I made a move toward the box and Teddy put a hand out, saying, "Gimme five bucks first." Then he laughed. "You shoulda seen the look on your face. Come on. I'm teasing. Help yourself." He hefted the box and passed it across the table. It was maybe three feet square, awkward but not heavy, the cardboard powdery with dust. The top had been sealed, but I could see where the packing tape had been cut and the flaps folded back together. I set the box on the seat beside me and pulled the flaps apart. The contents seemed hastily thrown together with no particular thought paid to the organization. It was rather like the last of the cartons packed in the moving process: stuff you don't dare throw out but don't really know what else to do with. A box like this could probably sit unopened in your basement for the next ten years, and nothing would ever stimulate a search for even one of the items. On the other hand, if you felt the need to inventory the contents, you'd still feel too attached to the items to toss the assortment in the trash. The next time you moved, you'd end up adding the box to the other boxes on the van, gradually accumulating sufficient junk to fill a . . . well, a storage bin.

I could tell at a glance these were articles I wanted. In addition to the grade school souvenirs, I spotted the high school diploma he'd mentioned, my yearbook, some textbooks, and, more important, file after file of mimeographed pages from my classes at the police academy. Thirty bucks was nothing for this treasury of remembrances.

Teddy was watching my face, trying to gauge the dollar signs in my reaction. I found myself avoiding eye contact lest he sense the extent of my interest. Stalling, I said, "Whose storage space was it? I don't believe you mentioned that."

"Guy named John Russell. He a friend of yours?"

"I wouldn't call him a friend, but I know him," I said. "Actually, that's an in-joke, like an alias. 'John Russell' is a character in an Elmore Leonard novel called *Hombre*."

"Well, I tried to get ahold of him, but I didn't have much luck. Way too many Russells in this part of the state. Couple of dozen Jonathans, fifteen or twenty Johns, but none were him because I checked it out."

"You put some time in."

"You bet. Took me couple hours before I gave it up and said nuts. I tried this whole area: Perdido, LA County, Orange, San Bernardino, Santa Teresa County, as far up as San Luis. There's no sign of the guy, so I figure he's dead or moved out of state."

I took a sip of my coffee, avoiding comment. The addition of milk and sugar made the coffee taste like a piece of hard candy.

Teddy tilted his head at me with an air of bemusement. "So you're a private detective? I notice you're listed as Millhone Investigations."

"That's right. I was a cop for two years, which is how I knew John."

"The guy's a cop?"

"Not now, but he was in those days."

"I wouldn't have guessed that . . . I mean, judging from the crap he had jammed in that space. I'da said some kind of bum. That's the impression I got."

"Some people would agree."

"But you're not one of 'em, I take it."

I shrugged, saying nothing.

Teddy studied me shrewdly. "Who's this guy to you?"

"What makes you ask?"

"Come on. What's his real name? Maybe I can track him down for you, like a missing persons case."

"Why bother? We haven't spoken in years, so he's nothing to me."

"But now you got me curious. Why the alias?"

"He was a vice cop in the late sixties and early seventies. Big dope busts back then. John worked undercover, so he was always paranoid about his real name."

"Sounds like a nut."

"Maybe so," I said. "What else was in the bin?"

He waved a hand dismissively. "Most of it was useless. Lawnmower, broken-down vacuum cleaner. There was a big box of kitchen stuff: wooden rolling pin, big wooden salad bowl, must have been three feet across the top, set of crockery bowls—what do you call it? That Fiesta Ware shit. I picked up a fair chunk of change for that. Ski equipment, tennis racquets, none of it in prime condition. There was an old bicycle, motorcycle engine, wheel cover, and some car parts. I figure Russell was a pack rat, couldn't let go of stuff. I sold most of it at the local swap meet; this was yesterday."

I felt my heart sink. The big wooden bowl had belonged to my Aunt Gin. I didn't care about the Fiesta

Ware, though that was hers as well. I was wishing I'd had the option to buy the wooden rolling pin. Aunt Gin had used it to make sticky buns—one of her few domestic skills—rolling out the dough before she sprinkled on the cinnamon and sugar. I had to let that one go; no point in longing for what had already been disposed of. Odd to think an item would suddenly have such appeal when I hadn't thought of it in years.

He nodded at the box. "Thirty bucks and it's yours."

"Twenty bucks. It's barely worth that. It's all junk."

"Twenty-five. Come on. For the trip down memory lane. Things like that you're never going to see again. Sentimental journey and so forth. Might as well snap it up while you have the chance."

I removed a twenty from my handbag and laid it on the table. "Nobody else is going to pay you a dime."

Teddy shrugged. "So I toss it. Who cares? Twenty-five and that's firm."

"Teddy, a dump run would cost you fifteen, so this puts you five bucks ahead."

He stared at the money, flicked a look to my face, and then took the bill with an exaggerated sigh of disgust with himself. "Lucky I like you or I'd be pissed as hell." He folded the twenty lengthwise and tucked it in his pocket. "You never answered my question."

"Which one?"

"Who's this guy to you?"

"No one in particular. A friend once upon a time . . . not that it's any of your business."

"Oh, I see. I get it. Now, he's 'a friend.' Inneresting development. You musta been close to the guy if he ended up with your things."

"What makes you say that?"

He tapped his temple. "I got a logical mind. Analytical, right? I bet I could be a peeper just like you."

"Gee, Teddy, sure. I don't see why not. The truth is I stored some boxes at John's while I was in the middle of a move. My stuff must have gotten mixed up with his when he left Santa Teresa. By the way, which storage company?"

His expression turned crafty. "What makes you ask?" he said, in a slightly mocking tone.

"Because I'm wondering if he's still in the area somewhere."

Teddy shook his head, way ahead of me. "No go. Forget it. You'd be wasting your time. I mean, look at it this way. If the guy used a phony name, he prob'bly also faked his phone number and his home address. Why contact the company? They won't tell you nothin'."

"I'll bet I could get the information. That's what I do for a living these days."

"You and Dick Tracy."

"All I'm asking is the name."

Teddy smiled. "How much's it worth?"

"How much is it *worth*?"

"Yeah, let's do a little business. Twenty bucks."

"Don't be silly. I'm not going to *pay* you. That's ridiculous."

"So make me an offer. I'm a reasonable guy."

"Bullshit."

"All I'm saying is you scratch my back and I'll scratch yours."

"There can't be that many storage companies in the area."

"Fifteen hundred and eleven, if you take in the neighboring counties. For ten bucks, I'll tell you which little town it's in."

"No way."

"Come on. How else you going to find out?"

"I'm sure I can think of something."

"Wanna bet? Five says you can't."

I glanced at my watch and slid out of the seat. "I wish I could chat, Teddy, but you have that appointment and I have to get to work."

"Whyn't you call me if you change your mind? We could find him together. We could form us a partnership. I bet you could use a guy with my connections."

"No doubt."

I picked up the cardboard box, made a few more polite mouth noises, and returned to my car. I placed the box in the passenger seat and then slid in on the driver's side. I locked both doors instinctively and blew out a big breath. My heart was thumping, and I could feel the damp of perspiration in the small of my back. "John Russell" was the alias for a former Santa Teresa vice detective named Mickey Magruder, my first ex-husband. What the hell was going on?

2

I SLOUCHED DOWN in my car, scanning the parking lot from my position at half mast. I could see a white pickup parked at the rear of the lot, the truck bed filled with the sort of buckets and tarps I pictured essential to a roofing magnate. An oversized toolbox rested near the back of the cab, and an aluminum extension ladder seemed to be mounted on the far side with its two metal antislip shoes protruding about a foot. I adjusted the rearview mirror, watching until Ted Rich came out of the coffee shop wearing his baseball cap and brown windbreaker. He had his hands in his pants pockets and he whistled to himself as he walked to the pickup and fished out his keys. When I heard the truck rumble to life, I took a moment to lean sideways out of his line of sight. As soon as he passed, I sat up again, watching as he turned left and entered the line of traffic heading toward the southbound freeway on-ramp.

I waited till he was gone, then got out of the VW and trotted to the public phone booth near the entrance to the parking lot. I placed his business card on the narrow

17

metal shelf provided, hauled up the phone book, and checked under the listings for United States Government. I found the number I was looking for and dug some loose change from the bottom of my shoulder bag. I inserted coins in the slot and dialed the number for the local post office branch printed on Rich's business card. The phone rang twice and a recorded message was activated, subjecting me to the usual reassurances. All the lines were busy at the moment, but my call would be answered in the order it was received. According to the recording, the post office really appreciated my patience, which shows you just how little they know about yours truly.

When a live female clerk finally came on the line, I gave her the box number for Overhead Roofing, possibly known as Ted's Roofs. Within minutes, she'd checked the rental agreement for his post office box and had given me the corresponding street address. I said thanks and depressed the plunger. I put another coin in the slot and punched in the phone number listed on the business card. As I suspected, no one answered, though Rich's machine did pick up promptly. I was happy to hear that Ted Rich was Olvidado's Number 1 certified master installer of fire-free roofing materials. The message also indicated that May was weatherproofing month, which I hadn't realized. More important, Teddy wasn't home and neither, apparently, was anyone else.

I returned to the car, fished an Olvidado city map from the glove compartment, and found the street listed on the ledger. By tracing the number and the letter coordinates, I pinpointed the location, not far from where I sat. Oh, happiness. I turned the key in the ignition, put the car in reverse, and in less than five minutes I was idling in front of Teddy's house, whence he operated his roofing business.

I found a parking spot six doors down and then sat in

the car while my good angel and my bad angel jousted for possession of my soul. My good angel reminded me I'd vowed to reform. She recited the occasions when my usual vile behavior had brought me *naught but grief and pain*, as she put it. Which was all well and good, but as my bad angel asserted, this was really the only chance I was going to have to get the information I wanted. If Rich had "shared" the name of the storage company, I wouldn't have to do this, so it was really all his fault. He was currently on his way to Thousand Oaks to give an estimate on some guy's roof. The round-trip drive would take approximately thirty minutes, with another thirty minutes thrown in for schmoozing, which is how men do business. The two of us had parted company at ten. It was now ten-fifteen, so (with luck) he wouldn't be back for another forty-five minutes.

I removed my key picks from my shoulder bag, which I'd left on the backseat under the pile of assorted clothes I keep there. Often in the course of surveillance work, I use camouflage garments, like a quick-change artist, to vary my appearance. Now I pulled out a pair of navy coveralls that looked suitably professional. The patch on the sleeve, which I'd had stitched to my specifications, read SANTA TERESA CITY SERVICES and suggested I was employed by the public works department. I figured from a distance the Olvidado citizens would never know the difference. Wriggling around in the driver's seat, I pulled the coveralls over my usual jeans and T-shirt. I tugged up the front zipper and tucked my key picks in one pocket. I reached for the matching clipboard with its stack of generic paperwork, then locked the car behind me and walked as far as Ted Rich's gravel drive. There were no vehicles parked anywhere near the house.

I climbed the front steps and rang the doorbell. I waited, leafing through the papers on the clipboard, making an official-looking note with the pen attached by a chain. I rang again, but there was no reply. *Quelle surprise.* I moved to the front window, shading my eyes as I peered through the glass. Aside from the fact that there was no sign of the occupant, the place had the look of a man accustomed to living by himself, an aura epitomized by the presence of a Harley-Davidson motorcycle in the middle of the dining room.

Casually, I glanced around. There was no one on the sidewalk and no hint of neighbors watching from across the way. Nonetheless, I frowned, making a big display of my puzzlement. I checked my watch to show that I, at least, was on time for our imaginary appointment. I trotted down the front steps and headed back along the driveway to the rear of the house. The backyard was fenced, and the shrubbery had grown up tall enough to touch the utility wires strung along the property line. The yard was deserted. Both sectional doors of the two-car garage were closed and showed hefty padlocks.

I climbed the back porch steps and then checked to see if any neighbors were busy dialing 9-1-1. Once assured of my privacy, I peeped in the kitchen window. The lights were off in the rooms within view. I tried the door handle. Locked. I stared at the Schlage, wondering how long it would take before it yielded to my key picks. Glancing down at knee height, I noticed that the bottom half of the door panel boasted a sizable homemade pet entrance. Well, what have we here? I reached down, gave the flap a push, and found myself staring at a section of kitchen linoleum. I thought back to Ted Rich's reference to his divorce and the death of his beloved pooch. The opening to the doggie door appeared to be large enough to accommodate me.

I set the clipboard on the porch rail and got down on my hands and knees. At five feet six inches and 118 pounds, I had only minor difficulties in my quest for admittance. Arms above my head, my body tilted to the diagonal, I began to ease myself through the opening. Once I'd succeeded in squeezing my head and shoulders through the door, I paused for a quick appraisal to assure myself there was no one else in residence. My one-sided view was restricted to the chrome-and-Formica dinette set, littered with dirty dishes, and the big plastic clock on the wall above. I inched forward, rotating my body so I could see the rest of the room. Now that I was halfway through the doggie door, it dawned on me that maybe I should have asked Rich if he'd acquired a new mutt. To my left, at eye level, I could see a two-quart water bowl and a large plastic dish filled with dry dog food. Nearby, a rawhide bone sported teeth marks that appeared to have been inflicted by a creature with a surly disposition.

Half a second later, the object of my speculation appeared on the scene. He'd probably been alerted by the noise and came skidding around the corner to see what was up. I'm not dog oriented by nature and I hardly know one breed from the next, with the exception of Chihuahuas, cocker spaniels, and other obvious types. This dog was big, maybe eighty pounds of lean weight on a heavily boned frame. What the hell was he doing while I was ringing the bell? The least he could have done was barked properly to warn me off. The dog was a medium brown with a big face, thick head, and a short, sleek coat. He was heavy through the chest and he had a dick the size of a hairy six-inch Gloria Cubana. A ruff of coarse hair was standing up along his spine, as though from permanent outrage. He stopped in his tracks and stood there, his expression a perfect blend of confusion and incredulity. I could almost see the question mark forming above his head. Apparently, in his experience, few human beings had tried to slither through his private entrance. I ceased struggling, to allow him time to assess the situation. I must not have represented any immediate threat because he neither lunged nor barked nor bit me cruelly about the head and shoulders. On the contrary, he seemed to feel that something was required of him in the way of polite behavior, though I could tell he was having trouble deciding what would be appropriate. He made a whining sound, dropped to his belly, and crept across the floor to me. I stayed where I was. For a while, we lay face-to-face while I suffered his meaty breath and he thought about life. Me and dogs always seem to end up in relationships like this.

"Hi, how're you," I said finally, in what I hoped was a pleasant tone (from the dog's perspective).

He put his head down on his paws and shot me a worried look.

I said, "Listen, I hope you don't mind if I slide on in, because any minute your neighbor's going to look out the window and catch sight of my hineybumper hanging out the doggie door. If you have any objections, speak now or forever hold your peace."

I waited, but the dog never even bared his gums. Using my elbows for leverage, I completed ingress, saying, "Nice dog," "What a good pooch," and similar kiss-ass phrases. His tail began to thump with hope. Maybe I was the little friend his dad had promised would come and play with him.

Once inside the kitchen, I began to rise to my feet. This, in the dog's mind, converted me into a beast that might require savaging. He leapt up, head down, ears back, beginning an experimental growl, his entire chest wall vibrating like a swarm of bees on the move. I sank down to my original submissive position. "Good boy," I murmured, humbly lowering my gaze.

I waited while the dog tested the parameters of his responsibility. The growling faded in due course. I tried again. Lifting onto my hands and knees seemed acceptable, but the minute I attempted to stand, the growling started up again. Make no mistake about it, this dog meant business.

"You're very strict," I said.

I waited a few moments and tried yet again. This time the effort netted me a furious bark. "Okay, okay." The big guy was beginning to get on my nerves. In theory, I was close enough to the doggie door to effect an escape, but I was fearful of going head first, thus exposing my rear end. I was also worried about going out feet first lest the dog attack my upper body while I was wedged in the opening. Meanwhile, the kitchen clock was ticking like a time bomb, forcing a decision. The curtain or the box? I could visualize Ted Rich barreling down the highway in my direction. I had to do *something*. Still on my hands and knees, I crawled forward a step. The dog watched with vigilance but made no menacing gesture. Slowly, I headed across the kitchen floor toward the front of the house. The dog tagged along beside me, his toenails clicking on the grimy linoleum, his full attention focused on my plodding journey. Already, I realized I hadn't really thought this thing through, but I'd been so intent on my ends, I hadn't fully formulated the means.

Babylike, in my romper, I traversed the dining room, bypassed the motorcycle, and entered the living room. This room was carpeted but otherwise contained little in the way of interest. I crawled down the hallway with the dog keeping pace, his head hanging down till his gaze was level with mine. I suppose I should state right here that what I was doing isn't routine behavior for a private eye. My conduct was more typical of someone intent on petty theft, too mulish and impetuous to use legitimate means (provided she could think of any). In the law enforcement sector, my actions would be classified as trespass, burglary, and (given the key picks in my pocket) possession of burglary tools—California Penal Code sections 602, 459, and 466 respectively. I hadn't stolen anything (yet) and the item I was after was purely intellectual, but it was nonetheless illegal to squirm through a doggie door and start crawling down a hall. Caught in the act, I'd be subject to arrest and conviction, perhaps forfeiting my license and my livelihood. Well, dang. All this for a man I'd left after less than nine months of marriage.

The house wasn't large: a bath and two bedrooms, plus the living room, dining room, kitchen, and laundry room. I must say the world is very boring at an altitude of eighteen inches. All I could see were chair legs, carpet snags, and endless stretches of dusty baseboard. No wonder house pets, when left alone, take to peeing on the rugs and gnawing on the furniture. I passed a door on the left that led back into the kitchen, with the laundry room to one side. When I reached the next door on the left, I crawled in and surveyed the premises, mentally wagging my tail. Unmade double bed, night table, chest of drawers, doggie bed, and dirty clothes on the floor. I did a U-turn and crawled into the room across the hall. Rich was using this one as a combination den and home office. Along the wall to my right, he had a row of banged-up file cabinets and a scarred oak desk. He also had a Barcalounger and a television set. The dog climbed on the recliner with a guilty look, watching to see if I was going to swat his hairy butt. I smiled my encouragement. As far as I was concerned, the dog could do anything he wanted.

I made my way over to the desk. "I'm getting up to take a peek, so don't get your knickers in a twist, okay?" By now, the dog was bored, and he yawned so hard I heard a little squeak at the back of his throat. Carefully, I eased into a kneeling position and searched the surface of the desk. There on a stack of papers lay the answer to my prayers: a sheaf of documents, among them the receipt for Rich's payment to the San Felipe Self-Storage Company, dated Saturday, May 17. I tucked the paper in my mouth, sank down on all fours, and crawled to the door. Since the dog had lost interest, I was able to make quick work of the corridor in front of me. Crawling rapidly, I rounded the corner and thumped across the kitchen floor. When I reached the back door, I grabbed the knob and pulled myself to my feet. Exploits like this aren't as easy as they used to be. The knees of my coveralls were covered with dust, and I brushed off some woofies with a frown of disgust. I took the receipt out of my mouth, folded it, and stuck it in the pocket of my coveralls.

When I glanced through the back door to make sure the coast was clear, I spotted my clipboard still sitting on the porch rail where I'd left it. I was just chiding myself for not tucking it someplace less conspicuous when I heard the sound of gravel popping and the front of Rich's pickup appeared in my field of vision. He pulled to a stop, cranked on the hand brake, and opened the truck door. By the time he got out, I'd taken six giant steps backward, practically levitating as I fled through the kitchen to the laundry room, where I slid behind the open door. Rich had slammed his door and was apparently now making his way to the back porch. I heard him clump up the back steps. There was a pause wherein he seemed to make some remark to himself. He'd probably found my clipboard and was puzzling at its import.

The dog had heard him, of course, and was up like a shot, hurtling for the back door as fast as he could. My heart was thumping so loud it sounded like a clothes dryer spinning a pair of wet tennis shoes. I could see my left breast vibrating against the front of my coveralls. I couldn't swear to this, but I think I may have wee-weed ever so slightly in my underpants. Also, I noticed the cuff of my pant leg was now protruding through the crack in the door. I'd barely managed to conceal myself when Rich clattered in the back door and tossed the clipboard on the counter. He and the dog exchanged a ritual greeting. On the part of the dog, much joyous barking and leaps; on Rich's part, a series of exhortations and commands, none of which seemed to have any particular effect. The dog had forgotten my intrusion, sidetracked by the merriment of having his master home.

I heard Rich move through the living room and proceed down the hall, where he entered his office and flipped on the television set. Meanwhile, the dog must have been tickled by a tiny whisper of recollection because he set off in search of me, his nose close to the floor. Hide and seek—what fun—and guess who was It? He rousted me in no time, spying my coveralls. Just to show how smart he was, he actually seemed to press one eye to the crack before he gave my pant leg a tug. He shook his head back and forth, growling with enthusiasm while he yanked on my cuff. Without even thinking, I poked my head around the door and raised a finger to my lips. He barked with enthusiasm, thus releasing me, and then he pranced back and forth hoping I would play. I have to say, it was pathetic to see an eighty-pound mutt having so much fun at my expense. Rich, unaware of the cause, bellowed orders to the pooch, who stood there torn between obedience to his master and the thrill of discovery. Rich called him again, and he bounded away with a series of exuberant yelps. Back in the den, Rich told him to sit and, apparently, he sat. I heard him bark once to alert his master there was game afoot.

I didn't dare delay. Moving with a silence I hoped was absolute, I slipped to the back door and opened it a crack. I was on the brink of escape when I remembered

my clipboard, which was resting on the counter where
Rich had tossed it. I paused long enough to grab it and
then I eased out the back door and closed it carefully behind me. I crept down the porch steps and veered left
along the drive, tapping the clipboard casually against
my thigh. My impulse was to bolt as soon as I reached
the street, but I forced myself to walk, not wanting to call
attention to my exodus. There's nothing so conspicuous
as someone in civilian clothes, running down the street as
though pursued by beasts.

3

THE DRIVE BACK to Santa Teresa was uneventful, though I was so juiced up on adrenaline I had to make a conscious effort not to speed. I seemed to see cops everywhere: two at an intersection directing traffic where a stoplight was on the fritz; one lurking near the on-ramp, concealed by a clump of bushes; another parked on the berm behind a motorist, who waited in resignation for the ticket to come. Having escaped from the danger zone, I was not only being meticulous about obeying the law but struggling to regain a sense of normalcy, whatever *that* is. The risk I'd taken at Teddy's house had fractured my perception. I'd become, at the same time, disassociated from reality and more keenly connected to it so that "real life" now seemed flat and strangely lusterless. Cops, rock stars, soldiers, and career criminals all experience the same shift, the plunge from soaring indomitability to unconquerable lassitude, which is why they tend to hang out with others of their ilk. Who else can understand the high? You get amped, wired, blasted out of your tiny mind on situational stimulants. Afterward, you have to talk yourself down, reliving your experience until the charge is off and events collapse back to their ordinary size. I was still awash with the rush, my vision shimmering. The Pacific pulsated on my left. The sea air felt as brittle as a sheet of glass. Like flint on stone, the late morning sun struck the waves in a series of sparks until I half expected the entire ocean to burst into flames. I turned on the radio, tuning the station to one with booming music. I rolled down the car windows and let the wind buffet my hair.

As soon as I got home, I set the cardboard box on the desk, pulled the storage company receipt from my pocket, and tossed the coveralls in the wash. I never should have broken into Teddy's house that way. What was I thinking? I was nuts, temporarily deranged, but the man had irritated me beyond reason. All I'd wanted was a piece of information, which I now possessed. Of course, I had no idea what to do with it. The last thing I needed was to reconnect with my ex.

We'd parted on bad terms, and I'd made a point of abolishing my memories of him. Mentally, I'd excised all reference to the relationship, so that now I scarcely allowed myself to remember his name. Friends were aware that I'd been married at the age of twenty-one, but they knew nothing of who he was and had no clue about the split. I'd put the man in a box and dropped him to the bottom of my emotional ocean, where he'd languished ever since. Oddly enough, while my second husband, Daniel, had betrayed me, gravely injuring my pride, he hadn't violated my sense of honor as Mickey Magruder had. While I may be careless about the penal code, I'm never casual about the law. Mickey had crossed the line, and he'd tried dragging me along with him. I'd moved on short notice, willing to abandon most of my belongings when I walked out the door.

The overload of chemicals began to drain from my

system, letting anxiety in. I went into my kitchenette and tranquilized myself with the ritual of a sandwich, smoothing Jif Extra Crunchy peanut butter on two slices of hearty seven-grain bread. I arranged six bread-and-butter pickles like big green polka dots on the thick layer of caramel-colored goo. I cut the finished sandwich on the diagonal and laid it on a paper napkin while I licked the knife clean. One virtue of being single is not having to explain the peculiarities of one's appetites in moments of stress. I popped open a can of Diet Coke and ate at the kitchen counter, perched on a stool with a copy of *Time* magazine, which I read back to middle. Nothing in the front ever seems to interest me.

When I finished, I crumpled the paper napkin, tossed it in the trash, and returned to my desk. I was ready to go through the box of memorabilia, though I half dreaded what I would find. So much of the past is encapsulated in the odds and ends. Most of us discard more information about ourselves than we ever care to preserve. Our recollection of the past is not simply distorted by our faulty perception of events remembered but skewed by those forgotten. The memory is like orbiting twin stars, one visible, one dark, the trajectory of what's evident forever affected by the gravity of what's concealed.

I sat down in my swivel chair and tilted back on its axis. I propped my feet on my desk, the box open on the floor beside me. A hasty visual survey suggested that the minute I'd walked out, Mickey'd packed everything of mine he could lay hands on. I pictured him carting the box through the apartment, snatching up my belongings, tossing them together in a heap. I could see dried-out toiletries, a belt, junk mail and old magazines rubber-banded in a bundle, five paperback novels, and a couple of pairs of shoes. Any other clothes I'd left were long gone. He'd probably shoved those in a trash bag and called the Salvation Army, taking satisfaction in the idea that many much-loved articles would end up on a sale table for a buck or two. He must have drawn the line at memorabilia. Some of it was here, at any rate, spared from the purge.

I reached in and fumbled among the contents, letting my fingers make the selection among the unfamiliar clusters, a grab bag of the misplaced, the bygone, and the abandoned. The first item I retrieved was a packet of old report cards, bound together with thin white satin ribbon. These, my Aunt Gin had saved for reasons that escaped me. She wasn't sentimental by nature, and the quality of my academic performance was hardly worth preserving. I was a quite average student showing no particular affinity for reading, writing, or arithmetic. I could spell like a champ and I was good at memory games. I liked geography and music and the smell of LePage's paste on black and orange construction paper. Most other aspects of school were terrifying. I hated reciting *anything* in front of classmates, or being called on perversely when my hand wasn't even raised. The other kids seemed to enjoy the process, while I quaked in my shoes. I threw up almost daily, and when I wasn't sick at school I would try to manufacture some excuse to stay home or go to work with Aunt Gin. Faced with aggression on the part of my classmates, I quickly learned that my most effective defense was to bite the shit out of my opponent. There was nothing quite as satisfying as the sight of my teeth marks in the tender flesh of someone's arm. There are probably individuals today who still bear the wrathful half moon of dental scars.

I sorted through the report cards, all of which were similar and shared a depressingly common theme. Scanning the written comments, I could see that my teachers were given to much hand wringing and dire warnings about my ultimate fate. Though cursed with "potential," I was apparently a child with little to recommend her. According to their notes, I daydreamed, wandered the classroom at will, failed to finish lessons, seldom volunteered an answer, and usually got it wrong when I did.

"Kinsey's bright enough, but she seems absentminded and she has a tendency to focus only on subjects of interest to her. Her copious curiosity is offset by an inclination to mind everybody else's business. . . ."

"Kinsey seems to have difficulty telling the truth. She should be evaluated by the school psychologist to determine . . ."

"Kinsey shows excellent comprehension and mastery of topics that appeal to her, but lacks discipline. . . ."

"Doesn't seem to enjoy team sports. Doesn't cooperate with others on class projects. . . ."

"Able to work well on her own."

"Undisciplined. Unruly."

"Timid. Easily upset when reprimanded."

"Given to sudden disappearances when things don't go her way. Leaves classroom without permission."

I studied my young self as though reading about a stranger. My parents had been killed in a car wreck on Memorial Day weekend. I'd turned five on May 5 that year, and they died at the end of that month. In September, I started school, armed with a lunch box, my tablet paper, a fat, red Big Bear pencil, and a lot of gritty determination. From my current vantage point, I can see the pain and confusion I hadn't dared experience back then. Though physically undersized and fearful from day one, I was autonomous, defiant, and as hard as a nut. There was much I admired about the child I had been: the ability to adapt, the resilience, the refusal to conform. These were qualities I still harbored, though perhaps to my detriment. Society values cooperation over independence, obedience over individuality, and niceness above all else.

The next packet contained photos from that same period. In class pictures, I was usually half a head shorter than anyone else in my class. My countenance was dark, my expression solemn and wistful, as if I longed to be gone, which of course I did. While others in the class stared directly at the camera, my attention was inevitably diverted by something taking place on the sidelines. In one photograph, my face was a blur because I'd turned my head to look at someone in the row behind me. Even then, life must have seemed more interesting slightly off-center. What I found unsettling was the fact I hadn't changed much in the years between.

I probably should have been out somewhere looking for new clients instead of allowing myself to be distracted by the past. What could have happened that would result in Mickey's belongings being sold at public auction? Not that it was any of my business, but then again, that's exactly what gave the question its appeal.

I went back to the cardboard box and pulled out an old tape recorder as big as a hardback book. I'd forgotten that old thing, accustomed by now to machines the size of a deck of cards. I could see a tape cassette inside. I pushed the PLAY button. No go. The batteries were probably already dead the day Mickey tossed it in the box with everything else. I opened my desk drawer and took out a fresh pack of C batteries, shoving four, end to end, into the back of the machine. I pushed PLAY again. This time the spindles began to turn and I heard my own voice, some rambling account of the case I was working at the time. This was like historical data sealed in a cornerstone, meant to be discovered later after everyone was gone.

I turned it off and set the tape machine aside. I reached into the box again. Tucked down along the side, I found ammo for the 9mm Smith & Wesson Mickey'd given me for a wedding present. There was no sign of the gun, but I could remember how thrilled I'd been with the gift. The finish on the barrel had been S & W blue, and the stock was checked walnut with S & W monograms. We'd met in November and married the following August. By then, he'd been a cop for almost sixteen years, while I'd joined the department in May, a mere three months before. I took the gift of a firearm as an indication that he saw me as a colleague, a status he accorded few women in those days. Now I could see there were larger implications. I mean, what kind of guy gives his young bride a semi-automatic on their wedding night? Impulsively, I pulled open my bottom drawer, searching for the old address book where I'd tucked the only forwarding information I'd ever had for him. The phone number had probably been relinquished and reassigned half a dozen times, the address just as long out of date.

I was interrupted by a knock. I hauled my feet off the desk and crossed to the door, peering through the port-hole to find my landlord standing on the porch. Henry was wearing long pants for a change, and his expression was distracted as he stared out across the yard. He'd turned eighty-six on Valentine's Day: tall and lean, a man who never actually seemed to age. He and his siblings, who were respectively eighty-eight, eighty-nine, ninety-five, and ninety-six, came from such vigorous genetic stock that I'm inclined to believe they'll never actually "pass." Henry's handsome in the manner of a fine antique, handcrafted and well constructed, exhibiting a polish that suggests close to nine decades of loving use. Henry has always been loyal, outspoken, kind, and generous. He's protective of me in ways that feel strange but are welcome, nonetheless.

I opened the door. "Hi, Henry. What are you up to? I haven't seen you for days."

"Thank goodness you're home. I have a dental appointment in"—he paused to glance at his watch—"approximately sixteen and three-quarter minutes, and both my cars are out of commission. My Chevy's still in the shop after that paint can fell on it, and now I discover the station wagon's dead. Can you give me a lift? Better yet, if you lend me your car, I can save you the trip. This is going to take awhile and I hate to tie you up." Henry's five-window butter-yellow 1932 Chevy coupe had suffered some minor damage when several paint cans shuddered off the garage shelf during a cluster of baby earthquakes late in March. Henry's meticulous about the car, keeping it in pristine condition. His second vehicle, the station wagon, he used whenever his Michigan-based sibs came to town.

"I'll give you a ride. I don't mind a bit," I said. "Let me grab my keys." I left the door ajar while I snagged my handbag from the counter and fished out the keys from the outer compartment. I picked up my jacket while I was at it and then pulled the door shut behind me and locked it.

We rounded the corner of the building and passed through the gate. I opened the passenger side door and moved around the front of the car. He leaned across the seat and unlocked the door on my side. I slid under the wheel, fired up the ignition, and we were under way.

"Great. This is great. I really appreciate this," Henry said, his tone completely false.

I glanced over at him, making note of the tension that had tightened his face. "What are you having done?"

"A crown 'ack 'ere," he said, talking with his finger stuck at the back of his mouth.

"At least it's not a root canal."

"I'd have to kill myself first. I was hoping you'd be gone so I could cancel the appointment."

"No such luck," I said.

Henry and I share an apprehension about dentists that borders on the comical. While we're both dutiful about checkups, we agonize over any work that actually has to be done. Both of us are subject to dry mouth, squirmy stomachs, clammy hands, and lots of whining. I reached over and felt his fingers, which were icy and faintly damp.

Henry frowned to himself. "I don't see why he has to do this. The filling's fine, really not a problem. It doesn't even hurt. It's a little sensitive to heat, and I've had to give up anything with ice—"

"The filling's old?"

"Well, 1942—but there's nothing *wrong* with it."

"Talk about make-work."

"My point exactly. In those days, dentists knew how to fill a tooth. Now a filling has a limited shelf life, like a carton of milk. It's planned obsolescence. You're lucky if it lasts you long enough to pay the bill." He stuck his finger in his mouth again, turning his face in my direction. "See this? Only fifteen years old and the guy's already talking about replacing it."

"You're kidding! What a scam!"

"Remember when they put fluoride in the city water and everybody thought it was a Communist plot? Dentists spread that rumor."

"Of course they did," I said, chiming in on cue. "They saw the handwriting on the wall. No more cavities, no more business." We went through the same duet every time either one of us had to have something done.

"Now they've cooked up that surgery where they cut half your gums away. If they can't talk you into that, they claim you need braces."

"What a *crock*," I said.

"I don't know why I can't have my teeth pulled and get it over with," he said, his mood becoming morose.

I made the usual skeptical response. "I wouldn't go that far, Henry. You have beautiful teeth."

"I'd rather keep 'em in a glass. I can't stand the drilling. The noise drives me crazy. And the scraping when they scale? I nearly rip the arms off the chair. Sounds like a shovel on a sidewalk, a pickax on concrete—"

"All right! Cut it out. You're making my hands sweat."

By the time I pulled into the parking lot, we'd worked ourselves into such a state of indignation, I was surprised he was willing to keep the appointment. I sat in the dentist's waiting room after Henry's name was called. Except for the receptionist, I had the place to myself, which I thought was faintly worrisome. How come the dentist only had one patient? I pictured Medicaid fraud: phantom clients, double-billing, charges for work that would never be done. Just a typical day in the life of Dr. Dentifrice, federal con artist and cheater with a large sadistic streak. I did give the guy points for having recent issues of all the best magazines.

From the other room, over the burbling of the fish tank, which is meant to mask the shrieks, I could hear the sounds of a high-speed drill piercing through tooth enamel straight to the pulsing nerve below. My fingers began to stick to the pages of *People* magazine, leaving a series of moist, round prints. Once in a while, I caught Henry's muffled protest, a sound suggestive of flinching and lots of blood gushing out. Just the thought of his suffering made me hyperventilate. I finally got so light-headed I had to step outside, where I sat on the mini-porch with my head between my knees.

Henry eventually emerged, looking stricken and relieved, feeling at his numbed lip to see if he was drooling on himself. To distract him on the ride home, I filled him in on the cardboard box, the circumstances under which it originated, Mickey's paranoia, the John Russell alias, and my own B&E adventure at Ted Rich's place. He liked the part about the dog, having urged me repeatedly to get one of my own. We had the usual brief argument about me and household pets.

Then he said, "So, tell me about your ex. You said he was a cop, but what's the rest of it?"

"Don't ask."

"But what do you think it means, his being delinquent with his storage fees?"

"How do I know? I haven't talked to him in years."

"Don't be like that, Kinsey. I hate it when you're stingy with information. I want the story on him."

"It's too complicated to get into. Maybe I'll tell you later, when I've figured it out."

"Are you going to follow up?"

"No."

"Maybe he got lazy about paying his bills," he said, trying to draw me in.

"I doubt it. He was always good about that stuff."

"People change."

"No, they don't. Not in my experience."

"Nor in mine, now that you mention it."

The two of us were silent for a block, and then Henry spoke up. "Suppose he's in trouble?"

"Serves him right if he is."

"You wouldn't help?"

"What for?"

"Well, it wouldn't hurt to check."

"I'm not going to *do* that."

"Why not? All it'd take is a couple of calls. What's it going to cost?"

"How do you know what it'd cost? You don't even know the man."

"I'm just saying, you're not busy . . . at least, as far as I've heard. . . ."

"Did I ask for advice?"

"I thought you did," he said. "I'm nearly certain you were fishing for encouragement."

"I was *not*."

"I see."

"Well, I wasn't. I have absolutely no interest in the man."

"Sorry. My mistake."

"You're the only person in my life who gets away with this shit."

When I got back to my desk, the first thing my eye fell on was my address book lying open to the *M*'s. I flipped the book shut and shoved it in a drawer, which I closed with a bang.

4

I SAT DOWN in my swivel chair and gave the carton a shove with my foot. I was tempted to chuck the damn thing, salvage the personal papers and dump the rest in the trash. However, having paid the twenty bucks, I couldn't bring myself to do it. It wasn't so much that I was cheap, though that was certainly a factor. The truth is, I was curious. I reasoned that just because I looked through the box didn't make me responsible for anything else. It certainly wouldn't *obligate* me to try to locate my ex. Sorting through the items would in no way compel me to take action on his behalf. If Mickey'd fallen on hard times, if he was in a jam of some kind, then so be it. *C'est la vie* and so what? It had nothing to do with me.

I pulled the wastebasket closer to the box, pushed the flaps back, and peered in. In the time I'd been gone, the elves and fairies still hadn't managed to tidy up the mess. I started tossing out loose toiletries: a flattened tube of toothpaste and a shampoo bottle with a thin layer of sludge pooled along its length. Something had leaked out and oozed down through the box, welding articles together like an insidious glue. I threw out a hodgepodge of over-the-counter medications, an ancient diaphragm, a safety razor, and a toothbrush with bristles splayed out in all directions. It looked like I'd used it to clean the bathroom grout.

From under the toiletries, I excavated a bundle of junk mail. When I picked up the stack, the rubber band disintegrated, and I plunked the bulk of it in the wastebasket. A few stray envelopes surfaced, and I pulled those from among the discarded magazines and dog-eared catalogs—bullshit from the look of them: a bank statement for an account I'd closed many years before, a department store circular, and a notice from Publisher's Clearing House telling me I'd been short-listed for a million bucks. The third envelope I picked up was a credit card bill that I *sincerely* hoped I paid. What a disgrace that would be, a blot on my credit rating. Maybe that's why American Express wasn't sending me any preapproved cards these days. And here I'd been feeling so superior. Mickey's payments might be delinquent, but not mine, she said.

I turned the bill over to open it. Stuck to the back was another envelope, this one a letter that must have arrived in the same post. I pulled the second envelope free, tearing the paper in the process. The envelope itself bore no return address, and I didn't recognize the writing. The script was tight and angular, letters slanting heavily to the left, as if on the verge of collapsing. The postmark read SANTA TERESA, APRIL 2, 1972. I'd left Mickey the day before, April Fool's Day, as it turned out. I removed the single sheet of lined paper, which was covered with the same inky cursive, as flattened as bent grass.

Kinsey,
 Mickey made me promise not to do this, but I think you should know. He was with me that night, sure, he

pushed the guy, but it was no big deal. I know because I saw it and so did a lot of other people whoer on his side. Benny was fine when he took off. Him and Mickey couldn't have connect after because we went back to my place and he was their till midnight. I told him I'd testify, but he says no because of Eric and his situation. He's complelty innocent and desperetly needs your help. What difference does it make where he was as long as he didn't do it? If you love him, you should take his part insted of being such a bitch. Being a cop is his whole life, please don't take that away from him. Otherwise I hope you find a way to live with yourself because your runing everything for him.

D.

I read the note twice, my mind blank except for a clinical and bemused response to all the misspellings and run-on sentences. I'm a snob about grammar and I have trouble taking anyone seriously who gets "there" possessives confused with "there" demonstratives. I didn't "rune" Mickey's life. It hadn't been up to me to save him from anything. He'd asked me to lie for him and I'd flatly refused. Failing that, he'd probably concocted this cover story with "D"—whoever she was. From the sound of it, she knew me, but I couldn't for the life of me remember her. D. That could be Dee. Dee Dee. Donna. Dawn. Diane. Doreen. . . .

Oh, shit. Of course.

There was a bartender named Dixie who worked in a place out in Colgate where Mickey and some of his cop buddies hung out after work. It wasn't uncommon for the guys to band together to do their after-hours drinking. In the early seventies, there were frequent watch parties at the end of a shift, revelries that sometimes went on until the wee hours of the morning. Both public and private drunkenness are considered violations of police discipline, as are extramarital affairs, failure to pay debts, and other scurrilous behavior. Such violations are punishable by the department, because a police officer is considered "on duty" at all times as a matter of public image and because tolerating such conduct might lead to similar infractions while the officer is formally at work. When complaints came in about the shift parties, the officers moved the drink fests from the city to the county, effectively removing them from departmental scrutiny. The Honky-Tonk, where Dixie worked, became their favorite haunt.

At the time I met Dixie, she must have been in her mid-twenties, older than I was by four or five years. Mickey and I had been married for six weeks. I was still a rookie, working traffic, while he'd been promoted to detective, assigned first to vice and then to burglary and theft under Lieutenant Dolan, who later moved on to homicide. Dixie was the one who organized the celebration for any transfer or promotion, and we all understood it was just one more excuse to party. I remembered sitting at the bar chatting with her while Mickey sucked back draft beers, playing pool with his cronies or trading war stories with the veterans coming back from Vietnam. At eighteen, he'd served a fourteen-month combat tour in Korea, and he was always interested in the contrast between the Korean War and the action in Vietnam.

Dixie's husband, Eric Hightower, had been wounded in Laos in April 1971, returning to the world with both legs missing. In his absence, she'd put herself through bartending school and she'd worked at the Tonk since the day Eric shipped out. After he came home, he'd sit there in his wheelchair, his behavior moody or manic, depending on his medications and his alcohol levels. Dixie kept him sedated on a steady regimen of Bloody Marys, which seemed to pacify his rage. To me, she seemed like a busy mother, forced to bring her kid to work with her. The rest of us were polite, but Eric certainly didn't do much to endear himself. At twenty-six, he was a bitter old man.

I used to watch in fascination while she assembled Mai Tais, gin and tonics, Manhattans, martinis, and revolting concoctions like pink squirrels and crème de menthe frappés. She talked incessantly, hardly looking at what she did, eyeballing the pour, spritzing soda or water from the bar hose. Sometimes she constructed four and five drinks at the same time without missing a beat. Her laugh was husky and low-pitched. She exchanged endless ribald comments with the guys, all of whom she knew by name and circumstance. I was impressed with her bawdy self-assurance. I also pitied her her husband, with his sour disposition and his obvious limitations, which I assumed extended into sex. Even so, it never occurred to me that she would screw around on him, especially with *my* husband. I must have been brain-dead not to notice—unless, of course, she was inventing this stuff to provide Mickey with the alibi that I'd declined to supply.

Dixie was my height, rail thin, with a long narrow face and an untidy tangle of auburn hair halfway down her back. Her brows were plucked, a wispy pair of arches that fanned out like wings from the bridge of her nose. Her eyes were darkly charcoaled, and she wore a fringe of fake lashes that made her eyes jump from her face. She was usually braless under her T-shirt, and she wore mini-skirts so short she could hardly sit down. Sometimes she veered off in the opposite direction, donning long granny dresses or India-print tunics over wide-legged pantlets.

I read her note again, but sure enough, the content was the same. She and Mickey had been having an affair. That seemed to be the subtext of her communication, though I found it hard to believe. He'd never given any indication he was even *interested* in her, or maybe he had and I'd been too dumb to pick up on it. How could she have stood there and chatted with me if the two of them were making it behind my back? On the other hand, the idea was not entirely inconsistent with Mickey's history.

Before we'd connected, he'd been involved in numerous affairs, but he was, after all, single and savvy enough to avoid emotional entanglements. In the late sixties, early seventies, sex was casual, recreational, indiscriminate, and uncommitted. Women had been liberated by the advent of the birth control pill, and dope had erased any further prohibitions. This was the era of love-ins, psychedelics, dropouts, war protests, body paint, assassinations, LSD, and rumors of kids so stoned their eyeballs got fried because they stared at the sun too long.

It was also the era in which law enforcement began to change. In 1964, the Supreme Court had ruled, in the matter of Escobedo *v.* Illinois, that the refusal by the police to honor Escobedo's request to consult his lawyer during the course of an interrogation constituted a violation of the Sixth Amendment. Two years later, 1966, in Miranda *v.* Arizona, the Supreme Court came down again on the side of the plaintiff, citing a breach of Sixth Amendment rights. From that point on, the climate in law enforcement underwent a shift, and the image of Dirty Harry was replaced by at least the *appearance* of restraint.

Mickey chafed at the limitations set by policy and, on a broader level, at legal restrictions he felt interfered with his effectiveness. He was an old-fashioned cop. He identified with the crime victim. In his mind, theirs were the only claims that counted. Let the perpetrator fend for himself. He hated having to protect the guilty, and he had no patience for the so-called rights of those arrested. I sometimes suspected he'd formed his attitudes from the reams of pulp fiction he'd read growing up. Please understand that none of this was evident to me when we first met. I was not only infatuated with his attitude but wide-eyed with admiration at what I mistook for worldliness. I suspect in Mickey's view certain rules and regulations simply didn't apply to him. He operated outside the standards most other cops finally came to accept. Mickey was accustomed to getting his way, experienced in what he called "certain time-honored methods for persuading a suspect to make himself agreeable in the matter of inculpatory statements." Mickey usually said this in a tone that made everybody laugh.

Mickey was revered by his fellow officers and, until that March, his departmental run-ins were focused on a series of minor infractions. He was late with his reports and occasionally insubordinate, though he seemed to have an instinct for how far he could push. He'd been the subject of two citizen's complaints: once for offensive language and once for excessive use of force. In both incidents the department investigated and found in his favor. Still, it didn't look good. His was an odd mix of the offbeat and the conventional. In his personal life, he was scrupulously honest—about his taxes, his bills, his personal debts. He was loyal to his friends and discreet with regard to others. He also honored his commitments, except (apparently) to me. He would never violate a confidence, never rat out a pal or a fellow officer. Among men, he was esteemed. With women, he was regarded with an admiration bordering on hero worship. I know because I did this myself, elevating his nonconformity to something praiseworthy instead of faintly dangerous.

Looking back on it, I can see that I didn't want to know the truth about him. I had graduated from the police academy in April of 1971 and was hired by the Santa Teresa Police Department as soon as I turned twenty-one in May. I'd met Mickey the previous November, and I was dazzled by the image he projected: seasoned, gruff, cynical, wise. Within months we fell in love, and by August we were married—all of this before either of us understood what the other was about. Once committed, I was determined to see him as the man I wanted him to be. I needed to believe. I saw him as an idol, so I accepted his version of events even when common sense suggested he was slanting the facts.

In the fall of 1971, after Mickey was reassigned to burglary and theft, he developed what was euphemistically referred to as a "personality conflict" with Con Dolan, who headed crimes against property. Lieutenant Dolan was an autocrat and a stickler for regulations, which caused the two of them to clash time and time again. Their differences put an end to Mickey's hopes for advancement.

Six months later, in the spring of 1972, Mickey resigned from the department to avoid yet another tangle with Internal Affairs. He was, at that time, under investigation for voluntary manslaughter after he'd been involved in a bar dispute. His altercation with a transient named Benny Quintero resulted in the man's death. This was March 17, St. Patrick's Day, and Mickey was off duty, drinking at the Honky-Tonk with a bunch of buddies, who supported his account. He claimed the man was drunk and abusive and exhibited threatening behavior. Mickey removed him bodily to the parking lot, where the two engaged in a brief shoving match. To hear Mickey tell it, he'd pushed the guy around some, but only in response to the drunk's attack. Witnesses swore he hadn't landed any blows. Benny Quintero left the scene, and that was the last anyone reported seeing him until his body was discovered the next day, beaten and bloody, dumped by the side of Highway 154. Internal Affairs launched an investigation, and Mickey's attorney, Mark Bethel, advised him to keep his mouth shut. Since Mickey was the prime suspect, facing the possibility of criminal charges, Bethel was doing what he could to cover his backside. IA can coerce testimony but is forbidden to share findings with the DA's office. There could be serious consequences all the same. Given the overarching need for honest officers, the department was determined to pursue the matter. Mickey resigned in order to avoid questioning. If he hadn't left when he did, he'd have been fired anyway for his refusal to respond.

The day Mickey turned in his badge, his weapon, and his radio, his fellow officers were incensed. Department regulations prohibited his superiors from making any public statement, and Mickey downplayed his departure, which made him look all the more heroic in the eyes of his comrades. The impression he gave was that, despite their treatment of him, his loyalty to the department overrode his right to defend himself against accusations completely contrived and unfair. So convincing was he that I believed him myself right up to the moment when he asked me to lie for him. A criminal investigation was initiated, which is where I came in. Apparently, there were four hours unaccounted for in Mickey's alibi for that night. He refused to say where he'd been or what he'd done between the time he left the Honky-Tonk and the time he arrived home. He was suspected of following the guy and finishing the job elsewhere, but Mickey denied the whole thing. He asked me to cover for him, and that's when I walked.

I left him April 1 and filed for divorce on the tenth of that month. Some weeks later, the findings from the coroner's exam revealed that Quintero, a Vietnam veteran, had suffered a service-related head injury. In combat, he'd been hit by sniper fire, and a stainless steel plate now served where a portion of his skull had been blown away. The official cause of death was a slow hemorrhage in the depths of his brain. Any minor blow could have generated the fatal seepage. In addition, the toxicology report showed a blood alcohol level of .15 with traces of amphetamine, marijuana, and cocaine. There was no actual evidence that Mickey had encountered Benny after their initial scuffle in the parking lot. The DA declined to file charges, so Mickey was off the hook. By then, of course, the damage had been done. He'd been separated from the city and he was, soon afterward, permanently separated from me. In the intervening years, my disenchantment had begun to fade. While I didn't want to see him, I didn't wish him ill. The last I'd heard he was doing personal security, a once-dedicated cop demoted to working night shift in an imitation cop's uniform.

I read the letter again, wondering what I would have done if I'd received it back then. I felt a ripple of anxiety coursing through my frame. If this was true, I had indeed contributed to his ruin.

I opened the drawer and took out my address book, which opened as if by magic to the page where he was listed. I picked up the handset and punched in the number. The line rang twice, and then I was greeted with a big two-tone whistling and the usual canned message telling me the number in the 213 area code was no longer in service. If I felt I'd reached the recording in error, I could recheck the number and then dial it again. Just to be certain, I redialed the number and heard the same message. I hung up, trying to decide if there were any other possibilities I should pursue.

5

I HADN'T VISITED the house on Chapel Street for a good fifteen years. I parked out in front and let myself into the yard through a small wrought-iron gate. The house was white frame, a homely story-and-a-half, with an angular bay window and a narrow side porch. Two second-story windows seemed to perch on the bay, and a simple wood filigree embellished the peaked roof. Built in 1875, the house was plain, lacking sufficient charm and period detail to warrant protection by the local historical preservationists. Out front, a stream of one-way traffic was a constant reminder of downtown Santa Teresa, only two blocks away. In another few years, the property would probably be sold and the house would finish its days as a secondhand furniture store or a little mom-and-pop business. Eventually, the building would be razed and the lot would be offered up as prime commercial real estate. I suppose not every vintage single-family dwelling can be spared the wrecker's ball, but a day will soon come when the history of the common folk will be entirely erased. The mansions of the wealthy will remain where they stand, the more ponderous among them converted for use by museums, art academies, and charitable foundations. A middle-class home like this would scarcely survive to the turn of another century. For the moment, it was safe. The front yard was well tended and the exterior paint looked fresh. I knew from past occasions the backyard was spacious, complete with a hand-laid brick patio, a built-in barbecue pit, and an orchard of fruit trees.

I pressed the front doorbell. A shrill note echoed harshly through the house. Peter Shackelford, "Shack," and his wife, Bundy, had been close friends of Mickey's long before we met. Theirs was a second marriage for both—Shack was divorced, Bundy widowed. Shack had adopted Bundy's four kids and raised them as his own. In those days, the couple entertained often and easily: pizza, potluck suppers, and backyard barbecues, paper plates, plastic ware, and bring-your-own-bottle, with everyone pitching in on cleanup. There were usually babies in diapers, toddlers taking off on cross-lawn forays. The older kids played Frisbee or raced around the yard like a bunch of hooligans. With all the parents on the scene, discipline was casual and democratic. Anyone close to the miscreant was authorized to act. In those days, I wasn't quite so self-congratulatory about my childless state, and I would occasionally keep an eye on the little ones while their parents cut loose.

Mickey and Shack had joined the Santa Teresa Police Department at just about the same time and had worked in close proximity. They were never partners, per se, but the two of them, along with a third cop named Roy "Lit" Littenberg, were known as the Three Musketeers. Lit and Shack were part of the crowd at the Honky-Tonk the year Mickey went down. I was hoping one or the other would know his whereabouts and his current status. I also needed confirmation of the letter's contents. I'd been convinced Mickey was guilty of the beating that resulted in Benny's death. I wasn't sure what I'd do if it turned out he'd had a legitimate alibi for that night. The idea made my stomach roil with anxiety.

Shack answered the door half a minute later, though it took him another ten seconds to figure out who I was. The delay gave me a chance to register the changes in him. In the period when I'd known him, he must have been in his late thirties. He was now in his early fifties and a good twenty-five pounds heavier. Gravity had tugged at all the planes in his face, now defined by a series of downward-turning lines: dense brows over drooping eyelids, sagging cheeks, a bushy mustache and heavy mouth curving down toward his double chin. His thick salt-and-pepper hair was clipped close to his head as though he were still subject to departmental regulations. He was wearing shorts, flip-flops, and a loose white T-shirt, the sagging neckline revealing a froth of white chest hair. Like Mickey, Shack had lifted weights three days a week, and there was still the suggestion of power in the way he carried himself.

"Hello, Shack. How are you?" I said, when I could see that my identity had been noted. I didn't bother to smile. This was not a social visit, and I guessed his feelings for me were neither friendly nor warm.

His tone when he spoke was surprisingly mild. "I always figured you'd show up."

"Here I am," I said. "Mind if I come in?"

"Why not?"

He stepped aside, allowing me to enter the front hall ahead of him. Given the echoes of the past, the quiet seemed unnatural. "Might as well follow me out back. I don't spend a lot of time in this part of the house." Shack closed the door and moved down the hall toward the kitchen.

Even the most cursory glance showed half the furniture was gone. In the living room, I spotted a coffee table, miscellaneous side tables, and a straight-back wooden chair. The silver-dollar-sized circles of matted carpeting indicated where the couch and easy chairs had once been. The built-in bookcases, flanking the fireplace, were now bereft of books. In their place, twenty-five to thirty framed photographs showed a myriad of smiling faces: babies, children, and adults. Most were studio portraits, but there were several enlargements of snapshots from family gatherings.

"Are you moving?"

He shook his head. "Bundy died six months ago," he said. "Most of the furniture was hers anyway. I let the kids take what they wanted. There's plenty left for my purposes."

"Is that them in the photographs?"

"Them and their kids. We got thirteen grandchildren among the four of them."

"Congratulations."

"Thanks. The youngest, Jessie . . . you remember her?"

"Dark curly hair?"

"That's her. The wild one in the bunch. She hasn't married to date, but she adopted two Vietnamese children."

"What's she do for a living?"

"Attorney in New York. She does corporate law."

"Do any of the others live close?"

"Scott's down in Sherman Oaks. They're spread out all over, but they visit when they can. Every six–eight months, I fire up the Harley and do a big round trip. Good kids, all of them. Bun did a hell of a job. I'm a sorry substitute, but I do what I can."

"What are you up to these days? I heard you left the department."

"A year ago this May. I don't do much of anything, to tell you the truth."

"You still lifting weights?"

"Can't. I got hurt. Had an accident on duty. Some drunk ran a red light and broadsided my patrol car. Killed him outright and knocked me all to hell and gone. I got a fractured fifth vertebra so I ended up taking an industrial retirement. A worker's comp claim."

"Too bad."

"No point complaining about things you can't change. The money pays the bills and gives me time to myself. What about you? I hear you're a P.I."

"I've been doing that for years."

He led me through the kitchen to the glassed-in porch that ran along the rear of the house. He seemed to live the way I did, confined to one area like a pet left alone while its owners are off at work. The kitchen was completely tidy. I could see a single plate, a cereal bowl, a spoon, and a coffee mug in the dish rack. He probably used the same few utensils, carefully washing up between meals. Why put anything away when you're only going to take it out and use it again? There was something homely about the presence of the dishes in the rack. From the look of it, he lived almost exclusively in the kitchen and enclosed porch. A futon, doubling as a couch, was set up at one end, blankets neatly folded with the pillows stacked on top. There was a TV on the floor. The rest of the porch was taken up with woodworking equipment: a lathe, a drill press, a router, a couple of C clamps, a vise, a wood chisel, a table saw, and an assortment of planes. He was in the process of refinishing two pieces. A chest of drawers had been stripped, pending further attention. A wooden kitchen chair had been laid on its back, its legs sticking out as stiffly as a dead possum's. Shack must sleep every night with the heady scent of turpentine, glue, tung oil, and wood shavings. He caught my look and said, "Virtue of being single. You can do anything you want."

I said, "Amen to that."

Once upon a time, Bundy had sewn the café curtains, hanging them on rods across the middle of the row of windows. The green and white checked cotton, probably permanent press, still looked fresh: crisp, carefully laundered, with little clip-on curtain rings. I found my eyes filling inexplicably with tears and had to feign attention to the backyard, which I could see through the glass. Many of the trees remained, as bent as old spines, curving toward the ground from a once-proud height. A saddle of purple morning glories was cinched to the fence, the chicken wire now swaybacked from the weight of the vines. The barbecue grill top had turned red-brown with rust, replaced by a portable kettle grill parked closer to the back steps.

Shack leaned against the wall with his arms folded across his chest. "So what's the reason for the call?"

"I'm looking for Mickey. The only number I have is a disconnect."

"You have business with him?"

"I may. I'm not sure. Do I need your approval before I telephone the man?"

Shack seemed amused. Bundy had always given him a hard time. Maybe he missed the rough and tumble of conversation. Live alone long enough and you forget what it's like. His smile faded slightly. "No offense, kiddo, but why not leave him alone?"

"I want to know he's okay. I don't intend to bother him. When's the last time you spoke?"

"I don't remember."

"I see. Do you have any idea what's going on with him?"

"I'm sure he's fine. Mickey's a big boy. He doesn't need anyone hovering."

"Fair enough," I said, "but I'd like the reassurance. That's all this is. Do you have his current phone or address?"

Shack shook his head and his mouth pulled down. "Nope. He initiates contact when it suits. In between calls, I make a point of leaving him alone. That's the deal we made."

"What about Lit?"

"Roy Littenberg died. The Big C took him out in less than six weeks. This was three years ago."

"I'm sorry to hear that. I liked him."

"Me too. I see his boy now and then: Tim. You'll never guess what he does."

"I give up."

"He bought the Honky-Tonk. Him and Bundy's boy, Scottie, pal around together whenever Scottie's in town."

I said, "Really. I don't remember meeting either one. I think both were off in Vietnam when Mickey and I were hanging out here." In Santa Teresa, all paths were destined to cross and recross eventually. Now the next generation was being folded into the mix. "Can you think of anyone else who might know what Mickey's up to?"

Shack studied me. "What's my motive in this?"

"You could be helping him."

"And what's yours?"

"I want the answer to some questions I should have asked back then."

"About Benny?"

"That's right."

His smile was shrewd. He cupped a hand to his ear. "Do I hear guilt?"

"If you like."

"A little late, don't you think?"

"Probably. I'm not sure. The point is, I don't need your permission. Now, will you help me or not?"

He thought about it briefly. "What about the lawyer who represented him?"

"Bethel? I can try. I should have thought of him. That's a good idea."

"I'm full of good ideas."

"You think Mickey was innocent?"

"Of course. I was there and I saw. The guy was fine when he left."

"Shack, he had a *plate* in his head."

"Mickey didn't hit him. He never landed a blow."

"How do you know he didn't go after him again? The two might have gotten into it somewhere else. Mickey wasn't exactly famous for his self-control. That was one of my complaints."

Shack wagged his head. The gesture turned into a neck roll, complete with cracking sound. "Sorry about that. I'm going to see the chiropractor later on account of this effing neck of mine. Yeah, it's possible. Why not? Maybe there was more to it than Mickey let on. I'm telling you what I saw, and it was no big deal."

"Fair enough."

"Incidentally—not that it's any of my business—but you should've stood by him. That's the least you could do. This isn't just me. A lot of the guys resented what you did."

"Well, I resented Mickey's asking me to lie for him. He wanted me to tell the DA he was in at nine o'clock that night instead of midnight or one A.M., whatever the hell time it was when he finally rolled in."

"Oh, that's right," he said snidely. "You never tell lies yourself."

"Not about murder. Absolutely not," I snapped.

"Bullshit. You really think Magruder beat a guy to death?"

"How do I know? That's what I'm trying to find out. Mickey was off course. He was intent on the Might and the Right of the law, and he didn't give a damn what he had to do to get the job done."

"Yeah, and you ask my opinion there should have been more like him. Besides, what I hear, you're not exactly one to be casting stones."

"I'll grant you that one. That's why I'm not in uniform today. But my butt wasn't on the line back then, *his* was. If Mickey had an alibi, he should have said so up front instead of asking me to lie."

Shack's expression shifted and he broke off eye contact. I said, "Come on, Shack. You know perfectly well where he was. Why don't you fill me in and we can put an end to this?"

"Is that why you're here?"

"In the main," I said.

"I can tell you this much: He wasn't on Highway 154 hassling a vet. He wasn't anywhere within miles."

"That's good. I believe you. Now could we try this? Mickey had a girlfriend. You remember Dixie Hightower? According to her, they were together that night 'getting it on,' to use the time-honored phrase."

"So he was sticking it to Dixie. Whoopee-do. So what? Everybody screwed around in those days."

"I didn't."

"Maybe not when you were married, but you were the same as everyone else . . . only maybe not as open or as honest."

I bypassed the judgment and went back to the subject under discussion. "Someone could have warned me."

"We assumed you knew. Neither of 'em went to any great lengths to cover up. Think of all the times you left the Honky-Tonk before him. What'd you think he was doing, going to night school? He was nailing her. Big deal. She was a bimbo tended bar. She wasn't any threat to you."

I swallowed my outrage, dismissing it as unproductive. I needed information, not an argument. Betrayal is betrayal, no matter when the truth of it sinks in. Whether Dixie was a threat to that marriage was beside the point. Even fourteen years later, I felt humiliated and incensed. I closed my eyes, detaching myself emotionally as though at the scene of a homicide. "Do you know for a fact he was with her that night?"

"Let's put it this way. I saw 'em leave the Tonk together. She was in her car. He was behind her in his. Nights her hubby was home, they checked into that dinky little motel out on Airport Road."

"Wonderful. How considerate of them. They were there that night?"

"Probably. I couldn't say for sure, but I'd be willing to bet."

"Why didn't *you* speak up for him?"

"I would have, for sure. I'd've gone to the wall, but I never had the chance. Mickey turned in his badge and that was the end of it. If you can't reach him, you can always ask her."

"Dixie?"

"Sure. She's around."

"Where?"

"You're the detective. Try the telephone book. She's still married to whosie-face . . . cripple guy. . . ."

"His name was Eric."

"That's right. Him and Dixie made a fortune and bought a mansion. Sixteen thousand square feet, something like that. Big."

"You're kidding."

"I'm not. It's the honest-to-God truth. They're living in Montebello on a regular estate."

"How'd he do that? The last I saw he was a hopeless drunk."

"He got into AA and straightened up his act. Once he sobered up, he figured out a way to build designer wheelchairs. Custom jobs with all the bells and whistles, depending on the disability. Now he's added sports chairs and prostheses. He has a plant in Taiwan, too, making parts for other companies. Donates a ton of stuff to children's hospitals across the country."

"Good for him. I'm glad to hear that. What about her? What's she doing with herself?"

"She's living the life of Riley, turned into Mrs. Gotrocks. Country club membership and everything. You look 'em up, tell 'em I said hi."

"Maybe I'll do that."

After I left Shack's, I went in to the office, where I opened the mail. There was nothing of interest and no pressing business. Most of my other cases were in limbo, pending callbacks or responses to written inquiries of various sorts. I tidied my desk and washed the coffeepot. I dusted the leaves on the fake ficus. I had no reason to stay, but I couldn't go home yet. I was restless, brooding about Mickey in a series of thought loops that went around and around. Had I erred? Had I acted in haste, jumping to conclusions because it suited me? By the time Quintero died, I was disenchanted with Mickey anyway. I wanted out of the marriage, so his involvement in Quintero's death provided the perfect excuse. But maybe that's all it was. Could he have resigned from the department to spare my pride and, at the same time, to avoid exposing Dixie? If Mickey was innocent, if I'd known where he was that night, the case might have gone differently and he might still be a cop. I didn't want to believe it, but I couldn't escape the thought.

I lay down on the carpet and flung an arm across my eyes. Was there really any point in obsessing about this? It was over and done with. Fourteen years had gone by. Whatever the truth, Mickey'd elected to resign. That was a fact. I'd left him, and our lives were irreparably changed. Why pursue the matter when there wasn't any way to alter what had happened?

What was at stake was my integrity, whatever sense of honor I possessed. I know my limitations. I know the occasional lapses I'm capable of, but a transgression of this magnitude was impossible to ignore. Mickey had lost what he'd loved best, and maybe that was simply his inevitable fate. Then again, if I'd been an unwitting accomplice to his downfall, I needed to own up to it and get square with him.

6

FORBES RUN WAS a meandering lane-and-a-half, a ribbon of pavement that snaked back and forth as it angled upward into the foothills. Massive branches of live oak hung out over the road. There were no houses visible, as far as I could see, but a series of markers suggested that large properties branched off at intervals. I watched the numbers progress, the signs leapfrogging from one side of the road to the other, alternating even and odd: 317, 320, 323, 326. The Hightowers' estate, at 329, was surrounded by a low fieldstone wall, accessible through wooden gates that opened electronically as soon as I pressed the button. Either the Hightowers were expecting someone or they didn't much care who appeared at their door.

The driveway extended perhaps a quarter of a mile and conjured up visions of a proper English manor house at the far end, a three-story Tudor with a steeply pitched slate roof. What I spotted, at long last, was nothing of the kind. The house was contemporary: long and low, hugging the ground, with an oversized roofline rising to a center peak. I could see four wide fieldstone chimneys, clusters of fan palms, and colossal black boulders the size of my car that must have erupted from Vesuvius and been transported to the grounds for effect. To the right, I could see a line of four garage doors.

I parked in the large circular parking area in front and made my way up the wide, sloping concrete walk. A woman, perhaps thirty, in tennis shoes, jeans, and a white T-shirt, was already standing in the open doorway, awaiting my arrival. This definitely wasn't Dixie, and I wondered for a fleeting moment if I'd come to the wrong house.

"Ms. Yablonsky?" she said.

"Actually, I'm not. I'm looking for Eric and Dixie Hightower. Am I in the right place?"

"Sorry. Of course. I thought you were someone else. We've been interviewing for staff positions, and the woman's half an hour late. Is Mrs. Hightower expecting you?" The woman herself remained nameless and without title: parlor maid, factotum, personal assistant. I guess she felt she was under no obligation to introduce herself.

"I'm an old friend," I said. I took out a business card and handed it to her.

She read the face of it, frowning. "A private detective? What's this about?"

"I'm hoping they can put me in touch with a mutual acquaintance. A guy named Mickey Magruder. My ex-husband."

"Oh. Why don't you come in and I'll tell Mrs. Hightower you're here."

"Is Eric home?"

"Mr. Hightower's out of town, but he should be home soon."

I stepped into the foyer, waiting uneasily while she disappeared from sight. I'm sometimes puzzled by wealth, which seems to have a set of rules of its own. Was I free to amble about or should I wait where I was? There was an angular stone bench positioned against one wall. The woman hadn't suggested I sit and I was loath to presume. Suppose it turned out to be a sculpture that collapsed under my weight? I did a one-eighty turn so I could scrutinize the place like a burglar-in-training, a little game I play. I noted entrances and exits, wondering about the possibility of a wall safe. If I were bugging the place, where would I tuck the surveillance equipment?

The floors were polished limestone, as pale as beach sand. I could see ancient marine creatures pressed into the surface, a tiny fossil museum at my feet. A wide corridor stretched off to the right. The ceiling was twelve feet high with floor-to-ceiling windows on one side. The facing walls were painted a snowy white and hung with a series of bright abstracts, oil paintings six feet tall, probably expensive and done by someone dead.

Before me, a pair of double doors stood open and I could see into the living room, easily thirty feet long. Again, the walls on the far side were floor-to-ceiling glass, this time with a panoramic view of pines, live oaks, giant ferns, eucalyptus, and the mountains beyond. I listened and, hearing nothing, tiptoed into the room to have a better look. The wood-beamed ceiling slanted upward to near-cathedral height. On the left, there was a marble-faced fireplace with a hearth twenty-six feet long. On the other end of the room, glass-enclosed shelves showcased a variety of art objects. To the left, I could see a built-in wet bar. The furniture was simple: large armless black leather couches and chairs, chrome-and-glass tables, a grand piano, recessed lighting.

I heard footsteps tap-tap-tapping down the hallway in my direction. I'd just managed to giant-step my way across the foyer to my original position when Dixie came into view. She wore skintight blue jeans, boots with spike heels, and a buff-colored blazer over a snowy white silk tank top. Her jewelry was Bakelite, two chunky bracelets that clattered on her narrow wrist. Now forty years old, she was still extremely thin: small hips, flat stomach, scarcely any butt to speak of. The shoulder pads in her jacket made it look like she was wearing protective gear. Her hair was pulled back away from her face, an oh-so-chic mess in a shade that suggested copious chemical assistance, a red somewhere between claret and burnt ocher. Gone were the false lashes and all the heavy black eyeliner. Curiously, the absence of makeup made her eyes seem much larger and her features more delicate. Her skin was sallow and there were dark circles under her eyes, lines in her forehead, cords showing in her neck. Hard to believe she hadn't yet availed herself of a little surgical refreshment. Even so, she looked glamorous. There was something brisk and brittle in the way she carried herself. She seemed to know who I was, using my name with an artificial warmth as she held out her hand. "Kinsey. How nice. What an incredible surprise. Stephie said you were here. It's been years."

"Hello, Dixie. You look great. I wasn't sure you'd remember me."

"How could I forget?" she said. "I'm sorry you missed Eric." Her gaze took me in without so much as a flicker of interest. Like her, I wore jeans, though mine were cut without style, the kind worn to wash cars or clean hair clots from the bathroom standpipe. In the years since I'd seen her, she'd risen in social stature, acquiring an almost indescribable air of elegance. No need to wear diamonds when plastic would do. Her jacket was wrinkled in the manner of expensive fabrics . . . linens and silks . . . you know how it is with that shit.

She glanced at her watch, which she wore on the inner

aspect of her wrist. The watch was forties vintage, stingy-sized crystal surrounded by little bitty diamonds on a band of black cording. I'd seen nicer versions at the swap meet, which just goes to show what I know about these things. Hers was probably rare, recognizable on sight by those who shopped in the tony places she did. "Would you like a drink?" she asked. "It's nearly cocktail time."

My watch said 4:10. I said, "Sure, why not?" I almost made a joke about crème de menthe frappés, but a black guy in a white jacket had materialized, a silver tray in hand. A bartender of her own? This was getting good.

She said, "What would you like?"

"Chardonnay sounds fine."

"We'll be out on the patio," she remarked, without directly addressing her faithful attendant. My, my, my. Another cipher accounted for in the nameless servant class. I noticed Dixie didn't need to specify what she'd be drinking.

I followed her through the stone-floored dining room. The table was a rhomboid of cherry, with sufficient chairs assembled for a party of twelve. Something odd was at work, and it took me a moment to figure out what it was. There were no steps, no changes in elevation, no area rugs, and no signs of wall-to-wall carpet within view. I thought of Eric in his wheelchair, wondering if the floors were left bare for his benefit.

It struck me as peculiar that Dixie hadn't yet questioned the reason for my unannounced arrival at her door. Maybe she'd been waiting for me all these years, rehearsing responses to numerous imaginary conversations. She'd always known she'd been screwing around with Mickey, whereas I'd just found out, which put me at a disadvantage. I don't often go up against other women in verbal combat. Such clashes are strange, but not without a certain prurient attraction. I thought of all the male-fantasy movies where women fight like alley cats, pulling at each other's hair while they roll around on the floor. I'd never had much occasion, but maybe that would change. I could feel myself getting in touch with my "inner" mean streak.

Dixie opened a sliding glass door and we passed out onto a spacious screened-in patio. The floor here was smooth stone, and the area was rimmed with a series of twenty-foot trees in enormous terra-cotta pots. The branches were filled with goldfinches, all twittering as they hopped from limb to limb. There was a grouping of upholstered patio furniture nearby, in addition to a glass-topped table and four thickly cushioned chairs. Everything looked spotless. I wondered where the little birdies dropped their tiny green and white turds.

"This is actually a combination greenhouse and aviary. These are specimen plants, proteas and bromeliads. South American," she said.

I murmured "gorgeous" for lack of anything better. I thought a bromeliad was a remedy for acid indigestion. She gestured toward the conversational grouping of chairs. From somewhere, I could already smell dinner in the making. The scent of sautéed garlic and onion, like a sumptuous perfume, floated in the air. Maybe one of those no-name indentured servants would appear with a tray of eats, little tidbits of something I could fall on and snarf down without using my hands.

As soon as we sat down, the man reappeared with drinks on his tray. He gave us each a tiny cloth napkin in case we urped something up. Dixie's beverage of choice was a martini straight up in a forties-style glass. Four green olives were lined up on a toothpick like beads on an abacus. We each took a sip of our respective libations. My Chardonnay was delicate, with a long, slow, vanilla finish, probably nothing from a screw-top bottle at the neighborhood Stop 'n' Shop. I watched her hold the gin on her tongue like a communion ritual. She set the glass down with a faint tap and reached into her blazer pocket to extract a pack of cigarettes and a small gold lighter. She lit the cigarette, inhaling with a reverence that suggested smoking was another sacrament. When she caught me observing her, she opened her mouth to emit a thick tongue of smoke that she then sucked up her nose. "You don't smoke these days?"

I shook my head. "I quit."

"Good for you. I'll never give it up myself. All this talk about health is fairly tedious. You probably exercise, too." She cocked her head in reflection, striking a bemused pose. "Let's see. What's in fashion at the moment? You lift weights," she said, and pointed a finger in my direction.

"I jog five days a week, too. Don't forget that," I said, and pointed back at her.

She took another sip of her drink. "Stephie tells me you're looking for Mickey. Has he disappeared?"

"Not as far as I know, but I'd like to get in touch with him. The only number I have turns out to be a disconnect. Have you heard from him lately?"

"Not for years," she said. A smile formed on her lips, and she checked her fingernails. "That's a curious question. I can't believe you'd ask me. I'm sure there are other folks much more likely to know."

"Such as?"

"Shack, for one. And who's the other cop? Lit something. They were always thick as thieves."

"I just talked to Shack, which is how I got to you. Roy Littenberg died. I didn't realize you and Eric were still in town."

She studied me for a moment through her cigarette smoke. Miss Dixie wasn't dumb, and I could see her analyze the situation. "Where's all this coming from?"

"All what?"

"You have something else in mind."

I reached down for my shoulder bag and removed the letter from the outside pocket. "Got your letter," I said.

"My letter," she repeated blankly, her gaze fixed on the envelope.

"The one you sent me in 1972," I said. "Mickey tossed it in a box with some other mail that must have come the same day. He failed to deliver it, so I never read the letter until today." For once, I seemed to have captured her full attention.

"You're not serious."

"I am." I held up the letter like a paddle in a silent auction: my bid. "I had no idea you were balling my beloved husband. You want to talk about that?"

She laughed and then caught herself. Her teeth were now as perfect as white horseshoes hinged together at the rear of her mouth. "Sorry. I'm sorry. I hope you won't take offense, but you're such a boob when it comes to men."

"Thanks. You know how I value your opinion."

"Nothing to be ashamed of. Most women don't have the first clue about men."

"And you do?"

"Of course." Dixie studied me over the ribbon of cigarette smoke, taking my measure with her eyes. She paused and leaned forward to tap off a cylinder of ash into a cut glass dish on the coffee table in front of her.

"What's your theory, Miss Dixie, if I may be so bold as to inquare?" I said, affecting a Southern accent.

"Take advantage of *them* before they take advantage of you," she said, her smile as thin as glass.

"Nice. Romantic. I better write that down." I pretended to make a note on the palm of my hand.

"Well, it's not *nice* but it's practical. In case you haven't noticed, most men don't give a shit about romance. They want to get in your panties and let it go at that. What else can I say?"

"That about covers it," I said. "May I ask, why him? There were dozens of cops at the Honky-Tonk back then."

She hesitated, apparently considering what posture to affect. "He was very good," she said, with a trace of a smile.

"I didn't ask for an evaluation. I'd like to know what went on."

"Why the attitude? You seem so . . . belligerent. In the end, you'd have left him anyway, so what do you care?"

"Indulge me," I said. "For the sake of argument."

She lifted one thin shoulder in a delicate shrug. "He and I were an item long before the two of you met. He broke it off for a while and then he came back. Why attach anything to it? We were not in love by any stretch. I might have *admired* him, but I can't say I liked him much. He had a rough kind of charm, but then again, you know that. I wouldn't even call it an affair in any true sense of the word. More like sexual addiction, a mutual service we performed. Or I should say, that's what it was for me. I don't know about him. It's a question of pathology. He probably couldn't help himself any more than I."

"Oh, please. Don't give me that horseshit about sexual addiction. What crap," I said. "Did it ever occur to you that wedding vows mean something?"

"Yours didn't seem to mean much. Until death do us part? At least I'm still married, which is more than you can say. Or am I wrong about that? Rude of me. You might have married someone else and had a whole passel of kids. I would have asked before now, but I didn't see a ring."

"Were you with him the night Benny Quintero died?"

Her smiled faded. "Yes." Flat. No hesitation, no emotion, and no elaboration.

"Why didn't he tell me?"

"Did you really want to know?"

"It would have helped. I'm not sure what I'd have done, but it might have made a difference."

"I doubt that. You were such a cocky little thing. Really, quite obnoxious. You knew it all back then. Mickey wanted you spared."

"And why is that?"

"He was crazy about you. I'm surprised you'd have to ask."

"Given the fact he was screwing you," I said.

"You knew his history the day you married him. Did you seriously imagine he'd be monogamous?"

"Why'd you take it on yourself to tattle when Mickey asked you not to?"

"I was afraid he'd get a raw deal—which he did, as it turns out."

"Did Eric know about Mickey?"

There was the tiniest flicker of hesitation. "We've come to an accommodation—"

"I'm not talking about now. Did he know back then?"

She took a long, deliberate drag on her cigarette while she formed her reply. "Life was difficult for Eric. He had a hard time adjusting after he got back."

"In other words, no."

"There was no emotional content between Mickey and me. Why inflict unnecessary pain?"

"How about so your respective spouses knew the truth about you? As long as there's no love—as long as it's simply sexual servicing, as you claim—why couldn't you tell us?"

She was silent, giving me a wide-eyed stare.

"The question isn't hypothetical. I really want to know,"

I said. "Why not be honest with us if your relationship meant so little?" I waited. "Okay, I'll help. You want the answer? Try this. Because we'd have kicked your respective butts and put an end to it. I don't know about Eric, but I have no tolerance for infidelity."

"Perhaps there are things about loyalty you never grasped," she said.

I closed my eyes briefly. I wanted to lift her front chair legs and flip her backward, just for the satisfaction of hearing her head thud against the stone floor. Instead, I silently recited what I remembered of the penal code: *An assault is an unlawful attempt, coupled with a present ability, to commit a violent injury on the person of another. . . . A battery is any willful and unlawful use of force or violence upon the person of another.*

I smiled. "You think it was okay to make fools of us? To gratify your whims at our expense? If you think *that's* loyalty, you're *really* fucked."

"You don't have to be crude."

Someone spoke from the far side of the patio. "Excuse me. Dixie?"

Both of us looked over. Stephie stood in the doorway.

For once, Dixie seemed embarrassed, and the color rose in her cheeks. "Yes, Stephie. What is it?"

"Ms. Yablonsky's here. Did you want to talk to her now or should I reschedule?"

Dixie exhaled with impatience, stubbing out her cigarette. "Have her wait in my office. I'll be there in a minute."

"Sure. No problem." Stephie closed the sliding glass door, watching for a moment before she moved away.

"This has gone far enough," Dixie said to me. "I can see you enjoy getting up on your high horse. You always liked claiming the moral high ground—"

"I do. That's correct. It's mine to claim in this case."

"When you've finished your drink, you can let yourself out."

"Thanks. This was fun. You haven't changed at all."

"Nor have you," she said.

7

I WAS HALFWAY down the driveway, heading toward the road, when I saw a vehicle coming my way. It was a custom van of a sort I hadn't seen before, sleek, black, and boxy, with Eric Hightower at the wheel. I'm not sure I would have recognized him if I hadn't been half expecting to see him anyway. I slowed the VW to a crawl and gave a tap to the horn as I rolled down my window. He drew alongside me and pulled to a stop, rolling his window down in response. Underneath the tank top he wore, his bulging shoulders and biceps looked smooth and tanned. In the old Honky-Tonk days, his gaze was perpetually glassy and his skin had the pallor of a man who'd made a science of mixing his medications with alcohol, LSD, and grass. Then, his beard had been sparse and he'd worn his straight black hair loose across his shoulders or pulled back in a ponytail and tied with a rag.

The man who studied me quizzically from the driver's side of the van had been restored to good health. His head was now shaved, his skull as neat as a newborn's. Gone were the beard and the bleary-eyed stare. I'd seen pictures of Eric in uniform before he left for Vietnam: young and handsome, twenty-one years old, largely untouched by life. After two tours of duty, he'd come back to the world looking gaunt and abused, ill-humored and withdrawn. He'd seemed to have a lot on his mind, but nothing he was capable of explaining to the rest of us. And none of us dared ask. One look at his face was sufficient to convince us that what he'd seen was hellish and wouldn't bear close scrutiny. In retrospect, I suspect he imagined us judgmental and disapproving when in truth we were frightened of what we saw in his eyes. Better to look away than suffer that torment.

"Can I help you?" he asked.

"Hi, Eric. Kinsey Millhone. We hung around together years ago at the Tonk out in Colgate."

I watched his features clear and then brighten when he figured out who I was. "Hey. Of course. No fooling. How're you doing?" He leaned his left arm out the window and we touched fingertips briefly, as close to a handshake as we could manage from separate vehicles. His dark eyes were clear. In his drinking days, he'd been scrawny, but the process of aging had added the requisite fifteen pounds. Success sat well on him. He seemed substantial and self-possessed.

I said, "You look great. What happened to your hair?"

He glanced at himself in his rearview mirror, running a hand across his smooth-shaven skull. "You like it? It feels weird. I did that a month ago and can't quite decide."

"I do. It's better than the ponytail."

"Well, ain't that the truth. What brings you here?"

"I'm looking for my ex-husband and thought you might have a line on him." The possibility seemed farfetched and I wondered if he'd press me on the subject, but he let it pass.

"Magruder? I haven't seen him in years."

"That's what Dixie said. I talked to Mickey's buddy, Shack, a little while ago and your names came up. You remember Pete Shackelford?"

"Vaguely."

"He thought you might know, but I guess not, huh."

Eric said, "Sorry I can't help. What's the deal?"

"I'm not really sure. It looks like I have a debt to settle with him and I'd like to clear it."

"I can ask around, if you want. I still see some of those guys at the gym. One of them might know."

"Thanks, but I can probably manage on my own. I'll call his lawyer, and if that fails I've got some other little ways. I know how his mind works. Mickey's devious."

Eric's gaze held mine, and I felt an unspoken communication scuttle between us like the shadow of a cloud passing overhead. His mood seemed to shift and he let the sweep of his arm encompass the tree-strewn property surrounding us on all sides. "So what do you think? Nine point nine acres and it's paid off—all mine. Well, half mine, given California's community property laws."

"It's beautiful. You've done well."

"Thanks. I had help."

"Dixie or AA?"

"I'd have to say both."

A plumber's truck appeared in the driveway, pulling up behind Eric's van. He glanced back and waved to let the driver know he was aware of him and wouldn't take all day. He turned back to me. "Why don't you turn the car around and come back to the house? We can all have dinner together and spend time catching up."

"I'd love to, but I'd better not. Dixie's got interviews and I have some things to take care of myself. Maybe another time. I'll give you a call and we can set something up." I put my car in gear.

"Great. Do that. You promise?"

"Scout's honor."

The driver of the truck behind him gave an impatient beep on his horn. Eric glanced back at him and waved again. "Anyway, nice to see you. Behave yourself."

"You too."

He rolled his window up, and I could see him accelerate with the help of a device on his steering wheel. It was the only reminder I'd had that he was a double amputee. He tapped his horn as he departed and I continued down the driveway, the two of us moving in opposite directions.

I headed into town, pondering the nature of the divine comedy. Two of my pet beliefs had been reversed in the past few hours. Given the brevity of my marriage to Mickey, I'd always assumed he'd been faithful. That notion turned out to be false so it was stricken from the record, along with any lingering confidence I felt. I'd also suspected—well, let's be honest about this—I'd been *convinced* Mickey'd played a part in Benny Quintero's death. It turned out he hadn't, so we could strike that one, too. Guilty of infidelity, innocent of manslaughter. Someone with talent could convert that to lyrics for a country-western tune. In some ways Dixie'd nailed it. Did I really want to know about this shit? I guess I didn't have a choice. The question was what to do with it?

The minute I hit the office, I hauled out the telephone book and leafed through the yellow pages to the section listing attorneys. I ran a finger down the column until I found Mark Bethel's name in a little box of its own. The ad read CRIMINAL DEFENSE and, under that heading, specified the following: Drugs, Molest, Weapons, White Collar, DUI, Theft/Fraud, Assault, Spousal Abuse, and Sex Crimes, which I thought just about covered it—except for murder, of course. Mark Bethel had been

Mickey's attorney when he resigned from the department, a move Mickey'd made on Mark's advice. I'd never been crazy about Mark, and after Mickey's unceremonious departure there was little reason for our paths to cross. On the odd occasion when I ran into him around town, we tended to be cordial, feigning a warmth neither of us felt. We were bound by old business, one of those uneasy alliances that survived more on form than content. Despite my lukewarm attitude, I had to admit he was an excellent attorney, though in the past few years he'd set his practice aside in his bid for public office—one Republican among many hoping for a shot at Alan Cranston's senate seat in the coming November elections. In the past ten years, his political ambitions had begun to emerge. He'd allied himself with the local party machine, ingratiating himself with Republicans by working tirelessly on Deukmejian's 1982 gubernatorial campaign. He'd opened his Montebello home for countless glitzy fund-raisers. He'd run for and won a place on the county board of supervisors; then he'd run for state assembly. Logically, his next step should have been a try for Congress, but he'd skipped that and entered the primary for a U.S. Senate seat. He must have felt his political profile was sufficient to net him the kind of votes he'd need to outstrip Ed Zschau. Fat chance, in my opinion, but then what did I know? I hate politicians; they lie more flagrantly than I do and with a lot less imagination. It helped that Bethel was married to a woman who had a fortune of her own.

I'd heard through the grapevine Laddie Bethel was bankrolling the major portion of his campaign. She'd made a name for herself locally as a fund-raiser of some persuasion for numerous charitable organizations. Whatever worthy cause she adopted, she certainly wasn't shy about sending me donation requests with a return envelope enclosed. Inevitably, there was a series of amounts to be circled: $2,500, $1,000, $500, $250. If the charitable event was an evening affair—"black tie optional" (in case your green one was at the cleaners)—I'd also be offered the opportunity to buy a "table" for my cronies at a thousand dollars a plate. Little did she know I was, by nature, so cheap that I'd sit there and pick the stamp off the prestamped envelope. In the meantime, Mark maintained an office and a secretary with his old law firm.

I dialed Mark Bethel's office, and his secretary answered, followed by an immediate "May I put you on hold?"

By the time I said sure, she was already gone. I was treated to a jazz rendition of "Scarborough Fair."

Mark's secretary clicked back on the line. "Thanks for holding. This is Judy. May I help you?"

"Yes, hi, Judy. This is Kinsey Millhone. I'm an old friend of Mark's. I think I met you at the Bethels' Christmas party a couple of years back. Is he there by any chance?"

"Oh, hi, Kinsey. I remember you," she said. "No, he's off at a committee meeting, probably gone for the day. You want him to call in the morning, or is there something I can do?"

"Maybe," I said. "I'm trying to get in touch with my ex-husband. Mickey Magruder was a client of his."

"Oh, I know Mickey," she said, and right away I wondered if she *knew* him in the biblical sense.

"Do you know if Mark has a current address and phone number?"

"Hold on and I'll check. I know we have something, because he called here a couple months ago and I spoke to him myself." I could hear pages rattling as she leafed through her book.

"Ah, here we go." She recited an address on Sepulveda, but the house number differed from the one I had. The digits were the same but the order was changed, which was typical of Mickey. In his semiparanoid state, he'd give the correct information but with the numbers transposed so you couldn't pin him down. He thought your address was your own damn business and phones were meant for *your* convenience, not anyone else's. If other people couldn't call him, what did he care? I don't know how he managed to receive his mail or have pizza delivered. Those were not issues he found interesting when his privacy was at stake. Judy chimed back in, and the phone number she recited was a match for the one I had in my book.

I said, "You can scratch that one out. I tried it a while ago, and it's a disconnect. I thought maybe Mickey moved or had the number changed."

I could hear her hesitate. "I probably shouldn't say this. Mark hates when I discuss a client, so please don't tell him I said this—"

"Of course not."

"When Mickey called—this would have been mid-March—he did ask to borrow money. I mean, he didn't ask *me*. This is just what I heard later, after Mark talked to him. Mark said Mickey'd had to sell his car because he couldn't afford the upkeep and insurance, let alone the gas. He's got financial problems even Mark couldn't bail him out of."

"That doesn't sound good. Did Mark lend him any money?"

"I'm not really sure. He might have. Mickey was always one of Mark's favorites."

"Could you check your message carbons and see if Mickey left a number where Mark could reach him?"

"I'll check if you like, but I remember asking at the time, and he said Mark would know."

"So Mark might have another number?"

"It's possible, I guess. I can ask and have him call you."

"I'd appreciate that. He can buzz me tomorrow and we'll take it from there." I left her my number and we clicked off.

My evening was unremarkable—dinner with Henry at Rosie's Tavern half a block away—after which I curled up with a book and read until I fell asleep, probably ten whole minutes later.

I turned off the alarm moments before it was set to ring. I brushed my teeth, pulled on my sweats, and went out for a three-mile jog. The bike path along the beach was cloaked in the usual spring fog, the sky a uniform gray, the ocean blended at the horizon as though a scrim of translucent plastic had been stretched taut between the two. The air temperature was perfect, faintly chill, faintly damp. I was feeling light and strong, and I ran with a rare sense of happiness.

Home again, I showered, dressed, and ate breakfast, then hopped in my car and hit the road for San Felipe with the receipt from the storage company tucked in my pocket. I'd dressed up to some extent, which in my case doesn't amount to much. I only own one dress: black, collarless, with long sleeves and a tucked bodice (which is a fancy word for front). This entirely synthetic garment, guaranteed wrinkle-free (but probably flammable), is as versatile as anything I've owned. In it, I can accept invitations to all but the snootiest of cocktail parties, pose as a mourner at any funeral, make court appearances, conduct surveillance, hustle clients, interview hostile witnesses, traffic with known felons, or pass myself off as a gainfully employed person instead of a freelance busybody accustomed to blue jeans, turtlenecks, and tennis shoes.

Before I departed, I'd taken a few minutes to complete a generic claim form that I'd dummied up from my days of working at California Fidelity Insurance. As I headed south on 101, I practiced the prissy, bureaucratic attitude I affect when I'm masquerading as someone else. Being a private investigator is made up of equal parts ingenuity, determination, and persistence, with a sizable dose of acting skills thrown in.

The drive to San Felipe took forty-five minutes. The scenery en route consisted largely of citrus and avocado groves, stretches of farmland, and occasional roadside markets selling—what else?—oranges, lemons, and avocados. I spotted the storage company from half a mile away. It was just off the main road, countless rows of two-story buildings, occupying two square blocks. The architectural style suggested a newly constructed California prison, complete with floodlights and tall chain-link fences.

I turned in at the gate. The buildings were identical: cinder block and blank doors, with wide freight elevators and a loading ramp at each end. The units were marked alphabetically and numerically in a system I couldn't quite decipher. The doors in each section appeared to be color-coded, but maybe that was simply an architectural flourish. It couldn't be much fun designing a facility that looked like cracker boxes arranged end to end. I passed a number of broad alleyways. Arrows directed me to the main office, where I parked and got out.

I pushed through the glass door to a serviceable space, maybe twenty feet by twenty with a counter running across the center. The area on the far side of the counter was taken up by rental-quality file cabinets and a plain wooden desk. This was not a multilayered company with the administration assuming any lofty position. The sole individual on duty apparently functioned as receptionist, secretary, and plant manager, sitting at a typewriter with a pencil in his mouth while he hunt-and-pecked his way through a memorandum of some sort. I guessed he was in his late seventies, round-faced and balding, with a pair of reading glasses worn low on his nose. I could see his belly bulging out like an infant monkey clinging closely to its mother's chest. "Be with you in just a second," he said, typing on.

"Take your time."

"How do you spell 'mischeevious'?"

"M-i-s-c-h-i-e-v-o-u-s."

"You sure? Doesn't look right."

"Pretty sure," I said.

When he'd finished, he stood up, separated the carbons, and tucked both the original and the copies in matching blue folders. He came over to the counter, hitching up his pants. "Didn't mean to keep you waiting, but I was on a tear," he said. "When business is slow, I write stories for my great-grandson. Kid's barely two and reads like a champ. Loves his pappaw's little booklets written just for him. This one's about a worm name of Wiggles and his escapades. Lot of fun for me, and you should see Dickie's little face light up. I figure one day I'll get 'em published and have 'em done up proper. I have a lady friend offered to do the illustrations, but somebody told me that's a bad idea. I guess these New York types like to hire their own artists."

"News to me," I said.

His cheeks tinted faintly and his tone of voice became shy. "I don't suppose you know an agent might take a look at this."

"I don't, but if I hear of one, I'll let you know."

"That'd be good. Meantime, what can I do for you?"

I showed him my California Fidelity Insurance identification, which bore an old photograph of me and the company seal of approval.

His gaze shifted from the photo to my face. "You oughta get you a new photo. This doesn't do you justice. You're a lot better looking."

"You really think so? Thanks. By the way, I'm Kinsey Millhone. And you're . . . ?"

"George Wedding."

"Nice to meet you."

"I hope you're not selling policies. I'd hate to disappoint, but I'm insured to the hilt."

"I'm not selling anything, but I could use some help." I hesitated. I had a story all ready. I intended to show him a homeowner's claim listing several items lost to flooding when some water pipes broke. Of course, this was all completely false, but I was hoping he'd react with sufficient moral indignation to set the record straight. What I wanted was the address and phone number Mickey'd used when he'd rented the space. I could then compare the information to facts already in my possession and thus (perhaps) figure out where the hell Mickey was. In my mind, on the way down, I'd spun the story out to a convincing degree, but now that I was here I couldn't bring myself to tell it. This is the truth about lying: You're putting one over on some poor gullible dunce, which makes him appear stupid for not spotting the deception. Lying contains the same hostile elements as a practical joke in that the "victim" ends up looking foolish in his own eyes and laughable in everyone else's. I'm willing to lie to pompous bureaucrats, when thwarted by knaves, or when all else fails, but I was having trouble lying to a man who wrote worm adventure stories for his greatgrandson. George was patiently waiting for me to go on. I folded the bogus claim in half until the bottom of the page rested a couple of inches from the top and the only lines showing were those containing the name, address, and telephone number of "John Russell." "You want to know the truth?"

"That'd be nice," he said blandly.

"Ah. Well, the truth is I was fired by CFI about three years ago. I'm actually a private investigator, looking for a man I was once married to." I pointed to John Russell's name. "That's not his real name, but I suspect the address may be roughly correct. My ex scrambles numbers as a way of protecting himself."

"Is this police business? Because my records are confidential, unless you have a court order. If you think this fellow was using his storage unit for illegal purposes . . . manufacturing drugs, for instance . . . you might talk me into it. Otherwise, no deal."

I could almost have sworn George was inviting me to fib, given that he'd laid out the conditions under which he might be persuaded to open his files to me. However, having started with the truth, I thought I might as well stick to my guns. "You're making this tough. I wish I could tell you otherwise, but this isn't related to any criminal activity—at least, as far as I know. Uhm . . . wow . . . this is hard. I'm not used to this," I said. "He and I parted enemies and it's just come to my attention I misjudged him badly. I can't live with my conscience until I square things with him. I know it sounds corny, but it's true."

"What'd you do?" George asked.

"It's not what I did. It's what I didn't do," I said. "He was implicated in a murder—well, not a murder, really, manslaughter is more like it. The point is I didn't wait to hear his side of it. I just assumed he was guilty and walked out on him. I feel bad about that. I promised 'for better or for worse' and gave him 'worse.' "

"So now what?"

"So now I'm trying to track him down so I can apologize. Maybe I can make amends . . . if it's not too late."

George's face was a study in caution. "I'm not entirely clear what you want from me."

I passed him the form, tilting my head to read the header along with him. I pointed to the relevant lines. "I think this is partly right. I've got two versions of this address. If yours matches this one or if you have another variation yet, I can probably determine which is correct."

He studied the name and address. "I remember this fellow. Went delinquent on his payments. We emptied his unit and auctioned everything off."

"That's what worries me. I think he's in trouble. Do you think you can help?"

I could see him vacillate. I left the clipboard up on the counter, angled in his direction. I could see his gaze retracing the lines of print. He moved to a file cabinet, scanned the labels on the drawer fronts, and opened the third one down. He pulled out a fat binder and laid it across the open drawer. He wet his thumb and began to leaf through. He found the relevant page, popped open the rings, removed a sheet of paper, and copied it, handing me the information without another word.

8

I RETURNED TO the office, where I spent the rest of the day paying bills, returning phone calls, and taking care of correspondence. There was no message from Mark Bethel. I'd try him again if I didn't hear from him soon. I locked my office at four-thirty, shoving my Los Angeles street map in the outer pouch of my bag. I left my car for the time being and walked over to the public library, where I checked the crisscross for the area encompassed by the three differing Sepulveda street numbers Mickey'd listed as his home address. It was impossible to determine the best candidate from looking at a map. I was going to have to make a run down there. It was time to satisfy myself as to his current situation, maybe even time for the two of us to talk. I had a big whack of money in my savings account. I was willing to offer my help if Mickey wasn't too proud to accept. I walked back to the office, where I picked up my car and made the short drive home. I didn't even have the details and I was already sick about the part I'd played in his slide from grace.

I arrived at my apartment to find two gentlemen

standing on my doorstep. I knew in a flash they were plainclothes detectives: neatly dressed, clean-shaven, their expressions bland and attentive, the perfect law enforcement presence on this May afternoon. I felt a spritz of electricity coursing through my frame. My hands were left tingling and the skin on my back suddenly felt luminous, like a neon sign flashing GUILT— GUILT—GUILT. My first thought was Teddy Rich had reported an intruder, that an officer had been dispatched, that he'd called for a tech who'd subsequently dusted for prints. Mine would have shown up on the inner and outer aspects of the pet door, on the edge of the desk, on the back doorknob, in other places so numerous I could hardly recall. I'd been a cop for two years and a P.I. since then. (I'd also been arrested once, but I don't want to talk about that now, thanks.)

The point is, my prints were in the system, and the computer was going to put me inside Teddy Rich's house. The cops would ask what I was doing there and what could I say? Was there an innocent explanation? I couldn't think of one to save me. The dog, of course, would pick me out of a police lineup, tugging at my pant leg, joyously barking, jumping, and slobbering on my shoes as they cuffed me and took me away. I could try to plea-bargain right up front or wait until sentencing and throw myself on the mercy of the court.

I hesitated on the walkway, my house keys in hand. Surely the cops had more pressing cases to pursue these days. Why would they even bother with a crime scene tech? The notion was absurd. These fellows might not be cops at all. Maybe Teddy figured out what I'd done and had sent these two goons to crush my elbows, my knees, and other relevant joints. Somewhat chirpily, I said, "Hi. Are you looking for me?"

The two of them seemed to be approximately the same

age: late thirties, trim, fit, one dark, the other fair. The blond carried a briefcase in his left hand like he was doing door-to-door sales. He spoke first. "Miss Millhone?" He wore a red plaid shirt under a tweed sport coat, his Adam's apple compressed by the knot in his solid red tie. His slacks were dark cotton, wrinkled across the crotch from sitting in the car too long.

"That's right."

He held out his right hand. "My name's Felix Claas. This is my partner, John Aldo. We're detectives with the Los Angeles Police Department. Could we talk to you?"

Aldo held out two business cards and a wallet he flipped open to expose his badge. Detective Aldo was a big guy with a muscular body, probably six-three, 240 pounds. He wore his dark hair slightly shaggy, and his dark eyes receded under wide dark eyebrows that came together at the bridge of his nose. His slacks were polyester, and he had a sport coat neatly folded and laid across one arm. His short-sleeved cotton shirt exposed a matting of silky hair on his forearms. He looked like a man who preferred wearing sweats. I'd heard his first name as "John," but I noticed on his business card the spelling was the Italian, Gian, and I made the mental correction. In the flush of apprehension, I'd already forgotten the first detective's name. I glanced down at the cards again. Felix Claas was the blond, Gian Aldo, the darker one.

Claas spoke up again, smiling pleasantly. His blond hair looked wet, parted on the side and combed straight back behind his ears. His eyebrows and lashes were an almost invisible pale gold, so that his blue eyes seemed stark. His lips were full and unusually pink. He had a cleft in his chin. "Great town you have here. The minute we crossed the county line, I could feel my blood pressure drop about fifteen points."

"Thanks. We're lucky. It's like this all year long. We get a marine layer sometimes in the summer months, but it burns off by noon so it's hard to complain." Maybe this pertained to an old case of mine.

Detective Aldo eased into the conversation. "We had a chat with Lieutenant Robb. I hope we haven't caught you at a bad time."

"Not at all. This is fine. You're friends of his?"

"Well, no, ma'am, we aren't. We've talked to him by phone, but we only met today. Seems like a nice guy."

"He's great. I've known Jonah for years," I said. "What's this about?"

"A case we've been working. We'd like to talk to you inside, if you don't object."

Detective Claas chimed in. "This shouldn't take long. Fifteen–twenty minutes. We'll be as quick as we can."

"Sure. Come on in." I turned and unlocked the front door, talking over my shoulder. "When'd you get up here?"

"About an hour ago. We tried calling your office, but they told us you'd left. We must have just missed you."

"I had some errands to run," I said, wondering why I felt I owed them an explanation. I stepped across the threshold and they followed me in. In the past few years, a number of investigations had taken me to Los Angeles. One of the cases I'd handled for California Fidelity had exposed me to a bunch of bad-asses. This was probably related. The criminal element form a special subset, the same names surfacing over and over again. It's always interesting to find out what the cruds are up to.

I took a mental photograph of my apartment, idly aware of how it must appear to strangers. Small, immaculate, as compact as a ship's interior complete with cubbyholes and built-ins. Kitchenette to the right; desk and seating arrangement to the left. Royal-blue shag carpet, a small spiral staircase leading to a loft above. I set my shoulder bag on one of the stools at the kitchen counter and moved the six steps into the living room.

The two detectives waited in the doorway deferentially.

"Have a seat," I said.

Aldo said, "Thanks. Nice place. You live alone?"

"As a matter of fact, I do."

"Lucky you. My girlfriend's a slob. There's no way I can keep my place looking this clean."

Claas sat down on the small sofa tucked into the bay window, setting his briefcase on the floor beside him. While Claas and Aldo seemed equally chatty, Claas was more reserved, nearly prim in his verbal manner, while Aldo seemed relaxed. Detective Aldo took one of the two matching director's chairs, which left me with the other. I sat down, feeling subtly maneuvered, though I wasn't sure why. Aldo slouched in the chair with his legs spread, his hands hanging between his knees. The canvas on the director's chair sagged and creaked beneath his shifting weight. His thighs were enormous, and his posture seemed both indolent and intimidating. Claas flicked him a look and he altered his posture, sitting up straight.

Claas turned his attention back to me. "We understand you were married to a former vice detective named Magruder."

I was completely taken aback. "Mickey? That's right. Is this about him?" I felt a tingle of fear. Connections tumbled together in a pattern I couldn't quite discern. Whatever was going on, it had to be associated with his current financial straits. Maybe he'd robbed a bank, scammed someone, or pulled a disappearing act. Maybe there was a warrant outstanding, and these guys had been assigned the job of tracking him down. I covered my discomfort with a laugh. "What's he up to?"

Claas's expression remained remote. "Unfortunately,

Mr. Magruder was the victim of a shooting. He survived . . . he's alive, but he's not doing well. Yesterday we finally got a line on him. At the time of the assault, he didn't have identification in his possession, so he was listed as a John Doe until we ran his prints."

"He was *shot*?" I could feel myself move the needle back to the beginning of the cut. Had I heard him correctly?

"Yes, ma'am."

"He's all right, though, isn't he?"

Claas's tone ranged somewhere between neutrality and regret. "Tell you the truth, it's not looking so good. Doctors say he's stable, but he's on life support. He's never regained consciousness, and the longer this goes on, the less likely he is to make a full recovery."

Or any at all was what I heard. I could feel myself blink. Mickey dying or dead? The detective was still talking, but I felt I was suffering a temporary hearing loss. I held a hand up. "Hang on. I'm sorry, but I can't seem to comprehend."

"There's no hurry. Take your time," Aldo said.

I took a couple of deep breaths. "This is weird. Where is he?"

"UCLA. He's currently in ICU, but he may be transferred to County, depending on his condition."

"He always had good insurance coverage, if it's a question of funds." The notion of Mickey at County didn't sit well with me. I was taking deep breaths, risking hyperventilation in my attempt to compose myself. "Can I see him?"

There was a momentary pause, and then Claas said, "Not just yet, but we can probably work something out." He seemed singularly unenthusiastic, and I didn't press the point.

Aldo watched me with concern. "Are you okay?"

"I'm fine. I'm just surprised," I said. "I don't know

what I thought you were doing here, but it wasn't this. I can't believe anything bad could ever happen to him. He was always a brawler, but he seemed invincible . . . at least to me. What happened?"

"That's what we're trying to piece together," Claas said. "He'd been shot twice, once in the head and once in the chest. A patrolman spotted him lying on the sidewalk a little after three A.M. The weapon, a semiautomatic, was found in the gutter about ten feet away. This was a commercial district, a lot of bars in the area, so it's possible Mr. Magruder got into a dispute. We have a couple of guys out now canvassing the neighborhood. So far no witnesses. For now, we're working backward, trying to get a line on his activities prior to the shooting."

"When *was* this?"

"Early morning hours of May fourteenth. Wednesday of last week."

Claas said, "Do you mind if we ask you a couple of questions?"

"Not at all. Please do."

I expected one of them to take out a notebook, but none emerged. I glanced at the briefcase and wondered if I was being recorded. Meanwhile, Claas was talking on. "We're in the process of eliminating some possibilities. This is mostly filling in the blanks, if you can help us out."

"Sure, I'll try. I'm not sure how, but fire away," I said. Inwardly, I flinched at my choice of words.

Claas cleared his throat. His voice was lighter, reedier. "When you last spoke to your ex-husband, did he mention any problems? Threats, disputes, anything like that?"

I leaned forward, relieved. "I haven't spoken to Mickey in fourteen years."

Something flickered between them, one of those wordless conversations married couples learn to conduct with their eyes. Detective Aldo took over. "You're the owner of a nine-millimeter Smith and Wesson?"

"I was at one time." I was on the verge of saying more but decided to rein myself in until I figured out where they were going. The empty box that had originally housed the gun was still sitting in the carton beside my desk, less than six feet away.

Claas said, "Can you tell us when you purchased it?"

"I didn't. Mickey bought that gun and gave it to me as a wedding gift. That was August of 1971."

"Strange wedding present," Aldo remarked.

"He's a strange guy," I said.

"Where's the gun at this time?"

"Beats me. I haven't laid eyes on it for years. I assumed Mickey took it with him when he moved to L.A."

"So you haven't seen the gun since approximately . . ."

I looked from Claas to Aldo as the obvious implications began to sink in. I'd been slow on the uptake. "Wait a minute. *That* was the gun used?"

"Let's put it this way: Yours was the gun that was found at the scene. We're still waiting for ballistics."

"You can't think I had anything to do with it."

"Your name popped up in the computer as the registered owner. We're looking for a starting point, and this made sense. If Mr. Magruder carried the gun, it's possible someone took it away from him and shot him with it."

"That puts *me* in the clear," I said facetiously. I felt like biting my tongue. Sarcasm is the wrong tack to take with cops. Better to play humble and cooperative.

A silence settled between the two. They'd seemed friendly and confiding, but I knew from experience there'd be a sizable gap between the version they'd given me and the one they'd withheld. Aldo took a stick of gum from his coat pocket and tore it in half. He tucked half in his pocket and slipped the paper wrapper and the foil from the other half. He slid the chewing gum in his mouth. He seemed disinterested for the moment, but I knew they'd spend the return trip comparing notes, matching their reactions and intuitions against the information I'd given them.

Claas shifted on the couch. "Can you tell us when you last spoke to Mr. Magruder?"

"It's Mickey. Please use his first name. This is hard enough as it is. He left Santa Teresa in 1972. I don't remember talking to him after we divorced."

"Can you tell us what contact you've had since then?"

"You just asked that. I've had none."

Claas's gaze fixed on mine, rather pointedly, I thought. "You haven't spoken to him in the past few months," he said—not a question, but a statement infused with skepticism.

"No. Absolutely not. I haven't talked to him."

While Detective Claas tried to hold my attention, I could see that Aldo was making a discreet visual tour of the living room. His gaze moved from item to item, methodically assessing everything within range. Desk, files, box, answering machine, bookshelves. I could almost hear him thinking to himself: *Which of these objects doesn't belong?* I saw his focus shift back to the cardboard box. So far, I hadn't said a word about the delinquent payments on Mickey's storage bin. On the face of it, I couldn't see how withholding the information represented any criminal behavior on my part. What justice was I obstructing? Who was I aiding and abetting? I didn't shoot my ex. I wasn't in custody and wasn't under oath. If it seemed advisable, I could always contact the detectives later when I "remembered" something relevant. All this went through my mind in the split second while I was busy covering my butt. If the two picked up on my uneasiness, neither said a word. Not that I expected them to gasp and exchange significant looks.

Detective Claas cleared his throat again. "What about him? Has he been in touch with you?"

I confess a little irritability was creeping into my response. "That's the same thing, isn't it, whether I talk to him or he talks to me? We divorced years ago. We don't have any reason to stay in touch. If he called, I'd hang up. I don't want to talk to him."

Aldo's tone was light, nearly bantering. "What are you so mad about? The poor guy's down for the count."

I felt myself flush. "Sorry. That's just how it is. We're not one of those couples that turned all lovey-dovey once the papers were signed. I have nothing against him, but I've never been interested in being his best friend . . . nor he mine, I might add."

"Same with my ex," he said. "Still, sometimes there's a piece of business—you know, a stock certificate or news of an old pal. You might forward the mail, even if you hate their guts. It's not unusual for one ex to drop the other a note if something relevant comes up."

"Mickey doesn't write notes."

Claas shifted in seat. "What's he do then, call?"

I could feel myself grow still. Why was he so determined to pursue the point? "Look. For the fourth or fifth time now, Mickey and I don't talk. Honest. Cross my heart. Scout's honor and all that. We're not enemies. We're not antagonistic. We just don't have that kind of relationship."

"Really. How would you characterize it? Friendly? Distant? Cordial?"

"What *is* this?" I said. "What's the relevance? I mean, come on, guys. You can't be serious. Why would I shoot my ex-husband with my own gun and leave it at the scene? I'd have to be nuts."

Aldo smiled to himself. "People get rattled. You never know what they'll do. We're just looking for information. Anything you can give us, we'd appreciate."

"Tell me your theory," I said.

"We don't have a theory," Claas said. "We're hoping to eliminate some angles. You could save us a lot of time if you'd cooperate."

"I'm *doing* that. This is what cooperation looks like, in case you're not accustomed to it. You're barking up the wrong tree. I don't even know where Mickey lives these days."

The two detectives stared at me.

"I'm telling you the truth."

Detective Claas asked the next question without reference to his notes. "Can you tell us where you were on March twenty-seventh?"

My mind went blank. "I haven't the faintest idea. Where were you?" I said. I could tell my hands were going to start shaking. My fingers were cold, and without even thinking about it, I crossed my arms and tucked my hands against my sides. I knew I looked stubborn and defensive, but I was suddenly unnerved.

"Do you have an appointment book you might check?"

"You know what? I think we should stop this conversation right now. If you're here because you think I was somehow involved in a shooting, you'll have to talk to my attorney because I'm done with this bullshit."

Detective Aldo seemed surprised. "Hey, come on. There's no call for that. We're not accusing you of anything. This is an exchange of information."

"What was exchanged? I tell you things, but what do you tell me? Or did I miss that part?"

Aldo smiled, undismayed by my prickliness. "We told you he was injured and you told us you never talked to

him. See? We tell you and then you tell us. It's like a dia-
logue. We're trading."

"Why did you ask where I was March twenty-
seventh? What's that about?"

Claas spoke up. "We checked his telephone bills.
There was a call to this number that lasted thirty minutes. We assumed the two of you talked. Unless someone
else lives here, which you've denied."

"Show me," I said. I held out my hand.

He leaned down and reached into the partially opened
briefcase, sliding out a sheaf of phone bills, which he
passed to me without comment. On top of the stack was
Mickey's bill for April, itemizing his March service. I
glanced at the header, noting that the phone number on
the account was the same one I had. At that point, his
February bill was already in arrears. The past-due notice
warned that if his payment wasn't received within ten
days, his service would be terminated. I let my eye drift
down the column of toll calls and long-distance charges
for March. Only two calls had been made, both to Santa
Teresa. The first was March 13, made to Mark Bethel's
office. I'd heard about that from Judy. The second was
to my number. Sure enough, that call was made on
March 27 at 1:27 P.M. and lasted, as specified, for a full
thirty minutes.

9

I'M NOT SURE how I got through the remainder of the conversation. Eventually the detectives left, with phony thanks on their part for all the help I'd given them, and phony assurances on mine that I'd contact them directly if I had anything more to contribute to their investigation. As soon as the door closed, I scurried into the bathroom, where I stepped into the empty bathtub and discreetly spied on them through the window. I kept just out of sight while Detectives Claas and Aldo, chatting in low tones, got into what looked like a county-issued car and drove away. I'd have given anything to know what they were saying—assuming the discussion was about Mickey or me. Maybe they were talking sports, which I don't give a rat's ass about.

As soon as they were gone, I returned to my desk and flipped back through my desk calendar to the page for March 27. That Thursday was entirely empty, as were the days on either side: no appointments, no meetings, no notation of events, professional or social. Typically, I'd have spent the day at the office, doing God knows what. I was hoping my desk calendar would jump-start my recollection. For the moment, I was stumped. All I knew was I hadn't talked to Mickey on March 27 or any other day in recent years. Had someone broken into my apartment? That was a creepy prospect, but what other explanation was there? Mickey could have dialed my number and spoken to someone else. It was also possible someone other than Mickey made the call from his place, establishing a connection that didn't actually exist. Who would go to such lengths? A person or persons who intended to shoot my ex-husband and have the finger point at me.

It rained during the night, one of those rare tropical storms that sometimes blow in from Hawaii without warning. I woke at 2:36 A.M. to the sound of heavy raindrops drumming on my skylight. The air gusting through the open window smelled of ocean brine and gardenias. May in California tends to be cool and dry. During the summer months following, vegetation languishes without moisture, a process of dehydration that renders the chaparral as fragile as ancient parchment. The rolling hills turn gold while the roadsides glow hazy yellow with the clouds of wild mustard growing along the berm. By August, the temperatures climb into the 80s and the relative humidity drops. Winds tear down the mountains and squeeze through canyons. Between the sundowners, the Santa Anas, and the desiccated landscape, the stage is set for the arsonist's match. Rains might offer temporary relief, delaying the inevitable by a week or two. The irony is that rain does little more than encourage growth, which in turn provides nature with additional combustible fuel.

By the time I woke again at 5:59, the storm had passed. I pulled on my sweats and went out for my run, returning to the apartment only long enough to toss a canvas duffel in the car and head over to the gym. I lifted weights for an hour, working my way through my usual routine. Though I'd only been back at the process for two months, I was seeing results, shoulders and biceps taking form again.

I was home at nine. I showered, ate breakfast, tossed some items in my fanny pack, grabbed my shoulder bag, left a note on Henry's door, and hit the road for L.A. Traffic was fast-moving, southbound cars barreling down the 101. At this time of day, the road was heavily populated with commercial vehicles: pickups and panel trucks, semis and moving vans, empty school buses, and trailers hauling new cars to the showrooms in Westlake and Thousand Oaks. As I crested the hill and eased down into the San Fernando Valley, I could see the gauzy veil of the smog that had already begun to accumulate. The San Gabriel Mountains, often obscured from view, were at least visible today. Every time I passed this way, new construction was under way. What looked like entire villages would appear on the crest of a hill, or a neighborhood of identical condominiums would emerge from behind a stand of trees. Billboards announced the availability of new communities previously unheard of.

Overhead, two bright yellow aircraft circled, one following the other in an aerial surveillance focused on those of us down below. The berm was littered with trash, and at one point I passed one of those perplexing curls of tire tread that defy explanation. Once I reached Sherman Oaks, I turned right on the San Diego Freeway. The foliage along the berm was whipped by the perpetual wind of passing vehicles. Several towering office buildings obstructed the view, like sightseers on a parade route with no consideration for others. I took the off-ramp at Sunset and drove east until the UCLA campus began to appear on my right. I turned right onto Hilgard, right again on Le Conte, and right onto Tiverton, where I paid for a parking voucher. There were no parking spots available in the aboveground lot. I began my descent into the underground levels, circling down and down until I finally found a spot on C-1. I locked my car and took the elevator up. The extensive grass and concrete plaza served both the Jules Stein Eye Clinic and the UCLA Hospital and Medical Center. I crossed to the main entrance and entered the lobby, with its polished granite walls and two-tone gray carpet with a smoky pink stripe along the edge. The reception area on the right was filled with people awaiting word of friends and family members currently undergoing surgery. Two teenage girls in shorts and T-shirts were playing cards on the floor. There were babies in infant seats and a toddler in a stroller, flushed and sweating in sleep. Others were reading newspapers or chatting quietly while a steady foot traffic of visitors crossed and recrossed the lounge. The lobby chairs and adjoining planters were boxy gray modules. On the left, the gift shop was faced in a curious hue somewhere between mauve and orchid. A large glass case contained sample floral arrangements in case you arrived to see someone without a posy in hand.

Dead ahead, above the information desk, the word INFORMATION was writ large. I waited my turn and then asked a Mrs. Lewis, the patient information volunteer, for Mickey Magruder's room. She was probably in her seventies, her eyelids crepey as a turtle's. Age had cut knife pleats in the fragile skin on her cheeks, and her lips were pulled together in a pucker, like a drawstring purse. She did a quick check of her files and began to shake her head with regret. "I don't show anybody by that name. When was he admitted, dear?"

"On the fourteenth. I guess he could be registered as Michael. That's how the name reads on his birth certificate."

She made a note of the name and consulted another source. Her knuckles were knotted with arthritis, but her cursive was delicate. "Well, I don't know what to tell you. Is it possible he's been discharged?"

"I doubt it. I heard he was in a coma in ICU."

"You know, he might have been taken to the Santa Monica facility on Sixteenth Street. Shall I put in a call to them?"

"I'd appreciate that. I drove all the way down from Santa Teresa, and I'd hate to go home without finding him."

I watched her idly as she dialed and spoke to someone on the other end. Within moments, she hung up, apparently without success. "They have no record of him there. You might try Saint John's Hospital or Cedars-Sinai."

"I'm almost certain he was brought here. I talked to police detectives yesterday, and that's what they said. He was admitted early Wednesday morning of last week. He'd been shot twice, so he must have been brought in through emergency."

"I'm afraid that doesn't help. All I'm given is the patient's name, room number, and medical status. I don't have information about admissions."

"Suppose he was transferred? Wouldn't you receive notice?"

"Ordinarily," she said.

"Look, is there anyone else I could talk to about this?"

"I can't think who unless you'd want to speak to someone in administration."

"Can't you check with Intensive Care? Maybe if you describe his injuries, they'll know where he is."

"Well," she said hesitantly, "there *is* a trauma social worker. She'd certainly have been alerted if the patient were the victim of a violent crime. Would you like me to call her?"

"Perfect. Please do. I'd appreciate your help."

By now, other people were lining up behind me, anxious for information and restless at the delay. Mrs. Lewis seemed reluctant, but she did pick up the phone again and make an in-house call. After the first couple of sentences, her voice dropped out of hearing range and she angled her face slightly so I couldn't read her lips. When she replaced the receiver, she wouldn't quite look at me. "If you'd care to wait, they said they'd send someone."

"Is something wrong?"

"Not that I know, dear. At the moment, the social worker's out of her office . . . probably on the floor somewhere. The ICU charge nurse is going to try paging her and get back to me."

"Then you're telling me he's here?"

The man behind me said, "Hey, come on, lady. Give us a break."

Mrs. Lewis seemed flustered. "I didn't say that. All I know is the social worker might help if you want to wait and talk to her. If you could just have a seat. . . ."

"Thanks. You won't forget?"

The man said, "Hell, I'll tell you myself."

I was too distracted to engage in a barking fest, so I let that one pass. I made my way over to an empty chair. Driving down to L.A., I hadn't pictured things turning out this way. I'd fancied a moment by Mickey's bed, some feeling of redemption, the chance to make amends. Now his latent paranoia was rubbing off on me. Had something happened to him? Had Detectives Claas and Aldo been holding out? It was always possible he'd been admitted under an assumed name. Crime victims, like celebrities, are often afforded the added measure of protection. If that were the case, I wasn't sure how I was going to sweet-talk my way into his alias. All I knew was I wouldn't budge until I got a lead on him.

Someone had left behind a tattered issue of *Sunset Magazine*. I began to leaf through, desperate for a diversion from my anxiety about him. I needed to get "centered." I needed serenity, a moment of calm, while I figured out whose butt I was going to kick and how hard. I settled on an article about building a brick patio, complete with layouts. Every ten or fifteen seconds I looked up, checking the clock, watching visitors, patients, and hospital personnel entering the lobby, emerging from the cafeteria, passing through the seeing-eye doors. It was important to dig out the area to a depth of six inches, adding back a layer of gravel and then a layer of sand before beginning to lay brick. I chose the herringbone pattern for my imaginary outdoor living space. Thirty minutes went by. I finished all the articles on horticulture and went on to check out the low-fat recipes utilizing phyllo and fresh fruit. I didn't want to eat anything that had to be kept under a moist towel before I baked it.

Someone sat down in the chair next to mine. I glanced over to find Gian Aldo, and he was pissed. The woman at the desk had clearly ratted me out. Aldo said, "I figured it was you. What the hell's going on? I get a call saying some woman's over here making a stink, trying to get Mickey's room number from a poor unsuspecting volunteer."

I felt the color rise in my cheeks. "I didn't 'make a stink.' I never even raised my voice. I came to see how he was. What's the big deal?"

"We asked to be notified if anyone came in asking for Magruder's room."

"How was I supposed to know? I'm concerned, worried sick. Is that against the law?"

"Depends on your purpose. You could've been the shooter . . . or had you thought about that?"

"Of course I thought about that, but I didn't shoot the

man," I said. "I was anxious about him and thought I'd feel better if I could see him."

Aldo's dark brows knit together and I could tell he was struggling to moderate his attitude. "You should have given us warning. We could have met you on arrival and saved you the time and aggravation."

"Your overriding purpose in life."

"Look, I was in the middle of a meeting when the call came through. I didn't have to rush right out. I could have let you sit and stew. It would have served you right." He stared off across the lobby. "Actually, my overriding purpose is protecting Magruder. I'm sure you can appreciate the risk, since we don't have the faintest idea who plugged him."

"I get that." I could see the situation from his perspective. This was an active investigation, and I'd gummed up the works by ignoring protocol. Since Mick was my ex and since mine was the gun that was found at the scene, my sudden appearance at the hospital didn't look that good. "I'm sorry. I get antsy for information and tend to cut to the chase. I should have called you. The fault was mine."

"Let's don't worry about that now." He glanced at his watch. "I have to get back to work, but if you want, I can take you up to ICU for a couple minutes first."

"I can't have time alone with him?"

"That's correct," he said. "For one thing, he's still unconscious. For another, it's my responsibility to keep him safe. I answer to the department, no ifs, ands, or buts. I don't mean to sound harsh, but that's the way it is."

"Let's get on with it then," I said, suppressing the surge of rebelliousness. Clearly, I'd have to yield to him in everything. This man was officially the keeper of the gate. Seeing Mickey was more important than bucking authority or winning arguments.

I got up when he did and followed him through the lobby, feeling like a dog trained to heel. We took a right down the corridor, saying nothing to each other. He pressed for the elevator. While we waited, he pulled out a package of gum and offered me a piece. I declined. He removed a stick for himself, tore it in half, peeled off the paper, and popped the gum in his mouth. The elevator doors slid open. I entered behind him, and we turned and faced front while we ascended. For once I didn't bother to memorize the route. There was no point in scheming to find Mickey on my own. If I pulled any shenanigans, Detective Aldo was going to nail my ass to the wall.

We entered the 7-E Intensive Care Unit, where the detective was apparently known by sight. While he had a brief conversation with the nurses at the desk, I had a chance to get my bearings. The atmosphere was curious: the lights slightly dimmed, the noise level reduced by the teal-and-gray patterned carpeting. I guessed at ten or twelve beds, each in a cubicle within visual range of the nurses' station. The beds were separated by light-weight green-and-white curtains, most of which were drawn shut. These were the patients who teetered on the edge, tethered to life by the slimmest of lines. Blood and bile, urine, spinal fluid, all the rivers in the body were being mapped and charted while the soul journeyed on. Sometimes, between breaths, a patient slipped away, easing into the greater stream from which all of us emerge and to which all must return.

Aldo rejoined me and steered me around the desk to the bed where Mickey lay. I didn't recognize the man, though a quick glance at Aldo assured me this was him. He wasn't breathing on his own. There was a wide band of tape across the lower portion of his face. His mouth was open, attached to a ventilator by a translucent blue tube about the same diameter as a vacuum cleaner hose.

The top half of the bed was elevated as if he were on permanent display. He lay close to one side, almost touching the side rails, which had been raised to contain him like the sides of a crib. He wore a watch cap of gauze. The bullet wound had left him with two blackened eyes, puffy and bruised as though he'd been in a fistfight. His complexion was gray. There was a tube in the back of one hand, delivering solutions from numerous bags hanging on an IV pole. I could count the drips one by one, a Chinese water torture designed to save life. A second tube snaked out from under the covers and into a gallon jug of urine accumulating under the bed. What hair I could see looked sparse and oily. His skin had a fine sheen of moisture. Years of sun damage were now surfacing like an image on film bathed in developing fluid. I could see soft down on the edges of his ears. His eyes weren't fully closed. Through the narrow slits I could watch him track an unseen movie or perhaps lines of print. Where was his mind while his body lay so still? I disconnected my emotions by focusing on equipment that surrounded his bed: a cart, a sink, a stainless steel trash can with a pop-up lid, a rolling chair, a glove dispenser, and a paper towel rack—utilitarian articles that hardly spoke of death.

The presence of Detective Aldo lent a strange air of unreality to our reunion. Mickey's chest rose and fell in a regular rhythm, a bellow's effect forcing his lungs to inflate. Under his hospital gown, I could see a tube top of white gauze bandages. When I'd met him, he was thirty-six. He was now almost fifty-three, the same age as Robert Dietz. For the first time I wondered if my involvement with Dietz had been an unwitting attempt to mend the breach with Mickey. Were my internal processes that obvious?

I stared at Mickey's face, watching him breathe, glancing at the blood pressure cuff that was attached to one arm. At intervals, the cuff would inflate and deflate itself, with a whining and a wheeze. The digital readout would then appear on the monitor above his head. His blood pressure seemed stable at 125 over 80, his pulse 74. It's embarrassing to remember love once the feeling's died, all the passion and romanticism, the sentimentality and sexual excess. Later, you have to wonder what the hell you were thinking of. Mickey had seemed solid and safe, someone whose expertise I admired, whose opinions I valued, whose confidence I envied. I'd idealized him without even realizing what I was doing, which was taking my projection as the stone cold truth. I didn't understand that I sought in him the qualities I lacked or hadn't yet developed. I'd have denied to the last breath that I was looking for a father figure, but of course I was.

I became conscious of Gian Aldo, who stared at Mickey with a silence similar to mine. What could either of us say beyond the trite and the obvious? I finally spoke up. "I should let you get back to work. I appreciate this."

"Any time," he said.

He walked me down through the hospital and across the plaza. I punched the elevator button and he waited with me dutifully. "I'm fine," I said, meaning he could leave.

"I don't mind," he said, meaning not-on-your-sweet-life.

When the elevator arrived, I got on and turned, giving him a little wave as the doors slid shut. I found my car, unlocked it, turned the key in the ignition, and put the gears in reverse. By the time I made the three circles upward to ground level, he was waiting in his car by the exit, his engine idling. I pulled out of the lot onto Tiverton, and when I reached Le Conte I turned left. Detective

Aldo did likewise, keeping pace with me as I headed toward the freeway. He was still asserting his control, as I was keenly aware. I could understand his desire to see me off, though I felt like the villain in a Western movie being escorted out of town. I kept track of his car in my rearview mirror—not that he made any effort to disguise his intent. West on Sunset, north on the 405, driving toward the 101, we formed a two-car motorcade at sixty miles an hour. I began to wonder if he was going to follow me all the way home.

I watched the cross streets go by: Balboa, White Oak, Reseda . . . did the man have no faith? What'd he think I was going to do, circle back to UCLA? At Tampa, I saw him lean forward and pick up his radio mike, apparently responding to a call. The subject must have been urgent because he suddenly veered off, crossing two lanes of traffic before he headed down the exit ramp. I kept my acceleration constant, my gaze fixed on the mirror to see if he'd reappear. Detective Aldo was a sneak, and I wouldn't put it past him to try a little misdirection. Winnetka, DeSoto, Topanga Canyon passed. It looked like he was gone. For once my angels were in agreement. One said, Nobody's perfect, and the other said, Amen.

I took the next off-ramp.

10

MICKEY HAD BEEN shrewd in listing an address on Sepulveda. According to the *Thomas Guide,* there are endless variations. Sepulveda Boulevard seems to spring forth in the north end of the San Fernando Valley. The street then traces a line south, often hugging the San Diego Freeway, all the way to Long Beach. The North and South Sepulveda designations seem to jump back and forth, claiming ever-shifting sections of the street as it winds from township to township. There are East and West Sepulveda Boulevards, a Sepulveda Lane, Sepulveda Place, Sepulveda Street, Sepulveda Eastway, East Sepulveda Fire Road, Sepulveda Westway. By juggling the numbers, Mickey could just about ensure that no one was ever going to pinpoint his exact location. As it happened, I'd collected three variations of the same four digits: 2805, 2085, and 2580.

I placed the addresses in numerical order, beginning with 2085, moving on to 2580, and then to 2805. I reasoned that even if finances had forced him to sell his car, he still had to get around. He might use a bike or public transportation traveling to and from his place of employment—unless, of course, he'd also lost his job. He probably did his shopping close to home, frequenting the local restaurants when he felt too lazy to prepare a meal, which (if the past was any indication) was most of the time. The detectives had mentioned the shooting had occurred in a commercial district with lots of bars close by. Already in my mind, a mental picture was forming. Mickey'd never owned a house, so I was looking for a rental, and nothing lavish, if I knew him.

I cruised the endless blocks of Sepulveda I'd selected. While this wasn't L.A. at its worst, the route was hardly scenic. There were billboards everywhere. Countless telephone poles intersected the skyline, dense strands of wire stretching in all directions. I passed gas stations, a print and copy shop, three animal hospitals, a 7-Eleven, a discount tire establishment. I watched the numbers climb, from a car wash to a sign company, from a construction site to a quick lube to an auto body shop. In this area, if you weren't in the market for lumber or fast food, you could always buy discount leather or stock up at the Party Smarty for your entertaining needs.

It wasn't until I reached the 2800 block in Culver City that I sensed this was Mickey's turf. The H-shaped three-story apartment building at 2805 had a rough plaster exterior, painted drab gray, with sagging galleries and aluminum sliding glass doors that looked like they'd be difficult to open. Stains, shaped like stalactites, streaked the stucco along the roofline. Weeds grew up through cracks in the concrete. A dry gully ran along the south side, choked with boulders and refuse. The wire fence marking the property line now leaned against the side of the apartment complex in a tangle of dead shrubs.

I drove past, scanning the nearest intersection, where I

saw an electronics shop, a photo lab, a paint store, a mini-mart, a pool hall, a twenty-four-hour coffee shop, two bars, and a Chinese restaurant, Mickey's favorite. I spotted a driveway, and at the first break in traffic I did a turn-around, coming up on the right side of the street in front of 2805. I found a parking place two doors away, turned off the engine, and sat in my car, checking out the ambience, if the concept isn't too grand. The building itself was similar to one Mickey occupied when the two of us first met. I'd been appalled then, as I was now, by his indifference to his environment. The sign out front specified *studios and 1 & 2 bedroom apartments* NOW RENT-ING, as if this were late-breaking news.

The landscaping consisted of a cluster of banana palms with dark green battered leaves that looked like they'd been slashed by a machete. Traffic in the area was heavy, and I found myself watching the cars passing in both directions, wondering if Detective Aldo was going to drive by and catch me at the scene. The very thought made me squirm. It's not as though he'd forbidden me to make an appearance, but he wasn't going to be happy if he figured it out.

I started the car and pulled away from the curb. I drove down half a block and turned right at the first corner and then right again, into the alley that ran be-hind the row of buildings and dead-ended at the gully. Someone had compressed the buckling wire fence so that one could cross the boundary and ease down into the ditch. I pulled in beside the garbage bins and made another U-turn, so that I now faced the alley entrance. I took a minute to grab my fanny pack from the back-seat and transfer my key picks, a penlight, my mini-tool kit, and a pair of rubber gloves. I clipped the fanny pack around my waist, locked the car, and got out.

I padded down the walkway between Mickey's building and the apartment complex next door. At night this area would be dark, since the exterior light fixtures were either dangling or missing altogether. A line of gray-painted water meters was planted along the side, real shin-bangers. By straining only slightly—which is to say, jumping up and down like a Zulu—I was able to peek in the windows through the wrought-iron burglar bars. Most of what I saw were bedrooms barely large enough for a king-sized bed. The occupants seemed to use the windowsills to display an assortment of homely items: cracker boxes, framed snapshots, mayonnaise jars filled to capacity with foil-wrapped condoms. In one unit, someone was nurturing a handsome marijuana plant.

Mickey's apartment building didn't have a lobby, but an alcove in the front stairwell housed a series of metal mailboxes with names neatly embossed on short lengths of red, blue, and yellow plastic. Even Mickey couldn't buck post office regulations. By counting boxes, I knew there were twenty apartments distributed on three floors, but I had no way to guess how many flats were the one- and two-bedroom units and how many were studios. His was unit 2-H. The manager was on the ground floor in 1-A to my immediate right. The name on the mailbox read HATFIELD, B & C. I decided to postpone contact until after I'd reconnoitered Mickey's place.

I went up the front stairs to the second floor, following the progression of front doors and picture windows that graced each flat. There were no burglar bars up here. Mickey's was the corner unit at the rear of the building on the right-hand side. There was a neat yellow X of crime-scene tape across his door. An official caution had been affixed advising of the countless hideous repercussions if crime-scene sanctity was breached. The gallery continued around the corner and ran along the back of the building, so that Mickey's rear windows over-looked the alleyway below and the gully to the right. A second set of stairs had been tacked on back here, probably to bring the building into compliance with fire department codes. Mickey probably considered this a mixed blessing. While the privacy offered a potential in-truder unimpeded access to his windows, it also gave Mickey an easy means of egress. When I peered over the railing, I could see my VW below like a faithful steed, so close I could have leapt down and galloped off at a moment's notice.

All Mickey's sliding glass windows were secured. Know-ing him, he'd tucked heavy wooden dowels into the in-side track so the windows would only slide back a scant six inches. The lock on his front door, however, seemed to be identical to those on the neighboring apartments. The manager must have discouraged swapping out the standard model for something more effective. I studied my surroundings. The alley was deserted and I saw no signs of any other tenant. I slipped on my rubber gloves and went to work with my pick. A friend in Houston had recently sent me a keen toy: a battery-operated pick that, once mastered, worked with gratifying efficiency. It had taken me a while to get the hang of it, but I'd practiced on Henry's door until I had the technique down pat.

The door yielded to my efforts in less than fifteen sec-onds, making no more noise than an electric toothbrush. I tucked the pick back in my fanny pack, loosened one end of the yellow tape, and stepped over the doorsill, turning only long enough to resecure the tape through the gap before I closed the door behind me. I checked my watch, allowing myself thirty minutes for the search. I figured if a neighbor had observed me breaking in, it would take the L.A. cops at least that long to respond to the call.

The interior was dim. Mickey's curtains were drawn, and sunlight was further blocked by the six-story building across the alley. Mickey still smoked. Stale fumes hung in the air, having permeated the carpet, the drapes, and all the heavy upholstered furniture. I checked the cigarette butts that had been left in the ashtrays, along with an array of wooden kitchen matches. All were the same Camel filters he'd been smoking for years, and none bore the telltale red rim suggesting female companionship. An Elmore Leonard paperback had been left on the arm of the sofa, open at the midpoint. Mickey had introduced me to Elmore Leonard and Len Deighton. In turn, I'd told him about Dick Francis, though I'd never known if he read the British author with the same pleasure I did. The walls were done in a temporary-looking pine paneling that was nearly sticky with the residue of cigarette tars. The living room and dining room formed an L. The furniture was clumsy—big overstuffed pieces of the sort you'd buy at a flea market or pick off the sidewalk, like an alley fairy, on collection day. There was a shredder against one wall, but the bin had been emptied. In Mickey's view of the world, no scrap of paper, no receipt, and no piece of correspondence should go into the trash without being scissored into tiny pieces. He probably dumped the bin at frequent intervals, using more than one trash can, so that a thief breaking in wouldn't have the means to reassemble vital documents. No doubt about it, the man was nuts.

I moved into the dining area, past four mismatched chairs and a plain wooden table that was littered with mail. I paused, picking through the stack that was piled at one end. I was careful not to sort the envelopes, though my natural inclination was to separate the bills from the junk. I spotted a number of bank statements, but there were no personal letters, no catalogs, and no credit card bills. I had little interest in his utility bills. What did I care how much electricity he used? I longed for a phone bill, but there were none to be found. The cops had lifted those. I picked up the handful of bank statements and slipped them down the front of my jeans into my underpants, where they formed a crackling paper girdle. I'd look at them later when I was home again. None of the other bills seemed useful so I left them where they were. Best to keep the federal mail-tampering convictions to a minimum.

Off the dining area, I entered a galley-style kitchen so small I could reach the far wall in two steps. Stove, apartment-sized refrigerator, sink, microwave oven. The only kitchen window was small and looked out onto the alley. On the counter, he kept a round glass fishbowl into which he tossed his extra packets of matches at the end of the night, a road map of his journey from bar to bar. The upper cabinets revealed a modest collection of Melamine plates and coffee mugs, plus the basic staples: dry cereal, powdered milk, sugar, a few condiments, paper napkins, and two sealed bottles of Early Times bourbon. The cupboards below were packed back to front with canned goods: soups, beans, Spam, tuna packed in oil, tamales, Spaghetti O's, applesauce, evaporated milk. In the storage space under the kitchen sink, I found an empty bourbon bottle in the trash. Tucked in among the pipes, I counted ten five-gallon containers of bottled water. This was Mickey's survival stock in case a war broke out or L.A. was invaded by extraterrestrials. The refrigerator was filled with things that smelled bad. Mickey had tossed in half-eaten items without the proper wrapping, which resulted in dark chunks of hardening cheddar cheese, a greening potato covered with wartlike sprouts, and half an air-dried tomato drawing in on itself.

I retraced my steps. To the left of the living room was

the door to the bedroom, with a closet and undersized bath beyond. The chest of drawers was filled with the usual jockey shorts and T-shirts, socks, handkerchiefs. The bed-table drawer contained some interesting items: a woman's diaphragm and a small spray bottle of cologne with a partial price label on the bottom. The cologne had apparently been purchased from a Robinson's Department Store, since I could still make out a portion of the identifying tag. I removed the top and took a whiff. Heavy on the lily of the valley that I remembered from the early days of our romance. Mickey's mother must have worn something similar. I remembered how he'd lay his lips in the hollow of my throat when I was wearing it myself. I put the cologne bottle down. There was a tissue paper packet about the size of a stick of gum. I unfolded the paper and picked up a thin gold chain threaded through the clasp of a small gold heart locket with an ever-so-tiny rose enameled in the center. Not to sound cynical, but Mickey'd given me one just like this about a week into our affair. Some men do that, find a gimmick or shtick that works once—the gift of a single red rose—and recycle the same gesture with every woman who comes along.

In a cleaning bag, he'd hung two dark-blue uniforms with patches on the sleeves. I slid a hand up under the bag and checked one of the light blue patches. *Pacific Coast Security* was stitched in gold around the rim. Also hanging in the closet were a couple of sport coats, six dress shirts, four pairs of blue jeans, two pairs of chinos, a pair of dark pants, and a black leather jacket I knew very well indeed. This was the jacket Mickey wore the first time we went out, the jacket he was wearing when he kissed me the first time. I was still living with Aunt Gin, so there was no way we could go inside to misbehave. Mickey backed me up against the trailer door, the leather in his jacket making a characteristic creaking sound. The kiss went on so long we both sank down along the frame. I was Eva Marie Saint with Marlon Brando—*On the Waterfront*—which is still one of the best screen kisses in recorded history. Not like love scenes nowadays where you watch the guy stick his tongue down the girl's throat, trying to activate her gag reflex. Mickey and I might've made love right there on the doorstep except we'd have been visible to everybody in the trailer park, which we knew was bad form, making us vulnerable to arrest.

I shook my head and closed the closet door while a sexual shiver ran down my frame. I tried the door next to it, which seemed to be an exit onto the rear gallery. The lock here was new. There was no key in the deadbolt, but it probably wasn't far. Mickey wouldn't make it easy for someone breaking into the apartment, but he'd want the key handy in case of fire or earthquake. I pivoted, letting my gaze move across the area, remembering his tricks. I knelt and felt my way along the edge of the carpeting. When I reached the corner, I gave the loosened carpet a tug. I lifted that section and plucked the key from its hiding place. I unlocked the back door and left it temporarily ajar.

I went back to the bedroom door and stood there, looking out at the living room. The cops had doubtless cruised through here once, sealing the apartment afterward, pending a more thorough investigation. I tried to see the place as they had, and then I looked at it again from personal experience. With Mickey, the question wasn't so much what was visible as what wasn't. This was a man who lived in a constant state of readiness and, as nearly as I could tell, his fears had only accelerated in the past fourteen years. In the absence of global conflict, he lived in anticipation of civil insurrection: unruly hordes

who would overrun the building, breaking into every
unit, clamoring for food, water, and other valuables like
toilet paper. So where were his weapons? How did he intend to defend himself?

I tried the kitchen first, tapping along the baseboards
for the sound of hollow spaces. I'd seen him install other
"safes"—compartments with false fronts where you
could tuck cash, guns, and ammunition. I started with
the kitchen sink. I took out all the gallon water containers, exposing the "floor" and rear wall of stained
plywood. I shone the penlight from top to bottom, side
to side. I could see four screw heads, one set in each
corner, darkened to match the panel. I unbuckled my
fanny pack, opened my mini-tool kit, took out a battery-
operated drill, and set about removing screws. A person
could develop carpal tunnel syndrome doing this the old-
fashioned way. Once the screws were out, the partition
yielded to gentle pressure, exposing a space that was six
to eight inches deep. Four handguns were mounted in a
rack on the rear wall, along with boxes of ammunition. I
replaced the panel with care and continued my search. I
considered this a fact-finding mission. Like the LAPD detectives, my prime purpose was determining just why
Mickey'd been shot. I didn't want to remove anything of
his unless I had to. Better to leave the items undisturbed
where possible.

At the end of thirty minutes, I'd uncovered three small
recesses hollowed out behind the switch plates in the
living room. Each contained a packet of identification
papers: birth certificate, driver's license, social security
card, credit cards, and currency. Emmett Vanover. Delbert Amburgey. Clyde Byler. None were names I recognized, and I assumed he'd invented them or borrowed
them from deceased persons whose vitals he'd gleaned

from public records. In every bogus document, Mickey's photo had been inserted. I left everything where it was and moved on. I'd also discovered that the back of the couch could be removed to reveal a space large enough to hide in. The paneling, while cheap, turned out to be securely fastened to the walls, but I did find tight rolls of crisp twenty-dollar bills tucked into either end of the big metal curtain rods in the living and dining rooms. A quick count suggested close to twelve hundred dollars.

In the bathroom, I removed a length of PVC, two inches in diameter, that had been set into the wall adjacent to the water lines. The pipe contained a handful of gold coins. Again, I left the stash where it was and carefully realigned the pipe in its original site. The only place I bombed out was one of his favorites, that being down the bathtub drain. He liked to drill a hole in the rubber stopper and run a chain up through the plug. He'd attach the relevant item to the chain, which he then left dangling down the drain with all the slimy hair and soap scum. This was usually where he kept his safe deposit key. I took a minute to lean over the rim of the tub. The rubber stopper was attached by a chain to the overflow outlet, but when I flashed the light into the drain itself, there was nothing hanging down the hole. Well, shoot. I consoled myself with the fact that I'd otherwise done well. Mickey probably had other secret repositories— maybe new ones I hadn't even thought about—but this was the best I could do in the time allotted. For now, it was time to clear the premises.

I let myself out the back door, using Mickey's key to lock the door behind me. I slipped the key in my pocket, stripped off my rubber gloves, and zipped them into my pack. I went downstairs and knocked at the manager's front door. I'd assumed that B & C Hatfield were a married couple, but the occupants turned out to be sisters. The woman who opened the door had to be in her eighties. "Yes?"

She was heavy through the middle, with a generously weighted bosom. She wore a sleeveless cotton sundress with most of the color washed away. The fabric reminded me of old quilts, a flour-sacking floral print in tones of pale blue and pink. Her breasts were pillowy, powdered with talcum, like two domes of bread dough proofing in a bowl. Her upper arms were soft, and I could see her stockings were rolled down below her knees. She wore slippers with a half-moon cut out of one to accommodate a bunion.

I said, "Mrs. Hatfield?"

"I'm Cordia," she said cautiously. "May I help you?"

"I hope so. I'd like to talk to you about Mickey Magruder, the tenant in Two-H."

She fixed me with a pair of watery blue eyes. "He was shot last week."

"I'm aware of that. I just came from the hospital, where I was visiting him."

"Are you the police detective?"

"I'm an old friend."

She stared at me, her blue eyes penetrating.

"Well, actually, I'm his ex-wife," I amended, in response to her gaze.

"I saw you park in the alley while I was sweeping out the laundry room."

I said, "Ah."

"Was everything in order?"

"Where?"

"Two-H. Mr. Magruder's place. You were up there quite a while. Thirty-two minutes by my watch."

"Fine. No problem. Of course, I didn't go in."

"No?"

"There was crime scene tape across the door," I said.

"Place was posted, too. Big police warning about the penalties."

"I saw that."

She waited. I would have continued, but my mind was blank. My thought process had shorted out, catching me in the space between truth and lies. I felt like an actor who'd forgotten her lines. I couldn't for the life of me think what to say next.

"Are you interested in renting?" she prompted.

"Renting?"

"Apartment Two-H. I assume that's why you went up."

"Oh. Oh, sure. Good plan. I like the area."

"You do. Well, perhaps we could let you know if the unit becomes available. Would you care to come in and complete an application? You seem discombobulated. Perhaps a drink of water?"

"I'd appreciate that."

I entered the apartment, stepping directly into the kitchen. I felt like I'd slipped into another world. Chicken was stewing on the back of the stove. A second woman, roughly the same age, sat at a round oak table with a deck of cards. To my right, I could see a formal dining room: mahogany table and chairs, with a matching hutch stacked with dishes. Clearly, the floor plan was entirely different from Mickey's. The temperature on the thermostat must have been set at 80, and the TV on the kitchen counter was blaring stock market quotes at top volume. Neither Cordia nor her sister seemed to be watching the screen. "I'll get you the application," she said. "This is my sister, Belmira."

"On second thought, why don't I take the application home with me? I can fill it out and send it back. It'll be simpler that way."

"Suit yourself. Have a seat."

I pulled out a chair and sat down across from Belmira, who was shuffling a tarot deck. Cordia went to the kitchen sink and let the faucet water run cold before she filled a glass. She handed me the water and then crossed to a kitchen drawer, where she extracted an application. She returned to her seat, handed me the paper, and picked up a length of multicolored knitting, six inches wide and at least fifteen inches long.

I took my time with the water. I made a study of the application, trying to compose myself. What was wrong with me? My career as a liar was being seriously undermined. Meanwhile, neither sister questioned my lingering presence.

Cordia said, "Belmira claims she's a witch, though you couldn't prove it by me." She peered toward the dining room. "Dorothy's around here someplace. Where'd she go, Bel? I haven't seen her for an hour."

"She's in the bathroom," Bel said, and turned to me. "I didn't catch your name, dear."

"Oh, sorry. I'm Kinsey. Nice meeting you."

"Nice to meet you, too." Her hair was sparse, a flyaway white with lots of pink scalp showing through. Under her dark print housedress, her shoulders were narrow and bony, her wrists as flat and thin as the handles on two soup ladles. "How're you today?" she asked shyly, as she pulled the tarot deck together. Four of her teeth were gold.

"I'm fine. What about yourself?"

"I'm real good." She plucked a card from the deck and held it up, showing me the face. "The Page of Swords. That's you."

Cordia said, "Bel."

"Well, it's true. This is the second time I pulled it. I shuffled the deck and drew this as soon as she stepped in, and then I drew it again."

"Well, draw something else. She's not interested."

I said, "Tell me about your names. Those are new to me."

Bel said, "Mother made ours up. There were six of us girls and she named us in alphabetical order: Amelia, Belmira, Cordia, Dorothy, Edith, and Faye. Cordi and I are the last two left."

"What about Dorothy?"

"She'll be along soon. She loves company."

Cordia said, "Bel will start telling your fortune any minute now. I'm warning you, once she gets on it, it's hard to get her off. Just ignore her. That's what I do. You don't have to worry about hurting her feelings."

"Yes, she does," Bel said feebly.

"Are you good at telling fortunes?"

Cordia cut in. "Not especially, but even a blind hog comes across an acorn now and then." She had taken up her knitting, which she held to the light, her head tilted slightly as the needles tucked in and out. The narrow piece of knitting trailed halfway down her front. "I'm making a knee wrap, in case you're wondering."

My Aunt Gin taught me to knit when I was six years old, probably to distract me in the early evening hours. She claimed it was a skill that fostered patience and eye-hand coordination. Now, as I watched, I could see that Cordia had dropped a few stitches about six rows back. The loops, like tiny sailors washed overboard, were receding in the wake of the knitting as each new row was added. I was about to mention it when a large white cat appeared in the doorway. She had a flat Persian face. She stopped when she saw me and stared in apparent wonderment. I'd seen a cat like that once before: long-haired, pure white, one green eye and one blue.

Bel smiled at the sight of her. "Here she is."

"That's Dorothy," Cordia said. "We call her Dort for short. Do you believe in reincarnation?"

"I've never sorted that one through."

"We hadn't either till this kitty came along. Dorothy always swore she'd be in touch with us from the Other Side. Told us for years, she'd find a way to come back. Then, lo and behold, the neighbor's cat had a litter the very day she passed on. This was the only female, and she looks just like Dort. The white hair, the one blue eye, the one green. Same personality, same behavior. Sociable, pushy, independent."

Bel chimed in. "The cat even passes wind the way Dorothy did. Silent but deadly. Sometimes we have to get up and leave the room."

I pointed to the knitting. "It looks like you dropped some stitches." I leaned forward and touched a finger to the errant loops. "If you have a crochet hook, I can coax them up the line for you."

"Would you? I'd like that. Your eyes are bound to be better than mine." Cordia bent over and reached into her knitting bag. "Let's see what I've got here. Will this do?" She offered me a J hook.

"That's perfect." While I began the slow task of working the dropped stitches up through the rows, the cat picked her way across the floor and jumped up in my lap. I jerked the knitting up and said, "Whoa!" Dorothy must have weighed twenty pounds. She turned her backside to me and stuck her tail in the air like a pump handle, exhibiting her little spigot while she marched in place.

"She never does that. I don't know what's got into her. She must like you," Belmira said, turning up cards as she spoke.

"I'm thrilled."

"Well, would you look at this? The Ten of Wands, reversed." Bel was laying out a reading. She placed the Ten of Wands with the other cards on the table in some mysterious configuration. The card she'd assigned me, the Page of Swords, had now been covered by the Moon.

I freed one hand and cranked Dorothy's tail down, securing it with my right arm as I pointed to the cards. "What's that one mean?" I thought the Moon might be good, but the sisters exchanged a look that made me think otherwise.

Cordia said, "I told you she'd do this."

"The Moon stands for hidden enemies, dear. Danger, darkness, and terror. Not too good."

"No kidding."

She pointed to a card. "The Ten of Wands, reversed, represents obstacles, difficulties, and intrigues. And this one, the Hanged Man, represents the best you can hope for."

"She doesn't want to hear that, Bel."

"I do. I can handle it."

"This card crowns you."

"What's that? I'm afraid to ask," I said.

"Oh, the Hanged Man is good. He represents wisdom, trials, sacrifice, intuition, divination, prophecy. This is what you want, but it isn't yours at present."

"She's trying to help with my knitting. You might at least leave her be until she finishes."

"I can do both," I said. Though, truthfully, Dorothy's presence was making the task difficult. The cat had rotated in my lap and now seemed intent on smelling my breath. She extended her nose daintily. I paused and breathed through my mouth for her. "What's that card?" I asked, while she butted my chin with her head.

"The Knight of Swords, which is placed at your feet. This is your own, what you have to work with. Skill, bravery, capacity, enmity, wrath, war, destruction."

"The wrath part sounds good."

"Not overall," Bel corrected. "Overall, you're screwed. You see this one? This card stands for pain, affliction, tears, sadness, desolation."

"Well, dang."

"Exactly. I'd say you're up poop creek without a roll of TP." Belmira turned up another card.

Dorothy climbed up on my chest, purring. She put her face in mine and we stared at each another. I glanced back at the tarot deck. Even I, believing none of this, could see the trouble I was in. Aside from the Hanged Man, there was a fellow burdened with heavy sticks, yet another fellow face down on the ground with ten swords protruding from his back. The card for Judgment didn't seem to bode well either, and then there was the Nine of Wands, which showed a cranky-looking man clinging to a staff, eight staves in a line behind him. That card was followed by a heart pierced with three swords, rain and clouds above.

By then, I'd succeeded in rescuing the lost stitches, and I reached around Dorothy to return the knitting to Cordia. I thought it was time to get down to business, so I asked Cordia what she could tell me about Mickey.

"I can't say I know all that much about him. He was extremely private. He worked as a bank guard until he lost his job in February. I used to see him going out in his uniform. He looked handsome, I must say."

"What happened?"

"About what?"

"How'd he lose his job?"

"He drank. You must have known that if you were married to him. Nine in the morning, he reeked of alcohol. I don't think he *drank* at that hour. This was left from the night before, fumes pouring through his skin. He never staggered, and I never once heard him slur his words. He wasn't loud or mean. He was always a gentleman, but he was losing ground."

"I'm sorry to hear that. I knew he drank, but it's hard to believe he reached a point where drinking interfered with his work. He was a cop in the old days when I was married to him."

"Is that right," she said.

"Was there anything else you could tell me about him?"

"He was quiet, no parties. Paid his rent on time until the last few months. No visitors except for the nasty fellow with all the chains."

I turned my attention from Dorothy. "Chains?"

"One of those motorcycle types: studs and black leather. He had a cowboy mentality, swaggered when he walked. Made so much noise it sounded like he was wearing spurs."

"What was that about?"

"I have no idea. Dort didn't like him. He was very rude. He knocked her sideways with his foot when she tried to smell his boot."

Bel said, "Oh, dear. This card represents the King of Cops . . . reversed again. That's not good."

I looked over with interest. "The King of Cops?"

"I didn't say cops, dear. I said Cups. The King of Cups stands for a dishonest, double-dealing man: roguery, vice, scandal, you name it."

Belatedly, I felt a flutter of uneasiness. "Speaking of which, what made you think I was a cop when I came to the door?"

Cordia looked up. "Because an officer called this morning and said a detective would be stopping by at two this afternoon. We thought it must be you since you were up there so long."

I felt my heart give a little hiccup, and I checked my

watch. Nearly two o'clock now. "Gee, I better hit the road and let the two of you get back to work," I said. "Um, I wonder if you could do me a little favor. . . ."

Bel turned up the next card and said, "Don't worry about it, dear. We won't mention you were here."

"I'd appreciate that."

"I'll take you out the other door," Cordia said. "So you can reach the alley without being seen. The detectives park in the front . . . at least, they did before."

"Why don't I leave you a number? That way you can get in touch with me if anything comes up," I said. I jotted down my number on the back of my business card. In return, Cordia wrote their number on the edge of the rental application. Neither questioned my request. With a tarot like mine, they must have assumed I was going to need all the help I could get.

11

ON THE WAY home, I stopped off at McDonald's and bought myself a QP with cheese, an order of fries, and a medium Coke. Once I'd picked Dorothy's hair off my lip, I steered with one hand while I munched with the other, all the time moaning with pleasure. It's pitiful to have a life in which junk food is awarded the same high status as sex. Then again, I tend to get a lot more of the one than I do of the other. I was back in Santa Teresa by four-fifteen. The only message on my machine was from Mark Bethel, who'd finally returned my Monday-afternoon call at eleven-thirty Wednesday morning.

I dialed his number, taking a moment to unzip my jeans and remove Mickey's mail from my underpants. Naturally, Mark was out, so I ended up talking to Judy. "You almost caught him. He left fifteen minutes ago."

"Shoot. Well, I'm sorry I missed him. I just got back from Los Angeles. I have news about Mickey and I may need his help. I'm in for the afternoon. If he has a chance to call, I'd love to talk to him."

"I'm afraid he's gone for the day, Kinsey, but if you

like you can catch him at seven tonight at the Lampara," she said, naming a downtown theater.

"Doing what?" I asked, though I had a fair idea. Mark Bethel was one of fourteen Republican candidates who'd be battling it out in the primary coming up on June 3, a scant twelve days off. I'd heard four of them had been invited to debate the issues at an event being sponsored by the League for Fair Government.

"This is a public debate: Robert Naylor, Mike Antonovich, Bobbi Fiedler, and Mark, talking about election issues."

"Sounds hot," I said, thinking, Who's kidding who? The California Secretary of State, March Fong Eu, was predicting the lowest voter turnout in forty-six years. Of the candidates Judy'd mentioned, only Mike Antonovich, the conservative L.A. County supervisor, had even a slim chance at winning. Naylor was an assemblyman from Menlo Park, the only Northern Californian in the race until Ed Zschau had stepped in. Zschau was the front-runner. Rumor had it that the *San Diego Union*, the *San Francisco Chronicle*, the *San Francisco Examiner*, and the *Contra Costa Times* were all coming out in support of him. Meanwhile, Bobbi Fiedler, a San Fernando Valley congresswoman and a seasoned politician, had had the rug pulled out from under her when a grand jury indicted her for allegedly bribing another candidate into leaving the race. The charges turned out to be groundless and had been dismissed, but her supporters had lost enthusiasm and she was having trouble recovering her momentum. As for Mark, this was his second fling at a statewide election, and he was busy pouring Laddie's money into TV spots in which he touted himself for running such a clean campaign. Like anyone gave a shit. The notion of sitting through some droning political debate was enough to put me in a coma of my own.

Meanwhile, Judy was saying, "Mark's been preparing for days, mostly on Prop Fifty-one. That's the Deep Pockets Initiative."

"Right."

"Also Props Forty-two and Forty-eight. He feels pretty strongly about those."

I said, "Hey, who wouldn't?" I pushed some papers around my desk, uncovering the sample ballot under the local paper and a pile of mail. Proposition 48 would put a lid on ex-officials' pensions. Yawn, snore. Prop 42 would authorize the state to issue $850 million in bonds to continue the Cal-Vet farm and home loan program. "I didn't know Mark was a veteran," I said, making conversation.

"Oh, sure, he enlisted in the army right after his college graduation. I'll send you a copy of his CV."

"You don't have to do that," I said.

"It's no trouble. I have a bunch of 'em going out in the mail. You know, he won a Purple Heart."

"Really, I had no idea."

While Judy nattered on, I found the comic section and read *Rex Morgan, M.D.*, which was at least as interesting. Judy interrupted herself, saying, "Shoot. There goes my other phone. I better catch that in case it's him."

"No problem."

As soon as I hung up, I propped my feet up on my desk and turned my attention to the mail I'd snitched. I picked up my letter opener and slit the envelopes. The bank statements showed regular paycheck deposits until late February, then nothing until late March, when he began to make small deposits at biweekly intervals. Unemployment benefits? I couldn't remember how that worked. There was probably a waiting period during which claims were processed and approved. In any event, the money he was depositing wasn't sufficient to cover his monthly expenses, and he was having to supplement the total out of his savings account. The current balance there was roughly $1,500. I'd found cash hidden on the premises, but no sign of his passbook. It would be nice to have that. I was surprised I hadn't come across it in my initial search. The monthly statements would have to do.

By comparing the activity in his savings and checking accounts, I could see the money jump from one to the other and then slide on out the door. Canceled checks indicated that he'd continued to pay as many bills as he could. His rent was $850 a month, which had last been paid March 1, according to the canceled check. Through the last half of February and the first three weeks of March, there were three checks made out to cash totaling $1,800. That seemed odd, given his financial difficulties, which were serious enough without pissing away his cash. The police probably had the April statement, so there was no way for me to tell if he'd paid rent on the first or not. My guess was that sometime in here he'd let his storage fees become delinquent.

By April, he was already in arrears on his telephone bill, and his service must have been cut before he had a chance to catch up. The cash he'd hidden probably represented a last resort, monies he was reluctant to spend unless his situation became desperate. Maybe his intent was to disappear, once all his other funds were depleted.

On the twenty-fifth of March, there was a one-time deposit of $900. I decided that was probably from the sale of his car. A couple of days later, on the twenty-seventh, there was a modest deposit of $200, which allowed him to pay his gas and electric bills. I did note that the $200 appeared the very day the call was made from his apartment to my machine. Someone paid him to use the phone? That would be weird. At any rate, he probably figured he could stall eviction for another month or two, at which point—what? He'd take his cash and phony documents and leave the state? Something about this gnawed at me. Mickey was a fanatic about savings. It was his contention that everyone should have a good six months' worth of income in the bank . . . or under the mattress, whichever seemed safer. He was such a nut on the subject, I'd made it a practice myself since then. He had to have another savings account somewhere. Had he put the money in a CD or a pension fund at his job? I wasn't even sure why he'd been fired. Was he drunk on duty? I sat and thought about that and then called directory assistance in Los Angeles and got the number for Pacific Coast Security in Culver City. I figured I had sufficient information to fake my way through. I knew his date of birth and his current address. His social security number would have been an asset, but all I remembered of it was the last four digits: 1776. Mickey always made a point about the numbers being the same as the year the Declaration of Independence was signed.

I dialed the number for Pacific Coast Security and listened to the phone ring, trying to figure out what I was going to say, surely not the truth in this case. When the call was picked up, I asked for Personnel. The woman who answered sounded like she was already halfway home for the day. It was close to five by now and she was probably in the process of clearing her desk. "This is Personnel. Mrs. Bird," she said.

"Oh, hi. This is Mrs. Weston in the billing department at UCLA Medical Center. We're calling with regard to a patient who's been admitted to ICU. We understand he's employed by Pacific Coast Security, and we're wondering if you can verify his insurance coverage."

"Certainly," she said. "The employee's name?"

"Last name Magruder. That's M-A-G-R-U-D-E-R. First name, Mickey. You may have him listed as Michael.

Middle initial B. Home address 2805 Sepulveda Boulevard; date of birth, sixteen September 1933. Admitted through emergency on May fourteenth. We don't have a complete social security number, but we'd love to pick that up from you."

I could hear the woman breathing in my ear. "We heard about that. The poor man. Unfortunately, like I told the detectives, Mr. Magruder no longer works for us. He was terminated as of February twenty-eighth."

"Terminated as in fired?"

"That's right."

"Well, for heaven's sake. What for?"

She paused. "I'm not at liberty to discuss that, but it had to do with d-r-i-n-k-i-n-g."

"That's too bad. What about his medical insurance? Is there any possibility his coverage was extended?"

"Not according to our records."

"Well, that's odd. He had an insurance card in his wallet when he was brought in, and we were under the impression his coverage was current. Is he employed by any other company in the area?"

"I doubt it. We haven't been asked for references."

"What about Unemployment. Has he applied for benefits? Because he may qualify for medical under SDI." Yeah, right, SDI. Like we were all so casual about State Disability Insurance we didn't even need to spell it out.

"I really can't answer that. You'd have to check with them."

"What about money in his pension fund? Did he have automatic debits to his savings out of each paycheck?"

"I don't see where that's relevant," she said. She was beginning to sound uneasy, probably wondering if this was a ruse of some kind.

"You would if you saw the way his bill was mounting up," I said tartly.

"I'm afraid I can't discuss it. Especially with the police involved. They made a big point of that. We're not supposed to talk to anyone about anything when it comes to him."

"Same here. We've been asked to notify Detective Aldo if anyone even asks for his room."

"Really? They didn't say anything like that to us. Maybe because he hadn't worked here for so long."

"Consider yourself lucky. We're on red alert. Did you know Mr. Magruder personally?"

"Sure. The company's not all that big."

"You must feel terrible."

"I do. He's a real sweet guy. I can't imagine why anyone would want to do that to him."

"Awful," I said. "What about his social security number? We have the last four digits . . . 1776 . . . but the emergency room clerk couldn't understand what he was saying so she missed the first portion. All I need are the first five digits for our records. The director's a real stickler."

She seemed startled. "He was conscious?"

"Oh. Well, I don't know, now you mention it. He must have been, at least briefly. How else would we have this much?" I sensed her debate. "It's in his best interest," I added piously.

"Just a minute." I heard her clicking her computer keys, and after a moment she read off the first five digits. I made a note. "Thanks. You're a doll. I appreciate that."

There was a pause, and then her curiosity got the better of her. "How's he doing?"

"I'm sorry, but I'm not allowed to divulge that information. You'd have to ask the medical staff. I'm sure you can appreciate the confidentiality of these matters, especially here at UCLA."

"Of course. Absolutely. Well, I hope he's okay. Tell him Ingrid said hi."

"I'll pass the word."

Once she'd hung up, I opened my desk drawer and took out a fresh pack of lined index cards. Time for clerical work. I began jotting down notes, writing as fast as I could, one item per card, piling them up as I went. I had a lot of catching up to do, days of accumulated questions. I knew some of the answers, but most of the lines I was forced to leave blank. I used to imagine I could hold it all in my head, but memory has a way of pruning and deleting, eliminating anything that doesn't seem relevant at the moment. Later, it's the odd unrelated detail that sometimes makes the puzzle parts rearrange themselves like magic. The very act of taking pen to paper somehow gooses the brain into making the leap. It doesn't always happen in the moment, but without the concrete notation, the data disappear.

I checked my watch. It was 6:05 and I was so cockeyed with weariness my clothes had begun to hurt. I turned the ringer off the phone, went up the spiral stairs, stripped, kicked my shoes off, wrapped myself in a quilt, and slept.

I woke at 9:15 P.M., though it felt like midnight. I sat up in bed, yawning, and tried to get my bearings. I felt weighted with weariness. I pushed the covers aside and went over to the railing. Below, on my desk, I could see the light on my answering machine blinking merrily. Shit. If not for that, I'd have crawled back in bed and slept through till morning.

I pulled a robe on and picked my way down the stairs barefoot. I pressed PLAY and listened to a message from Cordia Hatfield, the manager of Mickey's building. "Kinsey, I wonder if you could give us a call when you come in. There's something we think you should be aware of."

She'd called at 8:45, so I felt it was probably safe to return the call. I dialed the number, and Cordia picked up before I'd even heard the phone ring once. "Hello?"

"Cordia, is that you? This is Kinsey Millhone up in Santa Teresa. The phone didn't even ring."

"Well, it did down here. Listen, dear, the reason I called is that detective stopped by shortly after you left. He spent quite a bit of time up Two-H, and when he finished he came right here. He seemed perturbed, and he asked if anyone had gone in. We played dumb. He was quite insistent, but neither of us breathed a word."

"Ah. Was this the tall dark guy, Detective Aldo?"

"That's the one. We're old. What do we know, with all our brain cells gone? We didn't *lie* to him exactly, but I'm afraid we did skirt the truth a bit. I told him I was perfectly capable of taking in rent checks and calling the plumber if a toilet backed up, but I don't go skulking around, spying on the tenants. What they do is their business. Then I showed him my foot and told him, 'With this bunion, I'm lucky to get around. I can't be tromping up and down.' He changed the subject after that."

"What set him off?"

"He said something was missing, though he wouldn't say what. He had a boxload of items with him and told me he'd removed the crime tape. 'For all the good it did,' is how he put it. He was sour on the subject, I can tell you that."

"Thanks for the warning."

"You're entirely welcome. Main reason I called is you're free to enter the apartment, but it won't be long. The owners are pressing to get Mr. Magruder out of there. I guess the detective notified the management company, so they know he's in a coma. They snapped right to it, taking advantage of his condition. Shame on them. Anyway, if you're interested in *renting,* you should take a look."

"I may do that. I'd like that. When would be good?"

"The sooner the better. You're only two hours away."

"You're talking about *tonight*?"

"I think you'd be smart. The owners have already served him with a three-day pay or quit, so technically the sheriff could have a new lock on the door by tomorrow morning."

"Can't we do something to prevent that?"

"Not as far as I know."

"What if I pay what he owes, plus the next month's rent? Wouldn't that cancel the action?"

"I doubt it. Once a tenant starts paying late or doesn't pay at all, the owners would just as soon clear the place out and get someone else in."

I thought about the drive, rolling my eyes with dismay. "I wish I'd known this when I was down there earlier."

"If you're coming, you best hurry. It's entirely up to you, of course."

"Cordia, it's already close to nine-thirty. If I come down tonight, I'd still have to pack and get gas, which means I probably won't arrive before midnight." I didn't mention I was close to naked.

"That's not late for us. Bel and I only need four hours sleep, so we're up till all hours. The advantage in coming now is you'd have all the time you want and not a soul to disturb you."

"Mickey's neighbors won't notice if his lights are on?"

"Nobody pays attention. Most of these folk work so they're usually in bed by ten. And if it gets too late, you can always spend the night with us. We have the only three-bedroom unit in the building. The guest room is really Dort's, but I'm sure she wouldn't mind the company. We had quite a little chat about you after you left."

I let go of my resistance and took a deep breath. "All right. I'll do it. See you in a bit."

I changed into my jeans, turtleneck, and tennis shoes, which were light and silent, good for late-night work. At least I'd been inside Mickey's place and knew what to expect. I still had the key I'd removed from his back door, but I intended to take my pick in case the need arose. Since I had no intention of driving home in the wee hours of the morning, I got out my duffel and threw in the oversized T-shirt I wear as a nightie. I routinely carry a toothbrush, toothpaste, and fresh underwear in the bottom of my shoulder bag. The remainder of the space in the duffel I filled with tools: rubber gloves, my battery-operated pick, drill and drill bits, screwdriver, lightbulbs, pliers, needle-nose pliers, magnifying glass, and dental mirror, along with two flashlights, one standard and one on a long stem that could be angled for viewing those hard-to-reach places Mickey loved so much. I suspected I'd uncovered the majority of his hiding places, but I didn't want to take the chance, especially since this represented my last opportunity to snoop. I also took a second canvas duffel bag, folded and placed inside the first. I now planned to confiscate Mickey's contraband and hold it at my place until he could let me know what he wanted done with it.

I stopped at a service station to have my gas tank filled. While the guy cleaned the windshield and checked the oil, I popped into the "refreshment center" and bought myself a big nasty sandwich—cheese and mystery meat—and a large Styrofoam container of coffee that smelled only faintly scorched. I bought a separate carton of milk, poured out some of the black liquid, and refilled the cup to the brim with milk, then added two paper packets of sugar just to make sure my brain would be properly abuzz.

I was on my way by ten past ten, the VW windows rolled down, the engine whining with the effort of maintaining a constant 60 mph. I ate as I drove and somehow avoided spilling coffee down my front. There were a surprising number of cars on the road, interspersed with semis and RVs, all of us traveling at breakneck speeds. The sense of urgency was multiplied by the darkness that encompassed us, headlights and taillights forming ever-shifting patterns. In the stretch between Santa Teresa and Olvidado, the moon sat above the water like an alabaster globe resting on a pyramid of light. Along the shoreline, the waves were like loosely churning pearls tumbling through the surf. The ancient scent of seaweed drifted in the night air like a mist. Seaside communities appeared and disappeared as the miles accumulated. Hillsides, visible in the distance by day, were reduced to pinpoints of light that wound along the slopes.

I crested the Camarillo grade and coasted down the far side into the westernmost perimeter of the San Fernando Valley. There were no stars in sight. The Los Angeles light pollution gave the night sky a ghostly illumination, like an aurora borealis underlaid by smog. I cut south on the 405 as far as National, took the off-ramp and headed east. At Sepulveda, I hung a left and slowed, finally spotting Mickey's building in the unfamiliar night landscape. I parked out on the street, taking my shoulder bag and duffel. I locked the car behind me and prayed that the chassis, the wheels, and the engine wouldn't be dismantled and gone by morning.

The lights were on in the Hatfields' kitchen. I tapped at the door, and Cordia let me in. Bel was sleeping upright in her chair, so Cordia and I had a whispered conversation while she showed me the guest room with its adjoining bath. Dorothy followed like a puppy-cat, making sure she was in the center of any ongoing discussion. I had to pause more than once to rub behind her ears. I tossed my shoulder bag on the bed. Dorothy promptly claimed ownership, using all twenty pounds to squish and flatten the contents. The last I saw, she had settled like a chicken on a nestful of eggs.

12

I WENT UP the front stairs and along the gallery, lighting
my way with the larger of my flashlights. The two apartments I passed were shrouded in darkness, the sliding
glass windows open into what I was guessing were bedrooms. I continued around the corner, where I let myself
into Mickey's back door, using the key I'd lifted. I de-
bated about leaving the door locked or unlocked and decided to leave it locked. Ordinarily, I'd have opted to
leave the door ajar in case I had to make a hasty exit, but
I was feeling anxious and didn't like the possibility of
someone coming in on me unheard. I moved through the
apartment to the living room. The only light was a thin
shaft coming in from the gallery between drapery panels
in the dining L. I shone the flashlight beam like a sword,
cutting through the shadows. Since I'd been here earlier, the fingerprint technician had been busy with his
brushes, leaving powder residue on countless surfaces. I
made a quick foray through the dining area and kitchen,
then back through the bedroom and bathroom to make
sure I was alone.

I returned to the living room and secured the openings between the drapes. I pulled on my rubber gloves. Despite the fact the cops had come and gone, I didn't want to leave evidence that I'd been in the place. I like to think I'd learned something from my little trip through Ted Rich's doggie door. I turned on the overhead light, pausing to swap Mickey's 60-watt bulb for one of the 200-watt bulbs I'd brought with me. Even a cursory glance showed Detective Aldo had been there. Kitchen cabinets stood open. All the mail was missing, and the fishbowl full of matches had been upended on the dining room table. I pictured the police sorting through the collection for clues, carefully making notes about the bars and restaurants Mickey'd frequented. In truth, only about half the matchbooks would be from places he'd been. The rest were packets other people had acquired for him while traveling, a practice left over from his youth, when he'd assembled hundreds of such covers and mounted them in albums. Who knows why kids like to do shit like that?

I got down to work, methodically emptying the miniature safes he'd created behind the electrical plates. The three sets of phony IDs, the credit cards, and the currency went into my duffel. I spent a long time in his kitchen, sorting through containers with a fine-tooth comb, checking in and behind and under drawers. Once again, I removed the five-gallon water bottles from under the sink and unscrewed the back panel. This time I lifted out the handguns from the rack he'd built and put them in my duffel with the IDs.

I went into the bedroom and took the chenille bedspread and sheets off his bed. Tacky little thing that I am, I paused to check for evidence of recent sexual excess but found none. I pulled off the mattress and checked it carefully, looking for evidence that he'd opened a seam and restitched it. Good theory; no deal. I lay on my back and hunched my way under the bed, where I peeled back the gauzy material that covered the bottom of his box spring. I shone the flashlight across the underside, but no dice. I put the mattress back in place and then remade the bed. This was worse than hotel work, which I'd also done in my day.

I crawled the entire perimeter of wall-to-wall carpeting, pulling up section after section without finding much except a centipede that scared the hell out of me. I tried the bed-table drawer. The diaphragm was gone, as were the bottle of cologne and the tissue paper packet with the enameled heart and gold chain. Well, well, well. His latest inamorata must have heard about the shooting. She was certainly quick to erase the signs of their relationship. She must've had a key of her own, letting herself in sometime between my initial visit and this one. Could she be someone in the building? That was a notion worth exploring.

I spent a good thirty minutes in the bathroom, where I lifted the lid to the toilet tank and used my dental mirror and the angled flashlight to check for items concealed behind it. Nothing. I took all the toiletries out of the medicine cabinet and lifted the entire cabinet off the wall brackets to see if he'd hollowed out a space in the wall behind it. Nope. I checked inside the shower rod, checked the cheap-looking vanity for false fronts or concealed panels. I unscrewed the heater vent and tapped along the baseboards listening for hollow spots. I removed the PVC under the bathroom sink. The gold coins were still there. I loaded those in my duffel and replaced the length of pipe. No telling what the next tenant would make of it if the fake plumbing were discovered at some future date. In the hollow core of the toilet paper roll I found a hundred-dollar bill.

I went through his closet, checking his pockets, looking behind the hanging row of clothes for the possibility of a false wall at the rear. Nothing. The numerous zippered pockets in the black leather jacket were all empty. At the back of the closet, I found his answering machine, which he'd probably unplugged once his phone service was "disconnected or no longer in service." I opened the lid, but the cops had apparently taken the tape. I found one additional stash behind the closet switch plate. In a narrow slot that ran back along a stud, Mickey'd tucked a sealed number-ten envelope. I put it in my duffel for later scrutiny.

I had one other cache to unload that I'd saved until last. I went back into the living room and turned off the overhead light. I moved from window to window, looking out at the dark. It was two-thirty in the morning and, for the most part, windows in neighboring buildings were black. Occasionally I would see a light on, but the drapes would be drawn and no one was peeking through the slit. I picked up no movement in the immediate vicinity. Traffic noises had all but died.

I unhooked the two sets of drapes and lifted down the rods. I removed the finials, flashed a light down into the hollow core, and removed the cash. I replaced the rods and rehung the drapes, moving with a sudden sense of anxiety. I lifted my head. Had I heard something? Maybe the removal of the crime tape was done to tempt me, and Detective Aldo was outside waiting. He'd be thrilled to catch me with the duffel load of burglar tools, the handguns, and the phony documents. I kept the overhead light off, restricting myself to the use of my penlight as I went through the apartment, quickly gathering my tools, checking to see that I'd left no personal traces. The whole time I had the feeling I'd overlooked something obvious, but I knew I'd be pushing my luck to go back and try to figure it out. I was so focused on escape that I came close to missing the crunch of cinders and the putter of a motorcycle as it glided to a stop in the alleyway below.

Belatedly, I realized I'd picked up the muted roar as the motorcycle passed along the street out in front. The rider must have cut the switch at the entrance to the alley, coasting the rest of the way. I went over to the rear window and opened the drapes a crack. From that angle, I couldn't see much, but I was relatively certain someone was moving along the alley. I closed my eyes and listened. Within thirty seconds, I could hear the chink of boots on the stair treads, accompanied by a jingle as each step was mounted. The guy was coming up the back way. Possibly a tenant or a neighbor. I turned off my flashlight and followed the sounds of the guy's progress as he rounded the gallery along the back of the building and came up to Mickey's front door. I had hoped to hear him pass. Instead, I heard a tap and a hoarse whispering. "Hey, Mr. Magruder. Open up. It's me."

I passed through Mickey's bedroom and headed for the rear door, fumbling in my jeans pocket for the key. My hand was steady, but every other part of me was shaking so hard I couldn't hit the keyhole. I was afraid to use my flashlight because the guy had now moved to Mickey's bedroom window, where the tapping became sharper, a harsh clicking as though he might be rapping on the glass with a ring. "Open the fuck up and get your ass out here." He had moved the few steps to the front door, where he began to knock again. This time, the pounding was of the fee-fi-fo-fum variety and seemed to shake the intervening walls.

The next-door neighbor, whose bedroom must have been contiguous with Mickey's, yelled out his window, "Shaddup, you prick! We're tryin' to sleep in here."

The guy at the door said something even worse than

the F word, which I won't repeat. I could hear him jingle his way toward the neighbor's bedroom window, where I pictured him bashing through the glass with his fist. Sure enough, I heard the impact of his blow and the subsequent tinkling of glass, followed by a startled yelp from the tenant. I took advantage of this tender Hallmark moment to shine a quick light on the keyhole. I turned the key in the lock and was almost out the door when I stopped in my tracks. I'd never get into this apartment again. By morning the sheriff's deputy would arrive and the locks would be changed. While I could probably pick my way in, I didn't want to take the risk. Now that all the stashes had been cleaned out, there was only one thing of value. I set down the two duffels and returned to Mickey's closet, where I lifted the leather jacket from its hanger and shrugged myself into it, then grabbed the two duffels and eased out the back door, barely pausing long enough to lock it.

I was halfway down the back stairs when a face appeared above me. Over the wrought-iron railing, I saw shaggy corn-yellow hair, a long bony face, narrow shoulders, and a sunken chest in a blue denim jacket with the sleeves cut out. I slung one duffel over my shoulder, hugged the other to my body, and began to bound down the stairs, taking them two at a time while the guy in the jacket strode toward the landing. I reached the bottom of the stairs at the same moment he started down. I could hear every step he took because of the jingling of his boots, which must have been decorated with chains. I ran on tiptoe, keeping wide on the outside, conscious to avoid knocking into the water meters near the building.

The manager's apartment was fully dark by now, but Cordia, as promised, had left the back door unlocked. I turned the knob and opened the door to let myself in. My entrance was delayed briefly when the duffel over my shoulder got hung up on the door frame. I jerked it free and flung both duffels into the room. I was just turning to close the door when Dorothy streaked out through the narrow opening. She must have come running to see what I was up to and then couldn't resist making a bid for freedom. Once out, she stopped, astonished to find herself alone in the chilly dark at that hour. I heard a thumping noise and a resounding curse. The guy must have caught a foot on a water meter and gone down sprawling. I could hear him cussing as he recovered his gait and came limping down on us in a towering rage. If he caught up with Dorothy, he was going to wring her neck and fling her over the fence, thus forcing her return to this life in some other form. I grabbed her by the tail and dragged her backward while she struggled to gain purchase on the concrete with her outstretched claws. I hauled her, squawking, into the dark of the kitchen, closed the door, and bolted it in one motion.

I sank down on the floor, clutching her against me while my heart kept on banging and my breath came in gasps. I heard the jingling footsteps approach and come to a halt outside the Hatfields' door. The guy kicked the door hard enough to hurt himself. He must have had a flashlight with him, because a beam was soon being played across the far wall, briefly raking the kitchen table. The wand of light streaked back and forth. At one point, I could tell he'd angled up on tiptoe, trying to shine the light down into the darkened area where I was crouched. Meanwhile, Dorothy strained against my embrace and finally manage to wiggle free. I lunged, but she eluded me. She gave me a cranky look and then made a point of sashaying toward the dining room so that her path took her directly through his beam of light. There was a long, labored silence. I thought he'd break the door down, but he must have thought better of it.

Finally, I heard the scritch and jingle of his boots as they receded along the walkway.

I slumped against the door, waiting to hear his motorcycle start up and go screaming away in the night. There was no such reassuring sound. I finally staggered to my feet, retrieved the two duffels, and crept through the dining room toward the guest room. The nightlight in the hallway illuminated my way. The two other bedroom doors were closed, Cordia and Belmira having slept through the uproar in the enveloping silence of poor hearing. Once in the guest room, I kicked my shoes off and lay down on the bed, still wearing Mickey's jacket. Dorothy was already on the bed. The pillow turned out to be hers so I wasn't allowed the full use of it, just a few paltry inches around the edges. The still-indignant cat now felt compelled to wash from head to toe, comforting herself after the insult of having her tail pulled so rudely. The bedroom curtains were closed, but I found myself staring at them, fearful a fist would come smashing through the glass. Dorothy's steady licking took on a restful quality. The warmth of my body activated Mickey's personal scent from the lining of the jacket. Cigarette smoke and Aqua Velva. I stopped shivering and eventually fell asleep with Dorothy's feet resting neatly in my hair.

I woke to the smell of coffee. I was still wearing Mickey's jacket, but someone had placed a heavy afghan across my legs. I put a hand above my head, feeling across the pillow, but Dorothy was gone. The door was open a crack. Sunlight made the curtains glow. I looked at my watch and saw that it was close to eight. I put my feet over the side of the bed and ran a hand through my hair, yawning. I was getting too old to horse around at all hours of the night. I went into the bathroom and brushed my teeth, then showered and dressed again. In the end, I looked much as I had when I'd arrived.

Belmira was sitting at the kitchen table, watching a talk show, when I finally made my appearance. She was a tiny thing, quite thin, so short her feet barely touched the floor. Today, she wore a white bib apron over a red-and-white print housedress. She was shelling peas, the colander in her lap, a paper bag sitting next to her with the rim folded back. Dorothy was on the counter licking butter from the butter dish.

Bel smiled at me shyly. "Coffee's over there," she said. "The sheriff's deputy just arrived with the locksmith, so Cordia went upstairs to let them in. Did you sleep well?"

"I didn't get enough of it, but what I had was fine." I crossed to the coffeepot, an old-fashioned percolator sitting on the stove. There was a mug on the counter, along with a carton of milk. I poured a cup of coffee and added milk.

"Would you like to have an egg? We have cereal, too. Cordi made some oatmeal with raisins. That's what we have. Brown sugar's in the canister if you want to help yourself."

"I think I better go on up and see if I can catch Mickey's neighbors before they go off to work. I can always have breakfast once the deputy's gone." At the door, I looked back. "Did she say anything about a motorcycle parked in the alley?"

Belmira shook her head.

I took my coffee mug with me and headed for the stairs. I could see the sheriff's patrol car parked at the curb, not far from my VW, which as far as I could tell was still intact. The day was sunny and cool, the air already fragrant with the morning's accumulation of exhaust fumes. I passed along the second-floor gallery. A few neighbors had gathered to watch the locksmith at work. Maybe for them, this was a cautionary tale about paying the rent on time. Most seemed dressed for work except for one woman in her robe and slippers, who'd also brought her morning coffee with her. Like rubber-neckers passing a highway accident, they looked on, both repelled and attracted by the sight of someone else's misfortune. This was all faintly reminiscent of the fires that burned across the Santa Teresa foothills back in 1964. During the long smoky evenings, people had gathered on the street in clusters, sipping beer and chatting while the flames danced across the distant mountains. The presence of catastrophe seemed to break down the usual social barriers until the atmosphere was nearly festive.

Cordia Hatfield was keeping a careful eye on the situation, standing in the open doorway with a white sweater thrown over her shoulders. Her oversized blue-and-white checked housedress was worn ankle-length, and she sported the same pair of slippers with her bunion peeking out. She turned as I approached. "I see you found the coffee. How'd you sleep last night?"

"Dorothy was stingy with the pillow, but aside from that I did great."

"She was never one to share. Even when she came back, she insisted on having her old room. We were going to keep it closed up for guests, but she refused to use the litter box until she got her way."

Mickey's immediate neighbor, who appeared to be somewhere in his forties, emerged from his apartment, pulling on a tweed sport coat over a royal-blue Superman T-shirt. His shiny brown hair extended to his waist. He wore large metal-framed glasses with yellow lenses. A mustache and a closely trimmed beard bracketed a full complement of white teeth. His jeans were ripped and faded, and his cowboy boots had three-inch platform soles. Behind him, I could see the broken bedroom window, patched together now with cardboard and a jagged bolt of silver duct tape. He said, "Hey, Ms. Hatfield. How are you today?"

She said, "Morning. Just dandy. What happened to your window? That'll have to be repaired."

"Sorry about that. I'll take care of it. I called a glass company on Olympic, and they said they'd be out to take a look. Has Mickey been evicted?"

"I'm afraid so," she said.

The deputy clearly wasn't needed, so he returned to his car and went about his business. The locksmith beckoned to Cordia. She excused herself, and the two of them moved inside to have a consultation. The next-door neighbor had paused to watch the proceedings and he now greeted a couple who came out of the third apartment on that side. Both were dressed for work. The woman murmured something to her husband and the two continued toward the stairs. Mickey's neighbor nodded politely in my direction, acknowledging my presence.

I murmured, "Hi, how're you?"

"Good, thanks. What kind of crap is this? This dude's in a coma and they're changing the locks on him?"

"I guess the owners are pretty hard-nosed."

"They'd have to be," he said. "So how's Mickey doing? You a friend of his?"

"You could say that, I guess. We used to be married."

"No shit. When was this?"

"Early seventies. It didn't last long. I'm Kinsey, by the way. And you're . . ."

"Ware Beason," he said. "Everybody calls me Wary." He was still working to absorb the information about my marital connection to Mickey. "An ex-wife? How cool. Mickey never said a word."

"We haven't kept in touch. What about you? Have you known him long?"

"He's lived in that apartment close to fifteen years. I've been here six. Now and then I run into him at Lionel's Pub and we have a few beers. He feeds my fish if we have a gig someplace."

"You're a professional musician?"

Wary shrugged self-consciously. "I play keyboard in a combo. Mostly weekends here locally, though I sometimes play out of town as well. I also wait tables at a health food café down on National. I take it you heard about what happened?"

"I did, but it was purely by accident. I didn't even know he was in trouble until earlier this week. I'm from Santa Teresa. I tried calling from up there, but his phone was disconnected. I didn't think too much of it until a couple of detectives showed up and said he'd been shot. I was horrified."

"Yeah, me too. I guess it took 'em a while to figure out who he was. They showed up at my door about seven A.M. Monday. Big dark-haired guy?"

"Right. He's the one I talked to. I thought I better head on down in case there was something I could do."

"So how's he feeling? Have you seen him?"

"He's still in a coma so it's hard to say. I went over there yesterday and he didn't look too good."

"Damn. That's a shame. I should probably go myself, but I've been putting it off."

"Don't even bother unless you notify the cops. You can only visit with their permission, and then they keep someone with you in case you try to pull the plug."

"Jeez. Poor guy. I can't believe it."

"Me neither," I said. "By the way, what was that bunch of hollering last night? Did you hear it? It sounded like somebody went berserk and started banging on the walls."

"Hey, no shit. That was me he was yelling at. And look

what he did, bashed his fist through the glass. I thought he'd dive in after me, but he took off."

"What was he so mad about?"

"Who knows? He's some pal of Mickey's; at least, he acts that way. Mickey never seemed that glad to see him."

"How often did he show up?"

"Every couple of weeks. They must've had some kind of deal going, but I can't think what."

"How long has that gone on?"

"Maybe two–three months. I should probably put it this way: I never saw him before then."

"You know his name?"

Wary shook his head. "Nope. Mickey never introduced us. He seemed embarrassed to be seen with him, and who wouldn't be?"

"No shit."

"Guy's a scuzball, a real sleaze. Every time I see that show about America's Most Wanted, I start lookin' for his face."

"Literally? You think he's wanted by the cops?"

"If he's not, he will be. What a creep."

"That's odd. Mickey always hated lowlifes. He used to be a vice detective. We worked for the same department up in Santa Teresa."

"You're a cop too?"

"I was. Now I work as a P.I."

"A private investigator."

"That's right."

"Oh, I get it. You're looking into this."

"Not officially, no, but I *am* curious."

"Hey, I'm with you. Anything I can do to help, you just say."

"Thanks. What about the scuzball? Couldn't he be the one who shot Mickey? He sounds like a nut to me."

"Nah, I doubt it. If he did, he wouldn't come around pounding on the door, thinking Mickey'd be there. Guy who shot Mickey must have figured he was dead." Wary glanced at his watch. "I better get a move on. How long you going to be here?"

"I'm not sure. Another hour, I'd guess."

"Can I buy you breakfast? That's where I'm heading. There's a place around the corner. Wouldn't take more'n thirty minutes if you have to get back."

I did a quick debate. I hated to leave the premises, but there really wasn't anything more to do. Wary might prove to be useful. More important, I was starving. I said "sure" and then took a brief time-out to let Cordia know where I was going.

Wary and I headed down the front stairs, chatting as we went. Idly, he said, "If you want, after breakfast, I'll show you where he was shot. It's just a couple blocks away."

13

I'LL SKIP THE breakfast conversation. There's nothing so boring as listening to other people get acquainted. We chatted. We traded brief, heavily edited autobiographical sketches, stories about Mickey, theories about the motive for the shooting. In the meantime, I discovered that I liked Wary Beason, though I promptly erased all his personal data. As crass as it sounds, I didn't seriously think I'd ever see him again. Like the passenger sitting next to you on a cross-country plane ride, it's possible to connect with someone, even when the encounter has no meaning and no ultimate consequence.

I did appreciate his showing me the spot where Mickey was gunned down, a nondescript section of sidewalk in front of a coin and jewelry shop. The sign in the window advertised rare coins, rare stamps, pocket watches, antiques, and coin supplies. "We also make low-rate loans," the sign said. At 3 A.M. I didn't think Mickey'd been there to negotiate a loan.

Wary remained silent while I stood for a minute, looking out at the surrounding businesses. There was a pool hall across the street. I assumed the detectives had checked it out. Also the bar called McNalley's, half a block down.

"You mentioned you used to drink with Mickey at Lionel's. Is the pub close by?"

"Back in that direction," Wary said, gesturing.

"Any chance Mickey could have been there earlier that night?"

"No way. Mickey'd been eighty-sixed from Lionel's until he paid his tab." Wary took off his glasses and cleaned the yellow lenses on the hem of his T-shirt. He held his frames to the light so he could check for streaks, and then he put his glasses on again and waited to see what I would ask next.

"Where was he, then? You have a guess?"

"Well, he wasn't at McNalley's, because that's where I was. I know the cops checked the bars all up and down the street. They didn't learn a thing . . . or so they said."

"He was out doing something, and he was doing it on foot."

"Not necessarily. I mean, just because he'd sold his car doesn't mean he hoofed it. Somebody could've picked him up and taken him somewhere. Out for drinks or dinner. Could have been anyplace."

"Back up a minute. Do you happen to remember when he sold his car?"

"Couple of months back."

"You're talking about the end of March?"

"That sounds right. Anyway, the point is, nobody even saw him leave the building that night."

"So what's your theory?"

"Well, let's just say for the sake of argument he was in someone else's car. They go out for dinner or drinks and end up closing the place down. Two in the morning, they drive back to Culver City. He—"

"Or she," I inserted, promptly.

Wary smiled. "Right. . . . The shooter could have dropped Mickey at the corner and then driven down a block like he's on his way home. Shooter parks, waits in the dark while Mickey walks the intervening block. Minute he comes abreast, the shooter steps out and—*boom!*— plugs him twice. Shooter tosses the gun and takes off before anybody figures out what's up."

"You really think it happened like that?"

Wary shrugged. "It could have, that's all I'm saying. The cops canvassed all the bars and pool halls within a ten-block radius. Mickey hadn't been in any of 'em, but they know he'd been drinking *somewhere* because he had a blood alcohol of point one four."

"How'd you hear that?"

"The detective, the dark one, mentioned it in passing."

"Really. That's interesting. What'd they make of it, did anybody say?"

"No, and I didn't think to ask. Mickey always had a buzz on. He was probably pushing point one any given day of the week."

"He was legally drunk?"

"Legally plastered is a better way to put it. For a while, he straightened up. He went on the wagon, but it didn't last long. February he went on a bender, and I guess that's when he got himself fired from his job. He tried to straighten up again, after that, but without much success. He'd go a couple days and then fall right back. I give him credit. He did try. He just wasn't strong enough to do it by himself."

I was suddenly feeling restless and needed to move. I started walking again and Wary followed, catching up with me. I said, "What about the woman he was seeing?"

He gave me an odd look, equal parts surprise and embarrassment. "How'd you know about her?"

I tapped my temple. "A little birdie told me. You know who she was?"

"Nope. Never met her. Mickey made sure."

"How come?"

"Maybe he thought I'd try to hustle her myself."

"Did you actually see her?"

"In passing. Not to recognize later. She always came up the back stairs and let herself in that way."

"She had her own key?"

"She must have. Mickey never left his doors unlocked. Some days she showed up before he got home from work."

"What about her car? Did you ever see a vehicle parked out back?"

"Never looked. I figured it was his business. Why should I butt in?"

"How often was she there?"

"I'd say every two to three weeks. Not to be gross about it, but the walls in the building are not exactly soundproof. I have to say Mickey's alcohol intake never seemed to hamper him in the performance of his duties."

"How do you know it was him? Isn't there a chance he lent his apartment to someone else? Maybe he had a friend who needed a place to misbehave."

"Oh, no. It was him. I'd take an oath on that. He's been involved with this woman for at least a year."

"How do you know there was only one? He might have had a string of women."

"Well, it's possible, I guess."

"Any chance she lived in the building?" I asked.

"In *our* building? I doubt it. Mickey would've felt hemmed in by anybody living that close. He liked his freedom. He didn't like anybody checking up on him. Like sometimes—say, he was gone for the weekend—I might ask him, you know, How's the weekend, where'd you end up? Simple shit like that. Mickey wouldn't answer questions. If you pressed, he changed the subject."

"What about since the shooting? Do you think the woman's been there?"

"I really couldn't say for sure. I go to work at four and don't get home till after midnight. She could have gone in while I was off. Actually, come to think of it, I thought I heard her yesterday. Again last night, too, before that biker geek showed up. What an asshole. Glass company says it'll cost me a hundred bucks to get that fixed."

"Wary, that was me you heard last night. I went in and pulled his personal belongings before they had a chance to change the locks. I suspected his girlfriend'd been there, because a couple of personal articles I'd seen suddenly came up missing."

We'd reached the building by then. It was time to hit the road. I thanked him for his help. I made a note of his phone number and then gave him my business card with my home number jotted on the back. We parted company at the stairs.

I watched Wary go up, and then I went back to the Hatfields to collect the two duffels. They invited me for lunch, but I'd just finished breakfast and I was anxious to get back. We said our good-byes. I thanked them profusely, including Dort in my expressions of appreciation. I didn't dare be rude in case they were right about her incarnation.

Their door closed behind me, and I was just heading for my car when I chanced to glance over at the line of mailboxes under the stairs. Mickey's was crammed with mail. I stared, transfixed. Apparently, the cops had neglected to put a hold on the mail coming in. I wondered how many civil and criminal codes I'd violated so far. Surely, one more transgression wouldn't add that much to my sentence. I felt along the bottom of my shoulder bag, extracted my key picks, and went to work on the lock. This one was so easy it would have yielded to a hairpin, which I don't happen to carry. I pulled out the wad of mail and perused it in haste. The bulk of it consisted of an oversized pulp weekly devoted to survivalist lore: ads for mercenaries, articles about pending gun legislation, government cover-ups, and citizens' rights. I put the magazine back in the box so the contents would appear untouched. The remaining two envelopes I shoved in my shoulder bag for later consideration. I'll tell you right now, they turned out to be nothing, which disappointed me greatly. I hate risking jail time on behalf of third-class mail.

When I arrived in Santa Teresa at 1:35, I snagged the morning paper from the doorstep and let myself in. I tossed the paper on the counter, set the duffels on the floor, and crossed to my desk. There were several messages waiting on my answering machine. I played them, taking notes, aware that it was probably time to get down to paid employment. In the interest of earning a living, I drove over to the office and devoted the rest of the afternoon to servicing the clients with business pending. In any given month, I might juggle some fifteen to twenty cases, not all of them pressing. Despite the fact I had money in the bank, I couldn't afford to neglect matters already in the works. I'd just spent the past three days chasing down Mickey's situation. Now it was time to get my professional affairs in order. I had calls to return and receipts to tally and enter on the books. There were numerous invoices to be typed and submitted, along with the accompanying reports to write while my notes were still fresh. I also had a few stern letters to compose, trying to collect from slow-pays (all attorneys, please note), plus bills of my own to pay.

I was checking my calendar for the days ahead when I remembered the phone call made from Mickey's number to mine on March 27. I'd never checked my office schedule to see where I was that day. As with my day planner at home, that Thursday was blank. March 26 and 28 were both blank too, so I couldn't use either as a springboard for recollection.

At five-thirty, I locked up and drove back to my apartment through the Santa Teresa equivalent of rush-hour traffic, which meant it took me fifteen minutes to get home instead of the usual ten. The sun had finally burned through a lingering marine layer, and the heat in the vehicle was making me sleepy. I could tell I'd have to atone for my late-night activities. I parked down the street from my apartment and pushed through the gate. My place felt cozy, and I was relieved to be home. The emotional roller coaster of the past few days had generated an odd mood—weariness masquerading as depression. Whatever the source, I was feeling raw. I set my shoulder bag on a bar stool and went around the end of the counter into the kitchenette. I hadn't eaten since breakfast. I opened the refrigerator and stared at the empty shelves. When I thought about Mickey's cupboards, I realized my food supplies didn't look much better than his. Absurd that we'd married when we were simultaneously too much alike and much too different.

Soon after the wedding, I began to realize he was out of control . . . at least from the perspective of someone with my basically fearful nature. I wasn't comfortable with what I perceived as his dissipation and his self-indulgence. My Aunt Gin had taught me to be moderate—in my personal habits if not in my choice of cusswords. At first, Mickey's hedonism had been appealing. I remembered experiencing a nearly giddy relief at his gluttony, his love of intoxication, his insatiable appetite for sex. What he offered was a tacit permission to explore my lustiness, un-awakened until then. I related to his disdain for authority and I was fascinated by his disregard for the system, even while he was employed in a job dedicated to upholding law and order. I, too, had tended to operate outside accepted social boundaries. In grade school and, later, junior and senior high schools, I was often tardy or truant, drawn to the lowlife students, in part because they represented my own defiance and belligerence. Unfortunately, by the age of twenty, when I met Mickey, I was already on my way back from the outer fringes of bad behavior. While Mickey was beginning to embrace his inner demons, I was already in the process of retreating from mine.

Now—fifteen years later—it's impossible to describe how alive I was for that short period.

For dinner, I made myself an olive-pimento-cheese sandwich, using that divine Kraft concoction that comes in a jar. I cut the bread neatly into four fingers with the crusts intact and used a section of paper toweling as both napkin and plate. With this wholesome entrée, I sipped a glass of Chardonnay and felt thoroughly comforted. Afterward, I wadded up my dinnerware and tossed it in the trash. Having supped and done the dishes, I placed the two duffels on the counter and unloaded my tools and the booty I'd lifted from Mickey's the night before. I laid the items on the counter, hoping the sight of them would spark a new interpretation.

There was a knock at my door. I grabbed the newspaper and opened it, spreading it over the items as if I'd been reading with interest, catching up on events. I crossed to the door and peeked through the porthole to find my landlord standing on the porchlet with a plate of homemade brownies covered in plastic wrap. Henry's a retired commercial baker who now occupies his time catering tea parties for elderly widows in the neighborhood. He also supplies Rosie's restaurant with a steady line of baked goods: sandwich breads, dinner rolls, pies, and cakes. I confess I was not entirely happy to see him. While I adore him, I'm not always candid with him about my nocturnal labors.

I opened the door. We made happy noises at each other while Henry stepped in. I tried to steer him toward the sofa, hoping to divert his attention, but before I could even protest, he leaned over and closed the newspaper to make room for the plate. There sat the four handguns, the packets of phony documents, credit cards, and cash. To all appearances, I'd turned to robbing banks for a living.

He set the plate on the counter. "What's all this?"

I put a hand on his arm. "Don't ask. The less you know, the better. You'll have to trust me on this."

He looked at me quizzically, an expression in his eyes I hadn't seen before: trust and mistrust, curiosity, alarm. "But I want to know."

I had only a split second to decide what to say. "This is Mickey's. I lifted the stuff because a sheriff's deputy was scheduled to change the locks on his doors."

"Why?"

"He's being evicted. I had one chance to search, and I had to take advantage."

"But what *is* all this?"

"I have no idea. Look, I know how his mind works. Mickey's paranoid. He tends to hide anything of value. I went through his apartment systematically, and this is what I found. I couldn't leave it there."

"The guns are stolen?"

"I doubt it. Mickey always had guns. In all likelihood, they're legal."

"But you don't know that for sure. Mickey didn't authorize you to do this. Couldn't you end up in trouble?"

"Well, yeah, but I can't worry about that *now*. I didn't know what else to do. They were locking him out. This stuff was hidden in the walls, behind panels, in phony bathroom pipes. Meanwhile, he's in the hospital, completely out of it."

"What happens to his possessions? Doesn't he have furniture?"

"Tons. I'll probably offer to have things moved into storage until we see how he fares."

"Have you spoken to the doctors yet?"

"They're not going to talk to me. The cops put the lid on that possibility. Anyway, I made a big point of saying we've been out of touch for years. I can't come along afterward and ask for daily updates like I'm so distraught. They'd never believe me."

"But you said you weren't going to get involved in this."

"I know. I'm not. Well, I am a little bit. At the moment, I don't even know what's going on."

"Then leave it alone."

"It's too late for that. Besides, you're the one who said I ought to check it out."

"But you never listen."

"Well, I did this time."

"Will you listen if I tell you to butt out?"

"Of course. Once I know what it's about."

"Kinsey, this is clearly police business. You can't keep quiet about this stuff. You ought to call those detectives—"

"Nope. Don't want to. I'm not going to do that. I don't like those guys."

"At least, they can be objective."

"So can I."

"Oh, really?"

"Yes, *really*. Henry, don't do this."

"What am I doing?"

"You're disapproving of my behavior. It tears me up."

"As well it should."

I clamped my mouth shut. I was feeling stubborn and resistant. I was already in the thick of it and couldn't bail out. "I'll think about it some."

"You better do more than that. Kinsey, I'm concerned about you. I know you're upset, but this really isn't like you."

"You know what? It *is* like me. This is exactly who I am: a liar and a thief. You want to know something else? I don't feel bad about it. I'm completely unrepentant. More than that. I like it. It makes me feel alive."

A shadow crossed his face and something familiar seemed to scurry into hiding. He was silent for a moment and then said mildly, "Well. In that case, I'm sure you don't need any lectures from me."

He was gone before I could reply. The door closed quietly behind him. The plate of brownies remained. I could tell they were still warm because the air was filled with the scent of chocolate and the plastic wrap was foggy with condensation. I stood where I was. I felt nothing. My mind was blank except for the one assertion. I had to do this. I did. Something inside me had shifted. I could sense the muscles in my face set with obstinacy. There was no way I'd let go, no way I'd back away from this . . . whatever it was.

I sat down at the counter, propping my feet on the rung of the kitchen stool. I folded the newspaper neatly. I picked up the envelope and opened the seal. Inside were two passbooks for Mickey's savings accounts, six cash-register receipts, a Delta ticket envelope, and a folded sheet of paper. I examined the passbooks first. The first had once held a total of $15,000, but the account had been closed and the money withdrawn in January of 1981. The second savings account was opened that same January with a deposit of $5,000. This was apparently the money he'd been living on of late. I noticed that a series of $600 cash withdrawals corresponded to deposits in his checking account with the following discrepancy: Mickey would pull $600 and deposit $200, apparently keeping $400 in pocket change—"walking around" money, as he used to refer to it. I had to guess this was petty cash, used to pay his bar bills, his dinners out, items from the market. The six cash-register receipts were dated January 17, January 31, February 7, February 21, March 7, and March 21. The ink was faded, but the name of the establishment wasn't that hard to read: the Honky-Tonk. I was assuming he'd sold his car sometime in the third week in March because he'd deposited $900 in his checking account. The loss of his transportation might explain the sudden cessation of visits after so many regular Friday-night appearances. Why drive all the way to Santa Teresa to have a drink when there were bars in his neighborhood? I set the question aside since there was no way to answer it. Before examining the last item, I pulled out my index cards and made some notes. There's always the temptation to let this part slide, but I had to capture the data while everything was fresh in my mind.

Once I'd jotted down what I remembered, adding the cash count, credit card numbers, passbook numbers, and dates of receipts, I gave myself permission to proceed, opening the Delta ticket envelope, which really interested me. The flight coupons had been used. I removed the itinerary and the passenger receipt. Mickey had flown to Louisville, Kentucky, by way of Cincinnati on Thursday, May 8, returning late in the day on Monday, May 12. This impromptu five-day excursion had cost him more than $800 in plane fare alone.

I reached for the remaining item, a folded piece of

paper, and read the brief statement, which was dated January 15, 1981. This was a simple letter agreement between Mickey Magruder and Tim Littenberg, signed by the latter, in which he acknowledged receipt of the sum of $10,000, a no-interest loan with a five-year balloon payment due and payable five months ago— January 15, 1986.

I packed up the guns and other items, hid them in a safe place, and grabbed my jacket and handbag.

14

THE MAIN DRAG in Colgate is four lanes wide, lined with an assortment of businesses ranging from carpet stores to barbershops, with a gas station on every other corner and an automobile dealership on the blocks between. Colgate—sprawling, eclectic, and unpretentious—provides housing for those who work in Santa Teresa but can't afford to live there. The population count of the two communities is roughly the same, but their dispositions are different, like siblings whose personalities reflect their relative positions in the family matrix. Santa Teresa is the older of the two, stylish and staid. Colgate is the more playful, less insistent on conformity, more likely to tolerate differences among its residents. Few of its shops stay open after 6 P.M. Bars, pool halls, drive-in theaters, and bowling alleys form the exception.

The parking lot at the Honky-Tonk looked much as it had fourteen years before. Cars had changed. Whereas in the seventies the patrons were driving Mustangs and VW vans painted in psychedelic shades, streetlights now gleamed on Porsches, BMWs, and Trans Ams. Crossing the lot, I experienced the same curious excitement I'd felt when I was single and hunting. Given my current state of enlightenment, I wouldn't dream of circulating through the bar scene—barhopping, we called it—but I did in those days. In the sixties and seventies, that's what you did for recreation. That's how you met guys. That's how you got laid. What Women's Liberation "liberated" was our attitude toward sex. Where we once used sex for barter, now we gave it away. I marvel at the prostitutes we must have put out of business, doling out sexual "favors" in the name of personal freedom. What were we thinking? All we ended up with were bar bums afflicted with pubic vermin.

The Honky-Tonk had expanded, incorporating space formerly occupied by the adjacent furniture store that used to advertise liquidation sales every six to eight months. There was a line at the door, where one of the bouncers was checking IDs by running them through a scanner. Each patron, once cleared, was stamped HT on the back of the right hand, the HT of the Honky-Tonk apparently serving as clearance to drink. That way the waiters and bartenders didn't have to card each cherubic patron ordering rum and Coke—the drinker's equivalent of the training bra.

Now sporting my ink brand, I walked through a fog of cigarette smoke, trying to get a feel for the age and financial status of the crowd inside. There was a large infusion of college students, fresh-faced, uninhibited, their naïveté and bad judgment not yet having come home to roost. The rest were chronic singles, the same aging bachelors and divorcées who'd been eyeballing one another since I'd first buzzed through.

There was still sawdust on the floor. Between the dark-painted wainscoting and the pressed-tin ceiling, the walls were hung with old black-and-white photographs showing Colgate as it had been sixty years before: bucolic, unspoiled, rolling hills stretching out as far as the eye could see. The images were illuminated by gaudy beer signs, red and green neon tinting the vanished grasslands and sunsets.

There were also countless photographs of local celebrities and regulars, pictures taken on St. Patrick's Day, New Year's Eve, and other occasions when the Tonk closed its doors to the public and hosted private parties. I spotted two 8-by-11 photos of Mickey, Pete Shackelford, and Roy Littenberg. The first showed them in police uniform, standing at parade rest: solemn-faced, stiff-backed, serious about law and order. In the second, they were seasoned, men who'd become cynics, guys with old eyes who now smiled over cigarettes and highballs, arms flung casually across one another's shoulders. Roy Littenberg was the oldest by a good ten years. Of the three, he was now dead and Mickey was barely clinging to life. I wondered if there was a way to conjure them up out of memories and smoke—three cops, like ghosts, visible as long as I didn't turn and try to look at them directly.

Two long narrow rooms ran side by side, lined with wooden booths. Each had its own sound system, waves of music pounding against the senses as I moved from room to room. The first held the bar and the second a dance floor, surrounded by tables. The third room, since added, was sufficient to accommodate six pool tables, all of them occupied. The guys played Foosball and darts. The "girls" trooped in and out of the ladies' room, touching up their eye makeup, hiking up their pantyhose. I followed them in, taking advantage of an empty stall to avail myself of the facilities. I could hear two women in the adjoining stall, one barfing up her dinner while the other offered encouraging comments. "That's fine. Don't force it. You're doing great. It'll come." If I'd even heard

of it in my day, I'd have assumed Bulimia was the capital
of some newly formed Baltic state.

When I left the stall, there were four women in line
and another three in front of the mirrors. I waited for an
empty place at a sink, washing my hands while I checked
my reflection. The fluorescent lighting gave my otherwise unblemished skin a sickly appearance, emphasizing
the bags under my eyes. My hair looked like thatch. I
wore no lipstick, but that was probably just as well, as
the addition would have played up the yellow cast in
my aging complexion. I was wearing Mickey's black
leather jacket as a talisman, the same old blue jeans, and
a black turtleneck, though I'd traded my usual tennis
shoes for my usual boots. Mostly, I was dawdling, avoiding the moment when I'd have to perch on a bar stool
and buy myself a drink. The two young women emerged
from their stall, both of them thin as snakes. The barfer
pulled out a prepasted toothbrush and began to scrub. In
five years the stomach acid would eat through her tooth
enamel, if she didn't drop dead first.

I emerged from the ladies' room, passing the dance
floor on my left. I ventured over to the bar, where I
bought myself a draft beer. In the absence of available
bar stools, I drank the beer standing by myself, trying to
look like I was keeping an appointment. Now and then
I'd glance at my watch, like I was somewhat annoyed
because I didn't have all night. I'm sure many people
nearby were completely fooled by this. A few guys assessed me from a distance, not because I was "hot" but
because I represented fresh meat, waiting to be graded
and stamped.

I deleted my ego from the situation and tried to scrutinize the place from Mickey's point of view. What had possessed him to lend Tim Littenberg the money? Mickey
wasn't one to take risks like that. He kept his assets

liquid even if he earned very little in the way of interest. He was probably happiest making deposits to the
Curtain Rod Savings and Loan. Tim Littenberg—or his
dad—must have made a hell of a pitch. Nostalgia might
have played a part. Lit and his wife were never good with
money. They'd lived from paycheck to paycheck, over-
drawn, in debt, their credit cards maxed out. If Tim
had needed a stake, they probably didn't have the cash
to lend. Whatever the motivation, Mickey'd apparently
made the deal. The note had been signed and payment
had come due. I'd seen no evidence the loan had been repaid. Curious. Mickey certainly needed the money, and
the Honky-Tonk was clearly doing good business.

Near the wall, a bar stool became vacant and I eased
into the spot. My eyes strayed back to the mounted photographs and I studied the one hanging next to me. The
Three Musketeers again. In this one, Mickey, Shack, and
Lit were sitting at the bar, glasses aloft, offering a toast to
someone off to their left. Dixie was visible in the background, her eyes fastened on Mickey—a look both hungry
and possessive. Why hadn't I seen that at the time? What
kind of dunce was I? I squinted at the picture, taking in
the faces, one by one. Lit had always been the best-
looking of the three. He was tall, narrow through the
shoulders, long arms and legs, beautiful long fingers. I'm
a sucker for good teeth and his were even and white, except for one cuspid that sat slightly askew, giving his
smile a boyish appeal. His chin was pronounced, his bony
jaw wide at the apex. His Adam's apple danced when he
spoke. The last time I'd seen him was maybe four years
ago and then just in passing. His hair was thinning by
then. He'd been in his early sixties, and from what Shack
had said he was already in the midst of a struggle for
his life.

I rotated slightly on the bar stool and scanned the area,

hoping to see Tim. I'd never met Lit's son. Back when I was married to Mickey and hanging out with his parents, he was already grown and gone. He'd joined the army in 1970, and for the period in question he was off in Vietnam. In those days, a lot of STPD cops were ex-army, very gung-ho about the military, supportive of our presence in Southeast Asia. The public by then had lost patience with the war, but not in that circle. I'd seen pictures of Tim that his parents passed around. He always looked grubby and content, a cigarette between his lips, his helmet pushed back, his rifle resting against his knees. Lit would read portions of his letters in which he described his exploits. To me, he sounded reckless and defiant, a bit too enthusiastic, a twenty-year-old kid who spent his days stoned, who loved to kill "gooks" and brag about it later to his friends back home. He'd been brought up on charges after a particularly nasty incident involving two dead Vietnamese babies. Lit stopped saying much after that, and by the time of Tim's dishonorable discharge he'd fallen silent on the subject of his son. Maybe the Honky-Tonk was Lit's hope for Tim's rehabilitation.

Almost at once, my gaze settled on a guy I would have sworn was him. He was somewhere in his mid-thirties, close to my age, and bore at least a superficial resemblance to Roy Littenberg. He had the same lean face, the distinctive jaw and jutting chin. He wore a dark purple shirt and plain mauve tie under a dark sport coat, jeans, desert boots. I'd caught him in conversation with a waitress—probably a dressing down, since she seemed upset. She had straight black hair, very glossy in the light, cut at an angle, with a line of blunt-cut bangs across the front. She wore black eyeliner and very red lipstick. I pegged her in her thirties, though close up she might have been older. She nodded, her face stony, and moved away, heading in my direction. She gave her order to the bartender, fussing with her order pad to cover her agitation. Hands shaking, she lit a cigarette, took a long drag, and then blew the smoke out in a thin jet. She left the cigarette in an ashtray on the bar.

I swiveled slightly and spoke to her. "Hi. I'm looking for Tim Littenberg. Is he on the premises?"

She looked at me, her gaze dropping to my jacket and then quizzically to my face again. She hiked a thumb in his direction. "Purple shirt," she said.

Tim had turned to greet a fellow in a tweedy sport coat, and I saw him signal the bartender to comp the guy to a drink. The two shook hands and Tim patted his back in a friendly gesture that probably didn't have much depth. Roy Littenberg had been fair-haired. His son's coloring was dark. His mouth was pouty and his eyes were darker than his father's, deep-set, smudged with shadow. His smile, when it showed, never touched his eyes. His attention flicked restlessly from room to room. He must constantly estimate the status of his customers, gauging their ages, their levels of inebriation, screening each burst of laughter and every boisterous interchange for the possibility of violence. Every hour the Honky-Tonk was open, the crowd became looser and less inhibited, louder, more aggressive as the alcohol went down.

I watched him approach the bar, coming within a few feet of me. Nearby, the waitress turned abruptly with her tray to avoid contact with him. His gaze touched her and then drifted, caught mine, veered off, and then returned. This time his eyes held.

I smiled. "Hi. Are you Tim?"

"That's right."

I held a hand out. "I'm Kinsey. I knew your father years ago. I was sorry to hear he died."

We shook hands. Tim's smile was brief, maybe pained,

though it was impossible to tell. He was lean like his father, but where Lit's countenance was open and sunny, his son's was guarded. "Can I buy you a drink?"

"Thanks, I'm fine for now. The place really jumps. Is it always like this?"

He said, "Thursdays are good. Revving up for the weekend. This your first time in?" He was managing to conduct our conversation without being fully engaged. His face was slightly averted, his focus elsewhere: polite, but not passionate about the need to socialize.

"I was in years ago. That's how I knew your father. He was a great guy." This didn't seem to elicit any particular response. "Are you the manager?"

"The owner."

"Really. Oh, sorry. No offense," I said. "I could see you keeping a close eye out."

He shrugged.

I said, "You must know Mickey Magruder."

"Yeah, I know Mickey."

"I heard he'd bought a part interest in the place, so I was hoping to run into him. He's another cop from the old days. He and your dad were pals."

Tim seemed distracted. "Three Musketeers, right? I haven't seen him for weeks. Would you excuse me?"

I said, "Sure." I watched him cross the room to the dance floor, where he intervened in an exchange between a woman and her date. The guy was stumbling against her and she was struggling to keep him upright. Other couples on the dance floor were giving them a wide berth. The woman finally gave him a shove, both annoyed and embarrassed by his drunkenness. By the time Tim reached them, one of his bouncers had appeared and he began to walk the fellow toward the door, using the kind of elbow grip employed by street cops and mothers with small children acting up in department stores. The woman detoured to a table and snatched up her jacket and her handbag, prepared to follow. Tim intercepted her. A brief discussion ensued. I hoped he was persuading her to take a taxi home.

Moments later, he reappeared beside me, saying, "Sorry about that."

"I hope he's not getting in a car."

"The bouncer took his keys," he said. "We'll let him chill out in back and then see he gets home in one piece. He tends to hassle people when he's like that. Bad for business."

"I'll bet."

His smile was directed somewhere to my left. He gave my arm a pat. "I better go check on him. Hope to see you again."

"You can count on it," I said.

There was only a momentary hitch in his otherwise smooth delivery. "Good deal. Anything you want, you can let Charlie know." He caught the bartender's eye and pointed at me. The bartender nodded and, with that, Tim was gone.

I waited about a minute and then set my half-filled beer glass on the bar and made my way to the pay phones at the rear exit, near the office. I wanted to make sure I knew how to find him in his off-hours. I could have hung around until the place closed and followed him home, but I thought I'd try something more direct. I hauled out the phone book and looked up his address and phone number under *Littenberg, Tim and Melissa.*

I leaned to my left and looked down the shadowy corridor, where I could see three blank doors in addition to the one leading to the office. One of the busboys came in from outside, a draft of cold air following him in. I straightened up, put a coin in the slot, and dialed, listening to a recorded female voice that apprised me of the time to the minute and the second. I said *uh-huh, uh-huh*, like I was oh-so-interested. I watched until the busboy disappeared around the corner, moving into the bar.

The area was quiet. I replaced the handset and proceeded along the corridor, opening one door at a time. The first door exposed a mop closet: brooms, gallon containers of disinfectants, kitchen linens stacked on the shelves. The second door turned out to be the employees' lounge, lined with metal lockers and two sinks, an assortment of dumpy sofas, and a lot of ashtrays, most of which were full. No sign of the drunk; I wondered where he'd gone. The third door was locked. I leaned my head against the door, listening, but there was no sound.

Tim's office was just opposite. I crossed the corridor in two steps and gripped the doorknob with care. I turned it slowly to the right and pushed the door open the faintest crack. Tim was at his desk, his back to me, talking on the telephone. I couldn't hear his conversation. I sincerely hoped he wasn't busy putting out a contract on me. I eased the door shut and peeled my hand away from the knob to avoid any rattles and clicks. Time to get out. I really didn't want anyone to find me back here. I returned to the main corridor, where I checked in both directions. There was no evidence of an alarm system: no passive infrared beams, no numbered key pad by the rear exit. Interesting.

I drove home with an eye plastered to my rearview mirror. There was no reason in the world to think Tim's call had anything to do with me. He *had* made a beeline to the office after I'd mentioned Mickey's name, but that was the stuff of B-movies. Why would he rub me out? I hadn't done anything. I hadn't said a word about the ten grand he owed. I was saving that for next time. Actually, he could have paid it back, for all I knew.

It was only 10 P.M.: lots of traffic on the freeway and

none of it seemed sinister. Tim didn't know me from Adam, so he couldn't know where I lived or what kind of car I drove. Besides, Santa Teresa doesn't have any mobsters . . . at least as far as I know.

When I reached my neighborhood, I cruised the block, looking for a parking place that wasn't shrouded in darkness. I spotted only one unfamiliar car, a dark-toned Jaguar sitting at the curb across the street from my apartment. I pulled up around the corner onto Bay and waited to make sure no one had followed me. Then I locked up and walked the half block back. I was feeling foolish, but I still preferred to listen to my intuition. I knew the gate hinge would squeak, so I avoided it and approached by traversing the neighbor's yard along the wooden fence. Maybe I was being dumb, but I couldn't help myself.

When I reached the far side of Henry's garage, I lifted my head above the fence and looked. I'd left the back light on, but now my porchlet was in shadow. Henry's lights were out as well. A mist seemed to hover in the grass like smoke. I waited without moving, letting my eyes adjust to the dark. As in most cases, even the darkest night isn't without its ambient illumination. The moon was caught in the branches of a tree. Splashes of light spilled down in an irregular pattern. I listened until the crickets began to chirp again.

I divided Henry's backyard into segments and scanned them one by one. Nothing to my immediate left. Nothing near his back step. Nothing near the tree. The garage cast a triangle of blackness onto the patio so that not all his lawn furniture was visible. Still, I could have sworn I saw a form: the head and shoulders of someone sitting in one of his Adirondack chairs. It could have been Henry, but I didn't think so. I sank down below the fence. I reversed myself, easing back through the neighbor's yard to the street beyond. The leather boots I wore weren't designed for tiptoeing on wet grass, and I slipped as I crept along, hoping not to fall on my ass.

Once I gained the street, I had to wipe some doggie doo off my shoe heel, lest the odor alone make a target of me. I fumbled in the bottom of my bag until I found my penlight. I shielded the narrow beam with the palm of my hand and swept the Jaguar. All four doors were locked. I half expected the vanity plate to read HITZ R US. Instead, it said DIXIE. Well, that was interesting. I approached the backyard this time from the neighbor's property to the left of Henry's, first navigating up their driveway, then making a wide circle across Henry's yard along the rear flower beds. From this vantage point, I could see the silhouette of her tangled hair. She must have been dying to smoke. As I watched, her desire for a cigarette overrode her caution. I heard the flick of a lighter. She cupped a hand to her face and applied the flame to the end of a cigarette and inhaled with a nearly audible sigh of relief. No weapon, at any rate, unless she could wield one with her feet.

By then, I was close to the back of the Adirondack. "Gee, Dixie. Never light up. Now all the snipers in the neighborhood can get a bead on you."

She gasped, nearly levitating from her seat as she whipped her head around. She grabbed the arm of her chair and her handbag tumbled from her lap. I saw the cigarette fly off in the dark, the ember making a most satisfactory arc before it was snuffed in the wet grass. She was lucky she hadn't sucked it down her throat and choked to death. "Shit. Oh, shit! You scared the crap out of me," she hissed.

"What the hell are you doing here?"

She had a hand to her chest, trying to still her wildly banging heart. She bent at the waist, hyperventilating. I was singularly unimpressed with the possibility of heart failure. If her heart seized, she died. I was not going to do CPR on her. She was wearing what looked like a flight suit, a one-piece design with a zipper up the front. The oversized, baggy look was offset by the fact that she had the sleeves rolled midway up her arm, thus demonstrating how petite she was. She stooped to pick up her shoulder bag, which was battered leather, shaped like a mail carrier's pouch.

She tucked it under one arm. She put a hand to her forehead and then to her cheek. "I need to talk to you," she said, still sounding shaken.

"Had you thought about calling first?"

"I didn't think you'd agree to see me."

"So you wait in the dark? Are you *nuts*?"

"I'm sorry. I didn't mean to scare you. The old gentleman in the house was up when I arrived an hour ago. I could see him in the kitchen when I came around the corner, so I unscrewed the porch bulb. I didn't want him to notice and wonder what I was doing."

"What *are* you doing? I'm still not entirely clear."

"Could we go inside? I promise I won't stay long. I didn't bring a jacket and I'm freezing."

I felt a flash of annoyance. "Oh, come on," I said.

I set off across the yard. When I reached the porch, I gave the bulb a twist and saw the light come on. She followed me meekly. I took out my house keys and unlocked the door.

I took a moment to slip my shoes off. "Wipe your feet," I said crossly before I entered the living room.

"Sorry. Of course."

I pulled out a kitchen stool for her and then went around the kitchen counter and retrieved a brandy bottle from the liquor cabinet. I took out two jelly glasses and twisted the cork, pouring us both two fingers. I tipped my head back and flung the brandy to the back of my throat. I swallowed liquid fire, my mouth coming open, invisible flames shooting out. Damn, that was nasty, but it brought relief. I shuddered involuntarily the way I do when swilling NyQuil. I was calmer by the time I looked up at her. She'd chugalugged as I had, but she seemed better able to take the brandy in stride.

"Thanks. That's great. I hope you don't mind if I have a cigarette," she said, reaching into her bag as if with my consent.

"You can smoke outside. I don't want you smoking in here."

"Oh. Sorry," she said, and put the pack away.

"And quit apologizing," I said. She'd come here for something. Time to get on with it. I said, "Speak," like she was a dog about to demonstrate a trick.

Dixie closed her eyes. "What Mickey and I did was inexcusable. You have every right to be angry. I was obnoxious on Monday when you came to the house. I apologize for that, but I was disconcerted. I always assumed you'd received my letter and elected to do nothing. I guess I enjoyed blaming you for being disloyal. It was hard to give that up." She opened her eyes then and looked at me.

"Go on."

"That's it."

"No, it's not. What else? If that's all you wanted, you could have written me a note."

She hesitated. "I know you crossed paths with Eric on your way down the drive. I appreciated your keeping quiet on the subject of me and Mickey. You could have caused me a lot of trouble."

"*You* made the trouble. I didn't have anything to do with it."

"I'm aware of that. I know. But I've never been sure if Eric knew about what happened."

"He never mentioned it?"

"Nothing."

"Consider yourself lucky. I'd leave it at that, if I were you."

"Believe me, I will."

I felt myself subdivide, one part fully present, the other part watching from a distance. What she'd said so far was true, but there was bound to be more. Lacking my native talent in the liar-liar-pants-on-fire department, she couldn't help but color slightly, a bright coin of pink appearing on each cheek.

I said, "But what? You want assurances I'll keep my mouth shut from here on out?"

"I know I can't ask."

"That's correct. On the other hand, I don't know what purpose it would serve. Believe it or not, just because you 'done me wrong' doesn't mean I'd turn around and do likewise. Is there anything else?"

Dixie shook her head. "I should probably go." She picked up her handbag and began to search for her keys. "I know he invited you to dinner. Eric's always been fond of you. . . ."

I thought, *He has?*

"He's anxious to have you over, and I hope you'll agree. He might think it odd if you refused the invitation."

"Would you give it a rest. I haven't seen either one of you in fourteen years, so why would it seem odd?"

"Just think about it. Please? He said he'd probably call you early in the week."

"All right. I'll consider it, but no guarantees. It seems awkward to me."

"It doesn't have to be." She stood and held out a hand to me. "Thank you."

I shook hands with her, though I wondered in the moment if we'd made some unspoken pact. She moved to the door, turning back, her hand on the knob. "How'd you do in the search for Mickey? Any luck?" she asked.

"The day after I talked to you, a couple of LAPD detectives showed up on my doorstep. He was shot last week."

"He's dead?"

"He's alive but in bad shape. He may not survive."

"That's awful. That's terrible. What happened?"

"Who knows? That's why they drove up here to talk to me."

"Have they made an arrest?"

"Not yet. All I know about it is what they told me so far. He was found on the street a couple of blocks from his apartment. This was Wednesday of last week. He's been in a coma ever since."

"I'm . . . I don't know what to say."

"There's nothing required."

"Will you let me know what you hear?"

"Why would I do that?"

In a fragile voice, she said, "*Please?*"

I didn't bother to reply. Then she was gone, leaving me staring at the door. I resented her thinking she had equal grieving rights. More than that, I wondered what she was really up to.

15

FRIDAY MORNING, I woke up at 5:58, feeling logy and out of sorts. Every bone in my body was begging for more sleep, but I pushed aside the covers and reached for my sweats. I brushed my teeth and ran a comb through my hair, which was sticking out in all directions as though electrified. I paused near the gate and did an obligatory stretch. I started with a fast walk and then broke into a trot when I reached the beachfront park that runs along Cabana Boulevard.

The morning sky was dense with cloud cover, the air hazy. Without the full range of sunlight, all the warm reds and yellows had been leached from the landscape, leaving a muted palette of cool tones: blues, grays, taupe, dun, smoky green. The breeze blowing off the beach smelled of wharf pilings and seaweed. In the course of my run, I could feel the interior fog begin to lift. Intense exercise is the only legal high I know . . . except for love, of course. Whatever your inner state, all you have to do is run, walk, ride a bike, ski, lift weights, and suddenly your optimism's back and life seems good again.

Once recovered from my run, I drove over to the gym, which is seldom crowded at that hour, the pre-work fanatics having already come and gone. The gym itself is spartan, painted gunmetal gray, with industrial carpeting the same color as the asphalt in the parking lot outside. There are huge plate-glass mirrors on the walls. The air smells of rubber and sweaty armpits. The prime patrons are men in various stages of physical fitness. The women who show up tend to fall into two categories: the extremely lean fitness fiends, who trash themselves daily, and the softer women who arrive after any food-dominated holiday. The latter never last, but good for them anyway. Better to make *some* effort than do nothing for life. I fell somewhere between.

I started with leg extensions and leg curls, muscles burning as I worked. Abs, lower back, on to the pec deck and chest press, then on to shoulders and arms. Early in a workout, the sheer number of body parts multiplied by sets times the number of repetitions is daunting, but the process is curiously engrossing . . . pain being what it is. Suddenly I found myself laboring at the last two machines, alternating biceps and triceps. Then I was out the door again, sweaty and exhilarated. Sometimes I nearly wrench my arm from its socket patting myself on the back.

Home again, I turned on the automatic coffeepot, made the bed, showered, dressed, and ate a bowl of cereal with skim milk. Then I sat with my coffee and read the local paper. Usually, as the day wears on, my flirtation with good health is overrun by my tendency to self-abuse, especially when it comes to junk food. Fat grams are my downfall, anything with salt, additives, cholesterol, nitrates. Breaded and deep-fried or sautéed in butter, smothered in cheese, slathered with mayonnaise, dripping with meat juices—what foodstuff couldn't be improved by proper preparation? By the time I finished reading the paper, I was nearly dizzy with hunger and had to suck down more coffee to dampen my appetite. After that, all it took was a big gob of crunchy peanut butter I licked from the spoon while I settled at my desk. I'd decided to skip the office as I'd dutifully caught up with paperwork the day before.

I placed Detective Aldo's business card on the desk in front of me and put a call through to Mark Bethel. I'd actually given up hope of ever speaking to him in person. Sure enough, he'd popped down to Los Angeles for a campaign appearance. I told Judy about Mickey and she went through the usual litany expressing concern, shock, and dismay at life's uncertainties.

"Can Mark do anything to help?" she asked.

"That's why I called. Would you ask him if he'd talk to Detective Aldo and find out what's going on? They're not going to tell me, but they might talk to him since he's Mickey's attorney—or at least he was."

"I'm sure he'd do that. Do you have a number?"

I recited the number and gave her Detective Felix Claas's name as well. I also gave her Mickey's address in Culver City.

She said, "I'm making a note. He should be calling when he's finished. Maybe he can touch base with Detective Aldo while he's still in Los Angeles."

"Thanks. That'd be great."

"Is that it?"

"Just one more thing. Can you ask Mark what's going to happen to Mickey's bills? I'm sure they're piling up, and I hate to see his credit get any worse than it is."

"Got it. I'll ask. He'll think of something, I'm sure. I'll have him call you when he gets in."

"No need for that unless he has a question. Just let him know what we talked about and he can take it from there."

I sat at my desk, wondering what to do next. Once more, I hauled out the assorted items I'd lifted from Mickey's and studied them one by one. Phone bill, the Delta Airlines ticket envelope, receipts from the Honky-Tonk, savings passbooks, phony documents. Emmett Vanover . . . Delbert Amburgey . . . Clyde Byler, all with trumped-up personal data and a photo of Mickey's face plastered in the relevant spots. I went back to the plane ticket, which was issued in the name Magruder. The flight coupons were missing—I assumed, used for the trip—but the passenger receipt and itinerary were still in the ticket envelope. This was an expensive round trip for a guy with no job. What was the relevance, if any? The trip to Louisville might have been personal. Hard to know about that, since we hadn't talked in years. I laid the ticket on the desk beside the other items, lining them up in various configurations as though a story could be fabricated from the proper sequence of events.

When I was a kid, my Aunt Gin kept me supplied with activity books. The paper was always cheap, the games and puzzles designed to shut me up temporarily so she could read for an hour without my interrupting. I'd lie on the trailer floor with my big pencil and a box of crayons. Sometimes the instructions would entail the finding and circling of particular words in a gridwork of letters, sometimes a search for specific objects in a convoluted jungle picture. My favorite was dot-to-dot, in which you constructed a picture by connecting consecutively numbered points on the page. Tongue peeking out of the corner of my mouth, I'd laboriously trace the line from number to number until a picture emerged. I got so good at it, I could stare at the spaces between numbers and see the picture without ever setting pencil to paper. This didn't require much in the way of brains as the outline was usually simple: a teddy bear or a wagon or a baby duck, all dumb. Nonetheless, I can still remember the rush of joy when recognition dawned. Little did I know that at the age of five I was already in training for my later professional life.

What I was looking at here was simply a more sophisticated version of dot-to-dot. If I could understand the order in which the items were related, I could probably get some notion of what was going on in Mickey's life. For now, what I was missing were the links between events. What was he up to in the months before the shooting? The cops had to be pursuing many of these same questions, but it was possible I was in possession of information they lacked . . . having stolen it. In the rudimentary conscience I seemed to be developing, I knew I could always opt for the Good Citizen's Award by "sharing" with Detective Aldo. In the main, I don't hold back where cops are concerned. On the other hand, if I dug a little deeper, I might figure it out for myself, recapturing the thrill of discovery. There's nothing like the moment when everything finally falls into place. So why give that up when, with just a tiny bit more effort, I could have it all? (These are the sorts of rationalizations Ms. Millhone engages in when failing to do her civic duty.)

I hauled up my handbag and began to sift through the contents, coming up with Wary's phone number on the back of a business card. Maybe Mickey had said something to him about the trip. I picked up the phone and dialed Los Angeles. It was only ten-fifteen. Maybe I could catch him before he went off to breakfast. I had a vision of Wary's wire-rimmed glasses and his waist-length brown hair. Two rings. Three. When he finally answered, I could tell from his voice he'd been deeply asleep.

"Hey, Wary. How're you? Did I wake you?"

"No, no," he said valiantly. "Who's this?"

"Kinsey in Santa Teresa." Silence. "Mickey's ex."

"Oh, yeah, yeah. Got it. Sorry I didn't recognize your voice. How're you?"

"Fine. And you?"

"Doing great. What's up?" I could hear him lock his jaw in the effort to suppress a yawn.

"I have a quick question. Did Mickey say anything about the trip he made to Louisville, Kentucky?"

"What trip?"

"This was week before last. He departed May eighth and returned on the twelfth."

"Oh, that. I knew he was gone, but he never said where. Why'd he go?"

"How do I know? I was hoping *you'd* tell *me*. Given his finances, I'm having trouble understanding why he took off for five days. The plane ticket cost a fortune, and he probably had to add meals and a motel on top of that."

"Can't help you there. All I know is he went someplace, but he never said why. I didn't even know he left the state. Dude didn't like to fly. I'm surprised he'd get on a plane going anywhere."

"Did he talk to anyone else, someone in the building he might have mentioned it to?"

"Could have. I doubt it. It's not like he had buddies he confided in. Say, you know what might help? I just thought of this. Once his phone was disconnected, he used to pop in and borrow mine. Kind of pay-as-you-go, but he was always careful to keep square. I can find the numbers, if you want."

I closed my eyes, saying small prayers. "Wary, I'd be indebted to you for life."

"Hey, cool. I'm going to put the phone down and go look on my desk."

I heard a clunk and I was guessing the handset was now resting on his bed table while he padded around, probably bare-assed naked. A full minute passed, and then he picked up the phone again. "You still there?"

"Indeed."

"I got the statement right here. They bill on the fifteenth, so this was in yesterday's mail. I haven't even opened it yet. I know some calls he made were out-of-state because he left me ten bucks and said he'd pay the difference later when the bill came in."

"Really. Did you ever hear what was said?"

"Nope. I made it a point to leave the room. I figured it was private. You know him. He never explained anything, especially when it came to his work. He was stingy with exposition in the best of circumstances."

"What makes you think this was work?"

"His attitude, I guess. Cop mode, I'd call it. You could see it in his body, the way he carried himself. Even half in the bag, he knew his stuff." I could hear him shuffling papers. Distracted, he said, "I'm still looking. Have you heard anything?"

"About Mickey? Not lately. I guess I could call Aldo, but I'm afraid to ask."

"Here we go. Okay. Oh. There was just one. This's the seventh of May. Lookit here. You're right. He called Louisville." He read the number off to me. "Actually, he made two to the same number. The first was quick, less than a minute. The longer one—ten minutes—was shortly afterward."

I was frowning at the phone. "It must have been important to him if he flew out the next day."

"A man of action," he said. "Listen, I gotta get off the phone and go take a leak, but I'll be happy to call you back if I think of anything else."

"Thanks, Wary."

Once I hung up, I sat and stared at the phone, trying to "get centered," as we say in California. Ten-twenty here . . . that would make it one-twenty in Kentucky. I had no clue who he'd called, so I couldn't think of a ruse. I'd have to make it up as I went along. I dialed the number.

"Louisville Male High School. This is Terry speaking. May I help you?"

Male High School? Terry sounded like a student, probably working in the office. I was so nonplused I couldn't think of anything to say. "Oops. Wrong number." I put the handset back. Belatedly, my heart thumped. What was this about?

I took a couple of deep breaths and dialed again.

"Louisville Male High School. This is Terry speaking. May I help you?"

"Uh, yes. I wonder if I might speak to the assistant principal?"

"Mrs. Magliato? One minute." Terry put me on hold, and ten seconds later the line was picked up.

"Mrs. Magliato. May I help you?"

"I hope so. My name is Mrs. Hurst from the General Telephone offices in Culver City, California. A call was placed to this number from Culver City on May seventh, and the charges are currently in dispute. The call was billed to last-name Magruder, first name Mickey or Michael. Mr. Magruder indicates that he never made such a call, and we've been asked to identify the party called. Can you be of some assistance? We'd appreciate your help."

"What was that name again?"

I spelled it out.

She said, "Doesn't sound familiar. Hold on and I'll ask if anybody else remembers talking to him."

She put me on hold. I listened to a local radio station, but the sound was pitched too low for me to hear what was being said. She came back on the line. "No, I'm sorry. None of us talked to anyone by that name."

"What about the principal? Any possibility he might have taken the call himself?"

"For starters, it's a she and I already asked. The name doesn't ring a bell."

I thought about the names on the phony documents and pulled them closer. "Uh, what about the names Emmett Vanover, Delbert Amburgey, and Clyde Byler?" I repeated them before she asked, which seemed to piss her off.

"I know I didn't speak to any one of them. I'd remember the names."

"Could you ask the office staff?"

She sighed. "Just a moment," she said. She put a palm across the receiver and I could hear her relay the question. Muffled conversation ensued and then she removed her hand. "Nobody spoke to any of them either."

"No one from Culver City?"

"No-oo." She sang the word on two notes.

"Ah. Well, thanks anyway. I appreciate your time." I hung up the phone and thought about it for a minute. Who did Mickey talk to for ten minutes? It certainly wasn't her, I thought. I got up from the desk and went back to the kitchen, where I took out a butter knife and the jar of extra crunchy Jif. I took a tablespoon of peanut butter on the blade and spread it on the roof of my mouth, working it with my tongue until my palate was coated with a thin layer of goo. "Hello, this is Mrs. Kennison," I said aloud, in a voice that sounded utterly unlike me.

I returned to the phone and dialed the number again. When Terry answered, I asked the name of the school librarian.

"You mean Ms. Calloway?" she said.

"Oh, that's right. I'd forgotten. Could you transfer me?"

Terry was happy to oblige, and ten seconds later I was going through the same routine, only this time with a variation. "Mrs. Calloway, this is Mrs. Kennison with the district attorney's office in Culver City, California. A call was placed to this number from Culver City on May seventh, billed to last-name Magruder, first name Mickey or Michael—"

"Yes, I spoke to him," she said, before I could finish my tale.

"Ah. Oh, you did. Well, that's wonderful."

"I don't know if I'd call it *wonderful*, but it was pleasant. He seemed like a nice man: articulate, polite."

"Can you remember the nature of the query?"

"It was only two weeks ago. I may be close to retirement, but I'm not suffering from senile dementia—not yet, at any rate."

"Could you fill me in?"

"I could if I understood what this had to do with the district attorney's office. It sounds fishy as all get out. What'd you say your name was? Because I'm making a note of it, and I intend to check."

I hate it when people think. Why don't they just mind their own business and respond to my questions? "Mrs. Kennison."

"And the reason for the call?"

"I'm sorry, but I'm not at liberty to say. This is a legal matter, and there's a gag order in effect."

"I see," she said, as if she didn't.

"Can you tell me what Mr. Magruder wanted?"

"Why don't you ask him?"

"Mr. Magruder's been shot. He's in a coma at the moment. That's as much as I can tell you without being cited for contempt of court."

That seemed to work. She said, "He was trying to track down a former Male High School student."

"Can you give me the name?"

"What's your first name again?"

"Kathryn. Kennison. If you like, I can give you my number here and you can call me back."

"Well, that's silly. You could be anyone," she snapped. "Let's just get this over with. What is it you want?"

"Any information you can give me."

"The boy's name was Duncan Oaks, a 1961 graduate. His was an outstanding class. We still talk about that group of students."

"I take it you were the school librarian back then?"

"I was. I've been here since 1946."

"Did you know Duncan Oaks personally?"

"Everybody knew Duncan. He worked as my assistant in his sophomore and junior years. By the time he was a senior, he was the yearbook photographer, prom king, voted most likely to succeed—"

"He sounds terrific."

"He was."

"And where is he now?"

"He became a journalist and photographer for one of the local papers, the *Louisville Tribune,* long since out of business, I'm sorry to say. He died on assignment in Vietnam. The *Trib* got swallowed up by one of those syndicates a year later, 1966. Now whoever you are and whatever you're up to, I think I've said enough."

I thanked her and hung up, still completely unenlightened. I sat and made notes, using the cap of the pen to scrape the peanut butter from the roof of my mouth. Was this an heir search? Had Mickey taken on a case to supplement his income? He certainly had the background to do P.I. work, but what was he doing and who'd hired him to do it?

I heard a tap at my door and leaned over far enough to see Henry peering through the porthole. I felt a guilty pang about the night before. Henry and I seldom had occasion to disagree. In this case, he was right. I had no business withholding information that might be relevant to the police. *Really,* I was going to reform, I was almost sure. When I opened the door, he handed me a stack of envelopes. "Brought you your mail."

"Henry, I'm sorry. Don't be mad at me," I said. I tossed the mail on the desk and gave him a hug while he patted me on the back.

"My fault," he said.

"No, it's not. It's mine. You're entirely right. I was being obstinate."

"No matter. You know I worry about you. What's wrong with your voice? Are you catching cold?"

"I just ate something and it's stuck in my teeth. I'll call Detective Aldo today and tell him what I've found."

"I'd feel better if you did," he said. "Did I interrupt? We can do this another time if you're hard at work."

"Do what another time?"

"You said you'd give me a lift. The fellow from the body shop called to say the Chevy's ready."

"Sorry. Of course. It's taken long enough. Let me get my jacket and my keys."

On the way over to the body shop, I brought Henry up to date, though I was uncomfortably aware that even now I wasn't being completely candid with him. I wasn't lying outright, but I omitted portions of the story. "Which reminds me," I said. "Did I tell you about that call to my place?"

"What call?"

"I didn't think I'd mentioned it. I don't know what to make of it." I laid out the business about the thirty-minute call from Mickey's place to mine in late March. "I swear I never talked to him, but I can tell the detectives didn't believe me."

"What was the date?"

"March twenty-seventh, early afternoon, one-thirty. I saw the bill myself."

"You were with me," he said promptly.

"I was?"

"Of course. That was the day after the quakes that dumped the cans on my car. I'd called the insurance company and you followed me over to the shop. The claims adjuster met us there at one-fifteen."

"That was *that* day? How do you remember these things?"

"I have the estimate," he said and pulled it from his pocket. "The date's right here."

The incident returned in a flash. In the early morning hours of March 27 there'd been a series of temblors, a swarm of quakes as noisy as a herd of horses thundering across the room. I'd woken from a sound sleep with my entire bed shaking. The brightly lighted numbers on my digital alarm showed 2:06. Clothes hangers were tinkling, and all the glass in the windows rattled like someone rapping to get in. I'd been up like a shot, pulling on my sweats and my running shoes. Within seconds that quake passed, only to be followed by another. I could hear glass crashing in the sink. The walls had begun to creak from the strain of the rocking motion. Somewhere across the city, a transformer exploded and I was blanketed in darkness.

I'd grabbed my shoulder bag and fumbled down the spiral stairs while I groped in the depths for my penlight. I'd found it and flicked it on. The wash from the beam was pale, but it lighted my way. In the distance, I could hear sirens begin to wail. The trembling ceased. I'd taken advantage of the moment to snag my denim jacket and let myself out the door. Henry was already making his way across the patio. He carried a flashlight the size of a boom box, which he shone in my face. We spent the next hour huddled together in the backyard, fearful of returning indoors until we knew we were safe. The next morning, he'd discovered the damage to his five-window coupe.

I'd followed him to the body shop and an hour later I'd driven him home. When I'd returned to my apartment, my message light was blinking. I'd hit the REPLAY button, but there was only a hissing that extended until the tape ran out. I was mildly annoyed. I assumed it was pranksters and let it go at that. Henry was standing right there and heard the same thing I did; he suggested a malfunction when the power had been restored. I'd rewound the tape to erase the hiss and had thought no more about it. Until now.

16

As soon as I got home, I put a call through to Detective Aldo, eager to assert my innocence on this one small point. The minute he picked up the phone and identified himself, I launched right in. "Hi, Detective Aldo. This is Kinsey Millhone, up in Santa Teresa." Little Miss Cheery making friends with the police.

I was just embarking on my explanation of the March phone call when he cut me short. "I've been trying to get in touch with you for days," he said tersely. "This is to put you on notice. I know for a fact you violated crime-scene tape and entered that apartment. I can't prove it for now, but if I find one shred of evidence, we'll charge you with willful destruction or concealment of evidence and resisting a peace officer in the discharge of his duties, punishable by a fine not exceeding one thousand dollars, or by imprisonment in a county jail not exceeding one year, or by both. You got that straight?"

I'd opened my mouth to defend myself when he slammed down the phone. I depressed the plunger on my end and replaced the handset, my mouth as dry as sand. I felt such a hot flash of guilt and embarrassment, I thought I'd been catapulted into early menopause. I put a hand against my flaming cheek, wondering how he knew it was me. Actually, I wasn't the only one guilty of illegal entry. Mickey's phantom girlfriend had entered the premises at some point between my two visits, making off with her diaphragm, her necklace, and her spray cologne. Unfortunately, aside from the fact that I didn't know who she was, I couldn't accuse her without accusing myself as well.

I spent the rest of the day slinking around with my mental tail between my legs. I hadn't been so thoroughly rebuked since I was eight and Aunt Gin caught me smoking an experimental Viceroy cigarette. In this case, I was so heavily invested in Mickey's concerns, I couldn't afford to have my access to his life curtailed. I'd hoped clearing myself with Aldo in the matter of the phone call would net me information about the current status of his investigation. Instead, it was clear that his trust was so seriously eroded he'd never tell me a thing.

I used the early evening hours to pick my way through a plate of Rosie's stuffed beef rolls. She was pushing *vese porkolt,* which (translated from Hungarian) turned out to be heart and kidney stew. Remorseful as I felt, I was prepared to eat my own innards, but my stomach rebelled at the notion of vital piggie organs simmered with caraway seeds. I spent the hours after supper tending to my desk at home, atoning for my sins with lots of busywork. When all else fails, cleaning house is the perfect antidote to most of life's ills.

I waited until close to midnight to return to the Honky-Tonk. I wore the same outfit I'd worn the night before since it was previously smoked on and required laundering anyway. I'd have to hang Mickey's leather jacket on the line for days. This was now Friday night and, if memory still served me, the place would be packed with feverish weekend celebrants. Driving by, I could see the parking lot was jammed. I cruised the surrounding blocks and finally squeezed into a space just as a Ford convertible was pulling out. I walked the block and a half through the darkened Colgate neighborhood. This was an area that had once been devoted solely to single-family homes. Now a full third had been converted to small businesses: an upholsterer, an auto repair shop, and a beauty salon. There were no sidewalks along the street so I kept to the middle of the road and then cut through the small employee parking lot at the rear exit.

I circled the building to the entrance, where the line of people awaiting admittance seemed to be singles and couples in roughly equal numbers. I gave the bouncer my driver's license and watched him run it through his scanning device. I paid the five-dollar cover charge and received the inked benediction on the back of my right hand.

As I moved through the front room, I was forced to run the gauntlet of chain smokers standing four deep at the bar—shifty-eyed guys trying to look a lot hipper than they actually were. The music coming from the other room was live that night. I couldn't see the band, but the melody (or its equivalent) pounded, the beat distorted through the speakers to a tribal throb. The lyrics were indecipherable but probably consisted of sophomoric sentiments laid out in awkward rhyming couplets. The band sounded local, playing all their own tunes, if this one was any indication. I've picked up similar performances on local cable channels, shows that air at 3 A.M. as a special torture to the occasional insomniac like me.

I was already wishing I'd stayed at home. I'd have turned and fled if not for the fact that Mickey'd been here himself six consecutive Fridays. I couldn't imagine what he'd been doing. Maybe counting drinks, calculating Tim's profits, and thus computing his gross. Maybe Tim had cried poor, claiming he wasn't making sufficient money to repay the loan. If Tim's bartender happened to have his hand in the till, this could well be true. Bartenders have their little methods, and an experienced investigator, sitting at the bar, can simultaneously chat with other patrons and do an eyeball audit. If the bartender was skimming, it would have been in Mickey's best interests to spot the practice and blow the whistle on him. It was equally possible Mickey's presence was generated by another motive—a woman, for instance, or the need to escape his financial woes in L.A. Then, too, a heavy drinker doesn't really need an excuse to hit a bar anywhere.

I did the usual visual survey. All the tables were full, the booths bulging with customers packed four to a bench. The portion of the dance floor I could see from where I stood was so dense with moving bodies there was scarcely any room to spare. There was no sign of Tim, but I did see the black-haired waitress, inching through the mob in front of me. She held her tray aloft, balancing empty glasses above the reach of jostling patrons. She wore a black leather vest over nothing at all, her arms long and bare, the V of the garment exposing as much as it concealed. The dyed black of her hair was a harsh contrast to the milky pallor of her skin. A dark slash of lipstick made her mouth look grim. She leaned toward the bartender, calling her order over the generalized din.

There's a phenomenon I've noticed when I'm driving on the highway. If you turn and look at other drivers, they'll turn and look at you. Maybe the instinct is a holdover from more primitive days when being the object of scrutiny might mean you were in peril of being killed and consumed. Here, it happened again. Soon after I spotted her, she turned instinctively and caught my gaze. Her eyes dropped to Mickey's leather jacket. I shifted my attention, but not before I saw her expression undergo a change.

Thereafter, I was careful to avoid her, and I focused instead on what was going on nearby. I kept picking up an intermittent whiff of marijuana, though I couldn't trace the source. I started watching people's hands, since dopers seldom hold a joint the way they'd hold an ordinary cigarette. The average smoker tucks a cigarette in the V formed between the index and middle fingers, bringing the cigarette to the lips with the palm of the hand open. A doper with a joint makes an O-ring with the thumb and index finger, the doobie at the center, the three remaining fingers fanned out so the palm forms a shelter around the burning joint. Whether the intent is to shield the dope from the wind or from public view, I've never been able to determine. My own dope-smoking days are long since past, but the ceremonial aspects seem consistent to this day. I've seen a doper ask for a joint by simply forming that O and pressing it to his lips, a gesture that signals, Shall we smoke a little cannabis, my dear?

I began to circle the bar, moving casually from table to table until I spotted the fellow with a joint between his lips. He was sitting alone in a booth on the far side of the room, close to the corridor that led to the telephones and rest rooms. He was in his mid-thirties, vaguely familiar with his long, lean face. He was a type I'd found appealing when I was twenty: silent, brooding, and slightly dangerous. His eyes were light and close-set. He sported a mustache and goatee, both contributing to the look of borderline scruffiness. He wore a loose khaki-colored jacket and a black watch cap. A fringe of light hair extended well below his collar. He carried himself with a certain worldliness, something in the hunch of his shoulders and the mild knowing smile that flitted across his face.

Tim Littenberg emerged from the back corridor and paused in the doorway while he adjusted his cuffs. The two of them, the joint smoker and the bar owner, ignored each other with a casualness that seemed phony from my perspective. Their behavior reminded me of those occasions when illicit lovers run across each other in a social setting. Under the watchful eyes of their respective spouses, they'll make a point of avoiding contact, thus trumpeting their innocence, or so they think. The only problem is the aura of heightened awareness that underlies the act. Anyone who knows either can detect the charade. Between the man in the booth and Tim Littenberg there was an unmistakable air of self-consciousness. Both seemed to be watching the black-haired waitress, who seemed equally conscious of them.

Within minutes, she'd circled and arrived at the booth. Tim moved away without looking at her. The guy with the joint leaned forward on his elbows. He reached out and put a hand on her hip. He motioned for her to sit. She slid into the bench across from him with her tray between them as though the empty glasses might remind him she had other things to do. He took her free hand and began to talk earnestly. I couldn't see her face, but from where I stood she didn't seem relaxed or receptive to his message.

"You know that guy?" a voice said into my right ear.

I turned to find Tim leaning close to me, his voice amazingly intimate in the midst of loud music and high-pitched voices. I said, "Who?"

"The man you're watching, sitting in the booth over there."

"He seems familiar," I said. "Mostly, I was trying to remember where the rest rooms are."

"I see."

I stole a look at his face and then looked off in the other direction, deflecting the intensity with which he'd fixed his attentions on me. He said, "Remember Mickey's friend Shack?"

"Sure. We talked earlier this week."

"That's his son, Scottie. The waitress is his girlfriend, Thea. In case you're wondering," he added, with a hint of irony.

"You're kidding. That's Scott? No wonder he looked familiar. I've seen pictures of him. I take it you're still friends?"

"Of course. I've known Scottie for years. I don't like dope in my bar, but I don't want to make a fuss so I tend to ignore him when he's got a joint."

"Ah."

"I'm surprised you're back. Are you looking for someone in particular, or will I do?"

"I was hoping to find Mickey. I told you that last night."

"That's right. So you did. Can I buy you a drink?"

"Maybe when I finish this. I'm really fine for now."

He reached over and removed the beer glass from my hand and helped himself to a sip. "This is warm. Let me get you a fresh one in an icy mug." He caught the bartender's eye and lifted the glass, indicating a replacement. Tim was wearing a dark navy suit with a dress shirt that was oxblood red. His tie bore a pattern of diagonal wishbones, navy and red on a field of light blue. The musky bite of his aftershave filled the air between us. His pupils were pinpricks and his skin had a sheen. Tonight, instead of seeming restless and distracted, his demeanor was slow, every gesture deliberate as if he were slogging his way through mud. Well, well, well. What was he on? I felt a faint ridge of fear prickling up along my spine, like a cat in the presence of aliens.

I watched a frosty mug of beer being passed in my direction, hand over hand, like a bucket brigade. Tim placed the mug in my hand, at the same time resting his free hand against the middle of my back. He was standing too close, but in the press of the crowd it was hard to complain. I longed to back away, but there wasn't room. I said, "Thanks."

Again, he bent low and put his mouth close to my ear. "What's the story with Mick? This is twice you've been in."

"He lent me his jacket. I was hoping to return it."

"You and he have something going?"

"That's none of your business."

Tim laughed and his gaze glided off, easing toward Thea, who was just rising from the booth. Scott Shackelford was staring down at the table, pinching out the joint, which was barely visible between his fingers. Thea picked up her tray and began to push toward the bar, studiously avoiding the sight of Tim. Maybe she was still pissed off for what he'd said to her last night. I didn't want the beer, but I didn't see a place to set it down.

I said, "I'll be right back."

Tim touched my arm. "Where're you going?"

"To take a whiz. Is that okay?"

Again, he laughed, but it was not the sound of merriment.

I pushed my way through the crowd, praying he'd lose interest during the time I was gone. The first flat surface I saw, I put the beer glass down and walked on.

The rest room was undergoing one of those temporary lulls where I was the only person present. I crossed to the window and opened it a crack. A wedge of cold air slanted in, and I could see the smoke drift out. The quiet was like a tonic. I could feel myself resist the notion of ever leaving the room. If the window had been lower, I'd have crawled on out. I went into a stall and peed just for something to do.

I was standing at the sink, soaping my hands, when the door opened behind me and Thea walked in. She crossed to the adjacent sink and began washing her hands, her manner businesslike. I didn't think her arrival was an accident, especially when she could have used the employee's lounge around the corner. She caught my reflection in the mirror and gave me a pallid smile as if she'd just that moment noticed I was standing there. She said "Hi" and I responded in kind, letting her define the communication since she'd initiated it.

I pulled out a sheet of paper towel and dried my hands. She followed suit. A silence ensued and then she spoke up again. "I hear you're looking for Mickey."

I focused my attention, hoping she couldn't guess how very curious I was. "I'd like to talk to him. Have you seen him tonight?"

"I haven't seen him for weeks."

"Really? That seems odd. Somebody told me he was usually here on Fridays."

"Uh-uh. Not lately. No telling where he's at. He could be out of town."

"I doubt it. Not that he told me."

She took a lipstick from her pocket and twisted the color into view, sliding it across her lips. I read an article once in some glamour magazine—probably waiting for the dentist and hoping to distract myself—in which the author analyzed the ways women wear down a tube of lipstick. A flat surface meant one thing, slanted meant something else. I couldn't recall the theory, but I noticed hers was flat, the lipstick itself coming perilously close to the metal.

She screwed the lipstick back down and popped the top back on while she rubbed her lips together to even out the color. She corrected a slight mishap at the corner of her mouth, then studied her reflection. She tucked her coal-black hair behind her ears. Idly, she pursued the subject without any help on my part. "So what's your interest?" She used her tongue to remove a smudge of lipstick from her two front teeth.

"He's a friend."

She studied me with interest. "Is that why you have his jacket?"

"He's a *good* friend," I said, and then glanced down at myself. "You recognize this?"

"It sure looks like his. I spotted it when you were in here the other night."

"Last night," I said, as if she didn't know.

"Really. Did he give you that?"

"It's on loan. That's why I'm looking for him, to give it back," I said. "I tried calling, but his phone's been disconnected."

She'd taken out a mascara wand, leaning close to the mirror while she brushed through her lashes, leaving little dots of black. As long as she was wangling for information, I thought I'd wangle some myself.

I said, "What about you? Are you a friend of his?"

She shrugged. "I wait on him when he's in and we shoot the breeze."

"So nothing personal."

"I have a boyfriend."

"Was that him?"

"Who?"

"The guy in the watch cap, sitting at the booth out there?"

She stopped what she was doing. "As a matter of fact, yes. What makes you ask?"

"I was thinking to cop a joint when I saw you sit down. Is he local?"

She shook her head. "L.A." There was a pause and then she said, "How long have you dated Mickey?"

"It's kind of hard to keep track."

"Then this is recent," she said, turning the question into a statement to offset the inquisition.

I started fluffing at my hair the way she'd been fluffing hers. I leaned close to the mirror and checked some imaginary eye makeup, running the flat of one knuckle along the lower edge of one eye. She was still waiting for an answer. I looked at her blankly. "Sorry. Did you ask me something?"

She took a pack of unfiltered Camels from her jeans and extracted a cigarette. She applied a flame to the tip, using a wooden match she scratched on the bottom of her shoe. "I didn't know he was dating."

"Who, Mickey? Oh, please. He's always on the make. That's half his charm." I could picture the ashtray in his apartment, the numerous unfiltered Camel cigarette butts, along with the array of kitchen matches that looked just like hers. "He's so secretive. Jeez. You never know what he's up to or who he's doing these days."

She said, "I didn't know that about him." She turned to face me, leaning her backside against the sink with her weight on one hip.

I was warming to the subject, lies tumbling out with a tidy little mix of truth. "Take my word for it. Mickey doesn't give you a straight answer about anything. He's impossible that way."

"Doesn't that bother you?" she asked.

"Nah. I used to be jealous, but what's the point? Monogamy's not his thing. I figure what the hell? He's still a stud in his way. Take it or leave it. He's always got someone waiting in the wings."

"You live in L.A.?"

"I'm mostly here. Anytime I'm down, though, I stop by his place."

The information I was doling out seemed to make her restless. She said, "I have to get back to work. If you see him, tell him Thea said 'hi.' " She dropped the cigarette on the floor and stepped on it. "Let me know if you find him. He owes me money."

"You and me both, kid," I said.

Thea left the room. I confess I smirked when she banged the door shut. I caught sight of myself in the mirror. "You are such a little shit," I said.

I leaned on the sink for a minute, trying to piece together what I'd learned from her. Thea couldn't know about the shooting or she wouldn't have been forced to try to weasel information out of me. She must have hoped he was out of town, which would go a long way toward explaining why he hadn't been in touch with her. It wasn't difficult to picture her in a snit of some kind. There's no one as irrational as a woman on the make. She might seize the opportunity to screw around on her steady boyfriend, but woe betide the man who screwed around on *her*. Given the fact that Mickey's phone was out, she must have driven down to his apartment to collect her personal belongings. She certainly hadn't warmed to the idea that he and I were an item. I wondered how Scottie Shackelford would feel if he found out she was boffing Mick. Or maybe he knew. In which case, I wondered if he'd taken steps to put a stop to it.

17

I CAME OUT of the ladies' room and paused inside the doorway to the bar, glancing to my left. Scott Shackelford was no longer sitting in the booth. I spotted him at the bar, chatting with the bartender, Charlie. The crowd was beginning to thin out. The band had long ago packed up and departed. It was nearly one-forty-five and the guys looking to get laid were forced to zero in on the few single women who remained. The busboys were loading dirty glassware into plastic bins. Thea was now standing at the bar with Scott, using a calculator to add up her tips. I zipped up the front of Mickey's jacket. As I made my way to the front door, I became aware that she was watching me.

The chilly air was a relief after the smoky confinement of the bar. I could smell pine needles and loam. Colgate's main street was deserted, all the neighboring businesses long since shut down for the night. I cut through the parking lot on the way to my car, hands in my jeans pockets, the strap of my handbag hooked over my right shoulder. Streetlights splashed the pavement with pale

213

circles of illumination, emphasizing the darkness beyond their reach. Somewhere behind me, I heard the basso profundo rumble of a motorcycle. I looked over my shoulder in time to see a guy on a bike turning into the alley to the rear of the bar. I stared, walking backward, wondering if my eyes were deceiving me. I'd only caught a glimpse of him, but I could have sworn this was the same guy who'd shown up at Mickey's Wednesday night in L.A. As I watched, he cut the engine and, still astride, began to roll his bike toward the trash bins. A wan light shining down from the rear exit shone on his corn-yellow hair and glinted against the chrome of the bike. He lifted the bike backward onto the center stand, locked the bike, dismounted, and rounded the building, walking toward the main entrance with a jingling sound, his jacket flapping open. The body type was the same: tall, thin, with wide bony shoulders and a sunken-looking chest.

I dog-trotted after him, slowing as I reached the corner to avoid running into him. He'd apparently already entered the bar by the time I got there. The bouncer saw me and glanced at his watch with theatrical emphasis. He was in his forties, balding, big-bellied, wearing a sport coat that fit tightly through the shoulders and arms. I showed him the stamp on the back of my hand, demonstrating the fact I'd already been cleared for admittance. "I forgot something," I said. "Mind if I go back in real quick?"

"Sorry, lady. We're closed."

"It's only ten of two. There's still a ton of people inside. Five minutes. I swear."

"Last call was one-thirty. No can do."

"I don't want a *drink*. This is for something I left. It'll only take two minutes and I'll be right out again. Please, please, please?" I put my knees together and clasped my hands like a little child at prayer.

I saw him repress a smile, and he motioned me in with an indulgent rolling of his eyes. It's perplexing to realize how far you can get with men by pulling girlish shit. I paused, looking back at him as if my question had just occurred to me. "Oh, by the way . . . the fellow who just went in?"

He stared at me flatly, unwilling to yield anything more than he had.

I held a hand above my head. "About this tall? Denim jacket and spurs. He arrived on a motorcycle less than a minute ago."

"What about him?"

"Can you tell me his name? I met him a couple of nights ago and now I've forgotten. I'm too embarrassed to ask so I was hoping you'd know."

"He's a pal of the owner's. He's a two-bit punk. You got no business hanging out with a little shit like him."

"What about Tim? What's their relationship?"

He looked at his watch again, his tone shifting to exasperation. "Are you going to go in? Because technically we're closed. I'm not supposed to admit anyone after last call."

"I'm going. I'm going. I'll be out in a second. Sorry to be such a pest."

"Duffy something," he murmured. "Nice girl like you ought to be ashamed."

"I promise I am. You have no idea."

Once inside, I dropped the Gidget act and studied the faces within range of me. The overhead lights had come on and the busboys were now stacking chairs on the tabletops. The bartender was closing out the register and the party hearties seemed to be getting the hint. Thea and Scott were sitting in a booth. Both had cigarettes and fresh drinks: one for the road, to get their alcohol levels up. I crossed the front room, hoping to avoid calling attention to myself. Good luck with that. Three single guys gave me the toe-to-head body check, glancing away without interest, which I thought was rude.

I headed for the back corridor, operating on the assumption that Duffy Something was in Tim's office since I didn't see him anywhere else. I passed the ladies' room and the pay phones and turned right into the short hallway. The door to the employees' lounge stood open, and a couple of waitresses were sitting on the couch smoking while they changed their shoes. Both looked up at me, one pausing long enough to remove the cigarette from her lips. "You need help?" Smoke wafted out of her mouth like an SOS.

"I'm looking for Tim."

"Across the hall."

"Thanks." I backed away, wondering what to do next. I couldn't simply knock on his door. I had no reason to interrupt, and I didn't want the biker to get a look at me. I glanced at the door and then back at the two. "Isn't somebody in there with him?"

"No one important."

"I hate to interrupt."

"My, ain't we dainty? Bang on the door and walk in. It's no big deal."

"It's not that important. I'd rather not."

"Oh, shit. Gimme your name and I'll tell him you're here."

"Never mind. That's okay. I can catch him later." I backed up in haste, then scooted around the corner and out the back exit. I walked forward a few steps and then turned and stared. Where the front of the building was only one story tall, the rear portion was two. I could see lights on upstairs. A shift in the shadows suggested movement, but I couldn't be sure. What was going on up there?

No way to know unless I created the opportunity to pick my way in.

Meanwhile, I'd have given a lot to know what the biker was saying to Tim. From the location of Tim's office, I knew any exterior windows would have to be around the far corner to my left. I stood there, debating the wisdom of trying to eavesdrop. That corner of the building was shrouded in darkness, and it looked like I'd have to squeeze into the space between the Honky-Tonk and the building next to it. This was a feat that not only promised a bout of claustrophobia but the onslaught of hordes of domestic short-haired spiders the size of my hand. With my luck, the windowsills would be too high for peeking and the conversation too muffled for revelations of note. It was the thought of the spiders that actually clinched the vote.

I opted instead for a close-on inspection of the motorcycle. I fished out my penlight and flashed the beam across the bike. The make was a Triumph. The license plate was missing, but by law the registration should have been available on the bike somewhere. I ran a hand across the seat, hoping it would lift to reveal a storage compartment. I was in the process of the search when the rear door banged open and the two waitresses walked out. I shoved the penlight in my pocket and turned my attention toward the street, like I was waiting for someone. They moved off to my right, deep in conversation, crossing my line of vision without exhibiting any curiosity about what I was doing. As soon as they were gone, I turned off the penlight and slipped it in my bag.

Out in the street, the last of the bar patrons were straggling to their cars. I could hear doors slamming, car engines coughing to life. I abandoned the search and decided to return to my car. I jogged the two blocks, my shoulder bag banging against my hip. When I reached the VW, I unlocked the door and slid under the wheel. I stuck my key in the ignition, fired up the engine, and snapped on my headlights. I made an illegal U-turn and drove back to the Tonk.

Once in view of the place, I doused my headlights and pulled over to the right. I parked the car in the shadow of a juniper bush. I slouched down on my spine, keeping an eye on the rear exit over the rim of my sideview mirror. The biker showed up about ten minutes later. He mounted his bike, backed off his center stand, and dropped his weight down with a quick stomp that jolted his engine to life. He cranked the throttle with one hand, revving the bike until it roared in protest. He kept one foot on the ground while he pivoted his bike, the backside swinging wildly as he took off. I watched him slide through the stop sign and hang a left onto Main. By the time I could follow, he was easily five blocks ahead. Within minutes, I'd lost sight of him.

I cruised on for a while, wondering if he'd turned off on a side street close by. This was an area that consisted largely of single-family residences. The stretches of roadway between subdivisions and shopping malls were lined with citrus orchards. The Colgate Community Hospital appeared on my right. I turned left toward the freeway but saw no sign of the biker's taillight. If he'd already turned on the 101, he'd be halfway to town and I didn't have a prayer of catching up with him. I pulled over to the curb and shut off the ignition. I cranked down the driver's side window and tilted my head, listening for the distant racketing of the motorcycle in the still night air. Nothing at first and then . . . faintly . . . I picked up the rat-a-tat-tat, at a much reduced speed. The source of the sound was impossible to pinpoint, but he couldn't be far. Assuming it was him.

I started the VW and pulled out again. The road here

was four lanes wide, and the only visible side street went off to the left. There was a nursery on the corner. The sign read BERNARD HIMES NURSERY & TREE FARM: *Shade Trees, Roses, Fruit Trees, Ornamental Shrubs.* The street curved along beside the tree farm and around to the right again. As nearly as I remembered, there was no other exit, and anyone driving back there would be forced to return. The Santa Teresa Humane Society had its facility toward the far corners of the cul-de-sac, as did the County Animal Control. The other businesses were commercial enterprises: a construction firm, warehouses, a heavy-equipment yard.

I turned left, driving slowly, checking both sides of the street for signs of the biker. Passing the nursery on my right, I thought I saw a flicker of light, in a strobe effect, appearing through the thicket of specimen trees. I squinted, unsure, but the darkness now appeared unbroken and there was no sound. I drove on, following the street to its dead end, a matter of perhaps half a mile. Most of the properties I passed were either entirely dark or minimally lighted for burglar-repellent purposes. Twice, I caught sight of private security vehicles parked to one side. I imagined uniformed guards keeping watch, possibly with the help of attack-trained dogs. I returned to the main road without any clear-cut evidence the biker had come this way. It was now after two. I took the southbound on-ramp to the 101. Traffic was sparse, and I returned to my apartment without seeing him again.

Mercifully, the next morning was a Saturday and I owed myself nothing in the way of exercise. I pulled the pillows over my head, shutting out sound and light. I lay bundled under my quilt in an artificial dark, feeling like a small furry beast. At nine, I finally crawled out of my burrow. I brushed my teeth, showered, and shampooed the previous night's smoke from my hair. Then I wound down the spiral stairs and put on a pot of coffee before I fetched the morning paper.

Once I'd finished breakfast, I put a call through to Jonah Robb at home. I'd first encountered Jonah four years before when he was working missing persons for the Santa Teresa Police Department. I was checking on the whereabouts of a woman who later turned up dead. Jonah was separated from his wife, struggling to come to terms with their strange bond, which had started in junior high school and gone downhill from there. In the course of their years together, they'd separated so many times I think he'd lost count. Camilla worked him like a yo-yo. First, she'd kick him out; then she'd take him back or leave him for long periods, during which he wouldn't see his two daughters for months on end. It was in the midst of one of their extended separations that he and I became involved in a relationship. At some point I finally understood that he'd never be free of her. I broke off intimate contact and we reverted to friends.

He'd since been promoted to lieutenant and was now working homicide. We remained buddies of a sort, though I hadn't set eyes on him for months. The last time I'd run into him was at a homicide scene, where he confessed Camilla was pregnant—by someone else, of course.

"What's up?" he said, once I'd identified myself.

I gave him a rundown on the situation. The LAPD detectives had filled him in on the shooting, so he knew that much. I gave him a truncated version of my dealings with them and then filled in additional details: the money Tim owed Mickey, the biker appearing at his Culver City apartment and again at the Honky-Tonk.

Jonah said, "Did you get the license plate?"

"There wasn't one. I'm guessing the bike's stolen, but I

can't be sure. I can't swear he's connected to the shooting, but it seems too coincidental he'd show up in both places, especially since he's said to be a friend of Tim's. Can you ask Traffic to keep an eye out? I'd love to know who he is and how he's mixed up in this."

"I'll see what I can do and call you back," he said. "What's the story on the gun that was left at the scene? Was that really yours?"

"Afraid so," I said. "That was a wedding gift from Mickey, who purchased it in his name. Later, we switched the registration. It's a sweet little Smith and Wesson I haven't seen since the spring of '72, which is when I left. Maybe Mickey had it on him and the shooter took it away."

"How's he doing?"

"I haven't heard. I'll try calling in a bit, but the truth is, I don't want to ask for fear the news won't be good."

"I don't blame you. Scary shit. Is there anything else?"

"What's the word on the Honky-Tonk? What's going on out there?"

"Nothing that I've heard. As in what?"

"I don't know. It could be dope," I said. "I've been in there twice, and it feels *off* to me. I guess, at the back of my mind, I'm wondering if Mickey picked up on it too. I'm assuming he came up at first to bug Tim about the money owed. But why the return trips?"

"I'll ask around. It's possible the vice guys know something that I don't. What about yourself? How are you these days?"

"Doing great, considering I'm suspected of trying to kill my ex. Speaking of which, how's Camilla?"

"She's big. Baby's due July fourth, and according to the amnio it's a boy. We're excited about that."

"She's living with you?"

"Temporarily."

"Ah."

"Well, yeah. Her turd of a boyfriend abandoned her as soon as he found out she was pregnant. She's got nobody else."

"The poor thing," I said, in a tone of voice that went over his head.

"Anyway, it gives me a chance to spend time with the girls."

"That it does," I said. "Well, it's your life. Good luck."

"I'm going to need it," he said dryly, but he sounded pretty cheerful for a guy whose nuts were being slammed in a car door.

After he hung up, I dialed UCLA and asked for ICU. I identified myself to the woman who answered and asked about Mickey. She put me on hold. When she came back on, an eternity later, I realized I'd stopped breathing.

"He's about the same."

I said, "Thanks," and hung up quickly before she changed her mind.

I spent the bulk of the day in a fit of cleaning, armed with sponges and rags, a bucket of soapy water, a dust-cloth, and a vacuum cleaner, plus newspapers and vinegar water for the windows I could reach. The phone rang at four. I paused in my labors, tempted to let the answering machine pick up. Of course, curiosity got the better of me.

"Hey, Kinsey. Eric Hightower here. I hope I didn't catch you at a bad time."

"This is fine, Eric. How are you?"

"Doing good," he said. "Listen, Dixie and I are putting together a little gathering: cocktails and hors d'oeuvres. This is strictly impromptu, just a couple dozen folk, but we wanted you to come. Any time between five and seven."

I took advantage of the moment to open my mail, including the manila envelope Bethel's secretary had sent. Inside was his curriculum vitae. I tossed it in the wastebasket, then took it out again and stuck it in the bottom drawer. "You're talking about tonight?"

"Sure. We've got some friends in from Palm Springs so we're geared up anyway. Can you make it?"

"I'm not sure. Let me take a look at my calendar and call you right back."

"Bullshit. Don't do that. You're stalling while you think of an excuse. It's four now. You can hop in the shower and be ready in half an hour. I'll send the car at four-forty-five."

"No, no. Don't do that. I'll use my own."

"Great. We'll see you then."

"I'll do what I can, but I make no promises."

"If we don't see you by six, I'm coming after you myself."

As soon as he hung up, I let out a wail, picturing the house, the servants, and all their la-di-da friends. I'd rather have a root canal than go to these things. Why hadn't I just lied and told him I was tied up? Well, it was too late now. I put the cleaning gear away and trudged up the spiral stairs. I opened my closet door and stared at my dress. I admit to a neurotic sense of pride in only owning that one garment, except for times like this. I took the dress from the closet and held it up to the light. It didn't look too bad. And then a worse thought struck. What if *they* were all decked out in designer jeans? What if I was the only one who showed up in a dress made of a wrinkle-free synthetic fabric that scientific tests would later prove was carcinogenic? I'd end up looking like a social geek, which is what I am.

18

I DROVE INTO the parking area at the Hightowers' estate shortly after 6 P.M. The house was ablaze, though it wouldn't be dark for another hour yet. The evening was cool, 62 degrees, according to the report on my car radio. I parked my 1974 VW between a low-slung red Jaguar and a boxy chrome-trimmed black Rolls, where it sat looking faintly plaintive, a baby humpback whale swimming gamely among a school of sharks. In a final moment of cunning, I'd solved my fashion dilemma with the following: black flats, black tights, a very short black skirt, and a long-sleeved black T-shirt. I'd even applied a touch of makeup: powder, lip gloss, and a smudgy line of black along my lashes.

A middle-aged white maid in a black uniform answered the door chimes and ushered me into the foyer, where she offered to take my bag. I declined, preferring to retain it on the off chance I'd spy the perfect opportunity to flee the premises. I could hear a smattering of conversation, interspersed with the kind of laughter that suggests lengthy and unrestrained access to booze. The maid murmured a discreet directive and began to cross the living room in her especially silent maid's shoes. I followed her through the dining room and out into the screened atrium, where some fifteen to twenty people were already standing about with their drinks and cocktail napkins. A serving wench was circulating with a tray of hors d'oeuvres: teeny-weeny one-bite lamb chops with paper panties on the ends.

As is typical of California parties, there was a percentage of people dressed far better than I and a percentage dressed like bums. The very rich seem particularly practiced at the latter, wearing baggy chinos, shapeless cotton shirts, and deck shoes with no socks. The not-so-very-rich have to work a little harder, adding an abundance of gold jewelry that might or might not be fake. I tucked my bag against the wall behind a nearby chair and then stood where I was, hoping to get my bearings before the panic set in. I didn't know a soul and I was already flirting with the urge to escape. If I didn't see Eric or Dixie in the next twenty seconds, I'd ease right on out.

A black waiter in a white jacket appeared at my shoulder and asked if I'd like a drink. He was tall and freckle-faced, somewhere in his forties, his tone refined, his expression remote. His name tag said STEWART. I wondered what he thought of the Montebello social set and sincerely hoped he wouldn't take me for one of them. On second thought, there probably wasn't too much danger of that.

"Could I have Chardonnay?"

"Certainly. We're pouring Kistler, Sonoma-Cutrer, and a Beringer Private Reserve."

"Surprise me," I said, and then I tilted my head. "Don't I know you from somewhere?"

"Rosie's. Most Sundays."

I pointed in recognition. "Third booth back. You're usually reading a book."

"That's right. I work two jobs at the moment, and Sunday's the only day I have to myself. I got three kids in college and a fourth going off next year. By 1991, I'll be a free man again."

"What's the other job?"

"Telephone sales. I have a friend owns the company, and he lets me fill in when it suits my scheduling. His turnover's fast anyway, and I'm good at the spiel. I'll be back in a moment. Don't you go away."

"I'll be here."

Halfway across the room I caught sight of Mark Bethel in conversation with Eric, hunkered beside Eric's wheelchair. Eric had his back to me; Mark was just to the left of him and facing my way. Mark's face was long and his hairline was receding, which gave him a high-domed head with a wide expanse of brow. He wore glasses with tortoise-shell rims, behind which his eyes were a luminous gray. While technically not good-looking, the television cameras were amazingly kind to him. He'd removed his suit coat and, as I watched, I saw him loosen his tie and roll up the sleeves of his crisp white dress shirt. The gesture suggested that despite his buttoned-down appearance he was ready to go to work for his constituents. It was the sort of soft-focus image that would probably show up later in one of his commercials. The thrust of his campaign was shamelessly orchestrated: babies and old folk and the American flag waving over patriotic music. His opponents were portrayed in grainy black-and-white, overlaid with tabloid-type headlines decrying their perfidy. Mentally, I slapped myself around some for being such a cynic. Mark's wife, Laddie, and his son, Malcolm, were standing a few feet away, chatting with another couple.

Laddie was the exemplary political mate: mild, compassionate, so subtle in her affect that most people never guessed the power she held. Her eyes were a cool hazel, her dark hair streaked blond, probably to disguise any early hints of gray. Her nose was slightly too prominent, which saved her from perfection and thus endeared her to some extent. Never compelled to work, she'd devoted her time to a number of worthy causes—the symphony, the humane society, the arts council, and numerous charities. As hers was one of the few familiar faces present, I considered crossing the room and engaging her in conversation. I knew she'd at least *pretend* to be attentive, even if she couldn't quite remember who I was.

Malcolm, in another five years, was going to be a knockout. Even now, he was graced with a certain boy beauty: dark-haired and dark-eyed, with a succulent mouth and slouching, lazy posture. I'm a sucker for the type, though I tend to be careful about guys that good-looking as they often turn out to be treacherous. He seemed to have an awareness of the ladies, who were, likewise, more than casually aware of him. He wore desert boots, faded jeans, a pale blue dress shirt, and a navy blazer. He seemed poised, at ease, accustomed to attending parties given by his parents' snooty friends. He looked like a stockbroker in the making, maybe a commodities analyst. He'd end up on financial-channel talk shows, discussing short falls, emerging markets, and aggressive growth. Once off the air, the female anchor, ever bullish, would pursue him over drinks and then fuck his baby brains out, strictly no-load with no penalty for early withdrawal.

"Excuse me, dear."

I turned. The woman to my right handed me her empty glass, which I took without thinking. While she was clearly speaking in my direction, she managed to address me without direct eye contact. She was a gaunt and gorgeous fifty with a long flawless face and blown-about red hair. She wore a long-sleeved black silk body suit and blue jeans so tight I was surprised she could draw breath. With her flat tummy, tiny waist, and minuscule hips, my guess was she'd had sufficient liposuction to create an entire separate human being. "I need a refill. Gin and tonic. Make it Bombay Sapphire and no ice this round, please."

"Bombay Sapphire. No ice."

She leaned closer. "Darling, where's the nearest loo? I'm about to pee my pants."

"The loo? Let's see." I pointed toward the sliding glass doors that opened into the dining room. "Through those glass doors. Angle left. The first door on your right."

"Thanks ever so."

I set her empty glass in a potted palm, watching as she tottered away on her four-inch heels. She did as directed, passing through the glass doors to the dining room. She angled left to the first door, tilted her head, tapped lightly, turned the knob, and went in. Turned out to be a linen closet, so she walked right out again, looking mildly embarrassed and thoroughly confused. She spotted another door and corrected for her error with a quick look-around to see if anyone had noticed. She knocked and went in, then did an about-face, emerging from a closet filled with stereo equipment. Well, darn. I guess I know as much about the loo as I do about high-priced gins.

I eased my way through the crowd, intercepting Stewart, who was returning with my wine. The next time I saw the woman, she avoided me altogether, but she'd probably drop a hint to Dixie about having me removed. In the meantime, a young woman appeared with another tray of hors d'oeuvres, this time halved new potatoes the size of fifty-cent pieces, topped with a dollop of sour cream and an anthill of black caviar. Within minutes, everybody's breath was going to smell like fish.

Eric's conversation with Mark had come to an end. Across the room, I caught Mark's attention and he moved in my direction, pausing to shake a few hands en route. By the time he finally reached me, his public expression had been replaced by a look of genuine concern. "Kinsey. Terrific. I thought that was you. I've been trying to reach you," he said. "When'd you get here?"

"A few minutes ago. I figured we'd connect."

"Well, we don't have long. Laddie committed us to another party and we're just about to leave. Judy passed along the news about Mickey. What a terrible thing. How's he doing?"

"Not well."

Mark shook his head. "What a shitty world we live in. It's not like he didn't have enough problems."

"Judy said you talked to him in March."

"That's right. He asked me for help, in a roundabout way. You know how he is. By the way, I did talk to Detective Claas while I was down in L.A., though I didn't learn much. They're being very tight-lipped."

"I'll say. They certainly don't appreciate my presence on the scene."

"So I hear."

I could just imagine the earful he picked up from the LAPD. I said, "At this point, what worries me are Mickey's medical bills. As nearly as I can tell, he lost all his coverage when he was fired from his job."

"I'm sure that's not an issue. His bills can be paid from funds from Victims of Major Crimes, through the DA's office. It's probably been set in motion, but I'll be happy to check. By the way, I stopped off at Mickey's on my way back from L.A. I thought I should meet his landlady in case a question came up."

"Oh, great. Because the other thing I'm concerned about is this eviction. The sheriff's already been there and changed the locks."

"I gathered as much," he said. "Frankly, I'm surprised to see you take an interest. I was under the impression you hadn't spoken to him for years."

"I haven't, but it looks like I owe him one."

"How so?"

"You know I blamed him for Benny Quintero's death. Now I find out Mickey was with Dixie that night."

"I heard that story too, but I was never sure how much credit to attach."

"You're telling me they lied?"

"Who's to say? I've made it my practice not to speculate. Mickey didn't confide and I didn't press him for information. Fortunately, we never had to defend the point one way or the other."

I saw him glance in Laddie's direction, gauging their departure, which was imminent. Laddie had found Dixie and she was proffering regrets. Hugs, air kisses, and niceties were exchanged.

Mark said, "I better catch up. Give me a couple of days. I'll let you know about his bills. Glad we had a chance to chat." He gave my shoulder a squeeze and then joined Laddie and Malcolm, who waited in the dining room. Dixie followed them out, apparently intending to see them as far as the door.

Meanwhile, Eric had wheeled around and his face seemed to brighten at the sight of me. He pointed to a corner chair and then pushed himself in that direction. I nodded and followed, admiring his physique. His knit shirt fit snugly, emphasizing his shoulders and chest, along with his muscular arms. He looked like an ad for a fitness supplement. When he pivoted his chair, I could see the point where his thighs ended, six inches above the knees. He held a hand out to me. I leaned down and bussed his cheek before I took a seat. His aftershave was citrus and his skin was like satin. He said, "I didn't think you'd come."

"I probably won't stay long. I don't know a soul here except for Mark and his crew. The kid's attractive."

"And bright. Pity about his father. He's a waste of time."

"I thought you liked Mark."

"I do and I don't. He's phony as all get out, but aside from that he's great."

"That's a hell of an endorsement. What'd he do to you?"

Eric gestured dismissively. "Nothing. Forget it. He asked me to do a film clip for his ad campaign. Primary's only ten days off, and there's nothing like a cripple to pick up a few last-minute votes."

"Ooh, you're a cynic. You sound worse than I do. Did it ever occur to you he might see you as a shining example of success and achievement, overcoming the odds and similar sentiments?"

"No. It occurred to me he wants me on his team in hopes other Vietnam vets will follow suit. Prop Forty-two is his pet project. The truth is, he needs a banner issue because he's floundering. Laddie's not going to like it if he's trounced at the polls."

"What difference does it make? I didn't think he had a chance anyway."

"It's one thing to lose and another thing to lose *badly*. He doesn't want to look like a has-been right out of the gate."

"Easy come, easy go. They'll survive, I'm sure."

"Possibly."

"Possibly? I like that. What's that supposed to mean?"

I saw his gaze shift and glanced up in time to see Dixie return. "Things aren't always as they appear."

"The Bethels are unhappy?"

"I didn't say that."

"Incompatible?"

"I didn't say that, either."

"Then what? Come on. I won't repeat it. You've got me curious."

"Mark has places to go. He can't do that divorced. He needs Laddie's money to make it work."

"What about her? What's her stake in it?"

"She's more ambitious than he is. She dreams about the White House."

"You're not serious."

"I am. She grew up in the era of Jackie O and Camelot. While other girls played with Barbies, she was making a list of which rooms to redo."

"I had no idea."

"Hey, Mark wants it too. Don't get me wrong, but he'd probably be content with the Senate while she's longing for a place in all the history books. He won't make it this round—the competition's too fierce—but in four years, who knows? As long as he can rally support, he's probably got a shot at it one day. Meanwhile, if he starts looking like a loser, she might bump him and move on."

"And that's enough to keep their marriage afloat?"

"To a point. In the absence of passion, rampant ambition will suffice. Besides, divorce is a luxury."

"Oh, come on. Couples get divorced every day."

"Those are the people with nothing at stake. They can afford to set personal happiness above all else."

"As opposed to what?"

"The status quo. Besides, who wants to start over at

our stage in life? Are you eager to fling yourself into a new relationship?"

"No."

Eric smiled. "My sentiments exactly. I mean, think of all the stories you'd have to retell, the personal revelations, the boring family history. Then you'd have to weather all the hurt feelings and the fear and the stupid misunderstandings while you get to know the other person and they get to know you. Even if you take the risk and pour yourself heart and soul into someone new, the odds are your new love's a clone of the one you just dumped."

I said, "This is making me ill."

"It's really no big deal. You put up with things. You look the other way, and sometimes you have no choice but to bite your tongue. If both parties are committed—whatever their reasons—it can work."

"And what if both aren't committed?"

"Then you have a problem and you have to deal with it."

19

I'M GOING TO skip a bunch of stuff here because, really, who cares? We ate. We drank, and then we ate some more. I didn't spill, fart, fall down, or otherwise disgrace myself. I talked to the couple from Palm Springs, who turned out to be nice, as were most of the other folk. I listened with feigned interest to a lengthy discussion about vintage Jaguars and antique Rolls-Royces and another in which the participants told where they were when the last big local earthquake struck. Some of the answers were: the south of France, Barbados, the Galápagos Islands. I confessed I was in town, scrubbing out my toilet bowl, when a bunch of water slopped up and splashed my face. That got a big laugh. What a kidder, that girl. I felt I was just getting the hang of how to talk to the rich when the following occurred.

Stewart crossed the atrium with a bottle of Chardonnay and offered to fill my glass. I declined . . . I'd had plenty . . . but Dixie leaned toward him so he could refill hers. The collar of her silk shirt gaped briefly in the process, and I caught a glimpse of the necklace she wore in the hollow of her throat. Threaded on a gold chain was a tiny gold heart with a pink rose enameled in the center. I felt my smile falter. Fortunately, Dixie was looking elsewhere and didn't notice the change in my expression. I could feel my cheeks heat. The necklace was a duplicate of the one I'd seen in Mickey's bed-table drawer.

Now it was possible—remotely possible—he'd given her the necklace fourteen years before, in honor of the affair they were having back then. I set my glass on the table next to me and got to my feet. No one seemed to pay attention as I walked across the room. I passed through the doors into the dining room, where I spotted the same maid who'd answered the door.

I said, "Excuse me. Where's the nearest bathroom?" I couldn't, for the life of me, refer to it as the "loo."

"Turn right at the foyer. It's the second door on the right."

"I think someone's in there. Dixie said to use hers."

"Master bedroom's at the end of the hallway to the left of the foyer."

"Thanks," I said. As I passed the chair where I'd secured my handbag, I leaned down and picked it up. I moved through the living room and out into the foyer, where I turned left. I walked quickly, keeping my weight on my toes so the tap of my heels wouldn't advertise my passage. The double doors to the master bedroom stood open to reveal a room twice the size of my apartment. The pale limestone floors were the same throughout. All the colors here were muted: linens like gossamer, wall coverings of pale silk. There were two bathrooms, his 'n' hers, one on either side of the room. Eric's was nearer, fitted with an enormous roll-in shower and a wall-mounted bar to one side of the toilet. I turned on my heel and headed into the second.

Dixie's dressing table was a fifteen-foot slab of marble that stretched along one wall. There was a second wall of closets, a glass shower enclosure, a massive tub with Jacuzzi, and a separate dressing room with an additional U of hanging space. I closed the bathroom door behind me and started going through her belongings. This impulse to snoop was getting out of control. I just couldn't seem to keep my nose out of other people's business. The more obstacles the merrier. I found the cologne bottle in a cluster of ten others on a silver tray. On the bottom was the same partially torn label I'd seen at Mickey's. I sniffed at the spray. The scent was unmistakably the same.

I returned to the bedroom, where I crossed to the bed. I opened the top drawer in the first of the two matching bed tables. There sat the diaphragm case. I could hardly believe she was screwing him again . . . or was it *still*? No wonder she'd been nervous, prowling my backyard, angling for information about his current state. She must have wondered at his silence, wondered where he'd been the night she retrieved her personal items. Did she know he'd been shot? Hell, she might have done it herself if she'd found out about Thea. Maybe she was only quizzing me to determine what, if anything, I knew. I thought back to my conversation with Thea at the Honky-Tonk. Now I wondered if *she'd* seen the diaphragm et al., assuming it was mine while I'd assumed it belonged to her.

I closed the drawer and retraced my steps, emerging from the master suite just as Eric appeared, wheeling himself in my direction. I said, "Great bathroom. The maid sent me down here because the other was in use."

"I wondered where you went. I thought you left."

"I was just powdering my nose," I said, and then glanced at my watch. "Actually, I do have to go, now you mention it. I agreed to meet someone at eight, and it's almost that now."

"You have a date?"

"You don't have to sound so surprised."

He smiled. "Sorry. I didn't mean to pry."

"Could you give Dixie my thanks? I know it's rude not to do it personally, but I'd thought I'd slip out without making a fuss. Sometimes one person leaves and it starts an exodus."

"Sure thing."

"I appreciate the invitation. This was fun."

"We'll have to try it again. What's your schedule like next week?"

"My schedule?"

"I thought we'd have lunch, just the two of us," he said.

"Ah. I don't remember offhand. I'll check when I hit the office and call you on Monday."

"I'll be waiting."

Inwardly, I found myself backing away. Ordinarily, I don't imagine men are coming on to me, but his tone was flirtatious, which didn't sit well with me. I became especially chirpy as I made my retreat. Eric seemed amused by my discomfiture.

I was letting myself into my apartment some fifteen minutes later when I heard the last of a message being left on my machine. Jonah. I dropped my bag on the floor and snatched at the phone, but by then he'd hung up. I pressed the PLAY button and heard the rerun of his brief communication.

"Kinsey. Jonah here. It looks like we found your boy. Give me a call, and I'll fill you in on the nitty-gritty details. Not a very nice guy, but you probably know that already. I'm at home."

I looked up his home number and dialed with impatience, listening to ring after ring. "Come on, come on. . . ."

"Hello?"

Oh, shit. Camilla.

I said, "Could I speak to Lieutenant Robb? I'm returning his call."

"And who's this?"

"Kinsey Millhone."

Dead silence.

Then she said, "He's busy at the moment. Is this something I can help you with?"

"Not really. He has some information for me. Could I speak to him, please?"

"Just a minute," she said, not entirely happy about the situation. I heard a clunk as she placed the handset on the tabletop, then the tapping of her heels as she walked away. After that, I was treated to all the quaint, domestic sounds of the Robbs' Saturday night as they hung around the house. I could hear the television set in a distant room. Closer to the phone, one of his girls, probably Courtney, the older one, played chopsticks on an out-of-tune piano, never quite finishing her portion of the musical duet. I listened to countless repetitions of the first fifteen to twenty notes. The other daughter, whose name I forget, would chime in at the wrong spot, which caused the first girl to protest and start over again. The second child kept saying, "Stop it!" which the first girl declined to do. In the meantime, I could hear Camilla's comments to Jonah, who apparently hadn't been told there was a call for him. I could hear the sound of water running, the clattering of plates. I knew she was doing it deliberately, forcing me to eavesdrop on the small homely drama being played out for my benefit.

I whistled into the mouthpiece. I said "HELLO!" about six times, to no avail. I knew if I hung up, all I'd get was a busy signal when I tried calling back. *Clump, clump, clump.* I heard advancing footsteps on the hardwood floor. I yelled "HEY!" *Clump, clump, clump.* The footsteps receded. Another round of chopsticks was played. Shrieks from the girls. Chitchat between husband and wife. Camilla's seductive laughter as she teased Jonah about something. Once more I cursed myself for never learning how to do the piercing whistle you make when you put two fingers between your teeth. I'd pay six hundred dollars if someone could teach me that. Think of the taxis you could summon, the waiters you could signal across a crowded room. *Clump, clump, clump.* Someone approached the phone, and I heard Jonah remark with annoyance, "Hey, who left this off? I'm expecting a call."

I yelled "JONAH!" but not quickly enough to prevent his replacing the handset in the cradle. I redialed the number, but the line was busy. Camilla'd probably picked up another phone in haste, just to make certain I couldn't get through. I waited a minute and tried again. Still busy. On my fourth attempt, I heard the phone ring, only to have Camilla pick up again. This time she didn't even bother to say hello. I heard her breathe in my ear.

I said, "Camilla, if you don't put Jonah on the phone, I'm going to get in my car and drive over there right this minute."

She sang out, "Jonah? For you."

Four seconds later he said, "Hello?"

"Hi, Jonah. It's Kinsey. I just got home and picked up your message. What's going on?"

"Listen, you're going to love this. Bobbi Deems pulled your biker over last night when she saw he had a taillight out. Kid's name is Carlin Duffy, and it turns out he's driving with an expired Kentucky driver's license and expired registration. Bobbi cited him for both and impounded the bike."

"Where in Kentucky?"

"Louisville, she said. You want him, he'll be in court in thirty days."

"What about before then? Does he have a local address?"

"More or less. He claims he's living in a maintenance shed at that nursery off the 101 at the Peterson exit. Apparently, he works there part-time in exchange for rent, a claim the owner confirms. Meanwhile, Bobbi ran a background check on this crud, who's got a criminal history as long as your arm: arrests and convictions going back to 1980."

"For what?"

"Mostly nickel-and-dime stuff. He never killed anyone."

"I'm so relieved," I said.

"Let's see what we got here: wanton endangerment, criminal recklessness, theft, receiving stolen property, criminal mischief, trying to flee a halfway house where he was serving a ninety-day sentence for giving a false name to a police officer. The guy's not too bright, but he's consistent."

"Any outstanding warrants?"

"Nada. For the moment, he's clean."

"Too bad. It'd have been nice to have him picked up so I could talk to him."

"You'll definitely want to do that. Here's the best part. You ready? You want to know who his brother is? You'll never guess."

"I give up."

"Benny Quintero."

I could feel myself squint. "You're kidding me."

"It's true."

"How'd you figure that one out?"

"I didn't. Bobbi did. Apparently, Benny's name was listed as the owner on the bike registration, so Bobbi put

Duffy through his paces. She'd forgotten the story, but she remembered Benny's name. Duffy claims they're half brothers. His mom was originally married to Benny's dad, who died in World War Two. Ten years later, she moved to Kentucky, where she married Duffy's dad. He was born the next year, fifteen-year age gap between the two boys. Carlin was thirteen when Benny came out to California and got himself killed."

"Is that why he's here?"

"You'd have to ask him. I'm thinking it's a good bet, unless you happen to believe in coincidence."

"I don't."

"Nor do I."

"So where is he now?"

"Well, he can't be far off if he's hoofing it."

"He could have stolen a car."

"Always possible, I guess, though outside his area of expertise. Anyway, if you decide to go looking for him, take someone along. I don't like the idea of your seeing him alone."

"You want to go?"

"Sure, I'd love it. Wait a second." He put a hand across the mouthpiece. Camilla must have been hovering nearby, listening to every word, because she squelched the idea before he even had the chance to ask. He removed his hand from the mouthpiece, addressing me again. "I'm tied up tonight, but how's Monday. Does that work?"

"Sounds ducky."

"You'll call me?"

"Of course."

"I'll see you then," he said.

As soon as he clicked off, I grabbed my handbag and walked out the door. I wasn't going to wait until Monday. How ridiculous. Duffy could be long gone; I couldn't take the risk. I stopped for gas on the way out. The nursery was maybe ten minutes away, but the needle on my gas gauge was now pointing at E, and I wasn't sure how much driving I'd have to do catching up with him.

It was twenty of nine when I finally pulled into the parking lot at the nursery. The sign out front indicated the place was open until 9 P.M. on weekends. The property must have occupied some ten to fifteen acres, the land sandwiched between the highway on one side and the side street into which I'd turned. The gardening center was immediately in front of me, a low white glass-and-frame building that accommodated numerous bedding, landscape, and house plants, seeds, gardening books, bulbs, herbs, pottery, and gifts, for "that special someone with a talent for growing."

To the right, behind the chain-link enclosure, I could see an array of fountains and statuary for sale, ceramic, plastic, and redwood planters, along with big plastic bags of fertilizers, mulches, garden chemicals, and soil amendments. To the left, I could see a series of greenhouses, like opaque glass barracks, and, beyond them, row after row of trees, a shaggy forest of shadows stretching back toward the freeway.

Now that the sun was fully down, the lingering light had shifted to a charred black, permeated by the smell of sod. The area along the side street was well lighted, but the far reaches of the nursery were shrouded in darkness. I scrounged around in the backseat and found a medium-weight denim jacket that I hoped would offer warmth against the chill night air. I locked the car and went into the gardening center with its harsh fluorescent lights shining down on banks of seed packs and gaudy indoor blooms.

The girl at the counter wore a forest-green smock with the name *Himes* embroidered across the pocket. As I closed the door, she gave the air a surreptitious fanning. She was in her teens, with dry blond hair and heavy pancake makeup over bumpy cheeks and chin. The air smelled of a recently extinguished clove cigarette.

"Hi. I'm looking for Carlin. Is he here?"

"Who?"

"Carlin Duffy, the guy with the bike who's living in the shed."

"Oh, Duffy. He's not here. The cops took his bike and locked it in the impound lot. He said it's going to cost a bundle to get it out."

"Bummer."

"He was really pissed. What a bunch of pigs."

"The worst. You two are friends?"

She shrugged. "My mom doesn't like him. He's a bum, she says, but I don't see why it's his fault if he's new in town."

"How long's he been here?"

"Maybe five or six months. He came like right before Christmas, sometime right around in there. Mr. Himes caught this other guy, Marcel? Do you know him?"

"Uh-uh."

"Marcel stole a bunch of these plants and sold 'em on the street? Mr. Himes fired his sorry butt as soon as he found out."

"And Duffy got his job shortly afterward?"

"Well, yeah. Mr. Himes had no idea Marcel was cheating him until Duffy bought a dieffenbachia off him and brought it in," she said. "I mean, Duffy's smart. He figured it's a scam right off. He only paid Marcel I guess a buck or two and there's our tag . . . like for $12.99 . . . pasted on the side."

"What about Marcel? I bet he swore up and down he didn't do it, right?"

"Right. What a dork. He acted all crushed and upset,

like he's completely innocent. Oh, sure. He said he'd sue, but I don't see how he could."

"His word against Duffy's, and who's going to believe *him*. Is Marcel black, perchance?"

She nodded. "You know how they are," she said, rolling her eyes. For the first time, she assessed me. "How do you know Duffy?"

"Through his brother, Ben."

"Duffy has a brother? Well, that's weird," she said. "He told me his family's dead and gone."

"His brother's been dead for years."

"Oh. Too bad."

"What time will he be back?"

"Probably not until ten."

"Well, shoot," I said.

"Did he say he'd meet you here?"

"Nah. I saw him at the Tonk last night and then lost track of him."

"He's probably there tonight," she said helpfully. "You want to use the phone? You could have him paged. He's pals with the owner. I think his name is Tim."

"Really? I know Tim," I said. "Maybe I'll pop over there, since it isn't far. Meantime, if he comes in? Tell him I was here. I'd like to speak to him."

"About what?"

"About *what*?" I repeated.

"In case he asks," she said.

"It's sort of a surprise."

20

I CRUISED THROUGH the parking lot across from the Honky-Tonk and miraculously found a space about six slots down. It was not quite nine, and the Saturday-night boozers were just beginning to roll in. The Tonk wouldn't start jumping until ten o'clock when the band arrived. I crossed the street, pausing while a red-and-white panel truck idled near the garbage bins. No sign of the driver, but the logo on the side read PLAS-STOCK. I could see that second-floor lights were on in the building. Shifting shadows suggested someone moving around up there.

I continued on across the street, approaching the bar from the rear. Idly, I tried the back door, but it was locked. I guess it would be hard to insist on a cover charge out front if wily patrons could go around the back and get in for free. I moved to the front entrance. The bouncer remembered me from the night before so he waved off my ID and stamped the back of my hand. This was the third night in a row I'd checked into the place, and I was feeling like a regular. During the period when

Mickey and I were married, we were here four nights out of seven, which didn't seem odd at the time. He hung out with other cops, and that's what they did after work in those days. I was with Mickey so I did what he did as a matter of course. The Honky-Tonk was family, providing a social context for those of us without any other close ties. Looking back, I realize what an enormous waste of time it was, but maybe that was our way of avoiding each other, bypassing the real work of marriage, which is intimacy. I'm still lousy at being close, having so little practice in the past umpteen years.

I found a stool at the bar and ordered a beer. I sat with my back to the mirrored wall of glittering liquor bottles, one elbow on the bar, a foot swinging in time to whatever anonymous music played. I spotted Thea at just about the same time she spotted me. She held my gaze for a moment, her features drawn and tense. Gone was the leather vest that had exposed her long bare arms. In its place she wore a white turtleneck and tight jeans. Her belt was silver, the buckle shaped like a lock with a heart-shaped keyhole in the center. Preoccupied, she took an order from a table of four and then crossed to the bar, where she chatted with Charlie briefly before she moved toward me.

"Hello, Thea," I said. Close up, I realized she was pissed as hell. "Are you mad about something?"

"You can bet your sweet ass. Why didn't you tell me about Mickey? You *knew* he'd been shot and you never said a word."

"How'd you hear?"

"Scottie's father told us. You talked to me at least twice so you could have *mentioned* it."

"Thea, I wasn't going to walk in here cold and make that announcement. I didn't even know you were friends until you asked about his jacket. By then, I figured there was something more going on."

She shot an uneasy glance at a table near the poolroom door where Scottie was sitting, facing two men who had their backs to us. He'd apparently been watching us across the room. As if on cue, he excused himself to his companions and got out of his chair, then ambled in our direction with a beer bottle in his hand. I couldn't help but notice the change in his appearance. His mustache was neatly trimmed, and he'd shaved his goatee. He was also better dressed—nothing fancy, but attractive—cowboy boots, jeans, and a blue denim work shirt with the sleeves buttoned at the wrist. I thought he'd cut his hair, but as he drew near I could see he'd simply pulled it back and secured it in a rubber band.

Thea murmured, "Please don't say anything. He'd kill me if he knew."

"What time are you off? Can we meet and talk then?"

"Where?"

"What about that twenty-four-hour coffee shop over by the freeway?"

"Two A.M., but I can't promise—"

By then, Scottie'd reached us and we abandoned the exchange. His smile was pleasant, his tone mild. "Hi. How are you? I understand you're a friend of my dad's. I'm Scott Shackelford." He held out his right hand and we shook. I saw no indication that he was stoned or drunk.

"Nice meeting you," I said. "Tim told me who you were, but I didn't have the chance to introduce myself."

He put his left arm around Thea's neck in a companionable half nelson, holding the beer bottle just in front of her. The gesture was both casual and possessive. "I see you know Thea. How're you doin', babe," he said. He kissed her affectionately on the cheek.

Thea's eyes were on me as she murmured something noncommittal. She was clearly not all that crazy about the choke hold.

He turned back to me, his tone now tinged with concern. "We heard about Mickey. That's a hell of a thing. How's he doing?"

"He's fair. I called down there this afternoon, and the nurse said he's the same."

Scott shook his head. "I feel bad for the guy. I didn't know him well, but he used to come in here—what? Every couple of weeks?"

"About that," Thea said, woodenly.

"Anyway, it's been months."

"I heard he sold his car, so maybe he couldn't drive up as often," I said. I was trying think up a graceful excuse to extract myself. I'd only come here to find Duffy, and he was nowhere to be seen.

Scottie went on. "By the way, Tim said if you came in, he wants to talk to you."

"About what?"

"Beats me."

"Where is he?"

He looked around the room lazily, his mouth pulling down. "I'm not sure. I saw him a little while ago. Probably in his office if he's not out here somewhere."

"I'll try to catch him later. Right now—"

"Say, you know what? That's my dad and his friend at the table over there. Why don't you stop by and say hi?" He was pointing toward the two men he'd been sitting with.

I looked at my watch. "Oh, gee. I wish I had time, but I have to meet someone."

"Don't be like that. He'd like to buy you a drink. If anyone asks, Thea or Charlie can tell 'em where you're at, right, Thea?"

"I have to get back to work," she said. She eased out from under his arm and returned to the bar, where her order was waiting. She took the tray and moved off without looking back at us.

Scottie followed her with his eyes. "What's bugging her?"

"I have no idea. Look, I was just on my way to the ladies' room. I'll join you in a minute, but I really can't stay long."

"See you shortly," he said.

Scottie moved off toward the table. In retrospect, I decided he'd probably cleaned up his appearance in deference to his father. Pete Shackelford had always been a stickler about personal tidiness. I cut left toward the rest rooms. As soon as I was out of his line of sight, I headed down the corridor toward the rear exit. I had no intention of having a drink with Shack. He knew way too much about me and, as nearly as I could tell, he was already prepared to rat me out.

As I passed the short corridor where Tim's office was located, I stopped in my tracks. There was now a tarp flung across boxes stacked against the wall. Curious, I had a quick peek: ten sealed cartons with the Plas-Stock logo stamped on the sides. Clearly, this was a shipment unloaded from the panel truck currently idling outside. I dropped the corner into place. All four doors off that corridor were closed, but I could see a thin slit of light coming from under the third door on the left. That door was locked last I checked, and I couldn't help but wonder if it was locked again. I glanced around casually. I was alone in the hall and it wouldn't take but two seconds to see if it was secure. I eased to the left and placed my hand on the knob, taking care not to rattle it as I turned it in my hand. Ah. Unlocked. I wondered what was in there that required such security.

I pushed the door back, stuck my head in the opening. The floor area was only large enough to accommodate a set of stairs leading up and a padlocked door on the left, possibly a closet. I could see a dim light shining from the top of the narrow stairway. I stepped inside, closed the corridor door quietly behind me, and began to climb. It wasn't my intention to be sneaky, but I noticed I was walking on the outer edges of the treads, where there was less likelihood of creaking.

At the top of the stairs there was a landing about six feet square with a ladder affixed to one wall, probably leading to the roof. The only door off the landing was ajar, light flooding out from the space beyond. I pushed the door back. The room was huge, stretching off into the shadows, easily extending the length and breadth of the four large rooms below. The floor was linoleum, trampled in places where sooty footprints had permanently altered the color. I could see numerous electrical outlets along the walls and five or six large clean patches. The space was dense with the kind of dry heat that suggests poor insulation. The walls were unfinished plywood. There was a plain wooden table, two dozen folding chairs, a big garbage can jammed with scraps. I'd imagined cases of wine and beer stacked along the walls, but there was nothing. What had I pictured? Drugs, illegal aliens, child pornography, prostitution? At the very least, broken and outdated restaurant equipment, the old jukebox, the remains of New Year's Eve and St. Paddy's decorations from celebrations long past. This was boring.

I cruised the room, taking care to stay on the balls of my shoes. I didn't want anyone downstairs wondering who was clumping around up here. Still nothing of interest. I left the lights as I'd found them and crept back down the stairs. Again, I placed my hand carefully around the doorknob and turned it in silence. The hallway appeared empty. I exited the door, using my palm to blunt the click of its closing.

"Can I help you?"

Tim was standing in the shadows to the left of the door. I shrieked. I flung up my hands and my shoulder bag flew out of my grasp, contents tumbling out as it hit the floor. *"Shit!"*

Tim laughed. "Sorry. I thought you saw me. What were you doing?" He was casually dressed: jeans and a V-neck knit pullover.

"Nothing. I opened that door by mistake," I said. I dropped to my knees, trying to gather up items that seemed to be strewn everywhere. "Scottie said you wanted to see me. I was looking for your office. This door was unlocked. I tried the knob and it was open so I just went on in. I figured you might be upstairs, so I called out a big *yoo-hoo.*"

"Really. I didn't hear you."

He hunkered, setting my handbag upright. He began to toss the contents back in, while I watched in fascination. Fortunately, I wasn't carrying a gun and he didn't seem to register the presence of my key picks. He was saying, "I don't know how you women do this. Look at all this stuff. What's this?"

"Travel toothbrush. I'm a bit of a fanatic."

He smiled. "And this?" He held up a plastic case.

"Tampons."

As he picked up my wallet, it flipped open to my driver's license, which he glanced at idly. The photostat of my P.I. license was in the window opposite, but if he noticed he gave no indication. He tossed the wallet into the handbag. Shack had probably already blown my cover anyway.

"Here, let me do that," I said, happy to be in motion

lest he see my hands were shaking. Once we'd retrieved everything, I rose to my feet. "Thanks."

"You want to see what's up there? Here, come on. I'll show you."

"No, really. That's fine. I actually peeked at the space a few minutes ago. I was hoping you still had the old jukebox."

"Unfortunately, no. I sold that shortly after we bought the place. Great space up there, isn't it? We're thinking about expanding. We were using it for storage until it occurred to me there were better uses for that much square footage. Now all I have to do is get past fire department regulations—among other things."

"You'd do what, add tables?"

"Second bar and a dance floor. First, we have to argue with the city of Colgate and the county planning commission. Anyway, that's not what I wanted to talk to you about. You want to step into my office? We don't have to stand around out here talking in the dark."

"This is fine. I told Scottie I'd stop by his table and have a drink with his dad."

"We heard about Mickey."

"Word travels fast."

"Not as fast as you'd think. Shack tells us you were a cop once upon a time . . ."

"So what?"

Tim went right on. "We're assuming you're conducting an investigation of your own."

Thank you, Pete Fucking Shackelford, I thought. I tried to think how to frame my reply.

Meanwhile, Tim was saying, "We have a pal in L.A. who might be of help."

"Really. And who's that?"

"Musician named Wary Beason. Mickey's neighbor in Culver City."

Pointerlike, I could feel my ears prick up. "How do you know him?"

"Through his jazz combo. He's played here a couple times. He's very talented."

"Small world."

"Not really. Mickey told him we booked bands, so Wary got in touch and auditioned. We liked his sound."

"I'm surprised Wary didn't call you and tell you about the shooting."

"Yeah, we were too. We've been trying to reach him, but so far no luck. We thought you'd want to talk to him if you went to L.A."

"Maybe I'll do that. Mind if I ask you about a couple of things while I have you?"

"Sure. No problem."

"What's Plas-Stock?"

Tim smiled. "Plastic cutlery, plates, glassware, that kind of thing. We're doing a big buffet for the Memorial Day weekend. We'll comp you to it if you're interested. Anything else?"

"Did you ever pay Mickey the ten grand you owed him?"

His smile lost its luster. "How'd you hear about that?"

"I came across a reference to it in his papers. According to the note, payment was due in full on January fifteenth."

"That's right, but things were tight right about then so he gave me an extension. I pay him off in July."

"If he lives," I said. "Is that what he was doing when he came up here, negotiating the agreement?"

"Mickey's a drinker."

"I'm puzzled why he'd give you an extension when he's having financial problems of his own."

Tim seemed surprised. "Mickey has money problems? That's news to me. Last time I saw him, he didn't act like a guy with worries. You think the shooting had something to do with business?"

"I'm really not sure. I was curious why he was spending so much time up here."

Tim crossed his arms, leaning against the wall. "Don't quote me on this, especially not to Scottie, but if you want my opinion Mickey was hot to get in Thea's pants."

"What about her? Was she interested in him?"

"Let's put it this way: Not if she's smart. Scottie's not the kind of guy you mess with." I saw him lift his eyes to someone in the passage behind me. "You looking for me?"

"Charlie needs your approval on an invoice. The guy wants a check before he heads back to L.A."

"Be right there."

I glanced back. One of the other waitresses had already turned on her heel and disappeared.

Tim patted my arm. "I better take care of this. Whatever you want, it's on the house."

"Thanks."

I followed two steps behind Tim, entering the bar with another quick visual search for Duffy. Still no sign of him. Shack, at Scottie's table, caught sight of me and waved. I guessed there wasn't going to be a way to get out of this. Shack must have enjoyed the opportunity to burn me. Scottie turned to see who his dad was waving at, and then he motioned me over. I felt like a mule, stubbornly resisting even while I was being propelled in that direction.

Shack was sitting on the far side of the table, and he rose to his feet, saying, "Well, would you look who's here? We were just talking about you."

"I don't doubt that a bit."

"Sit down, sit down. Grab a seat."

The other fellow at the table rose and sank in his seat

respectfully, the physical equivalent of a gent tipping his hat to a lady.

I said, "I really can't stay long."

"Sure you can," Shack said. He reached over and grabbed a chair from a nearby table, pulling it up next to him. I sat down, resigned. Shack's gaze rested on his son, his satisfaction and pride giving a lift to his normally heavy features. He was wearing a plaid wool shirt, unbuttoned to accommodate his thick neck. His companion appeared to be in his fifties, gray hair cut close, weathered complexion suggesting years of sun exposure. Like Shack, he was heavyset, bulky through the shoulders, his belly protruding as if he were six months pregnant.

Shack hooked a thumb at him and said, "This is Del. Kinsey Millhone."

"Hello."

Del nodded and then half rose again and shook my hand across the table. "Del Amburgey. Nice to meet you," he said.

We went through that "how're-you-tonight" shit while I squirmed inwardly, trying to think of something bland to say. "Are you here for a visit, or are you local?"

"I live up in Lompoc, so it's a little bit of both. I come down here now and then to see what you big-city folks are up to."

"Not much."

Shack said, "Well, that's not entirely true. This little gal was a cop back when I was in uniform. Now she's a P.I. . . ."

"What's a P.I.?" Del asked.

"A private investigator," Shack said.

I thought I was going deaf. He talked on. I watched his mouth move, but the sound was gone. I didn't look at Scott, but I was acutely aware that he was taking in the information with something close to alarm. His expression didn't seem to change, but his face shut down. Out of the corner of my eye, I could see his hands resting on the table, still relaxed, his fingers loose on the beer bottle, which he tilted to his lips. Aside from the casualness of the gesture, his body was completely still. I tuned in to Shack's commentary, wondering if there were any way to contain the damage he was doing.

". . . just about the time Magruder left the department. What was that, '71?"

"The spring of '72," I said. He knew exactly when it was. We locked eyes briefly, and I could tell blowing my cover allowed him to enjoy a moment of revenge. Whatever I was up to, he would leave me fully exposed. Better take control, I thought, get a jump on the little shit. "That was when Mickey and I split up. I lost touch with him after that."

"Until recently," Shack amended.

I looked at Shack without comment.

He went blithely on. "I guess those two LAPD detectives drove up here and talked to you. They came around my place yesterday. They seemed to think you might've had a hand in it, but I told 'em I didn't see how. You showed up at my door Monday. I didn't think you'd call attention to yourself if you'd shot him the week before. You're not that dumb."

"That was a ruse and you fell for it," I said. I was smiling, but my tone of voice was snide.

"What brings you out to Colgate?"

"Mickey lent Tim ten grand. A no-interest loan with a five-year balloon. I was curious if the money was repaid when it came due." Scottie began to tap one foot, which caused his knee to jump. He crossed his legs, trying to cover his agitation.

"When was that?" Shack asked, still enough of a cop to pursue the obvious.

"January fifteenth. Just about the time Mickey started coming in," I said. "You didn't know about the loan?"

"You ready for a drink? I'm heading to the bar," Scottie said. He was on his feet, his eyes pinned on me.

"Nothing for me, thanks."

"What about you, Dad? Del?"

"I'll go another round. My turn to buy," he said. He leaned forward, hauling his wallet from his right rear pocket.

Scottie waved him off. "I'll take care of it. What's your pleasure? Another of the same?"

"That'd be great."

"Make that two," Shack said.

Once Scottie left, Shack changed the subject, engaging me in chitchat so banal I thought I'd scream. I endured about three minutes of his asinine conversation and then took advantage of Scott's absence to slide out of my seat.

"You leaving us?" Shack said.

"I have to meet someone. It's been nice seeing you."

"Don't rush off," he said.

I made no reply. Del and I exchanged nods. I shouldered my bag and turned, scanning the crowd as I made my escape. Still no sign of Duffy, which was just as well. I didn't want Tim or Scottie to see me talking to him.

21

THE OUTSIDE AIR was chilly. It was not even ten o'clock, and the main street of Colgate was streaming with traffic, car stereos thumping. The occupants seemed to number four and five to a car, windows rolled down, everyone looking for action of some undisclosed kind. I could hear a chorus of honks, and coming up on my right I saw a long pink stretch limo bearing a bride and groom. They were standing on the backseat, their upper torsos extending through the sliding moon-roof window. With one hand, the bride clung to her veil, which whipped out behind her like a trail of smoke. With her other hand, she held her bouquet aloft, her arm straight up in a posture that mimicked the Statue of Liberty. The groom appeared to be smaller, maybe eighteen years old, in a lavender tuxedo with a white ruffled shirt, purple bow tie, and cummerbund. His hair was cut close, his ears red-tipped with cold. Numerous cars tagged along behind the limo, all honking, most decorated with paper flowers, streamers, and clattering tin cans. Their destination seemed to be the Mexican restaurant down the block from the Tonk. Other drivers and pedestrians were honking and hooting happily in response to this moving pageant.

I found my car and got in, pulling into the line of traffic behind the last of the procession. Of necessity I drove slowly, forced to a crawl as car after car turned left into the restaurant parking lot, waiting for breaks in the traffic. Glancing over to my right, I spotted Carlin Duffy walking with his head down, his hands in his jacket pockets. I'd only seen the man twice, but his height and his yellow hair were unmistakable. Had he been at the Tonk and I'd missed seeing him? He appeared to be heading toward the nursery, a distance of perhaps a mile and a half. Like a gift, the man turned, extending his right hand, his thumb uppermost.

I pulled over, leaning across the seat to unlock the passenger door. He already seemed puzzled that anyone, let alone a woman, would give him a ride at that hour. I said, "I can take you as far as the 101 at Peterson. Will that do?"

"That'd be good."

Spurs jingling, he slid into the passenger seat and slammed the door. He looked back over his shoulder with a snort of derision. "You see them beaners? What a bunch of Pacos. Groom looks like he's thirteen. Probably knocked her up. He shoulda kept his pecker in his pocket."

"Nice talk," I said.

He looked at me with interest. At close range, his features seemed too pinched for good looks: narrow-set light eyes and a long thin nose. He had one goofy incisor that seemed to stick straight out. The rest of his teeth were a snaggle of overlapping edges, some rimmed with gold. The yellow in his hair was the result of peroxide, the roots already turning dark. He smelled funky, like wood smoke and dirty gym socks. He said, "I seen you before."

"Probably at the Honky-Tonk. I was just there."

"Me too. Took a bunch of money off some niggers playin' pool. What's your name?"

"I'm Kinsey. And you're Carlin Duffy. I've been looking for you."

He flashed a look in my direction and then stared out the windshield, his face shutting down. "Why's that?"

"You know Mickey Magruder."

He seemed to assess me and then looked out the side window, his tone dropping into a range somewhere between sullen and defensive. "I didn't have nothing to do with that business in L.A."

"I know. I thought we'd figure out what happened, just the two of us. Your friends call you Carlin?"

"It's Duffy. I'm not a fruit," he said. He looked at me slyly. "You're a lady cop, ain't you?"

"I used to be. Now I'm a private eye, working for myself."

"What d'you want with me?"

"I'd like to hear about Mickey. How'd the two of you connect?"

"Why should I tell you?"

"Why shouldn't you?"

"I don't know nothin'."

"Maybe you know more than you think."

He considered that, and I could almost see him shift gears. Duffy was the sort who didn't give anything away without getting something in return. "You married?"

"Divorced."

"Tell you what. Let's pick us up a six-pack and go back to your place. We can talk all you want."

"If you're on parole, an alcohol violation's the last thing you need."

Duffy looked at me askance. "Who's on parole? I done my bit and I'm free as a bird."

"Then let's go to your place. I have a roommate and I'm not allowed to bring in guests at this hour."

"I don't have a place."

"Sure you do. You're living in the maintenance shed at Bernie Himes's nursery."

He kicked at the floorboard, running an agitated hand through his hair. "Goddang! Now, how'd you know that?"

I tapped my temple. "I also know you're Benny Quintero's brother. Want to talk about him?"

I had by then passed the entrance to the nursery, heading across the freeway toward the mountains.

"Where you goin'?"

"To the liquor store," I said. I pulled into a convenience mart in a former gas station. I took a twenty from my shoulder bag and said, "It's my treat. Get anything you want."

He looked at the bill and then took it, getting out of the car with barely suppressed agitation. I watched him through the window as he went into the place and began to cruise down the aisles. There was nothing I could do if he cruised right out the side door and took off on foot. He probably decided there wasn't much point. All I had to do was drive over to the nursery and wait for him there.

The clerk at the counter kept a careful eye on Duffy, waiting for him to shoplift or maybe pull a gun and demand the contents of the cash drawer. Duffy removed two six-packs of bottled beer from the glass-fronted cooler on the rear wall and then paused on one aisle long enough to pick up a large bag of chips and a couple of other items. Once at the counter, he paid with my twenty and tucked the change in his pants pocket.

When he got back in the car, his mood seemed improved. "You ever try licorice and beer? I got us some Good and Plentys and a whole bunch of other shit."

"I can hardly wait," I said. "By the way, what's the accent, Kentucky?"

"Yes, ma'am."

"I'll bet it's Louisville, right?"

"How'd you know?"

"I have an instinct for these things."

"I guess so."

Having established my wizardry, I drove back over the freeway, turned right onto the side street, and pulled into the lot for the nursery. I parked in front of the gardening center, which was closed at this hour and bathed in a cold fluorescent glow. I locked my car, hefted my bag to my shoulder, and followed Carlin Duffy as he made his way down the mulch-covered path. This was like walking into a deep and well-organized woods, wide avenues cutting through crated and evenly spaced trees of every conceivable kind. Most were unrecognizable in the dark, but some of the shapes were distinctive. I could identify palms and willows, junipers, live oaks, and pines. Most of the other trees I didn't know by name, rows of shaggy silhouettes that rustled in the wind.

Duffy seemed indifferent to his surroundings. He trudged from one darkened lane to the next, shoulders hunched against the night air, me tagging along about ten steps behind. He paused when we reached the shed and fumbled in his pocket for his keys. The exterior was board-and-batten, painted dark green. The roofline was flat, with only one window in view. He snapped open the padlock and stepped inside. I waited until he'd turned on a light and then followed him in. The shed was approximately sixty feet by eighty, divided into four small rooms used to house the two forklifts, a mini-tractor, and a crane that must have been pulled into service for the planting of young trees. Anything more substantial would have required larger equipment, probably rented for the occasion.

The interior walls were uninsulated, the floor dirt and cinder crunching under our feet. One of the rooms had been hung with tarps and army surplus blankets, draped from the ceiling to form a tentlike substructure. Inside, I could see a canvas-and-wood cot with a rolled-up sleeping bag stashed at one end. We moved into the shelter, where illumination was provided by a bare hanging 60-watt bulb. There was also a space heater, a two-burner hot plate, and a mini-refrigerator about the size of a twelve-pack of beer. Duffy's clothes were hung on a series of nails pounded into the side wall: jeans, a bomber jacket, a wool shirt, black leather pants, a black leather vest, and two sweatshirts. Being fastidious by nature, I had to ponder the absence of visible clean underwear and a means of bathing and brushing his teeth. This might not be the sort of fellow one would want to have a lengthy chat with in a small unventilated space.

I said, "Cozy."

"It'll do. You can sit on the cot and I'll take this here."

"Thanks."

He placed the brown paper bag on an orange crate and removed the six-packs. He liberated two bottles and put the balance in his mini-refrigerator, leaving several on top. He reached in his pocket, took out a bottle opener, and flipped the caps from two beers. He set his bottle aside long enough to open the bag of chips and a can of bean dip, which he held out to me. I grabbed a handful of chips and put them in my lap, holding on to the can so I could help myself to dip.

"You want a paper plate for that?"

"This is fine," I said.

Having cleared the orange crate, he used it as a stool on which he perched. He opened his box of candy-coated licorice and tossed two in his mouth, sipping beer through his teeth with a little moan of delight. Before long, his teeth and his tongue were going to be blacker than soot. He leaned over and turned on the small electric space heater. Almost immediately, the coils glowed red and the metal began to tick. The narrow band of superheated air made the rest of the room seem that much colder by contrast. I confess, there was something appealing about this room within a room. It reminded me of "houses" I made as a kid, using blankets draped over tabletops and chairs.

"How'd you find me?" he asked.

"That was easy. You got pulled over and cited for a defective taillight. When they ran your name through the system, there you were in all your glory. You've spent a lot of time in jail."

"Well, now, see? That's such bullshit. Okay, so maybe sometimes I do something bad, but it's nothing *terrible.*"

"You never killed anyone."

"That's right. I never robbed nobody. Never used a gun . . . except the once. I never done drugs, I never messed with women didn't want to mess with me, and I never laid a hand on any kids. Plus I never done a single day of federal time. It's all city and county, mostly ninety-day horseshit. Criminal recklessness. What the fuck does that mean?"

"I don't know, Duffy. You tell me."

"Accidental discharge of a firearm," he said contemptuously. The crime was apparently so bogus, I was surprised he'd mention it. "It's New Year's Eve . . . this is a couple years now. I'm in this motel in E-town, having me a fine old time. I'm horsin' around, just like everyone else. I pop off a round, and the next thing you know, bullet goes through the ceiling and hits this lady in the ass. Why's that my fault?"

"How could it be?" I echoed, with equal indignance.

"Besides, jail's not so bad. Clean, warm. You got your volleyball, indoor tawlits, and your color television set. Food stinks, but medical care don't cost you a cent. I don't know what to do with myself half the time anyway. This pressure builds up and I blow. Jail's kind of like a time-out till I get my head on straight."

I said, "How old are you?"

"Twenty-seven. Why?"

"You're getting kind of old to be sent to your room."

"Probably so, I guess. I intend to straighten up my act, now I'm out here. Meantime, it's fun breakin' rules. Makes you feel free."

"I can relate to that," I said. "You ever hold a real job?"

He seemed mildly insulted that I'd question his employment history. "I'm a heavy equipment operator. Went to school down in Tennessee and got certified. Scaffolds, cranes, forklifts, dozers, you name it. Graders, backhoes, hydraulic shovels, boom lifts, anything Caterpillar or John Deere ever made. Ought to see me. I set up there in the cab and go to town." He spent a moment shifting gears with his mouth, using his beer bottle as a lever while he operated an imaginary loader.

"Tell me about your brother."

He set the empty bottle at his feet, leaning forward, elbows on his knees, his face animated. "Benny was the best. He looked after me better than my dad and momma. We done everything together, except when he went off to war. I was only six years old then. I remember when he come home. He'd been in the hospital and then rehab, on account of his head. After that, Momma said, he changed. She said he's moody and temperamental, kind of slow off the mark. Didn't matter to me; 1971, he bought the Triumph: three-cylinder engine, twin-style clutch. Wasn't new at the time, but it was hot. Nobody hardly fooled with Harley-Davidsons back then. None of them Jap bikes, neither. It was all BSA and Triumph." He motioned for me to hand him the chips and the can of bean dip.

"What brought him to California?"

"I don't know for sure. I think it had to do with his benefits, something about the VA fuckin' with his paperwork."

"But why not in Kentucky? They have VA offices."

Duffy cocked his head, crunching on potato chips while he wiped his lips with the back of his hand. "He knew someone out here he said could cut through the red tape. Hey, I got us some nuts. Reach me that bag."

I pushed the brown bag in his direction. He pulled out a can of peanuts and pulled the ring. He poured some into his palm and some into mine. I said, "Someone in the VA?"

"He never said who it was, or, if he did, I don't remember. I'se just a kid back then."

"How long was Benny here before he died?"

"Maybe a couple weeks. My momma flew out, brought his body back for burial, and had his bike shipped home. I still go to see him every chance I get. They got this whole section of Cave Hill Cemetery just for veterans."

"How much was she told about the circumstances of his death?"

"Some cop punched him out. They scuffled at the Honky-Tonk and Benny wound up dead."

"That must have been hard."

"You got that right. That's when I started havin' problems with the law," he said. "I did Juvie till I was finally old enough to be tried as an adult."

"When did you get out here?"

"Five–six months back. My dad died September. He had emphysema, smokin' three packs a day. Even at the end, he'd risk blowing hisself up, puffing on butts while he's hooked up to oxygen. Momma died a month later. I guess her heart give out on her while she was out rakin' leaves. I'd been over to the Shelby County jail on a DUI. Now that was bullshit for sure. I blew—what, point oh two over the limit? BFD is what I say. Anyway, once I finished out my time, I hitched my way home and here's the whole house is mine, plus furniture, motorcycle, and a bunch of other junk. Took me a long time to get the bike fixed up."

"Must have felt strange."

"Yeah, it did. I wandered around the place doing anything I felt like, though it wasn't any fun. I got lonesome. You spend time in jail, you get used to havin' other people near."

"And then what?"

"Well, Momma always kept Benny's room just like it was. Clothes on the floor, bed messed up the way he left it the day he come out here. I went through the place, just a cleanin' and sortin' and throwin' stuff out. Partly I was curious and partly I just needed me a little somethin' to do. I come across Benny's lockbox."

"What kind of lockbox?"

"Gray metal, about so-by-so." With his hands, he indicated a box maybe twelve inches by six. "It was under his bed, tucked up in the box springs."

"You still have it?"

"Naw. Mr. Magruder took it, so he probably hid it someplace."

"What was in the box?"

"Let's see. This press pass, belonged to a fellow named

Duncan Oaks. Also, Oaks's dog tags and this black-and-white snapshot of Benny and some guy we figured had to be Oaks."

Duncan Oaks again. I wondered if Mickey'd put the items in a safe deposit box. Mentally, I made a note. Next time I was down there, I'd have to try again if I could pick my way in. So far, I hadn't come across a safe deposit key, but maybe another search would yield results. "Tell me about your relationship with Mickey."

"Mr. Magruder's a good dude. I like him. He's a tough old bird. Once he knocked me on my ass so bad I won't never forget. Popped me smack in the jaw. I still got a tooth loose on account of it." He wiggled an incisor to demonstrate his point.

"Why'd you come out to California, to track him down?"

"Yes, ma'am."

"How'd you find him? He moved to Culver City fourteen years back. He's cagey about his phone number and his home address."

"Hell, don't I know? I got that from Tim, guy owns the Tonk. I tried the bar first because that's where the fight between him and my brother took place. I figured someone might remember him and tell me where he was."

"What was your intention?"

"To kill his ass, what else? I heard he's the one who punched Benny's lights out. After we talked, I begun to see things his way."

"Which was what?"

"He figured he was framed, and I'd agree with him."

"How so?"

"He had him an alibi. He was bonin' this married lady and didn't want to pull her into it, so he kept his mouth shut. I talked to this cop said he saw the whole thing.

Mostly, insults and pushing. The two never even struck a blow. I guess somebody come along later and beat the crap out of Benny. What kilt him was havin' that metal plate in his head. Blood seeped into his brain, and it swelled up like a sponge."

"Do you remember the cop's name?"

"Mr. Shackelford. I seen him at the Honky-Tonk earlier tonight."

"What about the snapshot in the box?"

"Two guys out in the boonies, gotta be Veetnam. Sojers in the background. Benny's wearin' fatigues and his big old army helmet he's decorated with this peace symbol. You know the one. Looks kind of like a wishbone with a thing stickin' out the end. Benny's got this shit-eatin' grin and he's flung his arm around the other fellow, who's bare to the waist. Other fellow has a cigarette hangin' off his lip. Looks like the dog tags he's wearin' are the same as the ones in the box."

"What's he look like?"

"You know, young, unshaved, with these big old dark brows and a black mustache: dirty-looking, like a grunt. Hardly any chest hair. Kind of pussyfied in that regard."

"Any names or dates on the back of the photograph?"

"No, but it's Benny clear as day. Had to be 1965, between August tenth when he shipped out and November seventeenth, which is when he got hit. Benny was at Ia Drang with the two/seven when a sniper got him in the head. He shoulda been medevacked out, but the choppers couldn't land because of all the ground fire. By time he got out, he said the dead and wounded was piled on each other like sticks of firewood."

"What was Mickey's theory?"

"He didn't tell me nothin'. Said he'd look into it is all I heard."

"Where's the lockbox now? I'd like to see the contents."

"Said he had a place. I learnt not to mess with him. He's the one in charge."

"Let's go back to Duncan Oaks. How does he fit in?"

"Beats me. I figure he's someone in Benny's unit."

"That's what Mickey was looking into. I know he placed a call to a high school in Louisville—"

"Manual, I bet. Benny went to Manual, played football and everything."

"Not Manual," I said. "It was Louisville Male High. He talked to the school librarian about Duncan Oaks. The next day, he hopped on a plane and flew east. Did you talk to him later, after he got back?"

"Never had a chance. I called a couple times. He never picked up his phone so I finally went down. I's madder than shit. I figured he's shining me on."

"You didn't know he'd been shot?"

"Uh-uh. Not then. Some guy down there told me. Fellow lived next door. I forget his name now, something queer."

"Wary Beason?"

"That's him. I busted out his winda, which is how we got acquainted." Duffy had the good grace to look sheepish about the window. He still didn't seem to realize I'd been on the premises that night.

I found myself staring at the dirt floor, trying to figure out what the hell was going on. How did the fragments connect? Tim Littenberg and Scott Shackelford were both in Vietnam, but the timing was off. Benny Quintero was there early in the war and then only briefly. Tim and Scottie went later, in the early seventies. Then there was Eric Hightower, whose second tour was cut short when he stepped on a mine and had his legs blown off. Again, that was long after Benny'd been shipped home. And why was any of it relevant to Mickey's being shot? I knew Mickey well enough to know he was on to *something*, but what?

"You with me or gone?"

I looked up to find Duffy staring at me with concern. I set aside my beer. "I think I'll butt out for now. I need time to absorb this. At the moment, I don't have a clue how any of it fits . . . or if it does," I said. "I may talk to you later when I've had a chance to think. You'll be around?"

"Here or the Tonk. You want me to walk you out?"

I said, "Please. It's dark as pitch out there."

22

I LET MYSELF into my apartment at eleven-fifteen, surprised to realize my entire conversation with Duffy had only taken an hour. I set up a pot of coffee and flipped the switch, letting it brew while I stretched some of the kinks out of my neck. I felt a faint headache perched between my eyes like a frown. I was longing for bed, but there was work to do yet. While the information was fresh, I opened my desk drawer and pulled out a new pack of lined index cards. Then I retrieved, from their hiding place, the various items I'd snitched from Mickey's.

I sat in my swivel chair, jotting down everything I could remember from the evening. Activities at the Honky-Tonk were turning out to be less sinister than I'd imagined. Maybe, as Tim had said, Mickey simply went there to drink and hustle Thea. I had to admit philandering would have been in character for him.

When the coffee was done, I got up from my chair and poured myself a mug, adding milk that seemed only mildly sour. I returned to my desk, where I remained on my feet, idly pushing at the index cards. There were still countless minor matters that didn't fit the frame: Mickey's being shot with my gun, the long hissing message on my answering machine. That had originated from his apartment the afternoon of March 27. Who'd called me and why? If Mickey, why not leave a message? Why let the tape simply run to the end? If it wasn't Mickey, then what was the purpose? To imply contact between us? It had certainly made me look bad in the eyes of the police.

I sat down at my desk and began to play with the cards. I had to assume Mickey was on the track of Benny Quintero's killer. That question would nag at him as long as he lived. Benny's death had never been officially ruled a homicide, but Mickey knew he'd been blamed, despite the fact that charges had never been filed. In light of his checkered history with the department, his involvement in the matter had called his credibility into question and further damaged his already tainted reputation. As he saw it, his only choice was to abandon the profession he'd loved. His life after that had never amounted to much: booze, women, a shabby apartment. He couldn't even hold on to the sorry job he'd found: Pacific Coast Security with its faux-cop uniform and dime-store badge. He must have dreamed of escape, creating a way out with his caches of money and his phony IDs. I turned over a few cards, making a column, sorting facts in no particular order.

Idly, I set two index cards on edge, using the weight of each to support the other. I added a third, leaving the right side of my brain in neutral while I constructed a maze. Building card houses was another way I'd amused myself as a kid. The first floor was easy, requiring patience and dexterity but not much else. To add a second story to the first, you had to append a flat layer of cards, deftly floating a "ceiling" on the substructure until the whole of it was covered. Then began the real work: starting again from square one. First balance two cards atop the structure below, using the pair for their mutual support. Then add a third at an angle to the first two. Then add a fourth, then a fifth. At any point in the process, as the overall dimensions increased, there was always the danger that the whole of it would collapse, tumbling in on itself like—well, a house of cards. Sometimes, perversely, I'd even done this myself, snapping a corner with my finger, watching as the cards deconstructed in slow motion like a demolition project.

I glanced at the card in my hand, reading the note on it before I added it to the pile. Carefully, I added another card to the maze. I paused to remove it, reading the datum again. I experienced a jolt of insight and felt myself blink. I'd seen a connection, two index cards suddenly appearing in conjunction. What a dummy I was that I hadn't seen it before! A name showed up twice and I could feel my perception shift. It was like the sharp dislocation of a temblor, coming out of nowhere, fading away soon after. What I spotted was the name Del Amburgey, the man to whom Shack had introduced me at the Tonk. Delbert Amburgey was also the name on one of Mickey's packets of fake IDs: California driver's license, credit cards, social security card.

I set the index cards aside, pulling out the documents with Mickey's face laminated on top of what were probably Delbert's vital statistics. I swiveled in my swivel chair and studied the effect. Did these documents belong to Delbert or had his identity been lifted? Was the date of birth real or bogus, borrowed or invented, and how had it been done? I knew credit card scammers often got into "Dumpster diving," coming up with charge slips or carbons, even credit card statements discarded once the monthly bills had been paid. The information on the statements could be used to generate additional credit. The scammer would apply for cards based on lines of credit previously established by the individual in question. Any number of new accounts might be opened in this way. With a name, address, and social security number, ATM cards could be obtained, along with blank checks or proceeds from insurance policies. The scammer would supply the credit company with a substitute address, so the owner of the card remained unaware that goods and services were being charged to his or her legitimate account. The cards could also be milked through a series of cash withdrawals. Once the credit limit was exceeded, the scammer could either make the minimum payment or move on, fencing items or selling them at a discount and pocketing the profits. Actually, counterfeit documents like those in Mickey's possession were worth money on the open market, where felons, illegal aliens, and the chronically bankrupt could buy a brand-new start in life with thousands of dollars of fresh credit at their disposal.

I went back to Mickey's financial statements. I studied his savings passbook, beginning to understand the regular withdrawals of six hundred dollars on dates that corresponded with his trips to the Tonk. I thought about Tim and the conversation we'd had about the second floor, where he was claiming he might add tables. In retrospect, I marveled at how carefully I'd been duped. He'd offered me the bait—the unlocked door—and the subsequent glimpse of what had appeared to be undeveloped floor space. I'd seen the bouncer scan the driver's licenses of those granted admission to the bar. Since the bar retained a copy of each credit card transaction, the numbers would have been easy enough to match to the driver's license data. I couldn't guess at the whole of it, but there were people who'd know.

I looked at my watch again. It was 1:55. I said, "Oh, shit." I'd told Thea I'd meet her as soon as she got off work at two. I leapt up, shoved all the cards in my desk drawer and locked it, put Mickey's phony IDs back in their hiding place. I grabbed my jacket and car keys. Within minutes, I was on 101, driving north again toward Colgate, restraining the temptation to put the gas pedal to the floor. Traffic was light, the freeway virtually deserted, but I knew this was the hour when the CHP would be out. I didn't need a traffic stop or a speeding ticket. I found myself talking out loud, encouraging the VW's performance, praying Thea would wait for me at the coffee shop until I arrived. The restaurant shared a parking lot with the bowling alley next door. Every slot was filled and I groaned as I circled, looking for a place. Finally, I left my car in a moderately legal spot. I cut the lights and the engine as I opened the car door and emerged. It was 2:13. I locked the car and then did a run/walk to the restaurant, pausing for breath as I hauled the door open and started looking for her.

Thea sat at a back booth, smoking a cigarette. The harsh fluorescent lighting washed all the lines from her face, leaving her expression as blank as Kabuki makeup.

I slid into the seat across the table from her. "Thanks for waiting," I said. "I was caught up in paperwork and lost track of the time."

"Doesn't matter," she said. "My life's rapidly turning to shit anyway. What's one more thing?"

She seemed curiously withdrawn. My guess was she'd had too much time to reconsider. At the Honky-Tonk earlier, I could have sworn she'd confide. People with problems are generally relieved at the chance to unburden themselves. Catch them at the right moment and they'll tell you anything you ask. I was kicking myself I hadn't had the opportunity to take her aside then.

I said, "Look, I know you're pissed off because I didn't own up to who I was—"

"Among other things," she said acidly. "I mean, give me a break. You're a private detective, plus you're Mickey's ex-*wife*?"

"But Thea, get serious. If I'd said that up front, would I have learned anything?"

"Probably not," she conceded. "But you didn't have to lie."

"Of course I did. That was the only means I had of getting at the truth."

"What's wrong with being straight? Or is that beyond you?"

"Me, straight! What about you? You're the one screwing Mickey behind Scott's back."

"You were screwing him too!"

"Nope. Sorry. Wasn't me."

She looked at me blankly. "But you said—"

"Uh-uh. You might have leapt to that conclusion, but I never said as much."

"You didn't?"

I shook my head.

She started blinking, nonplussed. "Then whose diaphragm was it?"

"Good question. I just got the answer to that myself. It looks like dear Mickey was screwing someone else."

"Who?"

"I think I'd better keep mum, at this point."

"I don't believe you."

"Which part? You know he was seeing someone. You saw the evidence yourself. Of course, if you weren't systematically betraying Scottie, you wouldn't have to worry about these things."

Her gaze hung on mine.

I said, "You don't have to look quite so glum. He did the same thing to me. That's just how he is."

"It's not that. I just realized I didn't mind so much when I thought it was you. At least you'd been married to him, so it didn't feel so bad. Is he in love with this other woman?"

"If he is, it didn't stop him from picking up on you."

"Actually, *I* pursued *him*."

"Oh, boy. I hate to say this, but are you nuts? The man's a barfly. He's unemployed, and he's older by—what, fifteen years?"

"He seemed . . . I don't know . . . sexy and protective. He's mature. Scottie's temperamental, and he's *so* self-involved. With Mickey, I felt safe. He loves women."

"Oh, sure. That's why he betrays us every chance he gets. He loves each one of us better than the last, often at the same time but never for long. That's how mature *he* is."

"You think he's going to be okay? I've been worried to death, but I can't get the hospital to say a word."

"I hope so, but really I have no idea."

"But you're hooked in, aren't you?"

"I guess. What feels strange is I'd put him out of my mind. Honest, I hadn't thought of him in years. Now that he's down, he seems to be everywhere."

"I feel the same. I keep looking for him. The door at the Tonk opens and I think he'll walk in."

"Why'd he keep coming back? Was it you or was something else going on?"

"Don't ask. I can't help you. I mean, I care about Mickey, but not enough to put my life on the line."

"Isn't it possible Scottie knows?"

"About Mickey and me?"

"That's what we're discussing," I said patiently.

"What makes you say that?"

"How do you know it wasn't Scott who shot Mickey?"

"He wouldn't do that. Anyway, his dad told us Mickey was gunned down two blocks from his apartment. Scottie doesn't even know where Mickey lives."

"Well, that's weak. I mean, think about it, Thea. Where was Scottie a week ago last Wednesday?"

"How should I know?"

"Was he with you?"

"I don't think so," she said. She stared at the table, going over it in her mind. "Tuesday, I was off. I wasn't feeling good."

"Did you talk to Scott on the phone?"

"No. I called and he was gone, so I left a message and he called me back the next day."

"In other words, he wasn't with you that Tuesday night or early Wednesday morning. We're talking May fourteenth."

Thea shook her head.

"What about the next day? Did you see him then?"

She stubbed out her cigarette. "I don't remember every single *day*."

"Start with what you do remember. When did you see Scottie last?"

Grudgingly, she said, "Monday. He and Tim had a meeting on Sunday. He drove up for the night and then left for L.A. the next day. I didn't see him again until the weekend. That was Saturday a week ago. He drove up here yesterday and goes back to L.A. tomorrow."

"What about you? Were you with Mickey at all on the night he was shot?"

She hesitated. "I went down to his apartment, but he was gone."

"Couldn't Scottie have followed you? He could have hung out in town. Once you got in your car, all he had to do was tail you to Mickey's."

She stared at me. "He wouldn't have done that. I know you don't like him, but that doesn't make him bad."

"Really. You told me he'd kill you if he ever found out."

"When I said he'd kill me it was . . . what do you call it—"

"Figurative."

"Figurative," she repeated. "Scottie wouldn't actually *shoot* anyone."

"Maybe his motive was something more serious."

"Like what?"

"A scam."

Thea's face underwent a shift. "I don't want to talk about this."

"Then let's change the subject. The first time I came in, Thursday of this week, Tim was pissed off at you. What was that about?"

"That's none of your business."

"Are Tim and Scottie partners?"

"You'd have to ask them."

"What kind of business?"

"I don't have a comment."

"Why? Are you involved in it too?"

"I gotta go," she said abruptly. I watched as she gathered up her jacket and her purse. She studiously avoided looking at me as she slid out of the booth.

It was 2:45 when I finally crawled into bed. I woke at 6 A.M. from long habit, nearly rolling out for my jog until I remembered it was Sunday. I lay for a moment, looking up at the skylight. The sun must have been close to rising because the sky was growing lighter as though a dimmer were being turned up. I felt oddly hung over for someone who'd drunk so little. It had to be the smoky bar, the conversation with Duffy, and tension between me and Thea, not to mention the late-night theorizing and driving around at all hours. I got up and brushed my teeth, took two aspirin with a big glass of water, and then returned to bed. In less than a minute, I was sleeping again. My bladder woke me at 10. I did an inner body survey, checking for symptoms of headache, nausea, and weariness. Nothing seemed to be amiss and I decided I could face life, but only with the promise of a nap later on.

I went through my usual morning routine: showered, donned my sweats, and made a pot of coffee. I read most of the Sunday paper, then wrapped myself in a quilt and settled on the couch with my book. Turned out to be nap time at 1 P.M. and I slept until 5. I climbed up the spiral stairs and checked myself in the bathroom mirror. My hair, as I suspected, was mashed flat on one side and sticking up in clumps on the other like dried palm fronds. I stuck my head under running water and emerged moments later with a more refined arrangement. I stripped off my sweats and pulled on a turtleneck and jeans, gym socks, my Sauconys, and Mickey's jacket. I picked up my shoulder bag, locked the door behind me, and crossed the patio to Henry's, where I tapped on his back door. There was no immediate response, but I realized the bathroom window was open a few inches, and I could hear sounds of a shower. Steam wafted out scented with soap and shampoo. I knocked on the window a familiar rat-a-tat-tat.

From inside, Henry yelled, "Yo!"

"Hey, Henry. It's me. I'm on my way to Rosie's for supper. Want to come?"

"I'll be there in a jiffy. Soon as I'm done in here."

I walked the half block to Rosie's, arriving at five-thirty, just as she was opening for business. We exchanged pleasantries, which in her case consisted of abrasive comments about my weight, my hair, and my marital status. I suppose Rosie's a mother figure, but only if you favor the sort that appear in Grimms' fairy tales. It was her avowed intention to fatten me up, get me a decent haircut, and a spouse. She knows perfectly well I've never met with success in that department, but she says *eventually* (meaning when I'm old and dotty, demented, and infirm) I'll need someone to look after me. I suggested a visiting nurse, but she didn't think that was funny. Then again, why should she? I was serious.

I sat down in my usual booth with a glass of puckery white wine. It's hellish to learn the difference between good wine and bad. Henry wandered in soon after, and we let Rosie browbeat us into a Sunday night supper that consisted of *savanyu marhahus* (hot pickled beef to you, pal) and *kirantott karfiol tejfolos martassal*, which is deep-fried cauliflower smothered in sour cream. While we mopped up our plates with some of Henry's homemade bread, I filled him in on the events of the past few days. I must say, the situation didn't seem any clearer when I'd laid it out to him.

"If Mickey and Mrs. Hightower are having an affair, her husband had as much reason to shoot him as Thea's boyfriend," he pointed out.

"Maybe so," I replied, "but I got the impression Eric had made his peace with her. I keep thinking there's more, something I haven't thought of yet."

"Can I do anything to help?"

"Not that I know, but thanks." I glanced up as the door opened and the waiter from the Hightowers' party came in with a hardback book under one arm. He wore a tweed sport coat over a black turtleneck, dark trousers, and loafers polished to a fare-thee-well. Having seen him in his white jacket serving drinks the night before, it took a moment to come up with his name.

I turned to Henry as I rose. "Can you excuse me for a minute? There's someone I need to talk to."

"Not a problem. I've been itching to finish this," he said. He brought out a neatly folded copy of the Sunday *New York Times* crossword puzzle and a ballpoint pen. I could see he was half done, completing the answers in a spiral pattern, starting at the edges and working toward the center. Sometimes he wrote in the answers leaving out every other letter because he liked the way it looked.

Stewart was passing the booth when he caught sight of me. "Well, hello. How are you? I wondered if you'd be here."

"Can I talk to you?"

"Be my guest," he said, gesturing toward the booth where he traditionally sat. I gave Henry's arm a squeeze, which he barely noticed, given his level of concentration. Stewart waited till I was seated and then sat down across from me, the book on the seat beside him.

"What's the book?" I asked.

He picked it up, holding the spine toward me so I could read the title, *The Conjure-Man Dies* by Rudolph Fisher. "I usually read biography, but I thought I'd try something new. Detective novel written in the early thirties. Black protagonist."

"Is it good?"

"Haven't decided yet. I'm just getting into it. It's interesting."

Rosie appeared. She stood by the table, her eyes fixed on the far wall, avoiding the sight of us. I noticed she was wearing slippers with her bright blue cotton muumuu.

Stewart reached for the menu and said, "Good evening, Rosie. How're you doing? Any specials I should hear about?"

"You tell him is good, the pickled beef," she said. Rosie can speak in perfect order the English when it suits her purposes. Tonight, for some reason, she was behaving like someone recently admitted to this country on a temporary visa. She seldom addresses men directly unless she's flirting with them. A similar inhibition applies to strangers and women, children, the hired help, and people who pop in and ask directions of her. She might answer your question, but she won't look.

I said, "The pickled beef is great. Fabulous. And the deep-fried cauliflower is not to be believed."

"I think I'll have that," Stewart said, setting aside the menu.

"What to drink?" she asked.

"Try the white wine. It's piquant. The perfect complement to pickled beef," I said.

"Sounds good. I'll try it."

Rosie nodded and departed while Stewart shook his head. "I wish I had the nerve to order something else. That Hungarian stuff is for the birds. I come here because it's quiet, especially on Sundays. I go home with indigestion keeps me up half the night. Now what can I do for you?"

"I need to ask you about the Hightowers."

"What about them?" he asked, with a caution that didn't bode well for me.

I took a deep breath. "Here's the deal," I said. "My ex-husband was shot in Los Angeles. This was in the early morning hours, May fourteenth. He's currently in a coma, with no clear indication he'll pull out of it. For various reasons too complicated to go into, I'm trying to figure out what happened. Obviously, the cops are too." I was watching his eyes: intelligent, attentive, giving nothing away. I went on. "Both the Hightowers know Mickey, and I'm trying to determine if there's a link."

"What's your question for me? Because some things I'll tell you and some I won't."

"I understand. Fair enough. What's your job?"

"My job?"

"Yeah, what do you actually do for them?"

"Chauffeur, handyman. I wait table sometimes."

"How long have you been there?"

"It'll be two years in June. Same as Clifton. He tends bar at parties like the one they had last night. Otherwise, he manages the house and handles general maintenance. All the major repairs are hired out, but it seems like there's always something broken or in need of adjustment."

"What about Stephanie? Does she work for both of them or just Dixie?"

"She's Mrs. H's personal assistant. She comes in Mondays and Thursdays, noon to five or five-thirty. Mr. H takes care of his business on his own. Phone calls and letters, personal appointments. He keeps it all up here," he said, tapping his head.

"I take it there's a cook, as well?"

"Cook and cleaning crew. There's two women do the laundry and another one does flowers. Plus the gardeners, the pool guy. I wash the cars and Mr. H's van. Clifton and the cook—her name's Ima—both live on the property. The rest of us live out and come in as needed."

"Which is when?"

"It varies. I'm usually not there during the week. Fridays and Saturdays I'm always on call, especially if the two of them are going out. Other times Mr. H prefers to drive himself. Mrs. H likes the car. They have a six-passenger limo she enjoys."

"Did you drive either one of them to Los Angeles last week?"

"I didn't, but that doesn't mean they didn't go down on their own."

"You know Mickey Magruder? Good-looking guy, in his fifties, an ex-cop?"

"Doesn't sound familiar. What's his connection?"

"We go way back, the four of us. More than fifteen years. Mickey and Dixie were having an affair back then. I have reason to believe they've rekindled the flame. I'm wondering if Eric knew."

Stewart thought briefly; then he shook his head. "I don't carry tales."

"I can appreciate that. Is there *anything* you can tell me?"

"I think you'd do better asking one of them," he said.

"What about the marriage? Do they get along okay?"

Again, Stewart paused, and I could see the conflict between his knowledge and his reticence. "Not of late," he said.

23

THAT WAS AS much as I was able to get from him. I must say I admired his loyalty, though it was frustrating. The evening wasn't completely unproductive. Henry's point was well taken. If jealousy was the motive for the shooting, the number of suspects had just increased. Eric Hightower was in the mix and Thea was another candidate, though not a particularly strong one. She'd risked a lot for Mickey, and while she professed her care and concern, that might have been laid on for my benefit. Dixie was another possibility. What would she have done if she'd discovered Mickey's affair with Thea?

The problem was, it all seemed so melodramatic. These people were grown-ups. I found it hard to picture any of them lurking in the shadows, plugging away at Mickey with my gun. It's not like you don't read about such things in the daily paper, but the scenario left too many things unexplained. For instance, who was Duncan Oaks? How was he related to events? Was Mickey on the trail of the person or persons responsible for Benny's fatal beating?

We left Rosie's at eight, Henry and I, walking home in

the dark without saying much. Once back in my apartment, I sat down at my desk yet again and reviewed my notes. Within minutes, I realized my heart wasn't in it. I made a pile of cards and shuffled, dealing myself a tarot reading of the data I'd collected. No insights emerged, and I finally packed it in. Maybe tomorrow I'd be smarter. There was always the outside chance.

Six A.M. Monday morning, I rolled out of bed, pulled on sweats, brushed my teeth, and went for a three-mile jog. The predawn light was gorgeous: the ocean luminous blue, the sky above it orange, fading to a thin layer of yellow, then a clear blue sky beyond. Along the horizon, the oil rigs sparkled like an irregular line of diamond scatter pins. The absence of cloud cover eliminated any special effects when the sun finally rose, but the day promised to be sunny and that was sufficient for me. When I finished the run, I headed over to the gym, where I variously stretched, curled, extended, crunched, hyperextended, pressed, pecked, pushed, shrugged, raised, pulled down, and pulled up weights. At the end of it, I felt keen.

I went home and showered, emerging from the apartment at nine in my jeans, ready to face the day. I drove my car north on 101, taking the off-ramp that put me in range of the county offices adjacent to the VA. I parked and went into the Architectural Archives, where I gave the Honky-Tonk's address and asked to see whatever drawings and blueprints they had on hand. I was given a set of progress prints showing the vicinity plan, site plan, demolition plan, foundation and framing plans, elevations, and electrical legend. It didn't take me long to find what I was looking for. I returned the prints and headed for the parking lot where I'd seen a pay phone.

I dialed directory assistance and asked for the number of the Secret Service in L.A., the offices of which were actually listed as part of the U.S. Treasury Department. In addition to the L.A. number, I was given a telephone number for the agency in Perdido. I charged the call to my credit card, punching in the Perdido number. The phone rang once.

"Secret Service," a woman said.

How secret could it be if she was willing to blurt it out that way?

I asked to speak to an agent and she put me on hold. I stared out across the parking lot, listening to the sibilant ebb and flow of traffic on the highway. The morning was clear, the temperature in the 50s. I imagined by afternoon that would warm to the usual 70s. The line was picked up moments later, and a flat-voiced gentleman introduced himself. "This is Wallace Burkhoff."

I said, "I wonder if you can help me. I'm calling because I suspect there's a credit-card scam being operated from a bar in Colgate."

"What kind of scam?"

"I'm not sure. A friend of mine—actually, my ex-husband—bought some phony documents from a fellow up here. I think the owner of the bar might be running a regular manufacturing plant." I told him about the Honky-Tonk: the scanning device for drivers' licenses and my guess about the matching of credit-card charge slips to names on licenses. On the surface, it sounded thin, but he listened politely as I talked on. "A couple of days ago I saw a truck on the premises. Ten cartons had been unloaded and stacked in the corridor. The boxes were marked Plas-Stock, which the owner told me was plastic glassware and cutlery."

"Not quite." Burkhoff laughed. "Plas-Stock specializes in commercial equipment for manufacturing plastic cards and blank card stock for medical ID cards and health club memberships."

"Really? My ex has three sets of fake IDs in his possession, including drivers' licenses, social security cards, and a fistful of credit cards. I'm reasonably certain some of the data came from a regular bar patron, because I was introduced to the guy, and the name and approximate date of birth are the same."

"What's his interest in acquiring phony IDs?"

"He's a former vice detective, and I think he picked up on the operation three or four months back. I mean, I can't swear this is true, but I have the receipts he kept from a series of visits to the place and I also have the phony documents with his picture plastered all over them."

"Would he be willing to talk to us?"

"He's currently out of commission." I told Agent Burkhoff about Mickey's condition.

"What about yourself?"

"Hey, I've already told you as much as I know. This is outside my area of expertise. I'm just making the call. You can do with it as you please."

"Where's their base of operation?"

"I think it's somewhere in the building. Yesterday, the owner set it up so I had a chance to see the second floor. It was empty, of course, but I did spot a number of electrical outlets. I don't know what kind of equipment would be in use—"

"I can tell you that," he said. "Optical scanners, encoding machines, shredders, embossers, tippers—that's what puts the gold on the newly embossed numbers—laminators, hologram punch devices. You see anything like that?"

"No, but I suspect they were operating in the space until a couple of days ago. I checked with the local architectural archives and took a look at the plans submitted when the owner applied for building permits. The structure's one of the few in town with a basement and my guess is they moved the operation down there."

"Give me the particulars and we'll check it out," he said.

I gave him the name and address of the Honky-Tonk and Tim's name and home address. I added Scottie's name to the mix, along with the dates Mickey'd been there and the names on the assortment of phony documents he had. "You need anything else?"

"Your name, address, and phone."

"I'd prefer not," I said. "But I'll make copies of the IDs and put those in the mail to you."

"We'd appreciate that."

I hung up, hauled out the telephone book, found my travel agent's number, and put a couple of coins in the slot. I told her I needed plane tickets for Louisville and gave her my budget limitations.

"*How* much?"

I said, "Five hundred dollars?"

She said, "You're joking."

I assured her I wasn't. She tapped the information into her computer. After much silence, many sighs, and some additional clicks, she told me the best she could do was an airline that had been in business for less than two years and was offering a no-frills flight to Louisville out of LAX with only two connections, Santa Fe and Tulsa. There was no advance seat assignment, no movie, and no meal service. She assured me the company hadn't filed for bankruptcy (yet) and hadn't reported any major flaming crashes to date. The point was I could get there for $577.

I had her book me on an early morning flight, leaving the return ticket open since I really had no idea how long my inquiry would take. Basically, I'd make it up as I went along. In addition to the plane fare, I reserved a rental car at the airport in Louisville. I'd find a motel when I got there, preferably something cheap. At the end of this, if nothing else, my debt of guilt with regard to Mickey would be paid in full. I went home, packed a duffel, and chatted briefly with Henry, letting him know I'd be gone for some indeterminate period. I also put a call through to Cordia Hatfield, telling her of my arrival later in the afternoon.

I stopped by the travel agent's and picked up my ticket, then drove over to the office, where I spent the balance of the morning getting life in order in case I didn't make it back. The drive to Culver City was uneventful, and I parked in the alley behind Mickey's building at 4:55. I left the duffel in the car, not wanting to seem presumptuous about staying overnight. Cordia had extended an invitation, but she hadn't seemed that thrilled.

I knocked on the Hatfields' door, wondering if they'd hear me over the blare of the TV set. I waited a moment and then knocked again. The sound was cut and Cordia opened the door.

I'd last seen the two sisters on Thursday, only four days before, but something in her manner seemed different. She stepped back, allowing me to enter. The apartment, as before, was uncomfortably warm, the temperature close to 80, windows fogged over with condensation. Steam curled from a pot simmering on the stove. The bubbling liquid was cloudy, and a collar of scum had collected on the surface. The air smelled of singed pork and something else, unfamiliar but faintly dunglike. The TV had been muted, but the picture remained: the late afternoon news with its steady diet of calamities. Belmira seemed transfixed. She sat at the kitchen table, tarot deck in hand, while under her chair, Dorothy chewed on a bony bundle of something crunchy and dead.

"Is this a bad time?" I asked.

"As good as any," Cordia said.

"Because I can come back later if it's more convenient."

"This is fine." She wore a long-sleeved cotton housedress in shades of mauve and gray with a smocklike apron over it, trailing almost to the floor. She turned to the stove, reaching for a slotted spoon that she used to adjust ingredients in the boiling water. Something floated to the surface: heart-shaped skull, short body, not a lot of meat on it. I could have sworn it was a squirrel.

"How have you two been?" I said, hoping for an answer that would clue me in.

"Good. We're fine. What can we do for you?"

Abrupt, to the point, not entirely friendly, I thought. "I'm on my way out of town, and I need to check Mickey's for something someone left with him."

Her tone was aggrieved. "Again? You were just up there last night. We saw lights on till close to midnight."

"At Mickey's? Not me. I was in Santa Teresa all weekend. I haven't been here since Thursday morning."

She looked at me.

"Cordia, I swear. If I'd wanted to get in, I'd have asked for the key. I wouldn't go in without permission."

"You did the first time."

"But that was before we met. You've been very helpful to me. I wouldn't do that behind your back."

"Suit yourself. I won't argue. I can't prove it."

"But why would I be here now if I'd already been in last night? That doesn't make sense."

She reached into her pocket and took out the key. "Return it when you're done and let's hope this is the last of it."

I took the key, aware that her manner was still stony and unyielding. I felt terrible.

Belmira said, "Oh, my dear!" She'd turned over four cards. The first was the Page of Swords, which I knew now was me. The remaining three cards were the Devil, the Moon, and Death. Well, that was cheering. Bel looked up at me, distressed.

Cordia moved quickly to the table and snatched up the cards. She crossed to the sink, opened the cabinet under it, and tossed the deck in the trash. "I asked you to quit reading. She doesn't believe in tarot. She told you that last week."

I said, "Cordia, really—"

"Go on up to the apartment and be done with it," she snapped.

Belmira's misery was palpable, but she didn't dare defy Cordia. Nor did I, for that matter. I tucked the key in my pocket and let myself out. Before the door closed behind me, I could hear Bel protesting her loss.

I unlocked Mickey's front door and let myself in. His drapes were still closed, blocking the light except for a narrow gap between panels where the late-afternoon sun cut like a laser, warming the interior. The air was dense with dust motes and carried the moldy scent of unoccupied space. I stood for a moment, taking in the scene. With no one to clean the place, many surfaces were still smudged with fingerprint powder. If someone had been in the apartment the night before, there were no obvious signs. I skipped the rubber gloves this time and did a quick walk-through. On the surface, it was just as I'd seen it last. I paused in the bedroom door. A small gauzy piece of cloth trailed out from under the bed. I got down on my hands and knees, lifted the bottom of the spread, and peeked under the bed. Someone had systemically removed the fabric covering the bottom of the box spring, and it lay on the carpet like a skin shed by a snake. I knelt by the bed and lifted one corner of the mattress. I could see a line where the fabric had been scored by something sharp. I lifted the bulk of the mattress, turning it over with the sheets still in place. The underside had been gutted, slit the entire length at ten-inch intervals. Stuffing boiled out, cotton tufts protruding where the thickness had been searched. There was something both sly and savage in the evisceration. I did what I could to restore the bed to a state of tidiness.

I checked the closet. Mickey's clothing had been slit in a similar fashion: seams and pockets slashed, linings ripped open, though the garments had been left hanging, apparently undisturbed. To the casual observer, nothing would appear amiss. The damage probably wouldn't have been discovered until Mickey returned or his belongings were moved to storage. I went back to the living room, noticing for the first time that the cushions on the couch appeared to be out of alignment. I turned them over and saw they'd been sliced open as well. Along the back of the couch, the fabric had been picked open at the seam. The damage would be apparent the first time the couch was moved, but, again, the vandalism wasn't evident on cursory inspection.

I checked both of the heavy upholstered chairs, getting down on the floor so I could squint at the underside. I lifted the chairs one at a time, tilting each forward to inspect the frames. On the bottom of the second chair, there was a rectangular cut in the padding. I removed the wedge of foam rubber. In the hole there was a gray metal box, six inches by twelve, like the one Duffy'd described. The lock had been badly damaged and yielded easily to pressure. Gingerly, I opened the lid. Empty. I sat back on my heels and said, "Mickey, you ass."

What a dumb hiding place! Given his ingenuity and paranoia, he could have done better than this. Of course, I'd searched the place twice and hadn't found the damn thing on either occasion, but *somebody* had. I was sick with disappointment, though there was clearly no remedy. I hadn't even heard about the lockbox until Saturday night. At the time, it hadn't occurred to me to drop everything and hit the road right then. Maybe if I had, I might have beat "somebody" to the punch.

Ah, well. It couldn't be helped. I'd simply have to do without. I could find a picture of Duncan Oaks in his high school yearbook, but I would have liked the dog tags and the press pass Duffy'd mentioned to me. There was something about an authentic document that served as a talisman, a totem object imbued with the power of the original owner. Probably superstition on my part, but I regretted the loss.

I returned the box to its niche, tilted the chair back into its upright position, and let myself out the front door, locking it behind me. I went down the steps and knocked on Cordia's door. She opened it a crack and I gave her the key. She took it without comment and closed the door again. Clearly, I wasn't being encouraged to spend the night with them.

I crept out to the alley, got in my car, and drove to the airport. I found a nearby motel, offering shuttle service every hour on the hour. I ate an unremarkable dinner in the nondescript restaurant attached to one end of the building. I was in bed by nine and slept until five-forty-five, when I rose, showered, threw on the same clothes, left my VW in the motel parking lot, and took the shuttle to LAX, where I caught my 7 A.M. plane. The minute the nonsmoking sign was turned off, all the passengers in the rear set their cigarettes on fire.

It was in the Tulsa airport, while I was waiting between planes, that I made a discovery that cheered me up no end. I had an hour to kill so I'd stretched out in a chair, my legs extended into the aisle in front of me. The position, while awkward, at least permitted a catnap, though later I'd probably require hundreds of dollars' worth of chiropractic adjustment. In the meantime, I was using Mickey's leather jacket as a pillow, trying to ease the strain on my neck. I turned over on my side, not easy to do while sitting upright. As I did so, I felt something lumpy against my face—metal zipper tab, button?—I didn't know what it was, except that it added an unacceptable level of discomfort. I sat up and checked the portion of the jacket that was under my cheek. There was nothing I could see, but by pinching the leather I could feel an object in the lining. I flattened the jacket on my lap, squinting at the seam where I could see an alteration in the stitching. I opened my shoulder bag and took out my nail scissors (the same ones I utilize for the occasional emergency haircut). I picked a few stitches loose and then used my fingers to widen the opening. Out slid Duncan Oaks's dog tags, the black-and-white snapshot, and the press card. Actually, the hiding place made perfect sense. Mickey'd probably worn this very jacket when he made the trip himself.

The dog tags bore Duncan Oaks's name and date of birth. Even all these years later, the chain was crusty with rust or blood. The snapshot was exactly as Duffy had described it. I set those items aside and studied the press card issued by the Department of Defense. The printing around the border said: LOSS OF THIS CARD MUST BE REPORTED AT ONCE. PROPERTY OF U.S. GOVERNMENT. Under the line that read *noncombatant's certificate of identity* was Duncan Oaks's name, and on the left was his picture. Dark-haired, unsmiling, he looked very young, which of course he was. The date of issue was 10 Sept. '65. Four years out of high school, he was no more than twenty-three years old. I studied his face. Somehow he seemed familiar, though I couldn't think why. I flipped the card over. On the back, he'd pasted a strip on which he'd written, *In case of emergency, please notify Porter Yount, managing editor, Louisville Tribune.*

24

My plane arrived in Louisville, Kentucky, at 5:20 P.M., at a gate so remote it appeared to be abandoned or under quarantine. I'd been in Louisville once before, about six months back, when a cross-country romp had ended in a cemetery, with my being the recipient of an undeserved crack on the head. In that case, as with this, I was out a substantial chunk of change, with little hope of recouping my financial losses.

As I passed through the terminal, I paused at a public phone booth and checked the local directory on the off chance I'd find Porter Yount listed. I figured the name was unusual and there couldn't be that many in the greater Louisville area. The high school librarian had told me the *Tribune* had been swallowed up by a syndicate some twenty years before. I imagined Yount old and retired, if he were alive at all. For once my luck held and I spotted the address and phone number of a Porter Yount, whom I assumed was the man I was looking for. According to the phone book, he lived in the 1500 block of Third Street. I made a note of the address and continued to the baggage claim level, where I forked over my credit card and picked up the keys to the rental car. The woman at Frugal gave me a sheet map and traced out my route: taking the Watterson Expressway east, then picking up I-65 North into the downtown area.

I found my car in the designated slot and took a moment to get my bearings. The parking lot was shiny with puddles from a recent shower. Given the low probability of rain any given day in California, I drank in the scent. Even the air felt different: balmy and humid with the late-afternoon temperatures in the low 70s. Despite Santa Teresa's proximity to the Pacific Ocean, the climate is desertlike. Here, a moist spring breeze touched at newly unfurled leaves, and I could see pink and white azaleas bordering the grass. I shrugged out of Mickey's jacket and locked it in the trunk along with my duffel.

I decided to leave the issue of a motel until after I'd talked to Yount. It was close to the dinner hour, and chances were good that I'd find him at home. Following instructions, I took one of the downtown off-ramps, cutting over to Third, where I took a right and crossed Broadway. I drove slowly along Third, scanning house numbers. I finally spotted my destination and pulled in at a bare stretch of curb a few doors away. The tree-lined street, with its three-story houses of dark red brick, must have been lovely in the early days of the century. Now, some of the structures were run-down, and encroaching businesses had begun to mar the nature of the area. The general population was doubtless abandoning the once-stately downtown for the featureless suburbs.

Yount's residence was two and a half stories of red brick faced with pale fieldstone. A wide porch ran along the front of the building. Three wide bay windows were stacked one to a floor. An air conditioner extended from an attic window. The street was lined with similar houses, built close to one another, yards and alleyways behind. In front, between the sidewalk and the street, a border of grass was planted with maples and oaks that must have been there for eighty to a hundred years.

I climbed three steps, proceeded along a short cracked walkway, and climbed an additional six steps to the glass door with its tiny foyer visible within. Yount's residence had apparently once been a single-family dwelling, now broken into five units, judging from the names posted on the mailboxes. Each apartment had a bell, connected to the intercom located near the entrance. I rang Yount's apartment, waiting two minutes before I rang again. When it became clear he wasn't answering, I tried a neighbor's bell instead. After a moment, the intercom crackled to life and an old woman clicked in, saying "Yes?"

I said, "I wonder if you can help me. I'm looking for Porter Yount."

"Speak up."

"Porter Yount in apartment three."

"What's the time?"

I glanced at my watch. "Six-fifteen."

"He'll be down yonder on the corner. The Buttercup Tavern."

"Thanks."

I returned to the sidewalk, where I peered up and down the street. Though I didn't see a sign, I spotted what looked like a corner tavern half a block down. I left my car where it was and walked the short distance through the mild spring air.

The Buttercup was dark, cloudy with cigarette smoke, and smelling of bourbon. The local news was being broadcast at low volume on a color TV set mounted in one corner of the room. The dark was further punctuated by neon signs in a series of advertisements for Rolling Rock, Fehr's, and Stroh's Beer. The tavern was paneled in highly varnished wood with red leather stools along the length of the bar. Most of the occupants at that hour seemed to be isolated individuals, all men, all smoking, separated from each other by as many empty stools as space allowed. Without exception, each turned to stare at me as I came in.

I paused just inside the door and said, "I'm looking for Porter Yount."

A fellow at the far end of the bar raised his hand.

Judging from the swiveling heads, my arrival was the most interesting event since the Ohio River flooded in 1937. When I reached Yount, I held my hand out, saying, "I'm Kinsey Millhone."

"Nice meeting you," he said.

We shook hands and I perched on the stool next to his. I said, "How are you?"

"Not bad. Thanks for asking." Porter Yount was heavyset, raspy-voiced, a man in his eighties. He was almost entirely bald, but his brows were still dark, an unruly tangle above eyes that were a startling green. At the moment, he was bleary-eyed with bourbon and his breath smelled like fruitcake. I could see the bartender drift in our direction. He paused in front of us.

Yount lit a fresh cigarette and glanced in my direction. He was having trouble with his focus. His mouth seemed to work, but his eyeballs were rolling like two green olives in an empty relish dish. "What'll you have?"

"How about a Fehr's?"

"You don't want Fehr's," he said. And to the bartender, "Lady wants a shot of Early Times with a water back."

"The beer's fine," I corrected.

The bartender reached into a cooler for the beer, which he opened and placed on the bar in front of me.

Yount said peevishly, "Give the lady a glass. Where's your manners?"

The bartender set a glass on the bar and Yount spoke to him again. "Who's cooking tonight?"

"Patsy. Want to see a menu?"

"Did I say that? This lady and I could use some privacy."

"Oh, sure." The bartender moved to the other end of the bar, accustomed to Yount's manner.

Yount shook his head with exasperation and his gaze slid in my direction. His head was round as a ball, sitting on the heft of his shoulders with scarcely any neck between. His shirt was a dark polyester, probably selected for stain concealment and ease of laundering. A pair of dark suspenders kept his pants hiked high above his waist. He wore dark socks and sandals, with an inch of shinbone showing. "Outfit okay? If I'd knowed you was coming, I'd've wore my Sunday best," he said, deliberately fracturing his grammar.

I had to laugh. "Sorry. I tend to look carefully at just about everything."

"You a journalist?"

I shook my head. "A private investigator. I'm trying to get a line on Duncan Oaks. You remember him?"

"Of course. You're the second detective to come in here asking after him this month."

"You talked to Mickey Magruder?"

"That's the one," he said.

"I thought as much."

"Why'd he send you? He didn't take me at my word?"

"We didn't talk. He was shot last week and he's been in a coma ever since."

"Sorry to hear that. I liked him. He's smart. First fella I met who could match me drink for drink."

"He's talented that way. At any rate, I'm doing what I can to follow up his investigation. It's tough, since I don't really know what he'd accomplished. I hope this won't turn out to be a waste of your time."

"Drinking's a waste of time, not talking to pretty ladies. What's the sudden interest in Oaks?"

"His name's cropped up in connection with another matter . . . something in California, which is where I'm from. I know he once worked for the *Tribune*. Your name was on his press pass, so I thought I'd talk to you."

"Fool's errand if I ever heard one. He's been dead twenty years."

"So I heard. I'm sorry for the repetition, but if you tell me what you told Mickey, maybe we can figure out if he's relevant."

Yount took a swallow of whiskey and tapped the ash off his cigarette. "He's a 'war correspondent'—pretty fancy title for a paper like the *Trib*. I don't think even the *Courier-Journal* had a correspondent back then. This was in the early sixties."

"Did you hire him yourself?"

"Oh, sure. He's a local boy, a blueblood, high society: good looks, ambition, an ego big as your head. More charisma than character." His elbow slid off the bar, and he caught himself with a jerk that we both ignored. Mentally, he seemed sharp. It was his body that tended to slip out of gear.

"Meaning what?"

"Not to speak ill of the dead, but I suspect he'd peaked out. You must know people like that yourself. High school's the glory days; after that, nothing much. It's not like he did poorly, but he never did as well. He's a fellow cut corners, never really earned his stripes, so to speak."

"Where'd he go to college?"

"He didn't. Duncan wasn't school-smart. He's a bright kid, made good grades, but he never cared much for academics. He had drive and aspirations. He figured he'd learn more in the real world so he nixed the idea."

"Was he right about that?"

"Hard to say. Kid loved to hustle. Talked me into paying him seventy-five dollars a week—which, frankly, we didn't have. Even in those days, his salary was a pittance, but he didn't care."

"Because he came from money?"

"That's right. Revel Oaks, his daddy, made a fortune in the sin trades, whiskey and tobacco. That and real estate speculation. Duncan grew up in an atmosphere of privilege. Hell, his daddy would've given him anything he wanted: travel, the best schools, place in the family business. Duncan had other fish to fry."

"For instance?"

He waved his cigarette in the air. "Like I said, he wangled his way into a job with the *Trib*, mostly on the basis of his daddy's influence."

"And what did he want?"

"Adventure, recognition. Duncan was addicted to living on the edge. Craved the limelight, craved risk. He wanted to go to Vietnam and report on the war. Nothing would do until he got his way."

"But why not enlist? If you're craving life on the edge, why not the infantry? That's about as close to the edge as you can get."

"Military wouldn't touch him. Had a heart murmur sounded like water pouring through a sluice. That's when he came to us. Wasn't any way the *Trib* could afford his ticket to Saigon. Didn't matter to him. He paid his own way. As long as he had access, he's happy as a clam. In those days, we're talking Neil Sheehan, David Halberstam, Mal Browne, Homer Bigart. Duncan pictured his byline in papers all across the country. He did a series of local interviews with newlyweds, army wives left behind when their husbands went off to war. The idea was to follow up, talk to the husbands, and see the fighting from their perspective."

"Not a bad idea."

"We thought it had promise, especially with so many of his classmates getting drafted. Any rate, he got his press credentials and his passport. He flew from Hong Kong to Saigon and from there to Pleiku. For a while, he was fine, hitching rides on military transports, any place they'd take him. To give him credit, I think he might have turned into a hell of a journalist. He had a way with words, but he lacked experience."

"How long was he there?"

"Couple months is all. He heard about some action in a place called Ia Drang. I guess he pulled strings—maybe his old man again or just his personal charm. It was a hell of a battle, some say the worst of the war. After that came LZ Albany: something like three hundred fellas killed in the space of four days. Must have found himself caught in the thick of it with no way out. We heard later he was hit, but we never got a sense of how serious it was."

"And then what?"

Yount paused to extinguish his cigarette. He missed the ashtray altogether and stubbed out the burning ember on the bar. "That's as much as I know. He's supposed to be medevacked out, but he never made it back. Chopper took off with a bellyful of body bags and a handful of casualties. Landed forty minutes later with no Duncan aboard. His daddy raised hell, got some high Pentagon official to launch an investigation, but it never came to much."

"And that's it?"

"I'm afraid so. You hungry? Ask me, it's time to eat."

"Fine with me," I said.

Porter gestured to the bartender, who ambled back in our direction. "Tell Patsy to put together couple of Hot Browns."

"Good enough," the man said. He set his towel aside, came out from behind the bar, and headed for a door I assumed led to Patsy in the kitchen.

Yount said, "Bet you never ate one."

"What's a Hot Brown?"

"Invented at the Brown Hotel. Wait and see. Now, where was I?"

"Trying to figure out the fate of Duncan Oaks," I said.

"He's dead."

"How do you know?"

"He's never been heard from since."

"Isn't it possible he panicked and took off on foot?"

"Absence of a body, anything's possible, I guess."

"But not likely?"

"I'd say not. The way we heard it later, the NVA were everywhere, scourin' the area for wounded, killing them for sport. Duncan had no training. He probably couldn't get a hundred yards on his own."

"I wonder if you'd look at something." I hauled up my bag from its place near my feet. I removed the snapshot, the press pass, and the dog tags embossed with Duncan's name.

Yount tucked his cigarette in the corner of his mouth, examining the items through a plume of smoke. "Same things Magruder showed me. How'd he come by them?"

"A guy named Benny Quintero had them. You know him?"

"Name doesn't sound familiar."

"That's him in the picture. I'm assuming this is Duncan."

"That's him. When's this taken?"

"Quintero's brother thinks Ia Drang. Benny was wounded November seventeenth."

"Same as Duncan," he said. "This'd have to be one of the last pictures of Duncan ever taken."

"I hadn't thought of that, but probably so."

Yount returned the snapshot, which I tucked in my bag.

"Benny's another Louisville boy. He died in Santa Teresa in 1972: probably a homicide, though there was never an arrest." I took a few minutes to detail the story of Benny's death. "Mickey didn't mention this?"

"Never said a word. How's Quintero tie in?"

"I can give you the superficial answer. His brother says he went to Manual; I'm guessing, at the same time Duncan went to Male. It seems curious he'd end up with Duncan's personal possessions."

Porter shook his head. "Wonder why he kept them?"

"Not a clue," I said. "They were in a lockbox in his room. His brother came across them maybe six months back. He brought them to California." I thought about it for a moment, and then I said, "What's Duncan doing with a set of dog tags if he was never in the service?"

"He had them made up himself. Appealed to his sense of theater. One more example of how he liked to operate: looking like a soldier was as good as being one. I'm surprised he didn't hang out in uniform, but I guess that'd be pushing it. Don't get me wrong. I liked Duncan, but he's a fella with shabby standards."

A woman, probably Patsy, appeared from the kitchen with a steaming ramekin in each of her oven-mitted hands. She put a dish in front of each of us and handed us two sets of flatware rolled in paper napkins. Yount murmured "thanks" and she said, "You're entirely welcome."

I stared at the dish, which looked like a lake of piping-hot yellow sludge, with a dusting of paprika and something lumpy underneath. "What *is* this?"

"Eat and find out."

I picked up my fork and tried a tiny bite. A Hot Brown turned out to be an open-faced sliced turkey sandwich, complete with bacon and tomatoes, baked with the most divine cheese sauce I ever set to my lips. I mewed like a kitten.

"Told you so," he said, with satisfaction.

When I was finished, I wiped my mouth and took a sip of beer. "What about Duncan's parents? Does he still have family in the area?"

Yount shook his head. "Revel died of a heart attack a few years back: 1974, if memory serves. His mother died three years later of a stroke."

"Siblings, cousins?"

"Not a one," he said. "Duncan was an only child, and his daddy was too. I doubt you'd find anyone left on his mother's side of the family either. Her people were from Pike County, over on the West Virginia border. Dirt poor. Once she married Revel, she cut all ties with them."

He glanced at his watch. It was close to 8 P.M. "Time for me get home. My program's coming on in two minutes."

"I appreciate your time. Can I buy your dinner?"

Yount gave me a look. "Obvious you haven't spent any time in the South. Lady doesn't buy dinner for a gent. That's his prerogative." He reached in his pocket, pulled out a wad of bills, and tossed several on the bar.

At his suggestion, I spent the night at the Leisure Inn on Broadway. I might have tried the Brown Hotel, but it looked way too fancy for the likes of me. The Leisure Inn was plain, a sensible establishment of Formica, nylon carpet, foam rubber pillows, and a layer of crackling plastic laid under the bottom sheet in case I wet the bed. I put a call through to the airline and discussed the options for my return. The first (and only) seat available was on a

3 P.M. flight the next day. I snagged it, wondering what I was going to do with myself until then. I considered a side visit to Louisville Male High, where Duncan had graduated with the class of 1961. Secretly, I doubted there was much to learn. Porter Yount had painted an unappealing portrait of the young Duncan Oaks. To me, he sounded shallow, spoiled, and manipulative. On the other hand, he was just a kid when he died: twenty-two, twenty-three years old at the outside. I suspect most of us are completely self-involved at that age. At twenty-two, I'd already been married and divorced. By twenty-three, I was not only married to Daniel but I'd left the police department and was totally adrift. I'd *thought* I was mature, but I was foolish and unenlightened. My judgment was faulty and my perception was flawed. So who was I to judge Duncan? He might have become a good man if he'd lived long enough. Thinking about it, I felt a curious secondhand sorrow for all the chances he'd missed, the lessons he never learned, the dreams he'd had to forfeit with his early death. Whoever he was and whatever he'd been, I could at least pay my respects.

At ten the next morning, I parked my rental car on a side street not far from Louisville Male High School, at the corner of Brook Street and Breckinridge. The building was three stories tall, constructed of dark red brick with white concrete trim. The surrounding neighborhood consisted of narrow red-brick houses with narrow walkways between. Many looked as if the interiors would smell peculiar. I went up the concrete stairs. Above the entrance, two gnomelike scholars were nestled in matching niches, reading plaques of some kind. The dates 1914 and 1915 were chiseled in stone, indicating, I supposed, the year the building had gone up. I pushed through the front door and went in.

The interior was defined by gray marble wainscoting, with gray-painted walls above. The foyer floor was speckled gray marble with inexplicable cracks here and there. In the auditorium, dead ahead, I could see descending banks of curved wooden seats and tiers of wooden flooring, faintly buckled with age. Classes must have been in session, because the corridors were empty and there was little traffic on the stairs. I went into the school office. The windows were tall. Long planks of fluorescent lighting hung from ceilings covered with acoustical tile. I asked for the school library and was directed to the third floor.

The school librarian, Mrs. Calloway, was a sturdy-looking soul in a calf-length denim skirt and a pair of indestructible walking shoes. Her iron-gray hair was chopped off in a fuss-free style she'd probably worn for years. Close to retirement, she looked like a woman who'd favor muesli, yoga, liniments, SAVE THE WHALES bumper stickers, polar-bear swims, and lengthy bicycle tours of foreign countries. When I asked to see a copy of the '61 yearbook, she gave me a look but refrained from comment. She handed me the *Bulldog* and I took a seat at an empty table. She returned to her desk and busied herself, though I could tell she intended to keep an eye on me.

I spent a few minutes leafing through the *Bulldog*, looking at the black-and-white portraits of the senior class. I didn't check for Duncan's name. I simply absorbed the whole, trying to get a feel for the era, which predated mine by six years. The school had originally been all male, but it had turned coed somewhere along the way. Senior pictures showed the boys wearing coats and ties, their hair in brush cuts that emphasized their big ears and oddly shaped heads. Many wore glasses with heavy black frames. The girls tended toward short hair and dark gray or black crew-neck sweaters. Each wore a simple strand of pearls, probably a necklace provided by the photographer for uniformity. By 1967, the year I graduated, the hairstyles were bouffant, as stiffly lacquered as wigs, with flipped ends sticking out. The boys had all turned into Elvis Presley clones. Here, in candid class photos, most students wore penny loafers and white crew socks, and the girls were decked out in straight or pleated skirts that hit them at the knee.

I breezed by the Good News Club, the Speech Club, the Art Club, the Pep Club, and the Chess Club. In views of classes devoted to industrial arts, home ec, and world science, students were clumped together pointing at wall maps or gathered around the teacher's desk, smiling and pretending to look interested. The teachers all appeared to be fifty-five and as dull as dust.

At Thanksgiving of that year, the fall of 1960, the annual Male–Manual game was played. Male High was victorious by a score of 20–6. "MALE BEATS MANUAL 20 TO 6, CLINCHES CITY & AAA CROWNS," the article said. "A neat, well-deserved licking of the duPont Manual Rams." Co-captains were Walter Morris and Joe Blankenship. The rivalry between the two high schools had been long and fierce, beginning in 1893 and doubtless continuing to the present. At that time, the record showed 39 wins for Male, 19 for Manual, and 5 games tied. At the bottom of the page, in the accompanying photograph of the Manual offense, I found a halfback named Quintero, weighing 162.

I went back to the first page and started through again. Duncan Oaks showed up in a number of photographs, dark-haired and handsome. He'd been elected vice president, prom king, and class photographer. His name and face seemed to crop up in many guises: the senior play, Quill and Scroll, Glee Club. He was a Youth Speaks delegate, office aide, and library assistant.

He hadn't garnered academic honors, but he had played football. I found a picture of him on the Male High team, a 160-pound halfback. Now that was interesting: Duncan Oaks and Benny Quintero had played the same position on opposing teams. They must have known each other, by reputation if nothing else. I thought about Porter Yount's comment that these were Duncan's glory years, that his life after this never approached the same heights. That might have been true for Quintero as well. In retrospect, it seemed touching that their paths had crossed again in Vietnam.

I turned to the front of the book and studied the picture of Duncan as prom king. He was wearing a tuxedo: shorn, clean-shaven, with a white boutonniere tucked into his lapel. I turned the page and studied the prom queen, wondering if they were boyfriend/girlfriend or simply elected separately and honored on the same occasion. Darlene LaDestro. Well, this was a type I'd known well. Long blond hair pulled up in a swirl on top, a strong nose, patrician air. She looked classy, familiar, like girls in my high school who came from big-time money. Though not conventionally pretty, Darlene was the kind of girl who'd age with style. She'd come back to class reunions having married her social equal, still thin as a rail, hair streaked tastefully with gray. Darlene LaDestro, what a name. You'd think she'd have dumped it the first chance she got, called herself Dodie or Dessie or—

A chill swept through me, and I made an involuntary bark of astonishment. Mrs. Calloway looked up, and I shook my head to indicate that I was fine . . . though I wasn't. No wonder Darlene looked familiar. She was currently Laddie Bethel, alive and well and living in Santa Teresa.

25

I POSTPONED MY return, moving the reservation from Wednesday afternoon to a morning flight on Thursday to give myself time to compile some information. I'd combed copies of the 1958, 1959, 1960, 1961, and 1962 yearbooks for reference to Mark Bethel but had found no mention of him. If Laddie'd known him in those days, it wasn't because he'd attended Louisville Male High. I made copious copies of the yearbook pages where Laddie and Duncan were featured, both together and separately, going all the way back to their freshman year. In many candid class pictures, the two were standing side by side.

I placed the stack of yearbooks on Mrs. Calloway's desk. I left the high school, driving through the area until I found a drugstore, where I bought a pack of index cards and a city map to supplement the simple sheet map I'd acquired from Frugal Rents. In the rental car again, I circled back to the public library, which was not far away. I inquired at the desk and was directed to the reference department. Then I got down to work. By cross-checking past city directories with past telephone books,

I found one LaDestro and made a note of the address. The 1959, 1960, and 1961 business directories indicated that Laddie's father, Harold LaDestro, had owned a machine shop on Market and listed his occupation as precision machinist and inventor. Because of Laddie's poise, her elegance, and her aristocratic airs, I'd assumed she came from money, but perhaps I was wrong. In those years, her father was a tradesman, and there was no hint whatever that his business interests extended beyond the obvious. From the yearbook, I knew she'd graduated with honors, but the list of her achievements made no mention of college plans. She might have enrolled at the University of Louisville, which was probably not expensive for local residents. It was also possible she'd attended a nearby business college, taking a secretarial course so she could work for her dad. That was the sort of thing a conscientious daughter might have done in those days.

But where had she met Mark? On a whim, I pulled out the 1961 phone book, where I found listings for twenty-one families with the last name of Bethel and four with the last name Oaks. There was only one Revel Oaks, and I made a note of that address. As for Bethels, I had another idea how to pin down Mark's family. I ran off copies of the phone book listings and pages from the relevant city directories, adding them to the copies I'd made of the yearbook information. I wasn't sure where I was going, but why not follow my nose? I'd already spent the money for plane fare to get here. I was stuck until flight time the next morning. What else was there to do?

I fired up the rental car and did a quick driving tour, starting with the Oaks family home on Fourth Street, still in the downtown area. The house was impressive: an immense three-story structure of stucco and stone, probably built in the late 1800s. The style fell midway between Renaissance and Baroque, with cornices, fluted columns, curved buttresses, a balustrade, and arched windows. The exterior color was uncommon: a dusky pink, washed with brown, as if the facade had been glazed by age to this mournful shade. From the sign on the lawn, the building was now occupied by two law firms, a court reporting firm, and a CPA. The property was large, the surrounding stone wall still visible, as well as the original gateposts. Two majestic oak trees shaded the formal gardens in the rear, and I could see a carriage house at the end of a cobbled driveway.

The LaDestros' address was less than two miles away, within a block of the university on a narrow side street. I checked for the number, but the house was gone, evidently razed to make way for expanding campus facilities. The remaining houses on the street tended to be elongated one-story boxes sheathed in dark red asphalt siding. Depressing. I couldn't imagine how Laddie'd been catapulted from these grim beginnings to her current wealth. Had she been married before? In those days, a rich husband was the obvious means by which a woman could elevate her social standing and improve her prospects. She certainly must have been eager to bail herself out of *this*.

While I was still in range of the central city, I located the Jefferson County clerk's office in the courthouse between Fifth and Sixth Streets on West Jefferson. The fellow at the desk couldn't have been more helpful when I told him what I needed: the marriage certificate for Darlene LaDestro and Mark Bethel, who I believed had been married in the summer of 1965. I couldn't give him the exact date, but I was remembering the line I'd picked up from Mark's secretary, Judy, who told me he'd enlisted in the army right after his college graduation. What would have been more natural than to marry Laddie that summer, before he went overseas? I was also operating on the theory that Laddie (aka Darlene LaDestro) was an obvious choice for one of Duncan's interviews. She was young, she was lovely, she was local. She would have been easy to approach, since they lived in the same town and he'd known her for years. Duncan's press credentials were dated September 10, 1965. If he'd talked to Laddie at all, it was probably sometime between her marriage, Mark's departure, and his own flight to Vietnam soon afterward.

Fifteen minutes later, I experienced one of those exhilarating moments of satisfaction when, sure enough, the clerk found the marriage record.

"Oh, wow. This is great. Isn't this *amazing*?" I said.

The clerk's look was jaded. "I'm completely stunned."

I laughed. "Well, I like being right, especially when I'm flying by the seat of my pants."

He leaned on the counter, his chin on his hand, looking on while I took out my cards and jotted down the information embedded in the form. The license was issued on June 3, 1965. Assuming it was good for thirty days, the wedding must have taken place within the month. Darlene LaDestro, age twenty-two and working as a bookkeeper, was the daughter of Harold and Millicent LaDestro and resided at the address listed in the 1961 telephone book. Mark Charles Bethel, age twenty-three, occupation U.S. Army, was the son of Vernon and Shirley Bethel with an address on Trevillian Way. Neither the bride nor the groom had been previously married.

Idly, the clerk said, "You know who he is, don't you?"

I looked up at him with interest. "Who, Mark Bethel?"

"No, LaDestro."

"I don't know a thing about him. What's the story?"

"He was awarded the patent for some kind of widget used on the Mercury space flights."

"And that's how he made his money?"

"Sure. He's still famous around here. Self-taught, eccentric. He didn't even have connections to the aerospace industry. He just worked on his own. I saw a picture of him once, and he looked like a pointy-headed geek. He'd been tinkering all his life without making a dime. In hock up to here, living in a dump. Everybody wrote him off as a nut, and then he comes along and aces out McDonnell-Douglas for the rights to the thing. He died a rich man. I mean, *very very* rich."

"Well, I'll be darned," I said. "What was it, the thing he patented?"

"Some doodad. Who knows? I heard it's in use to this day. The world is full of guys who design gizmos they never get credit for. LaDestro hired a patent attorney and took the big boys down."

"Incredible."

"His daughter sure lucked out. I hear she lives in California now on some fancy estate," he said. He pointed to the license. "You want a copy of that?"

"How much?"

"Two dollars for regular, five for certified."

"Regular's fine," I said.

I drove from Jefferson to Third, then hung a left on Broadway, driving east until it angled into Bardstown Road. I followed Bardstown Road through an area of town known as the Highlands. Once on Trevillian, I found the house where the Bethels had once lived. The white frame house looked comfortable, not large but well-maintained in a solid middle-class neighborhood, certainly superior to the one where Laddie'd grown up. I parked in front of the house, traversed the long sloping walk, and climbed the stairs to the porch. No one was home, but a simple check of the mailbox revealed that a family named Poynter now occupied the house. This was Donna Reed country: green shutters on the windows, pansies in the flower boxes, a tricycle on the sidewalk, and a dog bone lying in the yard. All the windowpanes sparkled, and the shrubs were crisply trimmed. As I looked on, a lean gray cat picked her way carefully across the newly cut lawn.

I returned to the car, where I sat and studied my map. Gauging the proximity of schools in the area, I decided Mark probably attended Highland Junior High and then Atherton or St. Xavier, the Catholic high school on Broadway. He might have gone to private school—I wasn't sure about that—but he struck me as the sort who'd take pride in his public school roots. Now what?

I leafed through the pages I'd assembled, letting my mind wander. I'd added a number of dots, but I still couldn't see all the lines connecting them. Duncan Oaks seemed pivotal. I sensed his presence like the hub of an enormous wheel. I could trace the hometown relationship between him and Benny Quintero. Contemporaries, two high school athletes who had played the same positions on opposing football teams, their paths had crossed years later on the bloody soil of Ia Drang. After that, Duncan Oaks had vanished but Quintero had survived, keeping Duncan's dog tags, his press credentials, and a snapshot. I could also tie Duncan Oaks to Laddie Bethel, born Darlene LaDestro, who'd attended high school with him. And here's where the machinations became more intricate. Laddie was now married to the attorney who'd represented my ex-husband, a suspect in Benny Quintero's beating death seven years later. If Duncan Oaks was the hub, maybe Mark Bethel was the axle driving subsequent events.

I started the car and headed back to my motel. Even without the links, a picture was forming, crude and unfocused, but one that Mickey must have seen as well. The problem was I had no proof a crime had been committed all those years ago, let alone that it had sparked consequences in the here-and-now. It simply stood to reason. *Some* combination of events had resulted in the killing of Benny Quintero and the shooting of Mickey Magruder. I had to fashion a story that encompassed all the players and made sense of their fates. If life is a play, then there's a logical explanation, an underlying tale that pulls the whole of it together, however clouded it first appears.

Before my plane the next morning, I put in a call to Porter Yount, asking if he could lay his hands on the columns Duncan Oaks had written before he went to Vietnam. Much hemming and hawing, but he said he'd see what he could do. I gave him my address and a great big telephone kiss, telling him to take care, I'd be in touch with him.

The flight home was uneventful, though it took up most of the day: Louisville to Tulsa, Tulsa to Santa Fe, Santa Fe to Los Angeles, where I shuttled to the motel, picked up my VW, and drove the ninety minutes home. Between the actual hours in the air, the wait between planes, and the commute at the end, I arrived in Santa Teresa at 4:30 P.M. I was feeling irritable: tired, hungry, flat-haired, oily-faced. I was also dehydrated from all the nuts I'd eaten in lieu of meals that day. I had to slap myself around some to keep from whining out loud.

The minute I got home, I sat down at my desk and removed Mark Bethel's curriculum vitae from the bottom drawer where I'd tucked it Saturday. On the front page, he'd listed his date and place of birth as Dayton, Ohio,

August 1, 1942. He'd graduated with a BA from the University of Kentucky in 1965. Under military experience, he listed U.S. Army, modestly omitting mention of his Purple Heart. I'd call Judy in the morning, my palate smeared with peanut butter, pretending to be a journalist so I could pin that down. If Mark had been at Ia Drang, I'd be one step closer to completing the picture, which was almost done.

I stripped, showered, and shampooed my hair. I brushed my teeth, got dressed again, and trotted down the spiral stairs.

My first thought was to have a conversation with Carlin Duffy, conveying a condensed version of what I'd learned in Louisville, though at this point I still didn't know quite what to make of it. I'd restrict myself to the facts, leaving out the speculations and suppositions I was still playing with. The contact was largely a courtesy on my part. He hadn't hired me. He wasn't paying me and I didn't feel I owed him an explanation. I was hoping, however, that he'd have something to contribute, some piece of the puzzle he hadn't thought to share. More to the point, I remembered Duffy's rage and frustration the night he'd shown up at Mickey's. I didn't relish a repeat performance and this was my way of protecting myself. Duffy's brother had died, and he had his stake in the matter.

I headed out to the nursery, where I found a parking slot in front of the gardening center. I prayed Duffy was on the premises instead of at the Honky-Tonk. The bar was open at this hour, but I didn't dare go back. I thought I'd better keep my distance in case Tim and Scottie realized I was the one who'd blown the whistle on them. It was close to five-thirty, still light out, and I made my way easily along the tree-lined paths. I could see the roofline of the shed at the rear of the lot, and I mentally marked my route. There was no direct passageway, and I angled back and forth between the crated trees.

When I reached the shed, I saw a compact yellow forklift parked in the entrance. Several large bags of mulch were stacked on the forks in front. Tall and boxy, the vehicle was an overblown version of the Tonka toys I'd played with when I was six. The phase had been shortlived, tucked somewhere between Legos and the demise of the baby doll I'd flattened with my trike. I moved into the shed, pushing aside the blanket Duffy'd hung to eliminate drafts. He'd passed out, lying shoeless on his cot. His mouth hung open and his snores filled the enclosure with bourbon fumes. He cradled an empty pint of Early Times against his chest. One sock was pulled half off, and his bare heel was exposed. He looked absurdly young for a fellow who'd spent half his life in jail. I thought, shit. I found a blanket and tossed it over him and then placed the dog tags, the press pass, the snapshot, and a note on the crate where he'd see it when he woke. The note said I'd be in touch the next day and fill him in on the trip. I backed out of the shed, leaving him to sleep off his drunken state.

I walked back to the car, thinking how often I identified with guys like him. As crude as he was with his racist comments, his tortured grammar, and his attitude toward crime, I understood his yearning. How liberating it was when you defied authority, flouted convention, ignoring ordinary standards of moral decency. I knew my own ambivalence. On the one hand, I was a true law-and-order type, prissy in my judgment, outraged at those who violated the doctrines of honesty and fair play. On the other hand, I'd been known to lie through my teeth, eavesdrop, pick locks, or simply break into people's houses, where I snooped through their possessions and took what suited me. It wasn't nice, but I savored every single minute of my bad girl behavior. Later, I'd feel guilty, but still I couldn't resist. I was split down the middle, my good angel sitting on one shoulder, Lucifer perched on the other. Duffy's struggle was the same, and while he leaned in one direction, I usually leaned in the other, searching for justice in the heart of anarchy. This was the bottom line as far as I was concerned: If the bad guys don't play by the rules, why should the good guys have to?

I drove back into town. It was now 5:50 and I was starving, of course, so I made a quick detour. I pulled up to the drive-in window at McDonald's and asked for a QP with cheese, a large order of fries, and a Coke to go. I was fairly humming with excitement as I waited for my bag of goodies. I'd go back to my apartment, change into my jammies, and curl up on my couch, where I'd watch junk TV while I ate my junk food. While I drove home, the car smelled divine, like a mobile microwave oven. I found a great parking place, locked the car, and let myself in through the squeaking gate. I rounded the corner, all atwitter at the notion of the pleasures to come. I stopped dead.

Detectives Claas and Aldo were standing on my front porch. This was a replay of our earlier encounter: same guys in their late thirties, one dark, the other fair, same sport coats. Claas carried the briefcase, just as he had before. Gian Aldo chewed gum. He'd had his dark hair trimmed short, but his eyebrows still met like a hedge across the bridge of his nose. I longed to fall on him with a pair of tweezers and pluck him bald.

I said, "What do you want?"

Detective Claas seemed amused. Now that was different. "Be nice. We drove all the way up here to have a chat with you."

I walked past him with my keys and unlocked the door. Detective Claas wore a hair product that smelled like a high school chemistry experiment. The two followed me in. I dropped my shoulder bag on the floor near my desk, taking a moment to check my answering machine. No messages.

I held up my McDonald's bag, the contents getting colder by the minute, as were my hopes. "I gotta eat first. I'm half dead."

"Have at it."

I crossed to the kitchen, moving around the counter to the refrigerator. I took out a chilled bottle of Chardonnay and sorted through the junk drawer until I found the opener. "You want wine? I'm having some. You might as well join me."

The two exchanged a look. It was probably against regulations, but they must have thought I'd be easier to get along with if I were all likkered up.

"We'd appreciate that. Thanks," Claas said.

I handed him the wine bottle and the opener, and he got to work while I set out three glasses and a paper plate. I dumped the fries out of the carton and fetched the ketchup bottle from the cabinet. "Help yourself," I said.

Detective Claas poured the wine and we stood there, eating lukewarm french fries with our fingers. They were completely limp by now, and we dropped them in our beaks like a trio of birdies eating albino worms. Ever gracious, I cut the QP into three equal parts and we gulped those down, too. After supper, we walked the six steps into the living room. This time I took the couch and let them settle into my director's chairs. I noticed Detective Claas kept his briefcase close at hand as he had before. I knew he had a tape recorder in there, and it made me want to lean down and address all my comments into the opening.

"So now what?" I said, crossing my arms against my chest.

Detective Aldo smiled. "We have some news we thought you might want to hear firsthand. We picked up a partial print on the Smith and Wesson and matched it to some prints that showed up in Magruder's place."

Claas said, "You remember a gray metal box concealed in the bottom of a chair?"

I could feel my mouth go dry. "Sure." No sound. I cleared my throat and tried again. "Sure."

"We got a real nice set on the inner rim of the lid, like someone pulled it open with their fingertips."

I was going to call his attention to the matter of subject-pronoun agreement, but I held my tongue. Instead, I said, "Who?" Was that an owl I heard?

Aldo spoke up again, clearly enjoying himself. "Mark Bethel."

I stared at him, blinking. "You're kidding. You gotta be *kidding*."

"He went in there Sunday night and left prints everywhere."

"That's great. I love it. Good for him," I said.

"We're not sure what he was looking for—"

I held a hand up. "I can tell you that," I said. I gave them a hasty summary of the work I'd done, including the discovery of Duncan Oaks's credentials in Mickey's jacket lining. "I can't believe he was dumb enough to leave his fingerprints. Has the man lost his mind?"

"He's getting desperate," Claas said. "He probably saw the print dust on all the surfaces and figured we were done."

"You dusted again?"

"Tuesday morning," Aldo said.

"But why? What possessed you?"

"We got a call from Cordia Hatfield. She'd seen lights on Sunday night. You swore it wasn't you, so she suspected it was him," Claas said.

"But how'd he get in?"

"With the key she'd given him. He'd stopped by last week and introduced himself as Magruder's attorney. He said he'd be paying Mickey's bills till he was on his feet, and he was hoping to pick up insurance policies and bank deposit slips. She gave him a key. Of course, he returned it later, but probably not before he'd had a copy made for himself," Claas said.

Detective Aldo spoke up. "I don't think the computer would have caught the match without the fresh set he left. Of course, we wasted a *lot* of time eliminating yours."

I could feel my cheeks heat. "Sorry about that."

Aldo wagged his finger, but he didn't seem all that mad.

Claas said, "We can also place Bethel in the area at the time of the shooting."

"You guys have been busy. How'd you do *that*?"

Claas was clearly pleased with himself. "On the thirteenth, Bethel was in Los Angeles for a TV appearance. The taping finished at ten. He checked into the Four Seasons on a late arrival and then went out again, returning in the early hours of the fourteenth. He might have slipped in unnoticed, but as it happened the valet car park was a supporter and recognized his face."

"Tell you what else," Detective Aldo said. "We got somebody saw them together that night."

"No."

"Oh, yes. We went through a bunch of matchbooks Magruder kept in a fishbowl. We found seven from a dive on Pico near the Pacific Coast Security offices. A gal at the bar remembered seeing them." Detective Aldo sat back, the wood and canvas chair creaking perilously under his weight. "What about you? What'd you pick up back east? Your landlord told us you made a trip to Louisville."

"That's right. I just got back today."

"Learn anything?"

"Actually, I did. I'm just piecing this together so I can't be sure, but here's what I know. Laddie Bethel went to high school in Louisville with a guy named Duncan Oaks. They were the prom king and queen in '61, the year they graduated. At some point, Laddie met Mark. They married in the summer of 1965, after he graduated from the University of Kentucky. Mark enlisted in the army right around the time Duncan Oaks was doing a series for the *Louisville Tribune*. I suspect Mark served in Vietnam, but I haven't pinned that down—"

"We can help on that. We haven't been exactly idle." Claas reached into his briefcase and removed a manila folder, which he opened, leafing through the contents. "Alpha Company, First Battalion, Fifth Cavalry."

"Well, great," I said. "I don't have a clue how it ties in, but maybe we'll figure that out. At any rate, Duncan had an idea for a series and began interviewing the soldiers' wives. His intention was to talk about the war from their differing perspectives, one off in Vietnam, the other stuck on the home front. I think Duncan and Laddie had a brief affair. Pure conjecture on my part. Within weeks, Duncan Oaks went to Vietnam. He and Mark must have crossed paths. In fact, Duncan probably sought him out for the second half of the interview."

"And?"

"That's as far as I can go."

Aldo said, "Maybe Mark fragged him. That's what it sounds like to me."

"Fragged?"

"You know, offed. Eliminated. Kilt him deader than a doornail. I mean, how hard could it be with bullets flying? It's not like the medics run ballistics tests."

I thought about it for a moment. "That's probably not a bad guess. Especially if Mark found out about the relationship between Duncan and his wife. . . ."

"Assuming there was one," Claas said.

"Well, yeah."

"Anyway, go on. Sorry for the interruption."

"I start faltering here and have to resort to waving my hands. I mean, I can put some of this together, but I don't have proof. Benny Quintero was another Louisville boy. I know Duncan and Benny were at Ia Drang together because I saw a picture of the two. According to my information, Duncan Oaks was wounded—by Mark, friendly fire, the NVA—we're never going to know, so we might as well skip that. In any event, he was loaded on a chopper filled with the wounded and the dead. By the time the chopper landed, he'd disappeared without a trace."

Aldo spoke up. "Maybe Mark's on the chopper and shoves him out the door. The guy falls—what? six to twelve hundred feet, landing in the jungle? Trust me, in two weeks there's nothing left but bones. From what you say, Oaks wasn't even in the army, so it's perfect. Who gives a shit about a fucking journalist?"

I said, "Right. The point is, I think Benny knew and that's why he held on to Duncan's ID. Again, I don't have proof, but it does make sense. Maybe he thought of a way to turn a profit on the deal."

Claas said, "What happened to Benny?"

"He was wounded by sniper fire and ended up with a metal plate in his head. In 1971, he came out to California; that much we know. Mickey and Benny got in a shoving match. A day later, someone beat Benny senseless and he ended up dead." I went on to detail Mickey's history of misbehavior and why he'd looked good for the beating when Internal Affairs stepped in.

Claas said, "I don't see the relevance."

"Mark was Mickey's attorney. He's the one who advised him to leave the department to avoid questioning."

"Got it."

Aldo leaned forward. "Speaking of which, how'd Bethel end up with your Smith and Wesson? That seems like a trick."

"I think Mickey sold it to him. I have a record of a deposit in March for two hundred dollars. Mark told me Mickey called and asked for money. I know Mickey better than that. I know he'd hoarded a stash of gold coins and bills, but that was probably not something he would have dipped into. He sold his car about then and he was probably off-loading his other possessions, trying to make ends meet. The minute Mark bought the gun, he must have seen his way clear, because it was on that same trip he made the phone call from Mickey's apartment to my machine. All he had to do was distract Mickey's attention, dial the number, and let the tape run on when my machine picked up."

"What if you'd been there?"

"Sorry wrong number, and he tries the call later. He knew Mickey and Duffy were as thick as thieves by then. Whatever his faults, Mickey's always been a hell of a detective. Mark must have known it was only a matter of time. He had a gun registered to me. He'd established a connection to me on Mickey's telephone bill. I'd be implicated anyway as soon as the gun registration came to light."

Aldo snorted. "Fuckin' devious."

Claas rubbed his hands together, then stretched his

arms out in front of him, his fingers laced with the palms turned outward until I heard his knuckles crack. "Well, boys and girls, I've enjoyed the bedtime stories. Too bad none of this'll fly in court."

"Oh, yeah. Which brings us to the next step," Aldo said, chiming in on cue. "Shall I tell her the plan?"

I said, "I don't like this. It sounds rehearsed."

"Exactly," Claas said. "So here's what we thought. Forget Vietnam. We're never going to get him for whacking Duncan Oaks. No weapons, no witnesses, so we're out of luck on that score."

Aldo said, "Quintero's another one. I mean, even if you prove it, the best you can hope for is a manslaughter bust, which is strictly bullshit."

I said, "Which brings us to Mickey."

"And to you," Claas said. He reached in his briefcase and pulled out the tape recorder. He held it so I could see.

I said, "I knew that was in there."

"But did you know how well it works?" He pressed REWIND and then PLAY, producing a clear, unobstructed recording of the conversation we'd just had. "We figure you can put this in your handbag, trot yourself off to Bethel's, and maybe help us out."

"You have an eavesdropping warrant?"

"No, we don't."

"Isn't that illegal? I thought you needed a court order. Whatever happened to the Fourth Amendment?" This from Kinsey Millhone, upholder of the Constitution.

"What you'd be doing is called a consent recording. It's done all the time by informants and undercover cops. As long as you're only taping comments someone makes to you, the court doesn't have a problem. Worst-case scenario—assuming what you get is juicy—you use the tape to refresh your own memory when you testify in court."

"Now I'm testifying?"

"If Mickey dies, you do. Right?"

I could feel my attention shift from Aldo to Claas, who said, "Look at it this way. We're building a case. We gotta have something concrete for the DA."

Aldo leaned forward. "That's what we're in business to do, get this cocksucker nailed, if you'll excuse my Greek."

"And Mark won't guess what I'm up to? He's not a fool," I said.

"He's Mickey's *attorney*. You're back from Kentucky with a shitload of information and you're filling him in. How can he resist? He wants to know what *you* know so he can measure the depth of the hole he's in. Of course, if he figures you're on to him, he'll want to pop you next."

"Thanks. That helps. Now I'm really feeling good about all this."

"Come on. It's no sweat. He's not going to do it in his own living room."

Aldo moved to the phone, holding the receiver out. "Give him a call."

"Now?"

"Why not? Tell him you have some stuff you want to talk to him about."

"Yeah," I said cautiously. "And then what?"

"We haven't made that part up yet."

26

THE BETHELS' ESTATE was on the outer edges of Montebello, perched on a bluff overlooking the Pacific Ocean. I'd spoken to Laddie on the phone and she'd given me directions to the house on Savanna Lane. Mark was out, but she said he'd be returning shortly. It worried me she hadn't voiced greater surprise or curiosity about the reason for my call. I'd mentioned the trip to Louisville, that I had something to discuss, preferably with the two of them, though I'd certainly value the opportunity to talk to her alone first. If she was alarmed about such a conversation, she gave no indication.

At seven on the dot, I pulled in at the gate. Detectives Claas and Aldo had followed me in their car, and they were parked in a grove of eucalyptus trees about a hundred yards off. I had the tape recorder in my bag, but I wasn't wired for sound so there was no way they could monitor the conversation once I was inside the house. No one (meaning them) seemed to think this would present a problem since I'd be in the Bethels' home with other people (meaning servants) on the premises. Our plan—if that's what you want to call it—was for them to hover on the sidelines, falling in behind me when I left the estate. Then we'd go back to my place, listen to the tape, and see if what we'd picked up constituted probable cause. If so, we'd find a judge who could sign a warrant for Mark's arrest on charges of assault with a deadly weapon and attempted murder in the shooting of Mickey Magruder. If not, we'd move to Plan B, on which we'd never quite agreed. On reflection, even Plan A seemed a bit half-assed, but I was there at the gate and I'd already pressed the button.

I expected to hear someone on the intercom asking for my name. Instead, there was silence. The gates simply swung open, allowing me entrance. I waved to the "boys" and put the car in gear. The driveway was long, curving off to the left. The land on either side was barren except for the grasses bending under the offshore winds. Occasionally, a tree broke the line of the horizon, a stark silhouette against the milder dark of the sky. I could see the lighted windows of the house, dazzling yellow and white, set in a bulky block of dark stone. I parked out in front on an enormous apron of gravel. I shut off the engine and sat taking in the sight of the house through the driver's side window.

The structure was curiously reminiscent of Duncan Oaks's house in Louisville. Despite the appearance of age, I knew construction had been completed only five years before, which might explain the absence of mature trees. The exterior was stone and stucco. Landscape lights washed the facade with its glaze of dusky pink underlaid with brown. In theory, the style was Mediterranean or Italianate, one of those bastard forms that Californians favor, but the arches above the windows seemed remarkably similar to their Kentucky counterpart. The front door was recessed, sheltered in a portico flanked by fluted columns. Even the balustrade was kindred in design. Was Laddie conscious of what she'd done or had she mimicked Duncan's house inadvertently? What is it that prompts us to reenact our unresolved issues? We revisit our wounds, constructing the past in hopes that this time we can make the ending turn out right.

The carriage lights on either side of the door came on. Reluctantly, I reached for my bag. I'd left the zippered compartment open, the tape recorder in easy range of my hand. I emerged from the car, crunched my way across the parking pad, and climbed the low front steps. Laddie opened the door before I had time to ring the bell. "Hello, Kinsey. How nice of you to drive all the way out here. I take it you had no trouble finding the place."

"Not at all. It's beautiful."

"We like it," she said mildly. "Can I take your jacket?"

"This is fine for now. It's cold."

She closed the door behind me. "Come on into the living room. I've got a nice fire burning. Will you have a drink? I'm having wine," she said. She was already walking toward the living room, her heels clicking smartly against the highly polished marble floors.

I followed her, saying, "I better not, but thanks. I had wine with dinner and that's my limit."

We stepped down into the living room, with its twelve-foot coffered ceiling. One entire wall of French doors looked onto a patio. The room was surprisingly light, done in shades of cream: the twenty- by twenty-four-foot area rug, the walls, the three plump matching love seats arranged in a U in front of the fireplace. There were touches of black in the throw pillows and lampshades, Boston ferns providing spots of green here and there. Maybe I could snitch some ideas for my spacious abode. The coffee table was a square of three-quarter-inch glass resting on three enormous polished brass spheres. A second wineglass sat near a bottle of Chardonnay in an insulated cooler. Laddie'd made quite a dent for someone drinking alone. I flicked on the tape recorder during the momentary lull as she picked up her wineglass and settled on one of the sofas that flanked the fireplace. The hearth was a glossy black granite that reflected the blaze. Really, I was taking notes—I had to have one of those.

I sat down opposite her, wondering how to begin. These transitions can be awkward, especially when you're trying to shift the discussion from niceties to the subject of murder.

She said, "What were you doing in Louisville? We used to go for the Derby, but it's been ages."

A maid came to the door. "I left Mr. Bethel's plate in the warming oven. Will there be anything else?"

"No, dear. That's fine. We'll see you in the morning."

"Yes, ma'am," the woman said, and then withdrew.

I said, "Actually, I went to Louisville on a research trip. Do you remember Benny Quintero, the fellow who was killed here a few years ago?"

"Of course. Mark represented Mickey."

"Well, as it happens, Benny was from Louisville. He went to Manual the same time you were at Louisville Male High."

Her lips parted in expectation. "What kind of research *was* this? I can't imagine."

"I keep thinking there's a connection between Benny Quintero's death and Mickey's being shot last week."

Laddie's frown was delicate. "That's quite a leap."

"Not really," I said, "though it does seem odd. Here the four of you come from the same hometown—"

"Four?"

"Sure. You, Mark, Benny, and Duncan Oaks. You remember Duncan," I said.

"Of course, but he's been gone for years."

"My point exactly," I said. Gee, this was going better than I'd thought. "During his stint in Vietnam, Mark was at Ia Drang, right?"

"You'd have to verify that with him, but I believe so."

"Turns out Benny was there too."

Laddie blinked. "I'm not following. What does any of this have to do with me?"

"Let me back up a step. Didn't Duncan Oaks interview you for the *Louisville Tribune?*"

She said, "Kinsey, what *is* this? I don't mean to be rude, but you're skipping back and forth and I'm confused. I really don't see the relevance."

"Just hear me out," I said. "Duncan was doing a series for the local paper. He interviewed army wives, like you, who'd been left behind—you know, talking about the war from their perspective. His idea was to tell the same story through the eyes of the husbands off fighting in Vietnam."

Laddie shook her head, shrugging. "I guess I'll have to take your word for it."

"At any rate, he did talk to you."

She took a sip of wine. "It's possible. I don't remember."

"Don't worry about the date. I've asked his editor to send a copy of the article. We can pin it down from that. Anyway, Duncan's editor says he flew to Vietnam in September of '65. He ran into Mark and Benny at Ia Drang, which was where Duncan disappeared." I was doling out pure theory, but I noticed she'd stopped offering much in the way of objections. "Seven years later Benny shows up in Santa Teresa with Duncan Oaks's ID. The next thing you know, Benny's been murdered. You see the link?"

"Benny wasn't *murdered.* You're overstating the situation. As I remember, Benny had a subdural hematoma, and his death was the result of an arterial bleed. Given the nature of his injury, it could have happened any time. Even the coroner's report said that."

"Really? You're probably right. You have quite a memory for the details," I said.

"Mark and I discussed it at the time. I suppose it stuck in my mind."

"Mickey's another link. He went off to Louisville on Thursday, May eighth. He came back on Monday, and in the wee hours of Wednesday morning he was shot, as you know."

Laddie's smile was thin. "Not to sound superior, but you're committing what's called a post hoc fallacy. Just because one event follows another doesn't mean there's a cause-and-effect relationship."

"I see. In other words, just because Benny knew something doesn't mean he died for it."

"Is this what you wanted to discuss with Mark?"

"In part."

"Then let's leave that. I'm sure it's more appropriate to wait till he comes in."

I said, "Fine. Could we talk about your relationship with Duncan?"

"I'd hardly call it a relationship. I knew him, of course. We went all through school together."

"Were you pals, confidants, boyfriend/girlfriend?"

"We were friends, that's all. There was never anything between us, if that's what you're getting at."

"Actually, it is," I said. "I thought since you were the king and queen of the senior prom, you might have been sweet on each other."

Laddie smiled, her composure restored. This was something she'd thought about; her version of the story was preassembled and prepackaged. "Duncan wasn't interested in me romantically, nor I in him."

"Too bad. He looked cute."

"He was cute. He was also extremely narcissistic, which I found obnoxious. There's nothing worse than a seventeen-year-old kid who thinks he's hot stuff."

"You don't think he was charismatic?"

"*He* thought he was," she said. "I thought he was conceited—nice, funny, but such a snob."

"What about your father?"

She looked at me askance. "My father? What's he have to do with this?"

"This is peripheral and probably none of my business—"

"None of this is your business," she said, bridling.

I smiled to show I hadn't taken offense. "I was told he was awarded a patent that earned him a lot of money. I gather, before that, he was considered a bit eccentric."

"If he was, so what? Make your point."

"I'm just thinking his fortune must have changed people's perception of you. Duncan's, in particular."

She was silent.

"Yes? No?"

"I suppose," she said.

"You went from being one down to one up where he was concerned. He sounds like the type who enjoyed a conquest—to prove he could do it, if nothing else."

"Are you trying to build a case for something?"

"I'm just trying to get a feel for what kind of guy he was."

"A dead one."

"Before that. You never had a fling with him?"

"Oh, please. Don't be silly. We never had an *affair*."

"Hey, an affair is six weeks or more. A fling can be anything from one night to half a dozen."

"I never had a fling with him, either."

"When did Mark leave for Vietnam? I know you married him in June. His orders came through . . ."

"July twenty-sixth," she said, biting off the words.

"The way I read the situation, Duncan was in Louis-ville after Mark shipped out. There you were, a young newlywed with a husband off at war. I'm sure you were lonely . . . needy. . . ."

"This is offensive. You're being extremely insulting, not only to me but to Mark."

"Insulting about what?" Mark said from the corridor. He shrugged out of his overcoat and tossed it over the back of a chair. He must have come in through the kitchen. His high forehead and receding hairline gave him an air of innocence, the same look babies have before they learn to bite and talk back. Laddie got up to greet him. I watched the two of them as he bussed her cheek.

He said, "Hang on a minute while I make a quick call." He crossed to the phone and dialed 9-1-1.

Laddie said, "What's going on?"

Mark raised a finger to indicate the dispatcher had picked up. "Hi, this is Mark Bethel. I'm at Four-forty-eight Savanna Lane. I've got a couple of guys parked in a car near the entrance to my gate. Could you have a patrol car cruise by? I really don't like the looks of them. . . . Thanks. I'd appreciate that." He replaced the handset and turned to Laddie and me with a shake of his head. "Probably harmless, a lovers' tryst, but just on the off chance they're casing the place. . ." He rubbed his palms together. "I could use a glass of wine."

I tried to picture Detectives Claas and Aldo busted by the local cops on a morals charge.

Laddie poured Chardonnay in a glass, holding it by the stem so as not to smudge the bowl. The trembling of her hand caused the wine to wobble in the glass. Mark didn't seem to notice. He took the glass and sat down, giving me his full attention. "I hope I didn't interrupt."

"We were talking about Benny Quintero," Laddie said.

"She's just back from Louisville, where she did some research."

"Benny. Poor guy."

I said, "I didn't realize you were all from the same town."

"Well, that's not strictly true. I was born in Dayton. My family moved to Louisville when I was six. I lived there till I went off to U of K."

"And you knew Benny then?"

"I knew *of* him, just as he must have known about me from football games."

"I didn't realize you played football."

"More or less," he said ruefully. "I went to Atherton, which was all girls for years. School didn't go coed until 1954. Even then, we seldom won a game against Manual or Male. Mostly, the players knew each other by reputation. I remember there was a guy named Byck Snell at Eastern. . . ."

"So Benny came to California and looked you up," I said.

"Right. He must have heard I was a lawyer and somehow got it in his head I could help him with his VA benefits. I mean, it's like I told him: just because I'm an attorney doesn't make me an expert. In those days, I knew next to nothing about the Veterans Administration. Now, of course, I'm educating myself on the issues because I can see what a difference I can make—"

I said, "Sounds like a campaign speech."

Mark smiled. "Sorry. At any rate, I couldn't seem to convince Benny of my ignorance. The whole thing was ludicrous, but I couldn't get him off it. The guy started stalking me, appeared at the office, appeared at the house. The phone started ringing at all hours of the night. Laddie was getting nervous, and I couldn't blame her. That's when I asked Mickey to step in and see what he could do."

"Meaning what?"

I could see him hesitate. "Well, you know, Mickey was a tough guy. I thought he could put the fear of God in him. I'm not saying Mickey meant to hurt him, but he did make threats."

"When?"

"During the incident in the Honky-Tonk parking lot."

"You talked to Benny after that?"

"Sure. He called me and he was furious. I said I'd talk to Mickey. I made a few calls but never managed to track him down, as you well know."

"Because he and Dixie were together," I said, helping him along.

"So they claimed. Frankly, I've always wondered. It seemed pretty damn convenient under the circumstances."

"So you're saying Mickey went back to Benny and beat the shit out of him."

"I'm saying it's possible. Mickey always had a temper. He hated it when some punk got the best of him."

"I hardly think Benny got the best of him. Shack says it was a shoving match with no blows exchanged."

"Well, that's true. Actually, I heard the same report from the other witnesses. The point is, Mickey came off looking bad, and for a guy like him that's worse."

"You know, this is the second time you've implicated Mickey."

"Hey, I'm sorry, but you asked."

"Why didn't you ever mention you knew Benny back in high school?"

"When did I have the chance? In those days, you barely spoke to me. And since then, believe me, I've been acutely aware you're not a fan of mine. We run into each other in public, you practically duck and hide, you're so anxious to avoid contact. Anyway, that aside, you weren't speaking to Mickey either, or he'd have told you the same thing."

I felt myself color at his accuracy. And here I thought I was so subtle. "Can I ask one more thing?"

"What's that?" Mark took a sip of his drink.

"After you joined the army, you were sent to Vietnam. Is that correct?"

"Absolutely. I'm proud of my service record."

"I'm sure you are," I said. "Benny Quintero was there and so was Duncan Oaks." I went on, giving him a hasty summation of what I'd learned from Porter Yount.

Mark's face took on the look of a man who's trying to pay attention while his mind is somewhere else. I could tell he was thinking hard, composing his response before I'd finished what I was saying. His resulting smile held an element of puzzlement. "You have to understand there were hundreds of guys who fought at Ia Drang. The one/five, the one/seven, the two/seven, the Second Battalion Nineteenth Artillery, the Two-twenty-seventh Assault Helicopter Battalion, the Eighth Engineer Battalion—"

"Got it," I said. "There were lots of guys. I got that, but Duncan was a journalist and he went out there specifically to talk to you because of the series he was writing. He must have told you he talked to Laddie. My guess is you'd felt threatened by him for years. He and Laddie were tight. She was poor in those days and never good enough for him, but I'll bet her classmates would tell me she'd had a crush on him, that she'd have given her eyeteeth for his attention—"

"That's absurd. That's ridiculous," Laddie interjected.

Mark made a motion with his hand that told her to hush, the sort of command you teach a dog in obedience training. She closed her mouth, but the significance of the gesture wasn't lost on her. Mark was clearly annoyed. "Let's get to the bottom line. What are you suggesting?"

"I'm suggesting the three of you connected up. You and Benny and Duncan Oaks."

Mark was shaking his head. "No. Wrong."

I said, "Yes. Right. I have a snapshot of the two of them, and you're visible in the background."

Laddie said, "So what?"

"I'll take care of this," he said to her. And then to me, "Go on. This is fascinating. Clearly, you've cooked up some theory and you're trying to make the pieces fit."

"I know how they fit. Duncan interviewed Laddie for the paper after you shipped out. By then, her daddy had money and Duncan couldn't resist. After all, a conquest is a conquest, however late it comes. The two had a fling and you found out about it. Either she 'fessed up or he told you himself—"

Laddie said, "I don't want to talk about this. It's over and done. I made a mistake, but it was years ago."

"Yeah, and I know who paid," I said caustically.

"Laddie, for God's sake, would you shut your mouth!" He turned back to me again, his face dark. "And?"

"And you killed him. Benny Quintero saw it and that's why he was hounding you. You set Mickey up. You killed Benny and made sure Mickey took the rap for it."

Mark's tone was light, but it wasn't sincere. "And you're saying what, that I shot Mickey too?"

"Yes."

He held his hands out, baffled. "Why would I do that?"

"Because he'd put it together the same way I have."

"Wait a minute, Kinsey. Duncan's body was never found, so for all you know he's alive and well. You think you can make a charge like this without evidence?"

"I have the snapshot. That helps."

"Oh, that's right. The snapshot. What crap. I think I better call your bluff. You have it with you?"

"I left it with a friend."

Mark snapped his fingers. "I forgot about Benny's brother. What's his name again? Duffy. Carlin Duffy. Now, there's a bright guy."

I said nothing.

He went on. "My sources tell me he's living in a shack at Himes Nursery. With his criminal history, it should be easy enough to put the screws to him."

"I thought you weren't worried."

"Call it cleanup," he said.

"Really. Now that you're running for public office, you have to bury your misdeeds, make sure the past won't rise up and bite you in the butt when you're least expecting it."

He pointed at me. "Bingo."

"Did you hate him that much?"

"Duncan? I'll tell you what pissed me off about that guy. Not so much that he screwed Laddie the minute my back was turned, but he showed up at Ia Drang, trying to pass himself off as a grunt. I had buddies—good friends, young guys—who died with valor, brave men who believed in what we were doing. I saw them die in agony, maimed and mutilated, limbs gone, gut-shot. Duncan Oaks was a sleaze. He had money and pretensions but not an ounce of decency. He deserved to die, and I was happy to help him out. Speaking of which, I'd like to have his personal effects."

"Effects?"

"Press pass, dog tags."

"I can't help you there. You'd have to talk to Duffy about those things."

From the depths of my shoulder bag, there was a small but distinct click as the tape ran out and the recorder shut itself off. Mark's gaze flicked down and then flicked up to my face. His smile faded, and I heard Laddie's sharp intake of breath. He held his hand out. "You want to give me that?"

"Hey, Dad?"

The three of us turned in unison. The Bethels' son, Malcolm, was standing in the door to the dining room.

"What is it?" Mark said, trying not to sound impatient with the kid.

"Can I take your Mercedes? I've got a date."

"Of course."

Malcolm continued to stand there. "I need the keys."

"Well, get a move on. We're in the middle of a conversation here," Mark said, waving him into the room.

Malcolm shot me a look of embarrassment as he entered the room. Impatiently, Mark removed his keys from his pocket, twisting the key from the ring as he separated it from the others. Meanwhile, I was staring at the kid. No wonder the photographs of Duncan Oaks had seemed familiar. I'd seen him . . . or his incarnation . . . in Laddie's son. The same youth, the same dark, distinctly handsome looks. Malcolm, at twenty, was the perfect blend of Duncan at seventeen and Duncan at twenty-three. I turned to Laddie, who must have known the final piece of the puzzle had fallen into place.

She said, "Mark." He glanced at her, and the two exchanged a quick piece of nonverbal communication.

"Where're you off to, Malcolm?" I said, ever the chipper one.

"I'm taking my girlfriend to a kegger out on campus."

"Great. I'm just leaving. I think I'll follow you out. I got lost coming in. Could you steer me in the right direction?"

"Sure, no problem. I'll be happy to," he said.

I kept a careful eye on the rear of Mark Bethel's black Mercedes as Malcolm drove slowly down the driveway ahead of me. In my rearview mirror, I saw another set of headlights come into view. Mark had apparently made a scramble for Laddie's BMW, a sporty red model perfect for a hit-and-run fatality or a high-speed chase. In front of me, Malcolm had just reached the gates, triggering the automatic mechanism buried in the drive. Slowly, the gates swung open. Out on the road, I spotted two Santa Teresa Sheriff's Department cars pulled onto the berm, lights flashing. Four deputies were in conversation with Detectives Claas and Aldo, who were just in the process of identifying themselves. Malcolm turned left onto Savanna and I followed in his wake. Detective Aldo caught my eye, but there was no way he could help until the deputies had finished with them. So much for Plan A.

I checked the rearview mirror. Mark was so close on my tail, I could see the smirk on his face. I hugged the back end of the Mercedes, figuring Mark wouldn't ram me or shoot as long as Malcolm was close by. Maybe I'd accompany Malcolm and his girlfriend to the kegger out on campus, have a beer, shoot the shit, anything to avoid Mark. We passed a cemetery on the left and slowed at the intersection by the bird refuge. Malcolm tapped his horn and gave a final wave, turning left on Cabana while I turned right and headed for the freeway.

I took the 101 north, keeping my speed at a steady 60 mph. I could see Mark keeping pace. Traffic was light. Not a cop on the road. I groped through my bag, fumbling among the contents with one hand while I steered with the other. I popped the used tape out, leaned over and opened the glove compartment, tossed the tape in, and closed it. I pulled a fresh cassette from the packet on the passenger seat and inserted it in the tape recorder. I didn't have my gun. I'm a private investigator, not a vigilante. Most of my work takes place in the public library or the hall of records. Generally speaking, these places aren't dangerous, and I seldom need a semiautomatic to protect myself.

Now what? I had, of course, invented the bit about Mark's being in the snapshot, visible as a backdrop to Duncan and Benny's reunion. If such a picture existed, it certainly wasn't in my hands ... or Duffy's, for that matter. I winced. The very notion had put Mark on a tear, thinking we had evidence of their association. Big damn deal. Even if we had such a picture, what would that prove? I should have kept my mouth shut. Poor Duffy didn't have a clue as to what misery was bearing down on him. The last time I'd seen him he was drunk as a coot, passed out on his cot.

I took the Peterson off-ramp and turned left at the light. I didn't bother to speed up or make any tricky moves. Mark didn't seem to be in any hurry either. He knew where I was going, and if I went somewhere else, he'd go to Himes anyway. I think he liked the idea of this slow-paced pursuit, catching up at his leisure while I was frantically casting about for help. I turned right onto the side street and right again into the nursery parking lot. Mine was the only car. The garden center was closed. The building's interior was dim except for a light here and there to discourage the odd burglar with a green thumb or an urge for potted plants. The rest of the acreage was blanketed in darkness.

I parked, locked the car, and headed off on foot. I confess I ran, having given up all pretense of being casual about these things. Glancing back, I could see the headlights of the Beamer as it eased into the lot. I was waiting for the sound of the car door slamming, but Mark had bumped his way across the low concrete barrier and was driving down the wide lanes between the crated trees. I cut back and forth, holding my shoulder bag against me to keep it from jostling as I increased my pace. Idly, I realized the maze of boxed trees had shifted. Lanes I remembered from earlier were gone or rotated on an axis, now shooting off on parallel routes. I wasn't sure if trees had been added, subtracted, or simply rearranged. Maybe Himes had a landscape project that required a half-grown arbor.

I yelled Duffy's name, hoping to alert him in advance of my arrival, but the sound seemed to be absorbed by the portable forest that surrounded me.

Mark was still barreling along behind me, but at least the narrow twists and turns were slowing him down. I felt like I was stoned, everything moving at half speed—including me. I reached the maintenance shed, heart thumping, breath ragged. The yellow forklift was now blocking the lane, parked beside the shed with a crated fifteen-foot tree hoisted on the forks. The shed door was open and a pale light spilled out on the path like water.

"Duffy?" I called.

The lights were on in his makeshift tent, but there was no sign of him. His shoes were missing and the blanket I'd laid over him was now crumpled on the floor. A cheap saucepan sat on the hot plate filled with a beige sludge that looked like refried beans. A plastic packet of flour tortillas sat, unopened, on the unused burner. The pan still felt warm so maybe he'd stepped out to take a leak. I heard the BMW skid to a halt.

"Duffy!"

I checked the top of the orange crate. Duncan Oaks's press pass, his dog tags, and the snapshot were still lying where I'd left them. Outside, I heard the car door slam, the sound of someone thumping in my direction. I gathered Duncan's things in haste, looking for a place to hide them before Bethel appeared. Quickly, I considered and discarded the idea of hiding the items in Duffy's clothes.

The shed itself was crude, with little in the way of furniture and no nooks or crannies. In the absence of insulation, I was looking at bare studs, not so much as a toolbox where I could stash the stuff. I shoved the items in my back pocket just as Mark appeared in the doorway, a gun in his hand.

"Oh, shit," I said.

"I'd appreciate your handing me the tape recorder and the tape."

"No problem," I said. I reached in my shoulder bag, took out the tape recorder, and held it out to him. While I watched, he tucked the tape recorder up against his body, pressed the EJECT button with his free hand, and extracted the cassette. He dropped the tape recorder on the dirt floor and crushed it with his foot. Behind him, I caught a flicker of movement. Duffy appeared in the doorway and then eased back out of sight.

"I don't get it," I said. I focused on Mark, making sure I didn't telegraph Duffy's presence with my eyes.

"Get what?" Mark was distracted. He tried to keep his eyes pinned on me while he held the gun and cassette in one hand and unraveled the tape with the other, pulling off the reel. Loops of thin, shiny ribbon were tangled in his fingers, trailing to the floor in places.

"I don't understand what you're so worried about. There's nothing on there that would incriminate you."

"I can't be sure what Laddie said before I showed."

"She was the soul of discretion," I said dryly.

Mark smiled in spite of himself. "What a champ."

"Why'd you kill Benny?"

"To get him off my back. What'd you think?"

"Because he knew you killed Duncan?"

"Because he saw me do it."

"Just like that?"

"Just like that. Call it a flash of inspiration. Six of us

were loaded with the body bags. Duncan was pissing and moaning, but I could tell he wasn't hurt bad. Fuckin' baby. Before we could lift off, the medic was killed by machine-gun fire. Benny seemed to be out of it. I'd been shot in the leg, and I'd taken a load of shrapnel in my back and side. Up we went. I remember the chopper shuddering, and I didn't think we'd make it under all the small arms fire. The minute we were airborne, I crawled over to Duncan, stripped him of his ID, ripped the tags off his neck, and tossed 'em aside. All the time the chopper lurched and vibrated like a crazy man was shaking it back and forth. Duncan lay there looking at me, but I don't think he fully understood what I was doing until I hoisted him out. Benny saw me, the shit. He pretended he'd passed out, but he saw the whole deal. By then, I was light-headed and rolled over on my side, sick with sweat. That's when Benny took the tags and hid 'em. . . ."

"I take it he pressed you too hard."

"Hey, I did what I could for him. In the end, I killed him as much for being dumb as trying to screw me over when he should have left well enough alone."

"And Mickey?"

"Let's cut the chitchat and get on with this." He snapped his fingers, pointing to the bag.

"I don't have a gun."

"It's Duncan's tags I want."

"I left the stuff sitting on the orange crate. Duffy must have taken it."

Mark snapped his fingers, gesturing for me to hand him the bag.

"I lied about the snapshot."

"GIVE ME THE FUCKIN' BAG!"

I passed him my shoulder bag and watched while he searched. His holding the gun necessitated working with the bag clamped against his chest. This made it tricky to inspect the interior while he kept an eye on me. Impatiently, he tipped the bag upside down, dumping out the contents. Somewhere nearby, I heard the low rumble of heavy equipment and I found myself praying, *Please, please, please.*

Mark heard it too. He tossed the bag to one side and motioned with the gun, indicating I should leave before him. I was suddenly afraid. While we talked, while we stood face-to-face, I didn't believe he'd kill me because I didn't think he'd have the nerve. My own fate had seemed curiously out of my hands. What mattered at that point was knowing the truth, finding out what had happened to Duncan and Benny and Mick. Now the act of turning my back was almost more than I could bear.

I moved toward the door. I could hear the deep growl of a diesel motor, some piece of machinery picking up speed as it advanced. My skin felt radiant. Anxiety snaked through my gut like summer lightning. I yearned to see what Mark was doing. I wondered if the gun was pointed at my back, wondered if he was, even then, in the process of releasing the safety, tightening his index finger on the trigger, speeding me to my death. Most of all, I wondered if the bullet would hit me before I heard the sound of the shot.

I heard the crack of sudden impact and glanced back, watching with astonishment as the shed wall blew in, boards splintering on contact as the tractor plowed through. Duffy's cot was crushed under the rolling track, which seemed to have the weight and destructive power of a moving tank. The front-mounted bucket banged into the space heater and sent it flying in my direction. I ducked my head, but the heater caught me in the back with an impetus that knocked me to my knees. As I scrambled to my feet, I looked over my shoulder. The entire rear wall of the shed had been demolished.

Duffy threw the tractor in reverse and backed out of the flattened structure, doing a three-point turn. I ran, emerging from the shed in time to see Mark jump into the BMW and jam the key in the ignition. The engine ground ineffectually, but never coughed to life. Duffy, in the tractor, bore down on the vehicle. From the grin on his face, I had to guess he'd disabled the engine. Mark took aim and fired at Duffy, perched high in the tractor cab. I was caught between the two men, and I paused, mesmerized by the violence unfolding. My heart burned in my chest and the urge to run was almost overpowering. I could see that Mark was corralled in the cul-de-sac formed by the wreckage of the shed, a row of crated trees, and the tractor, which was picking up speed again as Duffy accelerated. I was blocking his only avenue of escape.

Mark started running in my direction, apparently hoping to blow by me in his bid for freedom. He fired at Duffy again and the bullet zinged off the cab with a musical note. Duffy worked the lever that controlled the lift arm as the tractor bore down on him. I started running at Mark. He veered off at the last minute, reversing himself. He jumped up on one of the crates, hoping to crash through the trees to the aisle just behind. I caught him midair and shoved him. He bungled the leap, toppled backward, and fell on me. We went down in a heap. As he scuttled to his feet, I reached out and snagged his ankle, holding on for dear life. He staggered, half-dragging me into Duffy's path. Duffy stomped on the accelerator. I released Mark and rolled sideways. The tractor lurched forward, diesel engine rumbling, the bucket lever screeching as Duffy maneuvered it. Mark pivoted, trying to launch himself in the opposite direction, but Duffy bore down on him, the bucket extended like a cradle. Mark turned to face the tractor, gauging its momentum in hopes of dodging its mass. He fired another round, but it clanged harmlessly off the bucket. He'd badly misjudged Duffy's skill. The metal lip banged into Mark's chest with an impact that nearly lifted him off his feet, driving him back against the side wall of the shed. For a moment, he hung there, pinned between the bucket and the wall. He struggled, his weight pulling him down until the lip of the bucket rested squarely against his throat. Duffy looked over at me, and I could see his expression soften. He propelled the tractor forward, and Mark's neatly severed head thumped into the bucket like a cantaloupe.

It wasn't *quite* Plan B, but it would have to do.

Epilogue

THE BUST AT the Honky-Tonk didn't come down for another six months. A federal grand jury returned a fifteen-count indictment against Tim Littenberg and a twelve-count indictment against Scott Shackelford for manufacturing counterfeit credit cards, which carries a minimum five-year prison term and a $250,000 fine for each conviction. Both are currently free on bail. Carlin Duffy was arrested and charged with voluntary manslaughter and he's awaiting trial in the Santa Teresa County jail, with its volleyball, indoor tawlits, and color television sets.

Mickey died on June 1. Later, I sold his handguns, pooling the proceeds with the cash and gold coins I'd lifted from his apartment. Mickey'd never bothered to change his will and since I was named sole beneficiary, his estate (including some pension monies he'd tucked in a separate account, plus $50,000 in life insurance) came to me. Probably out of guilt, Pete Shackelford made good on the ten grand Tim Littenberg owed Mickey, so that in the end, there was quite a substantial sum that I turned over to the Santa Teresa Police Department to use as they saw fit. If he'd survived, I suspect Mickey would have been one of those miserly eccentrics who live like paupers and leave millions to charity.

As it happened, I sat with him, my gaze fixed on the monitor above his bed. I watched the staggered line of his beating heart, strong and steady, though his color began to fade and his breathing became more labored as the days went by. I touched his face, feeling the cool flesh that would never be warm again. After the rapture of love comes the wreckage, at least in my experience. I thought of all the things he'd taught me, the things we'd been to each other during that brief marriage. My life was the richer for his having been part of it. Whatever his flaws, whatever his failings, his redemption was something he'd earned in the end. I laid my cheek against his hand and breathed with him until the last breath. "You done good, kid," I whispered, when he was still at last.

Respectfully submitted,
Kinsey Millhone

SUE GRAFTON

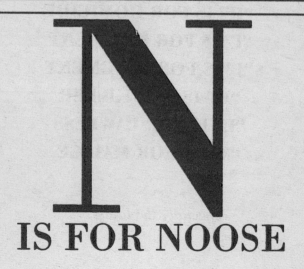

IS FOR NOOSE

Published by Fawcett Books.
Available at your local bookstore.